MISCHIEF

She started out as one of the most successful advertising copywriters of her generation. Fay Weldon's credits as a writer now include classic novels such as *The Life and Loves of a She-Devil* and *The Cloning of Joanna May*. In 2001 Fay was awarded a CBE for services to literature.

ALSO BY FAY WELDON

FICTION

The Fat Woman's Joke
Down Among the Women
Female Friends
Remember Me
Little Sisters
Praxis
Puffball
The President's Child
The Life and Loves of a She-Devil
The Shrapnel Academy
The Heart of the Country
The Hearts and Lives of Men
The Rules of Life
Leader of the Band
The Cloning of Joanna May
Darcy's Utopia
Growing Rich
Life Force
Affliction
Splitting
Worst Fears
Big Women
Rhode Island Blues
The Bulgari Connection
Mantrapped
She May Not Leave
The Spa Decamaron
The Stepmother's Diary
Chalcot Crescent
Kehua!
Habits of the House
Long Live the King
The New Countess

CHILDREN'S BOOKS

Wolf the Mechanical Dog
Party Puddle
Nobody Likes Me

SHORT STORY COLLECTIONS

Watching Me, Watching You
Polaris
Moon Over Minneapolis
Wicked Women
A Hard Time to Be a Father
Nothing to Wear & Nowhere to Hide

NONFICTION

Letters to Alice
Rebecca West
Sacred Cows
Godless in Eden
Auto Da Fay
What Makes Women Happy

MISCHIEF

Fay Weldon

First published in the UK in 2015 by Head of Zeus Ltd

9 7 5 3 1 2 4 6 8

A catalogue record for this book is available from the British Library.

Hardback ISBN: 9781784081027
eBook ISBN: 9781784081010

Typeset by PDQ

Printed and bound in Germany
by GGP Media GmbH, Pössneck

Head of Zeus Ltd
Clerkenwell House
45-47 Clerkenwell Green
London EC1R 0HT

WWW.HEADOFZEUS.COM

Contents

Introduction

During the four decades over which these stories were written the relationship between men and women in the West has changed out of all recognition. In the seventies women still endured the domestic tyranny of men, in the eighties we found our self-esteem, in the nineties we lifted our heads and looked about, and in the noughties – well, we went out to work. We had to.

The stories from the seventies, I notice, tend to be long and serious, those from the busy two thousands, shorter. Everyone's busy. By the 2014 novella, various chickens from these last decades have come home to roost, while social media and big pharma wreak their own special havoc. Some things don't change, of course. Like mother-love; and children learning to put up with second best. The wife may become the partner, but she goes on making, mending, patching broken lives the same as ever.

Reading through my hundred-odd stories was a disturbing experience. Delving into one's past writing is like delving into memories of one's own life for an autobiography – there is so much concentrated, even painful experience here. Fiction these stories may be, but the feeling-tones of yesterdays are bound to come surging back. Women's bodies go on betraying them, desire goes on trumping common sense. The sadistic male artist seems perennial, his poor masochistic moll up to her arms in soapsuds, admiring him.

Most of the tales in this book have been collected before; a few have appeared only in newspapers, magazines or on the radio. A couple are unpublished: the novella had an initial outing as an e-book but is paper published here for the first time. Most of them were written as interruptions of whatever novel I was writing at the time (*Alopecia*, for example, must have been a kind of interjection into the comparative frivolity of *Little Sisters*). It seems wiser to get new ideas out of my head and onto the page than keep them seething away inside it. These stories often read, I can see, more like concentrated mini novels than classic short stories.

It was only when I wrote my first short stories unasked for and uncommissioned that I could persuade myself that I was any kind of proper writer. Since I began writing fiction in 1966 I'd found myself writing non-stop in response to requests for television and radio dramas, stage plays, novels, fulfilling contracts and meeting deadlines. But perhaps the fact that I could do that was more to do with my training in advertising than from any genuine talent? Perhaps all I'd been doing was responding to requests in order to pay the rent and keep a family? Not initiating my own ideas like a proper writer? I trusted the incomparable Giles Gordon, my literary agent from 1966 until he died in 2003, to market what I produced. Which he unfailingly did. So I gained confidence.

Then the short began to creep surreptitiously into the long fiction. In *Leader of the Band* (1988) I added three only obliquely relevant short stories. And fiction crept into 'non-fiction': in *Letters to Alice on First Reading Jane Austen* (1984) I had to warn readers the 'I' in the book was not me, albeit she bore my name. In *Mantrapped* (2004) I stirred fiction into autobiography to work out whether one can truly separate the writer's personal life from what she makes up. I decided that you couldn't.

But I have always had a try-try-try-again approach to writing: nothing ends up quite as you meant it to, which is why one sighs and starts again, in the hope that this time you will get it right. Of course you never will. But this way you get an awful lot of different kinds of books written – to the despair of one marketing executive who shook her finger at me at a meeting and said, 'You write consistent product, we'll sell it.'

So many changes have come to pass in the last four decades to disturb the equanimity of the writer. By the nineties most of us were writing with computers – it was so fast, so easy, and the mouse outran the brain. Unconsidered first, not second, thoughts reached the page. Writing by hand went out of fashion. I held out until about 1995. I am not at all sure that the change to the digital text has been a blessing. The computer depends for its very existence on disambiguity; it deals with yes-no certainties. 'Perhaps' doesn't get a look in. Every sentence means what it says and only what it says, and the ease of change for the writer is so swift and unlaborious that any hint of paradox, any sense of the opaque, is removed.

And then the e-book came along, the naked text without the frills of publisher's advocacy, jacket, blurb, writer's photo: Look at me! Read this book! The text must now stand alone, without defences. Readers, who once liked to settle down with a good book when they had peace and time to think now increasingly read e-books when they are on the move. It's no surprise that plot-rich, contemplation-light genre novels leave literary novels lagging behind. 'Good' writing is so much to do with an aesthetic, with a resonance of language which is more apparent on paper than on a screen.

The Other Side always seems to hover over my work – alternative realities always threatening to break through, scaring us out of our wits and sometimes into them. In *The Ted Dreams* it finally steps into ours.

Fay Weldon
December 2014

MISCHIEF

Angel, All Innocence

There is a certain kind of unhappiness, experienced by a certain kind of woman married to a certain kind of man, which is timeless: outrunning centuries, interweaving generations, perpetuating itself from mother to daughter, feeding off the wet eyes of the puzzled girl, gaining fresh strength from the dry eyes of the old woman she will become – who, looking back on her past, remembers nothing of love except tears and the pain in the heart which must be endured, in silence, in case the heart stops altogether.

Better for it to stop, now.

Angel, waking in the night, hears sharp footsteps in the empty attic above and wants to wake Edward. She moves her hand to do so, but then stills it for fear of making him angry. Easier to endure in the night the nightmare terror of ghosts than the daylong silence of Edward's anger.

The footsteps, little and sharp, run from a point above the double bed in which Angel and Edward lie, she awake, he sleeping, to a point somewhere above the chest of drawers by the door; they pause briefly, then run back again, tap-tap, clickety-click. There comes another pause and the sound of pulling and shuffling across the floor; and then the sequence repeats itself, once, twice. Silence. The proper unbroken silence of the night.

Too real, too clear, for ghosts. The universe is not magic. Everything has an explanation. Rain, perhaps? Hardly. Angel can see the moon shine through the drawn blind, and rain does not fall on moonlit nights. Perhaps, then, the rain of past days collected in some blocked gutter, to finally splash through on to the rolls of wallpaper and pots of paint on the attic floor, sounding like footsteps through some trick of domestic acoustics. Surely! Angel and Edward have not been living in the house for long. The attic is still unpainted, and old plaster drops from disintegrating laths. Edward will get round to it sooner or later. He prides himself on his craftsman's skills, and Angel, a year married, has learned to wait and admire, subduing impatience in herself. Edward is a painter – of pictures, not houses – and not long out of art school, where he won many prizes. Angel is the lucky girl he has loved and married. Angel's father paid for the remote country house, where now they live in solitude and where Edward can develop his talents, undisturbed by the ugliness of the city, with Angel, his inspiration, at his side. Edward, as it happened, consented to the gift unwillingly, and for Angel's sake rather than his own. Angel's father Terry writes thrillers and settled a large sum upon his daughter in her childhood, thus avoiding death duties and the anticipated gift tax. Angel kept the fact hidden from Edward until after they were married. He'd thought her an ordinary girl about Chelsea, sometime secretary, sometime barmaid, sometime artist's model.

Angel, between jobs, did indeed take work as an artist's model. That was how Edward first clapped eyes upon her; Angel, all innocence, sitting nude upon her plinth, fair curly hair glinting under strong lights, large eyes closed beneath stretched blue-veined lids, strong breasts pointed upwards, stubby pale brush irritatingly and coyly hidden behind an angle of thigh that both gave Angel cramps and spoiled the pose for the students. So they said.

'If you're going to be an exhibitionist,' as Edward complained to her later in the coffee bar, 'at least don't be coy about it.' He took her home to his pad, that handsome, dark-eyed, smiling young man, and wooed her with a nostalgic Sinatra record left behind by its previous occupant; half mocking, half sincere, he sang love words into her pearly ear, his warm breath therein stirring her imagination, and the gentle occasional nip of his strong teeth in its flesh promising passion and pain beyond belief. Angel would not take off her clothes for him: he became angry and sent her home in a taxi without her fare. She borrowed from her flatmate at the other end. She cried all night, and the next day, sitting naked on her plinth, had such swollen eyelids as to set a student or two scratching away to amend the previous day's work. But she lowered her thigh, as a gesture of submission, and felt a change in the studio ambience from chilly spite to warm approval, and she knew Edward had forgiven her. Though she offered herself to multitudes, Edward had forgiven her.

'I don't mind you being an exhibitionist,' Edward said to her in the coffee bar, 'in fact that rather turns me on, but I do mind you being coy. You have a lot to learn, Angel.' By that time Angel's senses were so aroused, her limbs so languid with desire, her mind so besotted with his image, that she would have done whatever Edward wished, in public or in private. But he rose and left the coffee bar, leaving her to pay the bill.

Angel cried a little, and was comforted by and went home with Edward's friend Tom, and even went to bed with him, which made her feel temporarily better, but which she was to regret for ever.

'I don't mind you being a whore,' Edward said before the next studio session, 'but can't you leave my friends alone?'

It was a whole seven days of erotic torment for Angel before Edward finally spent the night with her: by that time her thighs hung loosely open in the studio. Let anyone see. Anyone. She did not care. The job was coming to an end anyway. Her new one as secretary in a solicitor's office began on the following Monday. In the nick of time, just as she began to think that life and love were over, Edward brought her back to their remembrance. 'I love you,' he murmured in Angel's ear. 'Exhibitionist slut, typist, I don't care. I still love you.'

Tap-tap, go the footsteps above, starting off again: clickety-click. Realer than real. No, water never sounded like that. What then? Rats? No. Rats scutter and scamper and scrape. There were rats in the barn in which Angel and Edward spent a camping holiday together. Their tent had blown away: they'd been forced to take refuge in the barn. All four of them. Edward, Angel, Tom and his new girlfriend Ray. Angel missed Edward one night after they all stumbled back from the pub to the barn, and searching for him in the long grass beneath an oak tree, found him in tight embrace with Ray.

'Don't tell me you're hysterical as well as everything else,' complained Edward. 'You're certainly irrational. You went to bed with Tom, after all.'

'But that was before.'

Ah, before, so much before. Before the declarations of love, the abandoning of all defence, all prudence, the surrendering of common sense to faith, the parcelling up and handing over of the soul into apparent safe-keeping. And if the receiving hands part, the trusted fingers lose their grip, by accident or by design, why then, one's better dead.

Edward tossed his Angel's soul into the air and caught it with his casual hands.

'But if it makes you jealous,' he said, 'why I won't… Do you want to marry me? Is that it? Would it make you happier?'

What would it look like when they came to write his biography? Edward Holst, the famous painter, married at the age of twenty-four – to what? Artist's model, barmaid, secretary, crime-writer's daughter? Or exhibitionist, whore, hysteric? Take your choice. Whatever makes the reader happiest, explains the artist in the simplest terms, makes the most successful version of a life. Crude strokes and all.

'Edward likes to keep his options open,' said Tom, but would not explain his remark any further. He and Ray were witnesses at the secular wedding ceremony. Angel thought she saw Edward nip Ray's ear as they all formally kissed afterwards, then thought she must have imagined it.

This was his overture of love: turning to Angel in the dark warmth of the marriage bed, Edward's teeth would seek her ear and nibble the tender flesh, while his hand travelled down to open her thighs. Angel never initiated their lovemaking.

No. Angel waited, patiently. She had tried once or twice, in the early days, letting her hand roam over his sleeping body, but Edward not only failed to respond, but was thereafter cold to her for days on end, sleeping carefully on his side of the bed, until her penance was paid and he lay warm against her again.

Edward's love made flowers bloom, made the house rich and warm, made water taste like wine. Edward, happy, surrounded Angel with smiles and soft encouragement. He held her soul with steady hands. Edward's anger came unexpectedly, out of nowhere, or nowhere that Angel could see. Yesterday's permitted remark, forgiven fault, was today's outrage. To remark on the weather to break an uneasy silence, might be seen as evidence of a complaining nature: to be reduced to tears by his first unexpected biting remark, further fuel for his grievance.

Edward, in such moods, would go to his studio and lock the door, and though Angel (soon learning that to weep outside the door or beat against it, moaning and crying and protesting, would merely prolong his anger and her torment) would go out to the garden and weed or dig or plant as if nothing were happening, would feel Edward's anger seeping out from under the door, darkening the sun, poisoning the earth; or at any rate spoiling her fingers in relation to the earth, so that they trembled and made mistakes and nothing grew.

The blind shakes. The moon goes behind a cloud. Tap, tap, overhead. Back and forth. The wind? No. Don't delude yourself. Nothing of this world. A ghost. A haunting. A woman. A small, desperate, busy woman, here and not here, back and forth, out of her time, back from the grave, ill-omened, bringing grief and ruin: a message that nothing is what it seems, that God is dead and the forces of evil abroad and unstoppable. Does Angel hear, or not hear?

Angel through her fear, wants to go to the bathroom. She is three months pregnant. Her bladder is weak. It wakes her in the night, crying out its need, and Angel, obeying, will slip cautiously out of bed, trying not to wake Edward. Edward needs unbroken sleep if he is to paint well the next day. Edward, even at the best of times, suspects that Angel tossing and turning, and moaning in her sleep, as she will, wakes him on purpose to annoy.

Angel has not yet told Edward that she is pregnant. She keeps putting it off. She has no real reason to believe he does not want babies: but he has not said he does want them, and to assume that Edward wants what other people want is dangerous.

Angel moans aloud: afraid to move, afraid not to move, afraid to hear, afraid not to hear. So the child Angel lay awake in her little white bed, listening to her mother moaning, afraid to move, afraid not to move, to hear or not to hear. Angel's mother was a shoe-shop girl who married the new assistant manager after a six-week courtship. That her husband went on to make a fortune, writing thrillers that sold by the million, was both Dora's good fortune and tragedy. She lived comfortably enough on alimony, after all, in a way she could never have expected, until dying by mistake from an overdose of sleeping pills. After that Angel was brought up by a succession of her father's mistresses and au-pairs. Her father Terry liked Edward, that was something, or at any rate he had been relieved at his appearance on the scene. He had feared an element of caution in Angel's soul: that she might end up married to a solicitor or stockbroker. And artists were at least creative, and an artist such as Edward Holst might well end up rich and famous. Terry had six Holst canvases on his walls to hasten the process. Two were of his daughter, nude, thigh slackly falling away from her stubby fair bush. Angel, defeated – as her mother had been defeated. 'I love you, Dora, but you must understand. I am not *in* love with you.' As I'm in love with Helen, Audrey, Rita, whoever it was: off to meetings, parties, off on his literary travels, looking for fresh copy and new backgrounds, encountering always someone more exciting, more interesting, than an ageing ex shoe-shop assistant. Why couldn't Dora understand? Unreasonable of her to suffer, clutching the wretched Angel to her alarmingly slack bosom. Could he, Terry, really be the only animation of her flesh? There was a sickness in her love, clearly; unaccompanied as it was by the beauty which lends grace to importunity.

Angel had her mother's large, sad eyes. The reproach in them was in-built. Better Dora's heart had stopped (she'd thought it would: six months pregnant, she found Terry in the housemaid's bed. She, Dora, mistress of servants! What bliss!) and the embryo Angel never emerged to the light of day.

The noise above Angel stops. Ghosts! What nonsense! A fallen lath grating and rattling in the wind. What else? Angel regains her courage, slips her hand out from beneath Edward's thigh preparatory to leaving the bed for the bathroom. She will turn on all the lights and run. Edward wakes; sits up.

'What's that? What in God's name's that?'
'I can't hear anything,' says Angel, all innocence. Nor can she, not now. Edward's displeasure to contend with now; worse than the universe rattling its chains.

'Footsteps, in the attic. Are you deaf? Why didn't you wake me?'
'I thought I imagined it.'

But she can hear them, once again, as if with his ears. The same pattern across the floor and back. Footsteps or heartbeats. Quicker and quicker now, hastening with the terror and tension of escape.

Edward, unimaginably brave, puts on his slippers, grabs a broken banister (five of these on the landing – one day soon, some day, he'll get round to mending them – he doesn't want some builder, paid by Angel, bungling the job) and goes on up to the attic. Angel follows behind. He will not let her cower in bed. Her bladder aches. She says nothing about that. How can she? Not yet. Not quite yet. Soon. 'Edward, I'm pregnant.' She can't believe it's true, herself. She feels a child, not a woman.

'Is there someone there?'

Edward's voice echoes through the three dark attic rooms. Silence. He gropes for and switches on the light. Empty, derelict rooms: plaster falling, laths hanging, wallpaper peeling. Floorboards broken. A few cans of paint, a pile of wallpaper rolls, old newspapers. Nothing else.

'It could have been mice,' says Edward, doubtfully.

'Can't you hear it?' asks Angel, terrified. The sound echoes in her ears: footsteps clattering over a pounding heart. But Edward can't, not any more.

'Don't start playing games,' he murmurs, turning back to

warmth and bed. Angel scuttles down before him, into the bathroom; the noise in her head fades. A few drops of urine tinkle into the bowl.

Edward lies awake in bed: Angel can feel his wakefulness, his increasing hostility towards her, before she is so much as back in the bedroom.

'Your bladder's very weak. Angel,' he complains. 'Something else you inherited from your mother?'

Something else, along with what? Suicidal tendencies, alcoholism, a drooping bosom, a capacity for being betrayed, deserted and forgotten?

Not forgotten by me, Mother. I don't forget. I love you. Even when my body cries out beneath the embraces of this man, this lover, this husband, and my mouth forms words of love, promises of eternity, still I don't forget. I love you, Mother.

'I don't know about my mother's bladder,' murmurs Angel rashly.

'Now you're going to keep me awake all night,' says Edward. 'I can feel it coming. You know I've nearly finished a picture.'
'I'm not going to say a word,' she says, and then, fulfilling his prophecy, sees fit to add, 'I'm pregnant.'

Silence. Stillness. Sleep?

No, a slap across nostrils, eyes, mouth. Edward has never hit Angel before. It is not a hard slap: it contains the elements of a caress.

'Don't even joke about it,' says Edward, softly.

'But I am pregnant.'

Silence. He believes her. Her voice made doubt impossible.

'How far?' Edward seldom asks for information. It is an act which infers ignorance, and Edward likes to know more than anyone else in the entire world.

'Three and a half months.'

He repeats the words, incredulous.

'Too far gone to do anything,' says Angel, knowing now why she did not tell Edward earlier, and the knowledge making her voice cold and hard. Too far gone for the abortion he will most certainly want her to have. So much for the fruits of love. Love? What's love? Sex, ah, that's another thing. Love has babies: sex has abortions.

But Angel will turn sex into love – yes, she will – seizing it by the neck, throttling it till it gives up and takes the weaker path. Love! Edward is right to be frightened, right to hate her.

'I hate you,' he says, and means it. 'You mean to destroy me.'

'I'll make sure it doesn't disturb your nights,' says Angel, Angel of the bristly fair bush, 'if that's what you're worrying about. And you won't have to support it. I do that, anyway. Or my father does.'

Well, how dare she! Angel, not nearly as nice as she thought.

Soft-eyed, vicious Angel.

Slap, comes the hand again, harder. Angel screams, he shouts; she collapses, crawls about the floor – he spurns her, she begs forgiveness; he spits his hatred, fear, and she her misery. If the noise above continues, certainly no one hears it, there is so much going on below. The rustlings of the night erupting into madness. Angel is suddenly quiet, whimpering, lying on the floor; she squirms. At first Edward thinks she is acting, but her white lips and taloned fingers convince him that something is wrong with her body and not just her mind. He gets her back on the bed and rings the doctor. Within an hour Angel finds herself in a hospital with a suspected ectopic pregnancy. They delay the operation and the pain subsides; just one of those things, they shrug. Edward has to interrupt his painting the next afternoon to collect her from the hospital.

'What was it? Hysteria?' he enquires.

'I dare say!'

'Well, you had a bad beginning, what with your mother and all,' he concedes, kissing her nose, nibbling her earlobe. It is forgiveness; but Angel's eyes remain unusually cold. She stays in bed, after Edward has left it and gone back to his studio, although the floors remain unswept and the dishes unwashed.

Angel does not say what is in her mind, what she knows to be true. That he is disappointed to see both her and the baby back, safe and sound. He had hoped the baby would die, or failing that, the mother would die and the baby with her. He is pretending forgiveness, while he works out what to do next.

In the evening the doctor comes to see Angel. He is a slight man with a sad face: his eyes, she thinks, are kind behind his pebble glasses. His voice is slow and gentle. I expect his wife is happy, thinks Angel, and actually envies her. Some middle-aged, dowdy, provincial doctor's wife, envied by Angel! Rich, sweet, young and pretty Angel. The efficient secretary, lovable barmaid, and now the famous artist's wife! Once, for two rash weeks, even an art school model.

The doctor examines her, then discreetly pulls down her nightie to cover her breasts and moves the sheet up to cover her crotch. If he were my father, thinks Angel, he would not hang my naked portrait on his wall for the entertainment of his friends. Angel had not known until this moment that she minded.

'Everything's doing nicely inside there,' says the doctor. 'Sorry to rush you off like that, but we can't take chances.'

Ah, to be looked after. Love. That's love. The doctor shows no inclination to go.

'Perhaps I should have a word with your husband,' he suggests. He stands at the window gazing over daffodils and green fields. 'Or is he very busy?'

'He's painting,' says Angel. 'Better not disturb him now. He's had so many interruptions lately, poor man.'
'I read about him in the Sunday supplement,' says the doctor.
'Well, don't tell him so. He thought it vulgarised his work.'

'Did you think that?'

Me? Does what I think have anything to do with anything?

'I thought it was quite perceptive, actually,' says Angel, and feels a surge of good humour. She sits up in bed.

'Lie down,' he says. 'Take things easy. This is a large house. Do you have any help? Can't afford it?'
'It's not that. It's just why should I expect some other woman to do my dirty work?'
'Because she might like doing it and you're pregnant, and if you can afford it, why not?'
'Because Edward doesn't like strangers in the house. And what else have I got to do with my life? I might as well clean as anything else.'

'It's isolated out here,' he goes on. 'Do you drive?'
'Edward needs peace to paint,' says Angel. 'I do drive but Edward has a thing about women drivers.'
'You don't miss your friends?'
'After you're married,' says Angel, 'you seem to lose contact. It's the same for everyone, isn't it?'

'Um,' says the doctor. And then, 'I haven't been in this house for fifteen years. It's in a better state now than it was then. The house was divided into flats, in those days. I used to visit a nice young woman who had the attic floor. Just above this. Four children, and the roof leaked; a husband who spent his time drinking cider in the local pub and only came home to beat her.'
'Why did she stay?'
'How can such women leave? How do they afford it? Where do they go? What happens to the children?' His voice is sad.

'I suppose it's money that makes the difference. With money, a woman's free,' says Angel, trying to believe it.

'Of course,' says the doctor. 'But she loved her husband. She couldn't bring herself to see him for what he was. Well, it's hard. For a certain kind of woman, at any rate.'

Hard, indeed, if he has your soul in his safe-keeping, to be left behind at the bar, in the pub, or in some other woman's bed, or in a seat in the train on his literary travels. Careless!

'But it's not like that for you, is it?' says the doctor calmly. 'You have money of your own, after all.'

Now how does he know that? Of course, the Sunday supplement article.

'No one will read it,' wept Angel, when Edward looked up, stony-faced from his first perusal of the fashionable columns. 'No one will notice. It's tucked away at the very bottom.'

So it was. 'Edward's angelic wife Angel, daughter of best-selling crime writer Terry Toms, has smoothed the path upwards, not just with the soft smiles our cameraman has recorded, but by enabling the emergent genius to forswear the cramped and inconvenient, if traditional, artist's garret for a sixteenth-century farmhouse in greenest Gloucestershire. It is interesting, moreover, to ponder whether a poor man would have been able to develop the white-on-white techniques which have made Hoist's work so noticeable: or whether the sheer price of paint these days would not have deterred him.'

'Edward, I didn't say a word to that reporter, not a word,' she

said, when the ice showed signs of cracking, days later.
'What are you talking about?' he asked, turning slow, unfriendly eyes upon her.
'The article. I know it's upset you. But it wasn't my fault.'

'Why should a vulgar article in a vulgar newspaper upset me?'

And the ice formed over again, thicker than ever. But he went to London for two days, presumably to arrange his next show, and on his return casually mentioned that he'd seen Ray while he was there.

Angel had cleaned, baked, and sewed curtains in his absence, hoping to soften his heart towards her on his return: and lay awake all the night he was away, the fear of his infidelity so agonising as to make her contemplate suicide, if only to put an end to it. She could not ask for reassurance. He would throw the fears so neatly back at her. 'Why do you think I should want to sleep with anyone else? Why are you so guilty? Because that's what you'd do if you were away from me?'

Ask for bread and be given stones. Learn self-sufficiency: never show need. Little, tough Angel of the soft smiles, hearing some other woman's footsteps in the night, crying for another's grief. Well, who wants a soul, tossed here and there by teasing hands, over-bruised and over-handled. Do without it!

Edward came home from London in a worse mood than he'd left, shook his head in wondering stupefaction at his wife's baking – 'I thought you said we were cutting down on carbohydrates' – and shut himself into his studio for twelve hours, emerging just once to say – 'Only a mad woman would hang curtains in an artist's studio, or else a silly rich girl playing at artist's wife, and in public at that' – and thrusting the new curtains back into her arms, vanished inside again.

Angel felt that her mind was slowing up, and puzzled over the last remark for some time before realising that Edward was still harking back to the Sunday supplement article.

'I'll give away the money if you like,' she pleaded through the keyhole. 'If you'd rather. And if you want not to be married to me I don't mind.' That was before she was pregnant.

Silence.

Then Edward emerged laughing, telling her not to be so ridiculous, bearing her off to bed, and the good times were restored. Angel sang about the house, forgot her pill, and got pregnant.

'You have money of your own, after all,' says the doctor.
'You're perfectly free to come and go.'
'I'm pregnant,' says Angel. 'The baby has to have a father.'
'And your husband's happy about the baby?'
'Oh yes!' says Angel. 'Isn't it a wonderful day!'

And indeed today the daffodils nod brightly under a clear sky. So far, since first they budded and bloomed, they have been obliged to droop beneath the weight of rain and mist. A disappointing spring. Angel had hoped to see the countryside leap into energy and colour, but life returned only slowly, it seemed, struggling to surmount the damage of the past: cold winds and hard frosts, unseasonably late. 'Or at any rate,' adds Angel, softly, unheard, as the doctor goes, 'he *will* be happy about the baby.'

Angel hears no more noises in the night for a week or so. There had been misery in the attic rooms, and the misery had ceased. Good times can wipe out bad. Surely!

Edward sleeps soundly and serenely: she creeps from bed to bathroom without waking him. He is kind to her and even talkative, on any subject, that is, except that of her pregnancy. If it were not for the doctor and her stay in the hospital, she might almost think she was imagining the whole thing. Edward complains that Angel is getting fat, as if he could imagine no other cause for it but greed. She wants to talk to someone about hospitals, confinements, layettes, names – but to whom?

She tells her father on the telephone – 'I'm pregnant.'

'What does Edward say?' asks Terry, cautiously.

'Nothing much,' admits Angel.

'I don't suppose he does.'

'There's no reason *not* to have a baby,' ventures Angel.

'I expect he rather likes to be the centre of attention.' It is the nearest Terry has ever got to a criticism of Edward.

Angel laughs. She is beyond believing that Edward could ever be jealous of her, ever be dependent upon her.

'Nice to hear you happy, at any rate,' says her father wistfully. His twenty-year-old girlfriend has become engaged to a salesman of agricultural machinery, and although she has offered to continue the relationship the other side of marriage,

Terry feels debased and used, and was obliged to break off the liaison. He has come to regard his daughter's marriage to Edward in a romantic light. The young bohemians!

'My daughter was an art school model before she married Edward Holst . . . you've heard of him? It's a real Rembrandt and Saskia affair.' He even thinks lovingly of Dora: if only she'd understood, waited for youth to wear itself out. Now he's feeling old and perfectly capable of being faithful to an ex shoe-shop assistant. If only she weren't dead and gone!

An art school model. Those two weeks! Why had she done it? What devil wound up her works and set poor Angel walking in the wrong direction? It was in her nature, surely, as it was in her mother's to follow the paths to righteousness, fully clothed.

Nightly, Edward studied her naked body, kissing her here, kissing her there, parting her legs. Well, marriage! But now I'm pregnant, now I'm pregnant. Oh, be careful. That hard lump where my soft belly used to be. Be careful! Silence, Angel. Don't speak of it. It will be the worse for you and your baby if you do.

Angel knows it.

Now Angel hears the sound of lovemaking up in the empty attic, as she might hear it in hotels in foreign lands. The couplings of strangers in an unknown tongue – only the cries and breathings universal, recognisable anywhere.

The sounds chill her: they do not excite her. She thinks of the mother of four who lived in this house with her drunken, violent husband. Was that what kept you by his side? The chains of fleshly desire? Was it the thought of the night that got you through the perils of the day?

What indignity, if it were so.

Oh, I imagine it. I, Angel, half-mad in my unacknowledged pregnancy, my mind feverish, and the doctor's anecdotes feeding the fever – I imagine it! I must!

Edward wakes.

'What's that noise?'
'What noise?'
'Upstairs.'
'I don't hear anything.'
'You're deaf.'
'What sort of noise?'

But Edward sleeps again. The noise fades, dimly. Angel hears the sound of children's voices. Let it be a girl, dear Lord, let it be a girl.

'Why do you want a girl?' asks the doctor, on Angel's fourth monthly visit to the clinic.

'I'd love to dress a girl,' says Angel vaguely, but what she means is, if it's a girl, Edward will not be so – what is the word? – hardly jealous, difficult perhaps. Dreadful. Yes, dreadful.

Bright-eyed Edward: he walks with Angel now – long walks up and over stiles, jumping streams, leaping stones. Young Edward. She has begun to feel rather old, herself.

'I am a bit tired,' she says, as they set off one night for their moonlit walk.

He stops, puzzled.

'Why are you tired?'
'Because I'm pregnant,' she says, in spite of herself.
'Don't start that again,' he says, as if it were hysteria on her part. Perhaps it is.

That night, he opens her legs so wide she thinks she will burst. 'I love you,' he murmurs in her nibbled ear, 'Angel, I love you. I do love you.' Angel feels the familiar surge of response, the holy gratitude, the willingness to die, to be torn apart if that's what's required. And then it stops. It's gone. Evaporated! And in its place, a new strength. A chilly icicle of non-response, wonderful, cheerful. No. It isn't right; it isn't what's required: on the contrary. 'I love you,' she says in return, as usual; but crossing her fingers in her mind, forgiveness for a lie. Please God, dear God, save me, help me save my baby. It is not me he loves, but my baby he hates: not me he delights in, but the pain he causes me, and knows he does. He does not wish to take root in me: all he wants to do is root my baby out. I don't love him. I never have. It is sickness. I must get well. Quickly.

'Not like that,' says Angel, struggling free – bold, unkind, prudish Angel – rescuing her legs. 'I'm pregnant. I'm sorry, but I am pregnant.'

Edward rolls off her, withdraws.

'Christ, you can be a monster. A real ball-breaker.'

'Where are you going?' asks Angel, calm and curious. Edward is dressing. Clean shirt; cologne. Cologne!

'To London.'
'Why?'
'Where I'm appreciated.'
'Don't leave me alone. Please.' But she doesn't mean it.
'Why not?'
'I'm frightened. Here alone at night.'
'Nothing ever frightened you.' Perhaps he is right.

Off he goes; the car breaking open the silence of the night. It closes again. Angel is alone.

Tap, tap, tap, up above. Starting up as if on signal. Back and forward. To the attic bed which used to be, to the wardrobe which once was; the scuffle of the suitcase on the floor. Goodbye. I'm going. I'm frightened here. The house is haunted. Someone upstairs, downstairs. Oh, women everywhere, don't think your misery doesn't seep into walls, creep downstairs, and then upstairs again. Don't think it will ever be done with, or that the good times wipe it out. They don't.

Angel feels her heart stop and start again. A neurotic symptom, her father's doctor had once said. It will get better, he said, when she's married and has babies. Everything gets better for women when they're married with babies. It's their natural state. Angel's heart stops all the same, and starts again, for good or bad.

Angel gets out of bed, slips on her mules with their sharp little heels and goes up the attic stairs. Where does she find the courage? The light, reflected up from the hallway, is dim. The noise from the attic stops. Angel hears only – what? – the rustling noise of old newspapers in a fresh wind. That stops, too. As if a film were now running without sound. And coming down towards Angel, a small, tired woman in a nightie, slippers silent on the stairs, stopping to stare at Angel as Angel stares at her. Her face marked by bruises.

'How can I see that,' wonders Angel, now unafraid, 'since there isn't any light?'

She flicks on the switch, hand trembling, and in the light, as she'd known, there is nothing to be seen except the empty stairs and the unmarked dust upon them.

Angel goes back to the bedroom and sits on the bed.

'I saw a ghost,' she tells herself, calmly enough. Then fear reasserts itself: panic at the way the universe plays tricks. Quick, quick! Angel pulls her suitcase out from under the bed – there are still traces of wedding confetti within – and tap-tap she goes, with sharp little footsteps, from the wardrobe to the bed, from the chest of drawers and back again, not so much packing as retrieving, salvaging. Something out of nothing!

Angel and her predecessor, rescuing each other, since each was incapable of rescuing herself, and rescue always comes, somehow. Or else death.

Tap, tap, back and forth, into the suitcase, out of the house.

The garden gate swings behind her.

Angel, bearing love to a safer place.

1976

Alopecia

It's 1972.

'Fiddlesticks,' says Maureen. Everyone else says 'crap' or 'balls', but Maureen's current gear, being Victorian sprigged muslin, demands an appropriate vocabulary. 'Fiddlesticks. If Erica says her bald patches are anything to do with Derek, she's lying. It's alopecia.'

'I wonder which would be worse,' murmurs Ruthie in her soft voice, 'to have a husband who tears your hair out in the night, or to have alopecia.'

Ruthie wears a black fringed satin dress exactly half a century old, through which, alas, Ruthie's ribs show even more prominently than her breasts. Ruthie's little girl Poppy (at four too old for playgroup, too young for school), wears a long, white (well, yellowish) cotton shift which contrasts nicely with her mother's dusty black.

'At least the husband might improve, with effort,' says Alison, 'unlike alopecia. You wake up one morning with a single bald patch and a month or so later there you are, completely bald. Nothing anyone can do about it.' Alison, plump mother of three, sensibly wears a flowered Laura Ashley dress which hides her bulges.

'It might be quite interesting,' remarks Maureen. 'The egghead approach. One would have to forgo the past, of course, and go all space age, which would hardly be in keeping with the mood of the times.'

'You are the mood of the times, Maureen,' murmurs Ruthie, as expected. Ruthie's simple adulation of Maureen is both gratifying and embarrassing, everyone agrees.

Everyone agrees, on the other hand, that Erica Bisham of the bald patches is a stupid, if ladylike, bitch.

Maureen, Ruthie and Alison are working in Maureen's premises off the Kings Road. Here Maureen, as befits the glamour of her station, the initiator of Mauromania, meets the media, expresses opinions, answers the phone, dictates to secretaries (male), selects and matches fabrics, approves designs and makes, in general, multitudinous decisions – although not, perhaps, as multitudinous as the ones she was accustomed to make in the middle and late sixties, when the world was young and rich and wild. Maureen is forty but you'd never think it. She wears a large hat by day (and, one imagines, night) which shades her anxious face and guards her still pretty complexion. Maureen leads a rich life. Maureen once had her pubic hair dyed green to match her fingernails – or so her husband Kim announced to a waiting (well, such were the days) world: she divorced him not long after, having lost his baby at five months. The head of the foetus, rumour had it, emerged green, and her National Health Service GP refused to treat her any more, and she had to go private after all – she with her Marxist convictions.

That was 1968. If the State's going to tumble, let it tumble. The sooner the better. Drop out, everyone! Mauromania magnifique! And off goes Maureen's husband Kim with Maureen's au pair – a broad-hipped, big-bosomed girl, good breeding material, with an ordinary coarse and curly brush, if somewhat reddish.

Still, it had been a good marriage as marriages go. And as marriages go, it went. Or so Maureen remarked to the press, on her way home (six beds, six baths, four recep., American kitchen, patio, South Ken) from the divorce courts. Maureen cried a little in the taxi, when she'd left her public well behind, partly from shock and grief, mostly from confusion that beloved Kim, Kim, who so despised the nuclear family, who had so often said that he and she ought to get divorced in order to have a true and unfettered relationship, that Maureen's Kim should have speeded up Maureen's divorce in order to marry Maureen's au pair girl before the baby arrived. Kim and Maureen had been married for fifteen years. Kim had been Kevin from Liverpool before seeing the light or at any rate the guru. Maureen had always been just Maureen from Hoxton, East London: remained so through the birth, rise and triumph of Mauromania. It was her charm. Local girl makes good.

Maureen has experience of life: she knows by now, having also been married to a psychiatrist who ran off with all her money and the marital home, that it is wise to watch what people do, not listen to what they say. Well, it's something to have learned. Ruthie and Alison, her (nominal) partners from the beginning, each her junior by some ten years, listen to Maureen with respect and diffidence.

'Mind you,' says Maureen now, matching up purple feathers with emerald satin to great effect, 'if I were Derek I'd certainly beat Erica to death. Fancy having to listen to that whining voice night after night. The only trouble is he's become too much of a gentleman. He'll never have the courage to do it. Turned his back on his origins, and all that. It doesn't do.'

Maureen has known Derek since the old days in Hoxton. They were evacuees together: shared the same bomb shelter on their return from Starvation Hall in Felixstowe – a boys' public school considered unsafe for the gentry's children but all right for the East Enders.

'It's all Erica's fantasy,' says Ruthie, knowledgeably. 'A kind of dreadful sexual fantasy. She *wants* him to beat her up so she trots round London saying he does. Poor Derek. It comes from marrying into the English upper classes, old style. She must be nearly fifty. She has that kind of battered-looking face.'

Her voice trails away. There is a slight pause in the conversation.

'Um,' says Alison.

'That's drink,' says Maureen, decisively. 'Poor bloody Derek. What a ball-breaker to have married.' Derek was Maureen's childhood sweetheart. What a romantic, platonic idyll! She nearly married him once, twice, three times. Once in the very early days, before Kim, before anyone, when Derek was selling books from a barrow in Hoxton market. Once again, after Kim and before the professor, by which time Derek was taking expensive photographs of the trendy and successful – only then Erica turned up in Derek's bed, long-legged, disdainful, beautiful, with a model's precise and organised face, and the fluty tones of the girl who'd bought her school uniform at

Harrods, and that was the end of that. Not that Derek had ever exactly proposed to Maureen; not that they'd ever even been to bed together: they just knew each other and each other's bed partners so well that each knew what the other was thinking, feeling, hoping. Both from Hoxton, East London: Derek, Maureen; and a host of others, too. What was there, you might ask, about that particular acre of the East End which over a period of a few years gave birth to such a crop of remarkable children, such a flare-up of human creativity in terms of writing, painting, designing, entertaining? Changing the world? One might almost think God had chosen it for an experiment in intensive talent-breeding. Mauromania, God-sent.

And then there was another time in the late sixties, when there was a short break between Derek and Erica – Erica had a hysterectomy against Derek's wishes; but during those two weeks of opportunity Maureen, her business flourishing, her designs world famous, Mauromania a label for even trendy young queens (royal, that is) to boast, rich beyond counting – during those two special weeks of all weeks Maureen fell head over heels classically in love with Pedro: no, not a fisherman, but as good as – Italian, young, open-shirted, sloe-eyed, a designer. And Pedro, it later transpired, was using Maureen as a means to laying all the models, both male and female (Maureen had gone into menswear). Maureen was the last to know, and by the time she did Derek was in Erica's arms (or whatever) again. A sorry episode. Maureen spent six months at a health farm, on a diet of grapes and brown rice. At the end of that time Mauromania Man had collapsed, her business manager had jumped out of a tenth-floor window, and an employee's irate mother was bringing a criminal suit against Maureen personally for running a brothel. It was all quite irrational. If the employee, a runaway girl of, it turned out, only thirteen, but looking twenty, and an excellent seamstress, had contracted gonorrhoea whilst in her employ, was that Maureen's fault? The judge, sensibly, decided it wasn't, and that the entire collapse of British respectability could not fairly be laid at Maureen's door. Legal costs came to more than £12,000: the country house and stables had to be sold at a knock-down price. That was disaster year.

And who was there during that time to hold Maureen's hand? No one. Everyone, it seemed, had troubles enough of their own. And all the time, Maureen's poor heart bled for Pedro, of the ridiculous name and the sloe eyes, long departed, laughing, streptococci surging in his wake. And of all the old friends and allies only Ruthie and Alison lingered on, two familiar faces in a sea of changing ones, getting younger every day, and hungrier year by year not for fun, fashion, and excitement, but for money, promotion, security, and acknowledgment.

The staff even went on strike once, walking up and down outside the workshop with placards announcing hours and wages, backed by Maoists, women's liberationists and trade unionists, all vying for their trumpery allegiance, puffing up a tiny news story into a colossal media joke, not even bothering to get Maureen's side of the story – absenteeism, drug addiction, shoddy workmanship, falling markets, constricting profits.

But Ruthie gave birth to Poppy, unexpectedly, in the black and gold ladies' rest room (customers only – just as well it wasn't in the staff toilets where the plaster was flaking and the old wall-cisterns came down on your head if you pulled the chain) and that cheered everyone up. Business perked up, staff calmed down as unemployment rose. Poppy, born of

Mauromania, was everyone's favourite, everyone's mascot. Her father, only seventeen, was doing two years inside, framed by the police for dealing in pot. He did not have too bad a time – he got three A-levels and university entrance inside, which he would not have got outside, but it meant poor little Poppy had to do without a father's care and Ruthie had to cope on her own. Ruthie of the ribs.

Alison, meanwhile, somewhat apologetically, had married Hugo, a rather straight and respectable actor who believed in women's rights; they had three children and lived in a cosy house with a garden in Muswell Hill: Alison even belonged to the PTA! Hugo was frequently without work, but Hugo and Alison managed, between them, to keep going and even happy. Now Hugo thinks Alison should ask for a rise, but Alison doesn't like to. That's the trouble about working for a friend and being only a nominal partner.

'Don't let's talk about Erica Bisham any more,' says Maureen. 'It's too draggy a subject.' So they don't.

But one midnight a couple of weeks later, when Maureen, Ruthie and Alison are working late to meet an order – as is their frequent custom these days (and one most unnerving to Hugo, Alison's husband) – there comes a tap on the door. It's Erica, of course. Who else would tap, in such an ingratiating fashion? Others cry 'Hi!' or 'Peace!' and enter.

Erica, smiling nervously and crookedly; her yellow hair eccentric in the extreme; bushy in places, sparse in others. Couldn't she wear a wig? She is wearing a Marks & Spencer nightie which not even Ruthie would think of wearing, in the house or out of it. It is bloodstained down the back. (Menstruation is not yet so fashionable as to be thus demonstrable, though it can be talked about at length.) A strong smell of what? alcohol, or is it nail varnish? hangs about her. Drinking again. (Alison's husband, Hugo, in a long period of unemployment, once veered on to the edge of alcoholism but fortunately veered off again, and the smell of nail varnish, acetone, gave a warning sign of an agitated, overworked liver, unable to cope with acetaldehyde, the highly toxic product of alcohol metabolism.)

'Could I sit down?' says Erica. 'He's locked me out. Am I speaking oddly? I think I've lost a tooth. I'm hurting under my ribs and I feel sick.'

They stare at her – this drunk, dishevelled, trouble-making woman.

'He,' says Maureen finally. 'Who's he?'
'Derek.'

'You're going to get into trouble, Erica,' says Ruthie, though more kindly than Maureen, 'if you go round saying dreadful things about poor Derek.'

'I wouldn't have come here if there was anywhere else,' says Erica.

'You must have friends,' observes Maureen, as if to say, Don't count us amongst them if you have.
'No.' Erica sounds desolate. 'He has his friends at work. I don't seem to have any.'
'I wonder why,' says Maureen under her breath; and then, 'I'll get you a taxi home, Erica. You're in no state to be out.'
'I'm not drunk, if that's what you think.'

'Who ever is,' sighs Ruthie, sewing relentlessly on. Four more blouses by one o'clock. Then, thank God, bed.

Little Poppy has passed out on a pile of orange ostrich feathers. She looks fantastic.

'If Derek does beat you up,' says Alison, who has seen her father beat her mother on many a Saturday night, 'why don't you go to the police?'
'I did once, and they told me to go home and behave myself.'
'Or leave him?' Alison's mother left Alison's father.
'Where would I go? How would I live? The children? I'm not well.' Erica sways. Alison puts a chair beneath her. Erica sits, legs planted wide apart, head down. A few drops of blood fall on the floor. From Erica's mouth, or elsewhere? Maureen doesn't see, doesn't care. Maureen's on the phone, calling radio cabs who do not reply.

'I try not to provoke him, but I never know what's going to set him off,' mumbles Erica. 'Tonight it was Tampax. He said only whores wore Tampax. He tore it out and kicked me. Look.'

Erica pulls up her nightie (Erica's wearing no knickers) and exposes her private parts in a most shameful, shameless fashion. The inner thighs are blue and mottled, but then, dear God, she's nearly fifty.

What does one look like, thigh-wise, nearing fifty? Maureen's the nearest to knowing, and she's not saying. As for Ruthie, she hopes she'll never get there. Fifty!

'The woman's mad,' mutters Maureen. 'Perhaps I'd better call the loony wagon, not a taxi?'

'Thank God Poppy's asleep.' Poor Ruthie seems in a state of shock.

'You can come home with me, Erica,' says Alison. 'God knows what Hugo will say. He hates matrimonial upsets. He says if you get in between, they both start hitting you.'

Erica gurgles, a kind of mirthless laugh. From behind her, mysteriously, a child steps out. She is eight, stocky, plain and pale, dressed in boring Ladybird pyjamas.

'Mummy?'

Erica's head whips up; the blood on Erica's lip is wiped away by the back of Erica's hand. Erica straightens her back. Erica smiles. Erica's voice is completely normal, ladylike.

'Hallo, darling. How did you get here?'
'I followed you. Daddy was too angry.'
'He'll be better soon, Libby,' says Erica brightly. 'He always is.'
'We're not going home? Please don't let's go home. I don't want to see Daddy.'

'Bitch,' mutters Maureen, 'she's even turned his own child against him. Poor bloody Derek. There's nothing at all the matter with her. Look at her now.'

For Erica is on her feet, smoothing Libby's hair, murmuring, laughing.

'Poor bloody Erica,' observes Alison. It is the first time she has ever defied Maureen, let alone challenged her wisdom. And rising with as much dignity as her plump frame and flounced cotton will allow, Alison takes Erica and Libby home and installs them for the night in the spare room of the cosy house in Muswell Hill.

Hugo isn't any too pleased. 'Your smart sick friends,' he says. And, 'I'd beat a woman like that to death myself, any day.' And, 'Dragging that poor child into it: it's appalling.' He's nice to Libby, though, and rings up Derek to say she's safe and sound, and looks after her while Alison takes Erica round to the doctor. The doctor sends Erica round to the hospital, and the hospital admits her for tests and treatment.

'Why bother?' enquires Hugo. 'Everyone knows she's mad.'

In the evening, Derek comes all the way to Muswell Hill in his Ferrari to pick up Libby. He's an attractive man: intelligent and perspicacious, fatherly and gentle. Just right, it occurs to Alison, for Maureen.

'I'm so sorry about all this,' he says. 'I love my wife dearly but she has her problems. There's a dark side to her nature – you've no idea. A deep inner violence – which of course manifests itself in this kind of behaviour. She's deeply psychophrenic. I'm so afraid for the child.'

'The hospital did admit her,' murmurs Alison. 'And not to the psychiatric ward, but the surgical.'

'That will be her hysterectomy scar again,' says Derek. 'Any slight tussle – she goes quite wild, and I have to restrain her for her own safety – and it opens up. It's symptomatic of her inner sickness, I'm afraid. She even says herself it opens to let the build-up of wickedness out. What I can't forgive is the way she drags poor little Libby into things. She's turning the child against me. God knows what I'm going to do. Well, at least I can bury myself in work. I hear you're an actor, Hugo.'

Hugo offers Derek a drink, and Derek offers (well, more or less) Hugo a part in a new rock musical going on in the West End. Alison goes to visit Erica in hospital.

'Erica has some liver damage, but it's not irreversible: she'll be feeling nauseous for a couple of months, that's all. She's lost a back tooth and she's had a couple of stitches put in her vagina,' says Alison to Maureen and Ruthie next day. The blouse order never got completed – re-orders now look dubious. But if staff haven't the loyalty to work unpaid overtime any more, what else can be expected? The partners (nominal) can't do everything.

'Who said so?' enquires Maureen, sceptically. 'The hospital or Erica?'

'Well,' Alison is obliged to admit, 'Erica.'

'You are an innocent, Alison.' Maureen sounds quite cross. 'Erica can't open her poor sick mouth without uttering a lie. It's her hysterectomy scar opened up again, that's all. No wonder. She's a nymphomaniac: she doesn't leave Derek alone month in, month out. She has the soul of a whore. Poor man. He's so upset by it all. Who wouldn't be?'

Derek takes Maureen out to lunch. In the evening, Alison goes to visit Erica in hospital, but Erica has gone. Sister says, oh yes, her husband came to fetch her. They hadn't wanted to let her go so soon but Mr Bisham seemed such a sensible, loving man, they thought he could look after his wife perfectly well, and it's always nicer at home, isn't it? Was it *the* Derek Bisham? Yes she'd thought so. Poor Mrs Bisham – what a dreadful world we live in, when a respectable married woman can't even walk the streets without being brutally attacked, sexually assaulted by strangers.

It's 1974.

Winter. A chill wind blowing, a colder one still to come. A three-day week imposed by an insane government. Strikes, power cuts, blackouts. Maureen, Ruthie and Alison work by candlelight. All three wear fun-furs – old stock, unsaleable. Poppy is staying with Ruthie's mother, as she usually is these days. Poppy has been developing a squint, and the doctor says she has to wear glasses with one blanked-out lens for at least eighteen months. Ruthie, honestly, can't bear to see her daughter thus. Ruthie's mother, of a prosaic nature, a lady who buys her clothes at C&A Outsize, doesn't seem to mind.

'If oil prices go up,' says Maureen gloomily, 'what's going to happen to the price of synthetics? What's going to happen to Mauromania, come to that?'

'Go up-market,' says Alison, 'the rich are always with us.'

Maureen says nothing. Maureen is bad tempered, these days. She is having some kind of painful trouble with her teeth, which she seems less well able to cope with than she can the trouble with staff (overpaid), raw materials (unavailable), delivery dates (impossible), distribution (unchancy), costs (soaring), profits (falling), re-investment (non-existent). And the snow has ruined the penthouse roof and it has to be replaced, at the cost of many thousands. Men friends come and go: they seem to get younger and less feeling. Sometimes Maureen feels they treat her as a joke. They ask her about the sixties as if it were a different age: of Mauromania as if it were something as dead as the dodo – but it's still surely a label which counts for something, brings in foreign currency, ought really to bring her some recognition. The Beatles got the MBE; why not Maureen of Mauromania? Throwaway clothes for throwaway people?

'Ruthie,' says Maureen. 'You're getting careless. You've put the pocket on upside-down, and it's going for copying. That's going to hold up the whole batch. Oh, what the hell. Let it go through.'

'Do you ever hear anything of Erica Bisham?' Ruthie asks Alison, more to annoy Maureen than because she wants to know. 'Is she still wandering round in the middle of the night?'

'Hugo does a lot of work for Derek, these days,' says Alison carefully. 'But he never mentions Erica.'

'Poor Derek. What a fate. A wife with alopecia! I expect she's bald as a coot by now. As good a revenge as any, I dare say.'

'It was nothing to do with alopecia,' says Alison. 'Derek just tore out chunks of her hair, nightly.' Alison's own marriage isn't going so well. Hugo's got the lead in one of Derek's long runs in the West End. Show business consumes his thoughts and ambitions. The ingenue lead is in love with Hugo and says so, on TV quiz games and in the Sunday supplements. She's underage. Alison feels old, bored and boring.

'These days I'd believe anything,' says Ruthie. 'She must provoke him dreadfully.'

'I don't know what you've got against Derek, Alison,' says Maureen. 'Perhaps you just don't like men. In which case you're not much good in a fashion house. Ruthie, that's another pocket upside-down.'

'I feel sick,' says Ruthie. Ruthie's pregnant again. Ruthie's husband was out of prison and with her for exactly two weeks; then he flew off to Istanbul to smuggle marijuana back into the country. He was caught. Now he languishes in a Turkish jail. 'What's to become of us?'

'We must develop a sense of sisterhood,' says Alison, 'that's all.'

Alison's doorbell rings at three in the morning. It is election night, and Alison is watching the results on television. Hugo (presumably) is watching them somewhere else, with the ingenue lead – now above the age of consent, which spoils the pleasure somewhat. It is Erica and Libby. Erica's nose is broken. Libby, at ten, is now in charge. Both are in their nightclothes. Alison pays off the taxi driver, who won't take a tip. 'What a world,' he says.

'I couldn't think where else to come,' says Libby. 'Where he wouldn't follow her. I wrote down this address last time I was here. I thought it might come in useful, sometime.'

It is the end of Alison's marriage, and the end of Alison's job. Hugo, whose future career largely depends on Derek's goodwill, says, you have Erica in the house or you have me.

Alison says, I'll have Erica. 'Lesbian, dyke,' says Hugo, bitterly. 'Don't think you'll keep the children, you won't.'

Maureen says, 'That was the first and last time Derek ever hit her. He told me so. She lurched towards him on purpose. She *wanted* her nose broken; idiot Alison, don't you understand? Erica nags and provokes. She calls him dreadful, insulting, injuring things in public. She flays him with words. She says he's impotent: an artistic failure. I've heard her. Everyone has. When finally he lashes out, she's delighted. Her last husband beat hell out of her. She's a born victim.'

Alison takes Erica to a free solicitor, who – surprise, surprise – is efficient and who collects evidence and affidavits from doctors and hospitals all over London, has a restraining order issued against Derek, gets Libby and Erica back into the matrimonial home, and starts and completes divorce proceedings and gets handsome alimony. It all takes six months, at the end of which time Erica's face has altogether lost its battered look.

Alison turns up at work the morning after the alimony details are known and has the door shut in her face. Mauromania. The lettering is flaking. The door needs repainting.

Hugo sells the house over Alison's head. By this time she and the children are living in a two-room flat.

Bad times.

'You're a very destructive person,' says Maureen to Alison in the letter officially terminating her appointment. 'Derek never did you any harm, and you've ruined his life, you've interfered in a marriage in a really wicked way. You've encouraged Derek's wife to break up his perfectly good marriage, and turned Derek's child against him, and not content with that you've crippled Derek financially. Erica would never have been so vindictive if she hadn't had you egging her on. It was you who made her go to law, and once things get into lawyers' hands they escalate, as who better than I should know? The law has nothing to do with natural justice, idiot Alison. Hugo is very concerned for you and thinks you should have mental treatment. As for me, I am really upset. I expected friendship and loyalty from you, Alison; I trained you and employed you, and saw you through good times and bad. I may say, too, that your notion of Mauromania becoming an exclusive fashion house, which I followed through for a time, was all but disastrous, and symptomatic of your general bad judgment. After all, this is the people's age, the sixties, the seventies, the eighties, right through to the new century. Derek is coming in with me in the new world Mauromania.'

Mauromania, meretricious!

A month or so later, Derek and Maureen are married. It's a terrific wedding, somewhat marred by the death of Ruthie – killed, with her new baby, in the Paris air crash, on her way home from Istanbul, where she'd been trying to get her young husband released from prison. She'd failed. But then, if she'd succeeded, he'd have been killed too, and he was too young to die. Little Poppy was at the memorial service, in a sensible trouser-suit from C&A, bought for her by Gran, without her glasses, both enormous eyes apparently now functioning well. She didn't remember Alison, who was standing next to her, crying softly. Soft beds of orange feathers, far away, another world.

Alison wasn't asked to the wedding, which in any case clashed with the mass funeral of the air-crash victims. Just as well. What would she have worn?

It's 1975.

It's summer, long and hot. Alison walks past Mauromania. Alison has remarried. She is happy. She didn't know that such ordinary everyday kindness could exist and endure. Alison is wearing, like everyone else, jeans and a T-shirt. A new ordinariness, a common sense, a serio-cheerfulness infuses the times. Female breasts swing free, libertarian by day, erotic by night, costing nobody anything, or at most a little modesty. No profit there.

Mauromania is derelict, boarded up. A barrow outside is piled with old stock, sale-priced. Coloured tights, fun-furs, feathers, slinky dresses. Passers-by pick over the stuff, occasionally buy, mostly look, and giggle, and mourn, and remember.

Alison, watching, sees Maureen coming down the steps. Maureen is rather nastily dressed in a bright yellow silk shift. Maureen's hair seems strange, bushy in parts, sparse in others. Maureen has abandoned her hat. Maureen bends over the barrow, and Alison can see the bald patches on her scalp.

'Alopecia,' says Alison, out loud. Maureen looks up. Maureen's face seems somehow worn and battered, and old and haunted beyond its years. Maureen stares at Alison, recognising, and Maureen's face takes on an expression of half-apology, half-entreaty. Maureen wants to speak.

But Alison only smiles brightly and lightly and walks on.

Alopecia

'I'm afraid poor Maureen has alopecia, on top of everything else,' she says to anyone who happens to enquire after that sad, forgotten figure, who once had everything – except, perhaps, a sense of sisterhood.

1976

The Man with No Eyes

Edgar, Minette, Minnie and Mona.

In the evenings three of them sit down to play Monopoly. Edgar, Minette and Minnie. Mona, being only five, sleeps upstairs, alone, in the little back bedroom, where roses, growing up over the porch and along under the thatch, thrust dark companionable heads through the open lattice window. Edgar and Minnie, father and daughter, face each other across the table. Both, he in his prime, she in early adolescence, are already bronzed from the holiday sun, blue eyes bright and eager in lean faces, dull red hair bleached to brightness by the best summer the Kent coast has seen, they say, since 1951 – a merciful God allowing, it seems, the glimmer of His smile to shine again on poor humiliated England. Minette, Edgar's wife, sits at the kitchen end of the table. The ladderback chair nearest the porch remains empty. Edgar says it is uncomfortable. Minnie keeps the bank. Minette doles out the property cards.

Thus, every evening this holiday, they have arranged themselves around the table, and taken up their allotted tasks. They do it almost wordlessly, for Edgar does not care for babble. Who does? Besides, Mona might wake, think she was missing something, and insist on joining in.

How like a happy family we are, thinks Minette, pleased,

shaking the dice. Minette's own face is pink and shiny from the sun and her nose is peeling. Edgar thinks hats on a beach are affected (an affront, as it were, to nature's generosity) so Minette is content to pay the annual penalty summer holidays impose on her fair complexion and fine mousy hair. Her mouth is swollen from the sun, and her red arms and legs are stiff and bumpy with midge bites. Mona is her mother's daughter and has inherited her difficulty with the sun, and even had a slight touch of sunstroke on the evening of the second day, which Edgar, probably rightly, put down to the fact that Minette had slapped Mona on the cheek, in the back of the car, on the journey down.

'Cheeks afire,' he said, observing his flushed and feverish child. 'You really shouldn't vent your neuroses on your children, Minette.'

And of course Minette shouldn't. Edgar was right. Poor little Mona. It was entirely forgivable for Mona, a child of five, to become fractious and unbiddable in the back of a car, cooped up as she was on a five-hour journey; and entirely unforgivable of the adult Minette, sitting next to her, to be feeling so cross, distraught, nervous and unmaternal that she reacted by slapping. Minette should have, could have diverted: could have sung, could have played Here is the Church, this Little Pig, something, anything, rather than slapped. Cheeks afire! As well they might be. Mona's with upset at her mother's cruel behaviour: Minette's, surely, with shame and sorrow.

Edgar felt the journey was better taken without stops, and that in any case no coffee available on a motorway was worth stopping for. It would be instant, not real. Why hadn't Minette brought a Thermos, he enquired, when she ventured to suggest they stopped. Because we don't *own* a Thermos, she wanted to cry, in her impossible mood, because you say they're monstrously over-priced, because you say I always break the screw; in any case it's not the coffee I want, it's for you to stop, to recognise our existence, our needs – but she stopped herself in time. That way quarrels lie, and the rare quarrels of Edgar and Minette, breaking out, shatter the neighbourhood, not to mention the children. Well done, Minette.

'Just as well we didn't go to Italy,' said Edgar, on the night of Mona's fever, measuring out, to calm the mother-damaged, fevered cheek, the exact dosage of Junior Aspirin recommended on the back of the packet (and although Minette's doctor once instructed her to quadruple the stated dose, if she wanted it to be effective, Minette knows better than to say so), dissolving it in water, and feeding it to Mona by the spoonful though Minette knows Mona much prefers to suck them – 'if this is what half an hour's English sun does to her.'

Edgar, Minette, Minnie and Mona. Off to Italy, camping, every year for the last six years, even when Mona was a baby. Milan, Venice, Florence, Pisa. Oh what pleasure, riches, glory, of countryside and town. This year, Minette had renewed the passports and replaced the sleeping bags, brought the Melamine plates and mugs up to quota, checked the Gaz cylinders, and waited for Edgar to reveal the date, usually towards the end of July, when he would put his ethnographical gallery in the hands of an assistant and they would pack themselves and the tent into the car, happy families, and set off, as if spontaneously, into the unknown; but this year the end of July went and the first week of August, and still Edgar did not speak, and Minette's employers were betraying a kind of incredulous restlessness at Minette's apparent lack of decision, and only then, on August 6, after a studied absent-mindedness lasting from July 31 to August 5, did Edgar say 'Of course we can't afford to go abroad. Business is rock-bottom. I hope you haven't been wasting any money on unnecessary equipment?'

'No, of course not,' says Minette. Minette tells many lies: it is one of the qualities which Edgar least likes in her. Minette thinks she is safe in this one. Edgar will not actually count the Melamine plates; nor is he likely to discern the difference between one old lumpy navy-blue sleeping bag and another unlumpy new one. 'We do have the money set aside,' she says cautiously, hopefully.

'Don't be absurd,' he says. 'We can't afford to drive the car round the corner, let alone to Venice. It'll only have sunk another couple of inches since last year, beneath the weight of crap as much as of tourists. It's too depressing. Everything's too depressing.' Oh Venice, goodbye Venice, city of wealth and abandon, and human weakness, glorious beneath sulphurous skies. Goodbye Venice, says Minette in her heart, I loved you well. 'So we shan't be having a holiday this year?' she enquires. Tears are smarting in her eyes. She doesn't believe him. She is tired, work has been exhausting. She is an advertising copywriter. He is teasing, surely. He often is. In the morning he will say something different.

'You go on holiday if you want,' he says in the morning. 'I can't. I can't afford a holiday this year. You seem to have lost all sense of reality, Minette. It's that ridiculous place you work in.' And of course he is right. Times are hard. Inflation makes profits and salaries seem ridiculous. Edgar, Minette, Minnie and Mona must adapt with the times. An advertising agency is not noted for the propagation of truth. Those who work in agencies live fantasy lives as to their importance in the scheme of things and their place in a society which in truth despises them. Minette is lucky that someone of his integrity and taste puts up with her. No holiday this year. She will pay the money set aside into a building society, though the annual interest is less than the annual inflation rate. She is resigned.

But the next day, Edgar comes home, having booked a holiday cottage in Kent. A miracle. Friends of his own it, and have had a cancellation. Purest chance. It is the kind of good fortune Edgar always has. If Edgar is one minute late for a train, the train leaves two minutes late.

Now, on the Friday, here they are, Edgar, Minette, Minnie and Mona, installed in this amazing rural paradise of a Kentish hamlet, stone-built, thatched cottage, swifts flying low across the triangular green, the heavy smell of farmyard mixing with the scent of the absurd red roses round the door and the night-stocks in the cottage garden, tired and happy after a day on the beach, with the sun shining and the English Channel blue and gentle, washing upon smooth pebbles.

Mona sleeps, stirs. The night is hot and thundery, ominous. Inflation makes the Monopoly money not so fantastic as it used to be. Minette remarks on it to Edgar.

'Speak for yourself,' he says. Minette recently got a rise, promotion. Edgar is self-employed, of the newly impoverished classes.

They throw to see who goes first. Minette throws a two and a three. Minnie, her father's daughter, throws a five and a six.

Minnie is twelve, a kindly, graceful child, watchful of her mother, adoring her father, whom she resembles.

Edgar throws a double six. Edgar chooses his token – the iron – and goes first.

Edgar, Minette, Minnie and Mona.

Edgar always wins the toss. Edgar always chooses the iron. (He is as good at housekeeping and cooking as Minette, if not better.) Edgar always wins the game. Minnie always comes second. Minette always comes last. Mona always sleeps. Of such stuff are holidays made.

Monopoly, in truth, bores Minette. She plays for Minnie's sake, to be companionable, and for Edgar's, because it is expected. Edgar likes winning. Who doesn't?

Edgar throws a double, lands on Pentonville Road, and buys it for £60. Minette hands over the card; Minnie receives his money. Edgar throws again, lands on and buys Northumberland Avenue. Minnie throws, lands on Euston Road, next to her father, and buys it for £100. Minette lands on Income Tax, pays £200 into the bank and giggles, partly from nervousness, partly at the ridiculous nature of fate.

'You do certainly have a knack, Minette,' says Edgar, unsmiling. 'But I don't know if it's anything to laugh about.'

Minette stops smiling. The game continues in silence. Minette lands in jail. Upstairs Mona, restless, murmurs and mutters in her sleep. In the distance Minette can hear the crackle of thunder. The windows are open, and the curtains not drawn, in order that Edgar can feel close to the night and nature, and make the most of his holiday. The window squares of blank blackness, set into the white walls, as on some child's painting, frighten Minette. What's outside? Inside, it seems to her, their words echo. The rattle of the dice is loud, loaded with some kind of meaning she'd rather not think about. Is someone else listening, observing?

Mona cries out. Minette gets up. 'I'll go to her,' she says.
'She's perfectly all right,' says Edgar. 'Don't fuss.'
'She might be frightened,' says Minette.
'What of?' enquires Edgar dangerously. 'What is there to be frightened of?' He is irritated by Minette's many fears, especially on holiday, and made angry by the notion that there is anything threatening in nature. Loving silence and isolation himself, he is impatient with those city-dwellers who fear them. Minette and Mona, his feeling is, are city-dwellers by nature, whereas Edgar and Minnie have the souls, the patience, the maturity of the country-dweller, although obliged to live in the town.
'It's rather hot. She's in a strange place,' Minette persists.

'She's in a lovely place,' says Edgar, flatly. 'Of course, she may be having bad dreams.'

Mona is silent again, and Minette is relieved. If Mona is having bad dreams, it is of course Minette's fault, first for having slapped Mona on the cheek, and then, more basically, for having borne a child with such a town-dweller's nature that she suffers from sunburn and sunstroke.

'Mona by name,' says Minette, 'moaner by nature.'

'Takes after her mother,' says Edgar. 'Minette, you forgot to pay £50 last time you landed in jail, so you'll have to stay there until you throw a double.'

'Can't I pay this time round?'

'No you can't,' says Edgar.

They've lost the rule book. All losses in the house are Minette's responsibility, so it is only justice that Edgar's ruling as to the nature of the game shall be accepted. Minette stays in jail.

Mona by name, moaner by nature. It was Edgar who named his children, not Minette. Childbirth upset her judgment, made her impossible, or so Edgar said, and she was willing to believe it, struggling to suckle her young under Edgar's alternately indifferent and chiding eye, sore from stitches, trying to decide on a name, and unable to make up her mind, for any name Minette liked, Edgar didn't. For convenience sake, while searching for a compromise, she referred to her first-born as Mini – such a tiny, beautiful baby – and when Edgar came back unexpectedly with the birth certificate, there was the name Minnie, and Minette gasped with horror, and all Edgar said was, 'But I thought that was what *you* wanted, it's what *you* called her, the State won't wait for ever for *you* to make up your mind; I had to spend all morning in that place and I ought to be in the gallery; I'm exhausted. Aren't you grateful for anything? You've got to get that baby to sleep right through the night somehow before I go mad.' Well, what could she say? Or do? Minnie she was. Minnie Mouse. But in a way it suited her, or at any rate she transcended it, a beautiful loving child, her father's darling, mother's too.

Minette uses Minnie as good Catholics use the saints – as an intercessionary power.

Minnie, see what your father wants for breakfast. Minnie, ask your father if we're going out today.

When Mona was born Minette felt stronger and happier. Edgar, for some reason, was easy and loving. (Minette lost her job: it had been difficult, looking after the six-year-old Minnie, being pregnant again by accident – well, forgetting her pill – still with the house, the shopping and the cleaning to do, and working at the same time: not to mention the washing. They had no washing machine, Edgar feeling, no doubt rightly, that domestic machinery was noisy, expensive, and not really, in the end, labour saving. Something had to give, and it was Minette's work that did, just in time to save her sanity. The gallery was doing well, and of course Minette's earnings had been increasing Edgar's tax. Or so he believed. She tried to explain that they were taxed separately, but he did not seem to hear, let alone believe.) In any case, sitting up in childbed with her hand in Edgar's, happy for once, relaxed, unemployed – he was quite right, the work did overstrain her, and what was the point – such meaningless, anti-social work amongst such facile, trendy non-people – joking about the new baby's name, she said, listen to her moaning. Perhaps we'd better call her Moaner. Moaner by name, Moaner by nature. Imprudent Minette. And a week later, there he was, with the birth certificate all made out. Mona.

'Good God, woman,' he cried. 'Are you mad? *You* said you wanted Mona. I took *you* at your word. I was doing what *you* wanted.'

'I didn't say that.' She was crying, weak from childbirth, turmoil, the sudden withdrawl of his kindness, his patience. 'Do you want me to produce witnesses?' He was exasperated.

She became pregnant again, a year later. She had an abortion. She couldn't cope, Edgar implied that she couldn't, although he never quite said so, so that the burden of the decision was hers and hers alone. But he was right, of course. She couldn't cope. She arranged everything, went to the nursing home by minicab, by herself, and came out by minicab the next day. Edgar paid half.

Edgar, Minette, Minnie and Mona. Quite enough to be getting on with.

Minette started going to a psychotherapist once a week. Edgar said she had to; she was impossible without. She burned the dinner once or twice – 'how hostile you are,' said Edgar, and after that cooked all meals himself, without reference to anyone's tastes, habits, or convenience. Still, he did know best. Minette, Minnie and Mona adapted themselves splendidly. He was an admirable cook, once you got used to garlic with everything, from eggs to fish.

Presently, Minette went back to work. Well, Edgar could hardly be expected to pay for the psychotherapist, and in any case, electricity and gas bills having doubled even in a household almost without domestic appliances, there was no doubt her earnings came in useful. Presently, Minette was paying all the household bills – and had promotion. She became a group head with twenty people beneath her. She dealt with clients, executives, creative people, secretaries, assistants, with ease and confidence. Compared to Edgar and home, anyone, anything was easy. But that was only to be expected. Edgar was real life. Advertising agencies – and Edgar was right about this – are make-believe. Shut your eyes, snap your fingers, and presto, there one is, large as life. (That is, if you have the right, superficial, rubbishy attitude to make it happen.) And of course, its employees and contacts can be easily manipulated and modified, as dolls can be, in a doll's house. Edgar was not surprised at Minette's success. It was only to be expected. And she never remembered to turn off the lights, and turned up the central heating much too high, being irritatingly sensitive to cold.

Even tonight, this hot sultry night, with the temperature still lingering in the eighties and lightning crackling round the edges of the sky, she shivers.

'You can't be cold,' he enquires. He is buying a property from Minnie. He owns both Get Out of Jail cards, and has had a bank error in his favour of £200. Minnie is doing nicely, on equal bargaining terms with her father. Minette's in jail again.
'It's just so dark out there,' she murmurs.
'Of course it is,' he said. 'It's the country. You miss the town, don't you?' It is an accusation, not a statement.

The cottage is on a hillside: marsh above and below, interrupting the natural path from the summit to the valley. The windows are open front and back as if to offer least interruption, throwing the house and its inhabitants open to the path of whatever forces flow from the top to the bottom of hills. Or so Minette suspects. How can she say so? She, the town dweller, the obfuscate, standing between Edgar and the light of his expectations, his sensitivity to the natural life forces which flow between the earth and him.

Edgar has green fingers, no doubt about it. See his tomatoes in the window-box of his Museum Street gallery? What a triumph!

'Couldn't we have the windows closed?' she asks.
'What for?' he enquires. 'Do *you* want the windows closed, Minnie?'
Minnie shrugs, too intent on missing her father's hotel on Northumberland Avenue to care one way or the other. Minnie has a fierce competitive spirit. Edgar, denying his own, marvels at it. 'Why do you want to shut out the night?' Edgar demands.
'I don't,' Minette protests. But she does. Yes, she does. Mona stirs and whimpers upstairs: Minette wants to go to her, close her windows, stop the dark rose heads nodding, whispering distress, but how can she? It is Minette's turn to throw the dice. Her hand trembles. Another five. Chance. You win £10, second prize in beauty contest.

'Not with your nose in that condition,' says Edgar, and laughs. Minnie and Minette laugh as well. 'And your cheeks the colour of poor Mona's. Still, one is happy to know there is a natural justice.'

A crack of thunder splits the air; one second, two seconds, three seconds – and there's the lightning, double-forked, streaking down to the oak-blurred ridge of hills in front of the house.

'I love storms,' says Edgar. 'It's coming this way.'
'I'll just go and shut Mona's window,' says Minette.
'She's perfectly all right,' says Edgar. 'Stop fussing and for God's sake stay out of jail. You're casting a gloom, Minette. There's no fun in playing if one's the only one with hotels.' As of course Edgar is, though Minnie's scattering houses up and down the board.

Minette lands on Community. A £20 speeding fine or take a Chance. She takes a Chance. Pay £150 in school fees.

The air remains dry and still. Thunder and lightning, though monstrously active, remain at their distance, the other side of the hills. The front door creaks silently open, of its own volition. Not a whisper of wind – only the baked parched air.

'Ooh,' squeaks Minnie, agreeably frightened.

Minette is dry-mouthed with terror, staring at the black beyond the door.

'A visitor,' cries Edgar. 'Come in, come in,' and he mimes a welcome to the invisible guest, getting to his feet, hospitably pulling back the empty ladderback chair at the end of the table. The house is open, after all, to whoever, whatever, chooses to call, on the way from the top of the hill to the bottom.

Minette's mouth is open: her eyes appalled. Edgar sees, scorns, sneers.

'Don't, Daddy,' says Minnie. 'It's spooky,' but Edgar is not to be stopped.
'Come in,' he repeats. 'Make yourself at home. Don't stumble like that. Just because you've got no eyes.'

Minette is on her feet. Monopoly money, taken up by the first sudden gust of storm wind, flies about the room. Minnie pursues it, half-laughing, half-panicking.

Minette tugs her husband's inflexible arm.

'Stop,' she beseeches. 'Don't tease. Don't.' No eyes! Oh, Edgar, Minette, Minnie and Mona, what blindness is there amongst you now? What threat to your existence? An immense peal of thunder crackles, it seems, directly overhead: lightning, both sheet and fork, dims the electric light and achieves a strobe-lighting effect of cosmic vulgarity, blinding and bouncing round the white walls, and now, upon the wind, rain, large-dropped, blows in through open door and windows.

'Shut them,' shrieks Minette. 'I told you. Quickly! Minnie, come and help –'

'Don't fuss. What does it matter? A little rain. Surely you're not frightened of storms?' enquires Edgar, standing just where he is, not moving, not helping, like some great tree standing up to a torrent. For once Minette ignores him and with Minnie gets door and windows shut. The rain changes its nature, becomes drenching and blinding; their faces and clothes are wet with it. Minnie runs up to Mona's room, to make that waterproof. Still Edgar stands, smiling, staring out of the window at the amazing splitting sky. Only then, as he smiles, does Minette realise what she has done. She has shut the thing, the person with no eyes, in with her family. Even if it wants to go, would of its own accord drift down on its way towards the valley, it can't.

Minette runs to open the back door. Edgar follows, slow and curious.

'Why do you open the back door,' he enquires, 'having insisted on shutting everything else? You're very strange, Minette.'

Wet, darkness, noise, fear make her brave.

'You're the one who's strange. A man with no eyes!' she declares, sharp and brisk as she sometimes is at her office, chiding inefficiency, achieving sense and justice. 'Fancy asking in a man with no eyes. What sort of countryman would do a thing like that? You know nothing about anything, people, country, nature. Nothing.'

I know more than he does, she thinks, in this mad excess of arrogance. I may work in an advertising agency. I may prefer central heating to carrying coals, and a frozen pizza to a fresh mackerel, but I grant the world its dignity. I am aware of what I don't know, what I don't understand, and that's more than you can do. My body moves with the tides, bleeds with the moon, burns in the sun: I, Minette, I am a poor passing fragment of humanity: I obey laws I only dimly understand, but I am aware that the penalty of defying them is at best disaster, at worst death.

Thing with no eyes. Yes. The Taniwha. The Taniwha will get you if you don't look out! The sightless blundering monster of the bush, catching little children who stumble into him, devouring brains, bones, eyes and all. On that wild Australasian shore which my husband does not recognise as country, being composed of sand, shore and palmy forest, rather than of patchworked fields and thatch, lurked a blind and eyeless thing, that's where the Taniwha lives. The Taniwha will get you if you don't watch out! Little Minette, Mona's age, shrieked it at her infant enemies, on her father's instructions. That'll frighten them, he said, full of admonition and care, as ever. They'll stop teasing, leave you alone. Minette's father, tall as a tree, legs like poles. Little Minette's arms clasped round them to the end, wrenched finally apart, to set him free to abandon her, leave her to the Taniwha. The Taniwha will get you if you don't watch out. Wish it on others, what happens to you? Serve you right, with knobs on.

'You know nothing about anything,' she repeats now. 'What country person, after dark, sits with the windows open and invites in invisible strangers? Especially ones who are blind.'

Well, Edgar is angry. Of course he is. He stares at her bleakly. Then Edgar steps out of the back door into the rain, now fitful rather than torrential, and flings himself upon his back on the grass, face turned to the tumultuous heavens, arms outspread, drinking in noise, rain, wind, nature, at one with the convulsing universe.

Minnie joins her mother at the door.

'What's he doing?' she asks, nervous.

'Being at one with nature,' observes Minette, cool and casual for Minnie's benefit. 'He'll get very wet, I'm afraid.'

Rain turns to hail, spattering against the house like machinegun bullets. Edgar dives for the safety of the house, stands in the kitchen drying his hair with the dish towel, silent, angrier than ever.

'Can't we go on with Monopoly?' beseeches Minnie from the doorway. 'Can't we, Mum? The money's only got a little damp. I've got it all back.'
'Not until your father puts that chair back as it was.'
'What chair, Minette?' enquires Edgar, so extremely annoyed with his wife that he is actually talking to her direct. The rest of the holiday is lost, she knows it.

'The ladderback chair. You asked in something from the night to sit on it,' cries Minette, over the noise of nature, hung now for a sheep as well as a lamb, 'now put it back where it was.'

Telling Edgar what to do? Impudence.

'You are mad,' he says seriously. 'Why am I doomed to marry mad women?' Edgar's first wife Hetty went into a mental home after a year of marriage and never re-emerged. She was a very trying woman, according to Edgar.

Mad? What's mad in a mad world? Madder than the dice, sending Minette to jail, back and back again, sending Edgar racing round the board, collecting money, property, power: pacing Minnie in between the two of them, but always nearer her father than her mother? Minnie, hot on Edgar's heels, learning habits to last a lifetime?

All the same, oddly, Edgar goes to the ladderback chair, left pulled back for its unseen guest, and puts it in its original position, square against the table.

'Stop being so spooky,' cries Minnie, 'both of you.'

Minette wants to say 'and now tell it go away –' but her mouth won't say the words. It would make it too much there. Acknowledgement is dangerous; it gives body to the insubstantial.

Edgar turns to Minette. Edgar smiles, as a sane person, humouring, smiles at an insane one. And he takes Minette's raincoat from the peg, wet as he already is, and races off through the wind to see if the car windows have been properly closed.

Minette is proud of her Bonnie Cashin raincoat. It cost one hundred and twenty pounds, though she told Edgar it was fifteen pounds fifty, reduced from twenty-three pounds. It has never actually been in the rain before and she fears for its safety. She can't ask Edgar not to wear it. He would look at her in blank unfriendliness and say, 'But I thought it was a raincoat. You described it as a raincoat. If it's a raincoat, why can't you use it in the rain? Or were you lying to me? It isn't a raincoat after all?'

Honestly, she'd rather the coat shrunk than go through all that. Silly garment to have bought in the first place: Edgar was quite right. Well, would have been had he known. Minette sometimes wonders why she tells so many lies. Her head is dizzy.

The chair at the top of the table seems empty. The man with no eyes is out of the house: Edgar, coat over head, can be seen through the rain haze, stumbling past the front hedge towards the car. Will lightning strike him? Will he fall dead? No.

If the car windows are open, whose fault? Hers, Minnie's?

'I wish you'd seen that Mona shut the car door after her.' Her fault, as Mona's mother. 'And why haven't you woken her? This is a wonderful storm.'

And up he goes to be a better mother to Mona than Minette will ever be, waking his reluctant, sleep-heavy younger daughter to watch the storm, taking her on his knee, explaining the nature and function of electrical discharge the while: now ignoring Minette's presence entirely. When annoyed with her, which is much of the time, for so many of Minette's attitudes and pretensions irritate Edgar deeply, he chooses to pretend she doesn't exist.

Edgar, Minette, Minnie and Mona, united, watching a storm from a holiday cottage. Happy families.

The storm passes: soon it is like gunfire, flashing and banging on the other side of the hills. The lights go out. A power line down, somewhere. No one shrieks, not even Mona: it merely, suddenly, becomes dark. But oh how dark the country is.

'Well,' says Edgar presently, 'where are the matches? Candles?'

Where, indeed. Minette gropes, useless, trembling, up and down her silent haunted home. How foolish of Minette, knowing there was a storm coming, knowing (surely!) that country storms meant country power cuts, not to have located them earlier. Edgar finds them; he knew where they were all the time.

They go to bed. Edgar and Minette pass on the stairs. He is silent. He is not talking to her. She talks to him.
'Well,' she says, 'you're lucky. All he did was make the lights go out. The man with no eyes.'

He does not bother to reply. What can be said to a mad woman that's in any way meaningful?

All night Edgar sleeps on the far edge of the double bed, away from her, forbidding even in his sleep. So, away from her, he will sleep for the next four or even five days. Minette lies awake for an hour or so, and finally drifts off into a stunned and unrefreshing sleep.

In the morning she is brisk and smiling for the sake of the children, her voice fluty with false cheer, like some Kensington lady in Harrods Food Hall. Sweeping the floor, before breakfast, she avoids the end of the table, and the ladderback chair. The man with no eyes has gone, but something lingers.

Edgar makes breakfast. He is formal with her in front of the children, silent when they are on their own, deaf to Minette's pleasantries. Presently she falls silent too. He adorns a plate of scrambled eggs with buttercups and adjures the children to eat them. Minette has some vague recollection of reading that buttercups are poisonous: she murmurs something of the sort and Edgar winces, visibly. She says no more.

No harm comes to the children, of course. She must have misremembered. Edgar plans omelette, a buttercup salad and nettle soup for lunch. That will be fun, he says. Live off the land, like we're all going to have to, soon.

Minette and Mona giggle and laugh and shriek, clutching nettles. If you squeeze they don't sting. Minette, giggling and laughing to keep her children company, has a pain in her heart. They love their father. He loves them.

After lunch – omelette with lovely rich fresh farm eggs, though actually the white falls flat and limp in the bowl and Minette knows they are at least ten days old, but also knows better than to say so, buttercup salad, and stewed nettles, much like spinach – Edgar tells the children that the afternoon is to be spent at an iron age settlement, on Cumber Hill. Mona weeps a little, fearing a hilltop alive with iron men, but Minnie explains there will be nothing there – just a few lumps and bumps in the springy turf, burial mounds and old excavations, and a view all round, and perhaps a flint or two to be found.

'Then why are we going?' asks Mona, but no one answers. 'Will there be walking? Will there be cows? I've got a blister.'

'Mona by name, moaner by nature,' remarks Edgar. But which comes first, Minette wonders. Absently, she gives Minnie and Mona packet biscuits. Edgar protests. Artificial sugar, manufactured crap, ruining teeth, digestion, morale. What kind of mother is she?

'But they're hungry,' she wants to say and doesn't, knowing the reply by heart. How can they be? They've just had lunch.

In the car first Mona is sick, then Minnie. They are both easily sick, and neatly, out of the car window. Edgar does not stop. He says, 'You shouldn't have given them those biscuits. I knew this would happen,' but he does slow down.

Edgar, Minette, Minnie and Mona. Biscuits, buttercups and boiled nettles. Something's got to give.

Cumber Hill, skirted by car, is wild and lovely: a smooth turfed hilltop wet from last night's rain, a natural fort, the ground sloping sharply away from the broad summit, where sheep now graze, humped with burial mounds. Here families lived, died, grieved, were happy, fought off invaders, perished: left something of themselves behind, numinous beneath a heavy sky.

Edgar parks the car a quarter of a mile from the footpath which leads through stony farmland to the hill itself, and the tracks which skirt the fortifications. It will be a long walk. Minnie declines to come with them, as is her privilege as her father's daughter. She will sit in the car and wait and listen to the radio. A nature programme about the habits of buzzards, she assures her father.

'We'll be gone a couple of hours,' warns Minette.
'That long? It's only a hill.'
'There'll be lots of interesting things. Flints, perhaps. Even fossils. Are you sure?'
Minnie nods, her eyes blank with some inner determination.
'If she doesn't want to come, Minette,' says Edgar, 'she doesn't. It's her loss.'

It is the first direct remark Edgar has made to Minette all day. Minette is pleased, smiles, lays her hand on his arm. Edgar ignores her gesture. Did she really think his displeasure would so quickly evaporate? Her lack of perception will merely add to its duration.

Their walking sticks lie in the back of the car – Minette's a gnarled fruit-tree bough, Edgar's a traditional blackthorn (antique, with a carved dog's head for a handle, bought for him by Minette on the occasion of his forty-second birthday, and costing too much, he said by five pounds, being twenty pounds) and Minnie's and Mona's being stout but mongrel lengths of branch from some unnamed and undistinguished tree. Edgar hands Mona her stick, takes up his own and sets off. Minette picks up hers and follows behind. So much for disgrace.

Edgar is brilliant against the muted colours of the hill a tall, long-legged rust-heaped shape, striding in orange holiday trousers and red shirt, leaping from hillock to hillock, rock to rock, black stick slashing against nettle and thistle and gorse. Mona, trotting along beside him, stumpy-legged, navy-anoraked, is a stocky, valiant, enthusiastic little creature, perpetually falling over her stick but declining to relinquish it.

Mona presently falls behind and walks with her mother, whom she finds more sympathetic than her father as to nettlesting and cowpats. Her hand is dry and firm in Minette's. Minette takes comfort from it. Soon Edgar, relieved of Mona's presence, is so far ahead as to be a dark shape occasionally bobbing into sight over a mound or out from behind a wall or tree.

'I don't see any iron men,' says Mona. 'Only nettles and sheep mess. And cow splats, where I'm walking. Only I don't see any cows either. I expect they're invisible.'
'All the iron men died long ago.'
'Then why have we come here?'
'To think about things.'
'What things?'
'The past, the present, the future,' replies Minette.

The wind gets up, blowing damply in their faces. The sun goes in; the hills lose what colour they had. All is grey, the colour of depression. Winter is coming, thinks Minette. Another season, gone. Clouds, descending, drift across the hills, lie in front of them in misty swathes. Minette can see neither back nor forward. She is frightened: Edgar is nowhere to be seen.

'There might be savage cows in there,' says Mona, 'where we can't see.'

'Wait,' she says to Mona, 'wait,' and means to run ahead to

find Edgar and bring him back; but Edgar appears again as if at her will, within earshot, off on a parallel path to theirs, which will take him on yet another circumnavigation of the lower-lying fortifications.

'I'll take Mona back to the car,' she calls. He looks astonished.

'Why?'

He does not wait for her answer: he scrambles over a hillock and disappears.

'Because,' she wants to call after him, 'because I am forty, alone and frightened. Because my period started yesterday, and I have a pain. Because my elder child sits alone in a car in mist and rain, and my younger one stands grizzling on a misty hilltop, shivering with fright, afraid of invisible things, and cold. Because if I stay a minute longer I will lose my way and wander here for ever. Because battles were fought on this hilltop, families who were happy died and something remains behind, by comparison with which the Taniwha, sightless monster of the far-off jungle, those white and distant shores, is a model of goodwill.'

Minette says nothing: in any case he has gone.

'Let's get back to the car,' she says to Mona.
'Where is it?' enquires Mona, pertinently.
'We'll find it.'
'Isn't Daddy coming?'
'He'll be coming later.'

Something of Minette's urgency communicates itself to Mona: or some increasing fear of the place itself. Mona leads the way back, without faltering, without complaint, between nettles, over rocks, skirting the barbed-wire fence, keeping a safe distance from the cows, at last made flesh, penned up on the other side of the fence.

The past. Minette at Mona's age, leading her weeping mother along a deserted beach to their deserted cottage. Minette's father, prime deserter. Man with no eyes for Minette's distress, her mother's despair. Little Minette with her arms clutched rigidly round her father's legs, finally disentangled by determined adult arms. Whose? She does not know. Her father walking off with someone else, away from the wailing Minette, his daughter, away from the weeping mother, his wife. Later, it was found that one of Minette's fingers was broken. He never came back. Sunday outings, thereafter, just the two of them, Minette and mother, valiantly striving for companionable pleasure, but what use is a three-legged stool with two legs? That's what they were.

The present? Mist, clouds, in front, behind; the wind blowing her misery back in her teeth. Minette and Mona stumble, hold each other up. The clouds part. There's the road: there's the car. Only a few hundred yards. There is Minnie, red hair gleaming, half-asleep, safe.

'England home and safety!' cries Minette, ridiculous, and with this return to normality, however baffling, Mona sits down on the ground and refuses to go another step, and has to be entreated, cajoled and bluffed back to the car.

'Where's Daddy?' complains Minnie. It is her children's frequent cry. That and 'Are you all right, Mummy?'
'We got tired and came back,' says Minette.

'I suppose he'll be a long time. He always is.'

Minette looks at her watch. Half-past four. They've been away an hour and a half.

'I should say six o'clock.' Edgar's walks usually last for three hours. Better resign herself to this than to exist in uneasy expectation.
'What will we do?'
'Listen to the radio. Read. Think. Talk. Wait. It's very nice up here. There's a view.'
'I've been looking at it for three hours,' says Minnie, resigned. 'Oh well.'
'But I'm hungry,' says Mona. 'Can I have an iced lolly?'
'Idiot,' says Minnie to her sister. 'Idiot child.'

There is nothing in sight except the empty road, hills, mist. Minette can't drive. Edgar thinks she would be a danger to herself and others if she learned. If there was a village within walking distance she would take the children off for tea, but there is nothing. She and Minnie consult the maps and discover this sad fact. Mona, fortunately, discovers an ants' nest. Minnie and Minette play I-Spy. Minette, busy, chirpy, stands four square between her children and desolation.

Five o'clock. Edgar reappears, emerging brilliantly out of the mist, from an unexpected direction, smiling satisfaction.

'Wonderful,' he says. 'I can't think why you went back, Minette.'
'Mummy was afraid of the cows,' says Mona.
'Your mother is afraid of everything,' says Edgar. 'I'm afraid she and nature don't get along together.'

They pile back into the car and off they go. Edgar starts to sing, 'One man went to mow.' They all join in. Happy families. A cup of tea, thinks Minette. How I would love a cup of immoral tea, a plate of fattening sandwiches, another of ridiculous iced cakes, in one of the beamed and cosy teashops in which the Kentish villages abound. How long since Minette had a cup of tea? How many years?

Edgar does not like tea – does not approve of eating between meals. Tea is a drug, he says: it is the rot of the English: it is a laughable substance, a false stimulant, of no nutritive value whatsoever, lining the stomach with tannin. Tea! Minette, do you want a cup of tea? Of course not. Edgar is right. Minette's mother died of stomach cancer, after a million comforting cups. Perhaps they did instead of sex? The singing stops. In the back of the car, Minette keeps silent; presently cries silently, when Mona, exhausted, falls asleep. Last night was disturbed.

The future? Like the past, like the present. Little girls who lose their fathers cry all their lives. Hard to blame Edgar for her tears: no doubt she makes Edgar the cause of them. He says so often enough. Mona and Minnie shall not lose their father, she is determined on it. Minette will cry now and for ever, so that Minnie and Mona can grow up to laugh – though no doubt their laughter, as they look back, will be tinged with pity, at best, and derision, at worst, for a mother who lives as theirs did. Minnie and Mona, saved from understanding.

I am of the lost generation, thinks Minette, one of millions. Inter-leaving, blotting up the miseries of the past, to leave the future untroubled. I would be happier dead, but being alive, of necessity, might as well make myself useful. She sings softly to the sleeping Mona, chats brightly to Minnie.

Edgar, Minette, Minnie and Mona. Nothing gives.

That night, when Mona is in bed, and Minnie has set up the Monopoly board, Edgar moves as of instinct into the ladderback chair, and Minette plays Monopoly, happy families, with the Man with no Eyes.

1977

Breakages

'We blossom and flourish
As leaves on a tree,
And wither and perish
But nought changeth thee –'

sang David's congregation in its laggardly, quavery voice. Some trick of acoustics made much of what happened in the church audible in the vicarage kitchen, where tonight, as so often, Deidre sat and darned socks and waited for Evensong to end.

The vicarage, added as a late Victorian afterthought, leaned up against the solidity of the Norman church. The house was large, ramshackle, dark and draughty, and prey to wet rot, dry rot, woodworm and beetle. Here David and Deidre lived. He was a vicar of the established Church; she was his wife. He attended to the spiritual welfare of his parishioners: she presided over the Mothers' Union and the Women's Institute and ran the Amateur Dramatic Society. They had been married for twenty-one years. They had no children, which was a source of acute disappointment to them and to Deidre's mother, and of understandable disappointment to the parish. It is always pleasant, in a small, stable and increasingly elderly community, to watch other people's children grow up, and sad to be deprived of that pleasure.

'Oh no, please,' said Deidre, now, to the Coronation Mug on the dresser. It was a rare piece, produced in anticipation of an event which had never occurred: the Coronation of the Duke of Windsor. The mug was, so far, uncracked and unchipped, and worth some three hundred pounds, but had just moved to the very edge of its shelf, not smoothly and purposively, but with an uneven rocking motion which made Deidre hope that entreaty might yet calm it, and save it from itself. And indeed, after she spoke, the mug was quiet, and lapsed into the ordinary stillness she had once always associated with inanimate objects.

'Immortal, invisible,
God only wise –
In light inaccessible –'

Deidre joined in the hymn, singing gently and soothingly, and trying to feel happy, for the happier she felt the fewer the breakages there would be and perhaps one day they would stop altogether, and David would never, ever find out that one by one, the ornaments and possessions he most loved and valued were leaping off shelves and shattering, to be secretly mended by Deidre with such skills as she remembered from the early days, before marriage had interrupted her training in china restoration, and her possible future in the Victoria and Albert Museum.

Long ago and far away. Now Deidre darned. David's feet were sensitive to anything other than pure, fine wool. Not for him the tough nylon mixtures that other men wore. Deidre darned.

The Coronation Mug rocked violently.

'Stop it,' said Deidre, warningly. Sometimes to appear stern was more effective than to entreat. The mug stayed where it was. But just a fraction further and it would have fallen.

Deidre unpicked the last few stitches. She was in danger of cobbling the darn, and there is nothing more uncomfortable to sensitive skin than a cobbled darn.

'You do it on purpose,' David would complain, not without reason. Deidre's faults were the ones he found most difficult to bear. She was careless, lost socks, left lids unscrewed, taps running, doors open, saucepans burning: she bought fresh bread when yesterday's at half price would do. It was her nature, she maintained, and grieved bitterly when her husband implied that it was wilful and that she was doing it to annoy. She loved him, or said so. And he loved her, or said so.

The Coronation Mug leapt off its shelf, arced through the air and fell and broke in two pieces at Deidre's feet. She put the pieces at the very back of the drawer beneath the sink. There was no time for mending now. Tomorrow morning would have to do, when David was out parish-visiting, in houses freshly dusted and brightened for his arrival. Fortunately, David seldom inspected Deidre's drawer. It smelt, when opened, of dry rot, and reminded him forcibly of the large sums of money which ought to be spent on the repair of the house, and which he did not have.

'We could always sell something,' Deidre would sometimes venture, but not often, for the suggestion upset him. David's mother had died when he was four; his father had gone bankrupt when he was eight; relatives had reared him and sent him off to boarding school where he had been sexually and emotionally abused. Possessions were his security.

She understood him, forgave him, loved him and tried not to argue.

She darned his socks. It was, today, a larger pile than usual. Socks kept disappearing, not by the pair, but singly. David had lately discovered a pillowslip stuffed full of them pushed to the back of the wardrobe. It was his wife's deceit which worried him most, or so he said. Hiding socks! That and the sheer careless waste of it all. Losing socks! So Deidre tried tying the socks together for the wash, and thus, in pairs, the night before, spun and dried, they had lain in the laundry basket. In the morning she had found them in one ugly, monstrous knot, and each sock oddly long, as if stretched by a hand too angry to know what it was doing. Rinsing had restored them, fortunately, to a proper shape, but she was obliged to darn where the stretching had worn the fabric thin.

It was always like this: always difficult, always upsetting. David's things were attacked, as if the monstrous hand were on her side, yet it was she, Deidre, who had to repair the damage, follow its source as it moved about the house, mending what it broke, wiping tomato purée from the ceiling, toothpaste from the lavatory bowl, replanting David's seedlings, rescrewing lids, closing doors, refolding linen, turning off taps. She scarcely dared leave the house for fear of what might happen in her absence, and this David interpreted as lack of interest in his parish. Disloyalty, to God and husband.

And so it was, in a way. Yet they loved each other. Man and wife.

Deidre's finger was bleeding. She must have cut it on the sharp edge of the broken Coronation Mug. She opened the table drawer and took out the first piece of cloth which came to hand, and wrapped her finger. The cold tap started to run of its own accord, but she ignored it. Blood spread out over the cloth but presently, fortunately, stopped.

Could you die from loss of blood, from a small finger cut?

The invisible hand swept the dresser shelf, knocking all sorts of treasures sideways but breaking nothing. It had never touched the dresser before, as if awed, as Deidre was, by the ever increasing value of its contents – rare blue and white pieces, frog mugs, barbers' bowls, lustre cups, a debatably Ming bowl, which a valuer said might well fetch five thousand pounds.

Enough to paint the vicarage, inside, and install central heating, and replaster walls and buy a new vacuum cleaner.

The dresser rattled and shook: she could have sworn it slid towards her.

David did not give Deidre a housekeeping allowance. She asked for money when she needed it, but David seldom recognised that it was in fact needed. He could not see the necessity of things like washing-up liquid, sugar, toilet rolls, new scourers. Sometimes she stole money from his pocket: once she took a coin out of the offertory on Sunday morning instead of putting a coin in it.

Why did she stoop to it? She loved him.

A bad wife, a barren wife, and a poor sort of person.

David came home. The house fell quiet, as always, at his approach. Taps stopped running and china rattling. David kissed her on her forehead.

'Deidre,' said David, 'what have you wrapped around your finger?'

Deidre, curious herself, unwrapped the binding and found that she had used a fine lace and cotton handkerchief, put in the drawer for mending, which once had belonged to David's grandmother. It was now sodden and bright, bright red.

'I cut my finger,' said Deidre, inadequately and indeed foolishly, for what if he demanded to know what had caused the wound? But David was too busy rinsing and squeezing the handkerchief under the tap to enquire. Deidre put her finger in her mouth and put up with the salt, exciting taste of her own blood.

'It's hopelessly stained,' he mourned. 'Couldn't you just for once have used something you wouldn't spoil? A tissue?'

David did not allow the purchase of tissues. There had been none in his youth: why should they be needed now, in his middle age?

'I'm sorry,' said Deidre, and thought, as she spoke, 'I am always saying sorry, and always providing cause for my own remorse.'

He took the handkerchief upstairs to the bathroom, in search of soap and a nailbrush. 'What kind of wife are you, Deidre?' he asked as he went, desperate.

What kind, indeed? Married in a register office in the days before David had taken to Holy Orders and a Heavenly Father more reliable than his earthly one. Deidre had suggested that they remarry in church, as could be and had been done by others, but David did not want to. Hardly a wife at all.

A barren wife. A fig tree, struck by God's ill temper. David's God. In the beginning they had shared a God, who was bleak, plain, sensible and kind. But now, increasingly, David had his own jealous and punitive God, whom he wooed with ritual and richness, incense and images, dragging a surprised congregation with him. He changed his vestments three times during services, rang little bells to announce the presence of the Lord, swept up and down aisles, and in general seemed not averse to being mistaken for God.

The water pipes shrieked and groaned as David turned on the tap in the bathroom, but that was due to bad plumbing rather than unnatural causes. She surely could not be held responsible for that, as well.

When the phenomena – as she thought of them – first started, or rather leapt from the scale of ordinary domestic carelessness to something less explicable and more sinister, she went to the doctor.

'Doctor,' she said, 'do mumps in adolescence make men infertile?'
'It depends,' he said, proving nothing. 'If the gonads are affected it well might. Why?'

No reason had been found for Deidre's infertility. It lay, presumably, like so much else, in her mind. She had had her tubes blown, painfully and unforgettably, to facilitate conception, but it had made no difference. For fifteen years twenty-three days of hope had been followed by five days of disappointment, and on her shoulders rested the weight of David's sorrow, as she, his wife, deprived him of his earthly immortality, his children.

'Of course,' he said sadly, 'you are an only child. Only children are often infertile. The sins of the fathers –' David regarded fecundity as a blessing; the sign of a woman in tune with God's universe. He had married Deidre, he vaguely let it be known, on the rebound from a young woman who had gone on to have seven children. Seven!

David's fertility remained unquestioned and unexamined. A sperm count would surely have proved nothing. His sperm was plentiful and he had no sexual problems that he was aware of. To ejaculate into a test-tube to prove a point smacked uncomfortably of onanism.

The matter of the mumps came up during the time of Deidre's menopause, a month or so after her, presumably, last period. David had been in the school sanatorium with mumps: she had heard him saying so to a distraught mother, adding, 'Oh mumps! Nothing in a boy under fourteen. Be thankful he has them now, not later.'

So he was aware that mumps were dangerous, and could render a man infertile. And Deidre knew well enough that David had lived in the world of school sanatoria after the age of fourteen, not before. Why had he never mentioned mumps?

And while she wondered, and pondered, and hesitated to ask, toothpaste began to ooze from tubes, and rose trees were up-rooted in the garden, and his seedlings trampled by unseen boots, and his clothes in the wardrobe tumbled in a pile to the ground, and Deidre stole money to buy mending glue, and finally went to the doctor.

'Most men,' said the doctor, 'confuse impotence with infertility and believe that mumps cause the former, not the latter.'

Back to square one. Perhaps he didn't know.

'Why have you *really* come?' asked the doctor, recently back from a course in patient–doctor relations. Deidre offered him an account of her domestic phenomena, as she had not meant to do. He prescribed Valium and asked her to come back in a week. She did.

'Any better? Does the Valium help?'
'At least when I see things falling, I don't mind so much.'
'But you still see them falling?'
'Yes.'
'Does your husband see them too?'

'He's never there when they do.'

Now what was any thinking doctor to make of that?

'We could try hormone replacement therapy,' he said.
'No,' said Deidre. 'I am what I am.'
'Then what do you want me to do?'

'If I could only feel angry with my husband,' said Deidre,

'instead of forever understanding and forgiving him, I might get it to stop. As it is, I am releasing too much kinetic energy.'

There were patients waiting. They had migraines, eczema and boils. He gave her more Valium, which she did not take.

Deidre, or some expression of Deidre, went home and churned up the lawn and tore the gate off its hinges. The other Deidre raked and smoothed, resuscitated and blamed a perfectly innocent child for the gate. A child. It would have taken a forty-stone giant to twist the hinges so, but no one stopped, fortunately, to think about that. The child went to bed without supper for swinging on the vicar's gate.

The wound on Deidre's finger gaped open in an unpleasant way. She thought she could see the white bone within the bloodless flesh.

Deidre went upstairs to the bathroom, where David washed his wife's blood from his grandmother's hankie. 'David,' said Deidre, 'perhaps I should have a stitch in my finger?'

David had the toothmug in his hand. His jaw was open, his eyes wide with shock. He had somehow smeared toothpaste on his black lapel. 'The toothmug has recently been broken, and very badly mended. No one told me. Did you do it?'

The toothmug dated from the late eighteenth century and was worn, cracked and chipped, but David loved it. It had been one of the first things to go, and Deidre had not mended it with her usual care, thinking, mistakenly, that one more crack amongst so many would scarcely be noticed.

'I am horrified,' said David.
'Sorry,' said Deidre.
'You always break my things, never your own.'
'I thought that when you got married,' said Deidre, with the carelessness of desperation, for surely now David would start an inspection of his belongings and all would be discovered, 'things stopped being yours and mine, and became ours.'
'Married! You and I have never been married, not in the sight of God, and I thank Him for it.'

There. He had said what had been unsaid for years, but there was no relief in it, for either of them. There came a crash of breaking china from downstairs. David ran down to the kitchen, where the noise came from, but could see no sign of damage.

He moved into the living room. Deidre followed, dutifully.

'You've shattered my life,' said David. 'We have nothing in common. You have been a burden since the beginning. I wanted a happy, warm, loving house. I wanted children.'

'I suppose,' said Deidre, 'you'll be saying next that my not having children is God's punishment?'
'Yes,' said David.
'Nothing to do with your mumps?'

David was silent, taken aback. Out of the corner of her eye Deidre saw the Ming vase move. 'You're a sadistic person,' said David eventually. 'Even the pains and humiliations of long ago aren't safe from you. You revive them.'

'You knew all the time,' said Deidre. 'You were infertile, not me. You made me take the blame. And it's too late for me now.'

The Ming vase rocked to the edge of the shelf: Deidre moved to push it back, but not quickly enough. It fell and broke.

David cried out in pain and rage. 'You did it on purpose,' he wept. 'You hate me.'

Deidre went upstairs and packed her clothes. She would stay with her mother while she planned some kind of new life for herself. She would be happier anywhere in the world but here, sharing a house with a ghost.

David moved through the house, weeping, but for his treasures, not for his wife. He took a wicker basket and in it laid tenderly – as if they were the bodies of children – the many broken and mended vases and bowls and dishes which he found. Sometimes the joins were skilful and barely detectable to his moving forefinger: sometimes careless. But everything was spoilt. What had been perfect was now second-rate and without value. The finds in the junk shops, the gifts from old ladies, the few small knick-knacks which had come to him from his dead mother – his whole past destroyed by his wife's single-minded malice and cunning.

He carried the basket to the kitchen, and sat with his head in his hands.

Deidre left without saying another word. Out of the door, through the broken garden gate, into the night, through the churchyard, for the powers of the dead disturbed her less than the powers of the living, and to the bus station.

David sat. The smell of rot from the sink drawer was powerful enough, presently, to make him lift his head.

The cold tap started to run. A faulty washer, he concluded. He moved to turn it off, but the valve was already closed. 'Deidre!' he called, 'what have you done with the kitchen tap?' He did not know why he spoke, for Deidre had gone.

The whole top of the dresser fell forward to the ground. Porcelain shattered and earthenware powdered. He could hear the little pings of the Eucharist bell in the church next door, announcing the presence of God.

He thought perhaps there was an earthquake, but the central light hung still and quiet. Upstairs heavy feet bumped to and fro, dragging, wrenching and banging. Outside the window the black trees rocked so fiercely that he thought he would be safer in than out. The gas taps of the cooker were on and he could smell gas, mixed with fumes from the coal fire where Deidre's darning had been piled up and was now smouldering. He closed his eyes.

He was not frightened. He knew that he saw and heard these things, but that they had no substance in the real world. They were a distortion of the facts, as water becomes wine in the Communion service, and bread becomes the flesh of the Saviour.

When next he opened his eyes the dresser was restored, the socks still lay in the mending basket, the air was quiet.

Sensory delusions, that was all, brought about by shock. But unpleasant, all the same. Deidre's fault. David went upstairs to sleep but could not open the bedroom door. He thought perhaps Deidre had locked it behind her, out of spite. He was tired. He slept in the spare room, peacefully, without the irritant of Deidre's warmth beside him.

In the morning, however, he missed her, and as if in reply to his unspoken request she reappeared, in the kitchen, in time to make his breakfast tea. 'I spent the night in the hospital,' she said. 'I went to casualty to have a stitch put in my finger, and I fainted, and they kept me in.'

Her arm was in a sling.

'I'm sorry,' he said. 'You should have told me it was a bad cut and I'd have been more sympathetic. Where did you put the bedroom key?'

'I haven't got it,' she said, and the teapot fell off the table and there were tea and tea leaves everywhere, and, one-armed, she bungled the business of wiping it up. He helped.

'You shouldn't put breakables and spillables on the edge of tables,' he reproached her. 'Then it wouldn't happen.'
'I suppose not.'
'I'm sorry about what I may have said last night. Mumps are a sore point. I thought I would die from the itching, and my friends just laughed.'
Itching? Mumps?
'Mumps *is* the one where you come out in red spots and they tie your hands to stop you scratching?'
'No. That's chickenpox,' she said.
'Whatever it was, if you're over fourteen you get it very badly indeed and it is humiliating to have your hands tied.'
'I can imagine.'

He wrung out the dishcloth. The tap, she noticed, was not dripping. 'I'm sorry about your things,' she said. 'I should have told you.'
'Am I such a frightening person?'
'Yes.'

'They're only things,' he said, to her astonishment. The house seemed to take a shift back into its ordinary perspective. She thought, that though childless, she could still live an interesting and useful life. Her friends with grown-up children, gone away, complained that it was as if their young had never been. The experience of childrearing was that, just that, no more, no less. An experience without much significance, presently over; as lately she had experienced the behaviour of the material world.

David insisted that Deidre must surely have the bedroom key, and was annoyed when she failed to produce it. 'Why would I lock you out of the bedroom?' she asked.

'Why would you do anything!' he remarked dourly. His gratitude for her return was fading: his usual irritation with her was reasserting itself. She was grateful for familiar ways, and as usual animated by them.

He went up the ladder to the bedroom window, and was outraged. 'I've never seen a room in such a mess,' he reported, from the top of the ladder, a figure in clerical black perched there like some white-ruffled crow. 'How you did all that, even in a bad temper, I can't imagine!'

The heavy wardrobe was on its side, wedged against the door: the bed was upside down: the chairs and light bulb broken, and the bedclothes, tumbled and knotted, had the same stretched and strained appearance as David's socks; and the carpet had been wrenched up, tossing furniture as it lifted, and wrung out like a dishcloth.

When the wardrobe had been moved back into place, the door was indeed found to be locked, with the key on the inside of the door, but both preferred not to notice that.

'I'm sorry,' said Deidre, 'I was upset about our having no children. That, and my time of life.'
'All our times of life,' he said. 'And as to your having no children, if it's anyone's fault, it's God's.'

Together they eased the carpet out of the window and down onto the lawn, and patiently and peaceably unwrung it. But the marks of the wringing stayed, straying for ever across the bedroom floor, to remind them of the dangers of, for him, petulance, and for her, the tendency to blame others for her own shortcomings.

Presently the Ming vase was mended, not by Deidre but by experts. He sold it and they installed central heating and had a wall knocked out there, a window put in here, and the washer on the kitchen tap mended, and the dry rot removed so that the sink drawer smelled like any other, and the broken floorboard beneath the dresser replaced. The acoustics in the kitchen changed, so that Deidre could no longer hear David's services as she sat by the fire, so she attended church rather more often; and David, she soon noticed, dressed up as God rather less, and diverted his congregation's attention away from himself and more towards the altar.

1978

Weekend

By seven-thirty they were ready to go. Martha had everything packed into the car and the three children appropriately dressed and in the back seat, complete with educational games and wholewheat biscuits. When everything was ready in the car Martin would switch off the television, come downstairs, lock up the house, front and back, and take the wheel.

Weekend! Only two hours' drive down to the cottage on Friday evenings: three hours' drive back on Sunday nights. The pleasures of greenery and guests in between. They reckoned themselves fortunate, how fortunate!

On Fridays Martha would get home on the bus at six-twelve and prepare tea and sandwiches for the family: then she would strip four beds and put the sheets and quilt covers in the washing machine for Monday: take the country bedding from the airing basket, plus the books and the games, plus the weekend food – acquired at intervals throughout the week, to lessen the load – plus her own folder of work from the office, plus Martin's drawing materials (she was a market researcher in an advertising agency, he a freelance designer) plus hairbrushes, jeans, spare T-shirts, Jolyon's antibiotics (he suffered from sore throats), Jenny's recorder, Jasper's cassette player and so on – ah, the so on! – and would pack them all, skilfully and quickly, into the boot. Very little could be left in the cottage during the week. ('An open invitation to burglars': Martin) Then Martha would run round the house tidying and wiping, doing this and that, finding the cat at one neighbour's and delivering it to another, while the others ate their tea; and would usually, proudly, have everything finished by the time they had eaten their fill. Martin would just catch the BBC2 news, while Martha cleared away the tea table, and the children tossed up for the best positions in the car. 'Martha,' said Martin, tonight, 'you ought to get Mrs Hodder to do more. She takes advantage of you.'

Mrs Hodder came in twice a week to clean. She was over seventy. She charged two pounds an hour. Martha paid her out of her own wages: well, the running of the house was Martha's concern. If Martha chose to go out to work – as was her perfect right, Martin allowed, even though it wasn't the best thing for the children, but that must be Martha's moral responsibility – Martha must surely pay her domestic stand-in. An evident truth, heard loud and clear and frequent in Martin's mouth and Martha's heart.

'I expect you're right,' said Martha. She did not want to argue. Martin had had a long hard week, and now had to drive. Martha couldn't. Martha's licence had been suspended four months back for drunken driving. Everyone agreed that the suspension was unfair: Martha seldom drank to excess: she was for one thing usually too busy pouring drinks for other people or washing other people's glasses to get much inside herself. But Martin had taken her out to dinner on her birthday, as was his custom, and exhaustion and excitement mixed had made her imprudent, and before she knew where she was, why there she was, in the dock, with a distorted lamppost to pay for and a new bonnet for the car and six months' suspension.

So now Martin had to drive her car down to the cottage, and he was always tired on Fridays, and hot and sleepy on Sundays, and every rattle and clank and bump in the engine she felt to be somehow her fault.

Martin had a little sports car for London and work: it could nip in and out of the traffic nicely: Martha's was an old estate car, with room for the children, picnic baskets, bedding, food, games, plants, drink, portable television and all the things required by the middle classes for weekends in the country. It lumbered rather than zipped and made Martin angry. He seldom spoke a harsh word, but Martha, after the fashion of wives, could detect his mood from what he did not say rather than what he did, and from the tilt of his head, and the way his crinkly, merry eyes seemed crinklier and merrier still – and of course from the way he addressed Martha's car.

'Come along, you old banger you! Can't you do better than that? You're too old, that's your trouble. Stop complaining. Always complaining, it's only a hill. You're too wide about the hips. You'll never get through there.'

Martha worried about her age, her tendency to complain, and the width of her hips. She took the remarks personally. Was she right to do so? The children noticed nothing: it was just funny lively laughing Daddy being witty about Mummy's car. Mummy, done for drunken driving. Mummy, with the roots of melancholy somewhere deep beneath the bustling, busy, everyday self. Busy: ah so busy!

Martin would only laugh if she said anything about the way he spoke to her car and warn her against paranoia.

'Don't get like your mother, darling.' Martha's mother had, towards the end, thought that people were plotting against her. Martha's mother had led a secluded, suspicious life, and made Martha's childhood a chilly and a lonely time. Life now, by comparison, was wonderful for Martha. People, children, houses, conversations, food, drink, theatres – even, now, a career. Martin standing between her and the hostility of the world – popular, easy, funny Martin, beckoning the rest of the world into earshot.

Ah, she was grateful: little earnest Martha, with her shy ways and her penchant for passing boring exams – how her life had blossomed out! Three children too – Jasper, Jenny and Jolyon – all with Martin's broad brow and open looks, and the confidence born of her love and care, and the work she had put into them since the dawning of their days.

Martin drives. Martha, for once, drowses.

The right food, the right words, the right play. Doctors for the tonsils: dentists for the molars. Confiscate guns: censor television: encourage creativity. Paints and paper to hand: books on the shelves: meetings with teachers. Music teachers. Dancing lessons. Parties. Friends to tea. School plays. Open days. Junior orchestra.

Martha is jolted awake. Traffic lights. Martin doesn't like Martha to sleep while he drives.

Clothes. Oh, clothes! Can't wear this: must wear that. Dress shops. Piles of clothes in corners: duly washed, but waiting to be ironed, waiting to be put away.

Get the piles off the floor, into the laundry baskets. Martin doesn't like a mess.

Creativity arises out of order, not chaos. Five years off work while the children were small: back to work with seniority lost. What, did you think something was for nothing? If you have children, mother, that is your reward. It lies not in the world.

Have you taken enough food? Always hard to judge.

Food. Oh, food! Shop in the lunch hour. Lug it all home. Cook for the freezer on Wednesday evenings while Martin is at his car maintenance evening class, and isn't there to notice you being unrestful. Martin likes you to sit down in the evenings. Fruit, meat, vegetables, flour for home-made bread. Well, shop bread is full of pollutants. Frozen food, even your own, loses flavour. Martin often remarks on it. Condiments. Everyone loves mango chutney. But the expense!

London Airport to the left. Look, look, children! Concorde? No, idiot, of course it isn't Concorde.

Ah, to be all things to all people: children, husband, employer, friends! It can be done: yes, it can: super woman. Drink. Home-made wine. Why not? Elderberries grown thick and rich in London: and at least you know what's in it. Store it in high cupboards: lots of room: up and down the step-ladder. Careful! Don't slip. Don't break anything.

No such thing as an accident. Accidents are Freudian slips: they are wilful, bad-tempered things.

Martin can't bear bad temper. Martin likes slim ladies. Diet.

Martin rather likes his secretary. Diet. Martin admires slim legs and big bosoms. How to achieve them both? Impossible. But try, oh try, to be what you ought to be, not what you are. Inside and out.

Martin brings back flowers and chocolates: whisks Martha off for holiday weekends. Wonderful! The best husband in the world: look into his crinkly, merry, gentle eyes; see it there. So the mouth slopes away into something of a pout. Never mind. Gaze into the eyes. Love. It must be love. You married him. *You*. Surely *you* deserve true love?

Salisbury Plain. Stonehenge. Look, children, look! Mother, we've seen Stonehenge a hundred times. Go back to sleep.

Cook! Ah cook. People love to come to Martin and Martha's dinners. Work it out in your head in the lunch hour. If you get in at six-twelve, you can seal the meat while you beat the egg white while you feed the cat while you lay the table while you string the beans while you set out the cheese, goat's cheese, Martin loves goat's cheese, Martha tries to like goat's cheese – oh, bed, sleep, peace, quiet.

Sex! Ah sex. Orgasm, please. Martin requires it. Well, so do you. And you don't want his secretary providing a passion you neglected to develop. Do you? Quick, quick, the cosmic bond. Love. Married love.

Secretary! Probably a vulgar suspicion: nothing more. Probably a fit of paranoia, à la mother, now dead and gone. At peace. R.I.P.
Chilly, lonely mother, following her suspicions where they led.

Nearly there, children. Nearly in paradise, nearly at the cottage. Have another biscuit.

Real roses round the door.

Roses. Prune, weed, spray, feed, pick. Avoid thorns. One of Martin's few harsh words.

'Martha, you can't not want roses! What kind of person am I married to? An anti-rose personality?'

Green grass. Oh, God, grass. Grass must be mown. Restful lawns, daisies bobbing, buttercups glowing. Roses and grass and books. Books.

Please, Martin, do we have to have the two hundred books, mostly twenties' first editions, bought at Christie's book sale on one of your afternoons off? Books need dusting.

Roars of laughter from Martin, Jasper, Jenny and Jolyon. Mummy says we shouldn't have the books: books need dusting!

Roses, green grass, books and peace.

Martha woke up with a start when they got to the cottage, and gave a little shriek which made them all laugh. Mummy's waking shriek, they called it.

Then there was the car to unpack and the beds to make up, and the electricity to connect, and the supper to make, and the cobwebs to remove, while Martin made the fire. Then supper – pork chops in sweet and sour sauce ('Pork is such a *dull* meat if you don't cook it properly': Martin), green salad from the garden, or such green salad as the rabbits had left. ('Martha, did you really net them properly? Be honest, now!': Martin) and sauté potatoes. Mash is so stodgy and ordinary, and instant mash unthinkable. The children studied the night sky with the aid of their star map. Wonderful, rewarding children!

Then clear up the supper: set the dough to prove for the bread: Martin already in bed: exhausted by the drive and lighting the fire. ('Martha, we really ought to get the logs stacked properly. Get the children to do it, will you?': Martin) Sweep and tidy: get the TV aerial right. Turn up Jasper's jeans where he has trodden the hem undone. ('He can't go around like *that*, Martha. Not even Jasper': Martin)

Midnight. Good night. Weekend guests arriving in the morning. Seven for lunch and dinner on Saturday. Seven for Sunday breakfast, nine for Sunday lunch. ('Don't fuss, darling. You always make such a fuss': Martin) Oh, God, forgotten the garlic squeezer. That means ten minutes with the back of a spoon and salt. Well, who wants *lumps* of garlic? No one. Not Martin's guests. Martin said so. Sleep.

Colin and Katie. Colin is Martin's oldest friend. Katie is his new young wife. Janet, Colin's other, earlier wife, was Martha's friend. Janet was rather like Martha, quieter and duller than her husband. A nag and a drag, Martin rather thought, and said, and of course she'd let herself go, everyone agreed. No one exactly excused Colin for walking out, but you could see the temptation.

Katie versus Janet.

Katie was languid, beautiful and elegant. She drawled when she spoke. Her hands were expressive: her feet were little and female. She had no children.

Janet plodded round on very flat, rather large feet. There was something wrong with them. They turned out slightly when she walked. She had two children. She was, frankly, boring. But Martha liked her: when Janet came down to the cottage she would wash up. Not in the way that most guests washed up – washing dutifully and setting everything out on the draining board, but actually drying and putting away too. And Janet would wash the bath and get the children all sat down, with chairs for everyone, even the littlest, and keep them quiet and satisfied so the grown-ups – well, the men – could get on with their conversation and their jokes and their love of country weekends, while Janet stared into space, as if grateful for the rest, quite happy.

Janet would garden, too. Weed the strawberries, while the men went for their walk; her great feet standing firm and square and sometimes crushing a plant or so, but never mind, oh never mind. Lovely Janet; who understood.

Now Janet was gone and here was Katie.

Katie talked with the men and went for walks with the men, and moved her ashtray rather impatiently when Martha tried to clear the drinks round it.

Dishes were boring, Katie implied by her manner, and domesticity was boring, and anyone who bothered with that kind of thing was a fool. Like Martha. Ash should be allowed to stay where it was, even if it was in the butter, and conversations should never be interrupted.

Knock, knock. Katie and Colin arrived at one-fifteen on Saturday morning, just after Martha had got to bed. 'You don't mind? It was the moonlight. We couldn't resist it. You should have seen Stonehenge! We didn't disturb you? Such early birds!'

Martha rustled up a quick meal of omelettes. Saturday night's eggs. ('Martha makes a lovely omelette': Martin) ('Honey, make one of your mushroom omelettes: cook the mushrooms separately, remember, with lemon. Otherwise the water from the mushrooms gets into the egg, and spoils everything.') Sunday supper mushrooms. But ungracious to say anything.

Martin had revived wonderfully at the sight of Colin and Katie. He brought out the whisky bottle. Glasses. Ice. Jug for water. Wait. Wash up another sinkful, when they're finished. 2 a.m.

'Don't do it tonight, darling.'
'It'll only take a sec.' Bright smile, not a hint of self-pity. Self-pity can spoil everyone's weekend.
Martha knows that if breakfast for seven is to be manageable the sink must be cleared of dishes. A tricky meal, breakfast. Especially if bacon, eggs, and tomatoes must all be cooked in separate pans. ('Separate pans mean separate flavours!': Martin)

She is running around in her nightie. Now if that had been Katie – but there's something so *practical* about Martha. Reassuring, mind; but the skimpy nightie and the broad rump and the thirty-eight years are all rather embarrassing. Martha can see it in Colin and Katie's eyes. Martin's too. Martha wishes she did not see so much in other people's eyes. Her mother did, too. Dear, dead mother. Did I misjudge you?

This was the second weekend Katie had been down with Colin but without Janet. Colin was a photographer: Katie had been his accessoriser. First Colin and Janet: then Colin, Janet and Katie: now Colin and Katie!

Katie weeded with rubber gloves on and pulled out pansies in mistake for weeds and laughed and laughed along with everyone when her mistake was pointed out to her, but the pansies died. Well, Colin had become with the years fairly rich and fairly famous, and what does a fairly rich and famous man want with a wife like Janet when Katie is at hand?

On the first of the Colin/Janet/Katie weekends Katie had appeared out of the bathroom. 'I say,' said Katie, holding out a damp towel with evident distaste, 'I can only find this. No hope of a dry one?' And Martha had run to fetch a dry towel and amazingly found one, and handed it to Katie who flashed her a brilliant smile and said, 'I can't bear damp towels. Anything in the world but damp towels,' as if speaking to a servant in a time of shortage of staff, and took all the water so there was none left for Martha to wash up.

The trouble, of course, was drying anything at all in the cottage. There were no facilities for doing so, and Martin had a horror of clothes lines which might spoil the view. He toiled and moiled all week in the city simply to get a country view at the weekend. Ridiculous to spoil it by draping it with wet towels! But now Martha had bought more towels, so perhaps everyone could be satisfied. She would take nine damp towels back on Sunday evenings in a plastic bag and see to them in London.

On this Saturday morning, straight after breakfast, Katie went out to the car – she and Colin had a new Lamborghini; hard to imagine Katie in anything duller – and came back waving a new Yves St Laurent towel. 'See! I brought my own, darlings.'

They'd brought nothing else. No fruit, no meat, no vegetables, not even bread, certainly not a box of chocolates. They'd gone off to bed with alacrity, the night before, and the spare room rocked and heaved: well, who'd want to do washing-up when you could do that, but what about the children? Would they get confused? First Colin and Janet, now Colin and Katie?

Martha murmured something of her thoughts to Martin, who looked quite shocked. 'Colin's my best friend. I don't expect him to bring anything,' and Martha felt mean. 'And good heavens, you can't protect the kids from sex for ever; don't be so prudish,' so that Martha felt stupid as well. Mean, complaining, and stupid.

Janet had rung Martha during the week. The house had been sold over her head, and she and the children had been moved into a small flat. Katie was trying to persuade Colin to cut down on her allowance, Janet said.

'It does one no good to be materialistic,' Katie confided. 'I have nothing. No home, no family, no ties, no possessions. Look at me! Only me and a suitcase of clothes.' But Katie seemed highly satisfied with the me, and the clothes were stupendous. Katie drank a great deal and became funny. Everyone laughed, including Martha. Katie had been married twice. Martha marvelled at how someone could arrive in their mid-thirties with nothing at all to their name, neither husband, nor children, nor property and not mind.

Mind you, Martha could see the power of such helplessness. If Colin was all Katie had in the world, how could Colin abandon her? And to what? Where would she go? How would she live? Oh, clever Katie.

'My teacup's dirty,' said Katie, and Martha ran to clean it, apologising, and Martin raised his eyebrows, at Martha, not Katie.

'I wish *you'd* wear scent,' said Martin to Martha, reproachfully. Katie wore lots. Martha never seemed to have time to put any on, though Martin bought her bottle after bottle. Martha leapt out of bed each morning to meet some emergency – miaowing cat, coughing child, faulty alarm clock, postman's knock – when was Martha to put on scent? It annoyed Martin all the same. She ought to do more to charm him.

Colin looked handsome and harrowed and younger than Martin, though they were much the same age. 'Youth's catching,' said Martin in bed that night. 'It's since he found Katie.' Found, like some treasure. Discovered; something exciting and wonderful, in the dreary world of established spouses.

On Saturday morning Jasper trod on a piece of wood ('Martha, why isn't he wearing shoes? It's too bad': Martin) and Martha took him into the hospital to have a nasty splinter removed. She left the cottage at ten and arrived back at one, and they were still sitting in the sun, drinking, empty bottles glinting in the long grass. The grass hadn't been cut. Don't forget the bottles. Broken glass means more mornings at the hospital. Oh, don't fuss. Enjoy yourself. Like other people. Try.

But no potatoes peeled, no breakfast cleared, nothing. Cigarette ends still amongst old toast, bacon rind and marmalade. 'You could have done the potatoes,' Martha burst out. Oh, bad temper! Prime sin. They looked at her in amazement and dislike. Martin too.

'Goodness,' said Katie. 'Are we doing the whole Sunday lunch bit on Saturday? Potatoes? Ages since I've eaten potatoes. Wonderful!'

'The children expect it,' said Martha.

So they did. Saturday and Sunday lunch shone like reassuring beacons in their lives. Saturday lunch: family lunch: fish and chips. ('So much better cooked at home than bought': Martin) Sunday. Usually roast beef, potatoes, peas, apple pie. Oh, of course. Yorkshire pudding. Always a problem with oven temperatures. When the beef's going slowly, the Yorkshire should be going fast. How to achieve that? Like big bosom and little hips.

'Just relax,' said Martin. 'I'll cook dinner, all in good time. Splinters always work their own way out: no need to have taken him to hospital. Let life drift over you, my love. Flow with the waves, that's the way.'

And Martin flashed Martha a distant, spiritual smile. His hand lay on Katie's slim brown arm, with its many gold bands.

'Anyway, you do too much for the children,' said Martin. 'It isn't good for them. Have a drink.'

So Martha perched uneasily on the step and had a glass of cider, and wondered how, if lunch was going to be late, she would get cleared up and the meat out of the marinade for the rather formal dinner that would be expected that evening. The marinaded lamb ought to cook for at least four hours in a low oven; and the cottage oven was very small, and you couldn't use that and the grill at the same time and Martin liked his fish grilled, not fried. Less cholesterol.

She didn't say as much. Domestic details like this were very boring, and any mild complaint was registered by Martin as a scene. And to make a scene was so ungrateful.

This was the life. Well, wasn't it? Smart friends in large cars and country living and drinks before lunch and roses and bird song – 'Don't drink *too* much,' said Martin, and told them about Martha's suspended driving licence.

The children were hungry so Martha opened them a can of beans and sausages and heated that up. ('Martha, do they have to eat that crap? Can't they wait?': Martin)

Katie was hungry: she said so, to keep the children in face. She was lovely with children – most children. She did not particularly like Colin and Janet's children. She said so, and he accepted it. He only saw them once a month now, not once a week.

'Let me make lunch,' Katie said to Martha. 'You do so much, poor thing!'

And she pulled out of the fridge all the things Martha had put away for the next day's picnic lunch party – Camembert cheese and salad and salami and made a wonderful tomato salad in two minutes and opened the white wine – 'not very cold, darling. Shouldn't it be chilling?' – and had it all on the table in five amazing competent minutes. 'That's all we need, darling,' said Martin. 'You are funny with your fish-and-chip Saturdays! What could be nicer than this? Or simpler?'

Nothing, except there was Sunday's buffet lunch for nine gone, in place of Saturday's fish for six, and would the fish stretch? No. Katie had had quite a lot to drink. She pecked Martha on the forehead, 'Funny little Martha,' she said. 'She reminds me of Janet. I really do like Janet.' Colin did not want to be reminded of Janet, and said so. 'Darling, Janet's a fact of life,' said Katie. 'If you'd only think about her more, you might manage to pay her less.' And she yawned and stretched her lean, childless body and smiled at Colin with her inviting, naughty little girl eyes, and Martin watched her in admiration.

Martha got up and left them and took a paint pot and put a coat of white gloss on the bathroom wall. The white surface pleased her. She was good at painting. She produced a smooth, even surface. Her legs throbbed. She feared she might be getting varicose veins.

Outside in the garden the children played badminton. They were bad-tempered, but relieved to be able to look up and see their mother working, as usual: making their lives for ever better and nicer: organising, planning, thinking ahead, side-stepping disaster, making preparations, like a mother hen, fussing and irritating: part of the natural boring scenery of the world.

On Saturday night Katie went to bed early: she rose from her chair and stretched and yawned and poked her head into the kitchen where Martha was washing saucepans. Colin had cleared the table and Katie had folded the napkins into pretty creases, while Martin blew at the fire, to make it bright. 'Good night,' said Katie.

Katie appeared three minutes later, reproachfully holding out her Yves St Laurent towel, sopping wet. 'Oh dear,' cried Martha. 'Jenny must have washed her hair!' And Martha was obliged to rout Jenny out of bed to rebuke her, publicly, if only to demonstrate that she knew what was right and proper. that meant Jenny would sulk all weekend, and that meant a treat or an outing midweek, or else by the following week she'd be having an asthma attack. 'You fuss the children too much,' said Martin. 'That's why Jenny has asthma.' Jenny was pleasant enough to look at, but not stunning. Perhaps she was a disappointment to her father? Martin would never say so, but Martha feared he thought so.

An egg and an orange each child, each day. Then nothing too bad would go wrong. And it hadn't. The asthma was very mild. A calm, tranquil environment, the doctor said. Ah, smile, Martha, smile. Domestic happiness depends on you. 21 x 52 oranges a year. Each one to be purchased, carried, peeled and washed up after. And what about potatoes. 12 x 52 pounds a year? Martin liked his potatoes carefully peeled. He couldn't bear to find little cores of black in the mouthful. ('Well, it isn't very nice, is it?': Martin)

Martha dreamt she was eating coal, by handfuls, and liking it.

Saturday night. Martin made love to Martha three times.

Three times? How virile he was, and clearly turned on by the sounds from the spare room. Martin said he loved her. Martin always did. He was a courteous lover; he knew the importance of foreplay. So did Martha. Three times.

Ah, sleep. Jolyon had a nightmare. Jenny was woken by a moth. Martin slept through everything. Martha pottered about the house in the night. There was a moon. She sat at the window and stared out into the summer night for five minutes, and was at peace, and the went back to bed because she ought to be fresh for the morning.

But she wasn't. She slept late. The others went out for a walk. They'd left a note, a considerate note: 'Didn't wake you. You looked tired. Had a cold breakfast so as not to make too much mess. Leave everything 'til we get back.' But it was ten o'clock, and guests were coming at noon, so she cleared away the bread, the butter, the crumbs, the smears, the jam, the spoons, the spilt sugar, the cereal, the milk (sour by now) and the dirty plates, and swept the floors, and tidied up quickly, and grabbed a cup of coffee, and prepared to make a rice and fish dish, and a chocolate mousse and sat down in the middle to eat a lot of bread and jam herself. Broad hips. She remembered the office work in her file and knew she wouldn't be able to do it. Martin anyway thought it was ridiculous for her to bring work back at the weekends. 'It's your holiday,' he'd say. 'Why should they impose?' Martha loved her work. She didn't have to smile at it. She just did it.

Katie came back upset and crying. She sat in the kitchen while Martha worked and drank glass after glass of gin and bitter lemon. Katie liked ice and lemon in gin. Martha paid for all the drink out of her wages. It was part of the deal between her and Martin – the contract by which she went out to work. All things to cheer the spirit, otherwise depressed by a working wife and mother, were to be paid for by Martha. Drink, holidays, petrol, outings, puddings, electricity, heating: it was quite a joke between them. It didn't really make any difference: it was their joint money, after all. Amazing how Martha's wages were creeping up, almost to the level of Martin's. One day they would overtake. Then what?

Work, honestly, was a piece of cake.

Anyway, poor Katie was crying. Colin, she'd discovered, kept a photograph of Janet and the children in his wallet. 'He's not free of her. He pretends he is, but he isn't. She has him by a stranglehold. It's the kids. His bloody kids. Moaning Mary and that little creep Joanna. It's all he thinks about. I'm nobody.'

But Katie didn't believe it. She knew she was somebody all right. Colin came in, in a fury. He took out the photograph and set fire to it, bitterly, with a match. Up in smoke they went. Mary and Joanna and Janet. The ashes fell on the floor. (Martha swept them up when Colin and Katie had gone. It hardly seemed polite to do so when they were still there.) 'Go back to her,' Katie said. 'Go back to her. I don't care. Honestly, I'd rather be on my own. You're a nice old-fashioned thing. Run along then. Do your thing, I'll do mine. Who cares?'
'Christ, Katie, the fuss! She only just happens to be in the photograph. She's not there on purpose to annoy. And I do feel bad about her. She's been having a hard time.'
'And haven't you, Colin? She twists a pretty knife, I can tell you. Don't you have rights too? Not to mention me. Is a little loyalty too much to expect?'

They were reconciled before lunch, up in the spare room. Harry and Beryl Elder arrived at twelve-thirty. Harry didn't like to hurry on Sundays; Beryl was flustered with apologies for their lateness. They'd brought artichokes from their garden. 'Wonderful,' cried Martin. 'Fruits of the earth? Let's have a wonderful soup! Don't fret, Martha. I'll do it.'

'Don't fret.' Martha clearly hadn't been smiling enough. She was in danger, Martin implied, of ruining everyone's weekend. There was an emergency in the garden very shortly – an elm tree which had probably got Dutch elm disease – and Martha finished the artichokes. The lid flew off the blender and there was artichoke purée everywhere. 'Let's have lunch outside,' said Colin. 'Less work for Martha.'

Martin frowned at Martha: he thought the appearance of martyrdom in the face of guests to be an unforgivable offence.

Everyone happily joined in taking the furniture out, but it was Martha's experience that nobody ever helped to bring it in again. Jolyon was stung by a wasp. Jasper sneezed and sneezed from hay fever and couldn't find the tissues and he wouldn't use loo paper. ('Surely you remembered the tissues, darling?': Martin)

Beryl Elder was nice. 'Wonderful to eat out,' she said, fetching the cream for her pudding, while Martha fished a fly from the liquefying Brie ('You shouldn't have bought it so ripe, Martha': Martin) – 'except it's just some other woman has to do it. But at least it isn't *me*.' Beryl worked too, as a secretary, to send the boys to boarding school, where she'd rather they weren't. But her husband was from a rather grand family, and she'd been only a typist when he married her, so her life was a mass of amends, one way or another. Harry had lately opted out of the stockbroking rat race and become an artist, choosing integrity rather than money, but that choice was his alone and couldn't of course be inflicted on the boys.

Katie found the fish and rice dish rather strange, toyed at it with her fork, and talked about Italian restaurants she knew. Martin lay back soaking in the sun: crying, 'Oh, this is the life.' He made coffee, nobly, and the lid flew off the grinder and there were coffee beans all over the kitchen especially in amongst the row of cookery books which Martin gave Martha Christmas by Christmas. At least they didn't have to be brought back every weekend. ('The burglars won't have the sense to steal those': Martin)

Beryl fell asleep and Katie watched her, quizzically. Beryl's mouth was open and she had a lot of fillings, and her ankles were thick and her waist was going, and she didn't look after herself. 'I love women,' sighed Katie. 'They look so wonderful asleep. I wish I could be an earth mother.'

Beryl woke with a start and nagged her husband into going home, which he clearly didn't want to do, so didn't. Beryl thought she had to get back because his mother was coming round later. Nonsense! Then Beryl tried to stop Harry drinking more home-made wine and was laughed at by everyone. He was driving, Beryl couldn't, and he did have a nasty scar on his temple from a previous road accident. Never mind.

'She does come on strong, poor soul,' laughed Katie when they'd finally gone. 'I'm never going to get married,' – and Colin looked at her yearningly because he wanted to marry her more than anything in the world, and Martha cleared the coffee cups.

'Oh don't *do* that,' said Katie, 'do just sit *down*, Martha, you make us all feel bad,' and Martin glared at Martha who sat down and Jenny called out for her and Martha went upstairs and Jenny had started her first period and Martha cried and cried and knew she must stop because this must be a joyous occasion for Jenny or her whole future would be blighted, but for once, Martha couldn't.

Her daughter Jenny: wife, mother, friend.

1978

Delights of France
or
Horrors of the Road

Miss Jacobs, I don't believe in psychotherapy. I really do think it's a lot of nonsense. Now it's taken me considerable nerve to say that – I'm a rather mild person and hate to be thought rude. I just wouldn't want to be here under false pretences: it wouldn't be fair to you, would it?

But Piers wants me to come and see you, so of course I will. He's waiting outside in your pretty drawing room: I said he should go, and come back when the session was up: that I'd be perfectly all right but he likes to be at hand in case anything happens. Just sometimes I do fall forward, out of my chair – so far I haven't hurt myself. Once it was face-first into a feather sofa; the second was trickier – I was with Martin – he's my little grandchild, you know, David's boy, the only one so far – at the sandpit in the park and I just pitched forward into the sand. Someone sent for an ambulance but it wasn't really necessary – I was perfectly all right, instantly. Well, except for this one big permanent fact that my legs don't work.

I'm a great mystery to the doctors. Piers has taken me everywhere – Paris, New York, Tokyo – but the verdict seems to be the same: it's all in my head. It is a hysterical paralysis. I find this humiliating: as if I'd done it on purpose just to be a nuisance. I'm the last person in the world to be a nuisance!

Did you see Piers? Isn't he handsome? He's in his mid-fifties, you know, but so good-looking. Of course he has an amazing brain – well, the whole world knows that – and I think that helps to keep people looking young. I have a degree in Economics myself – unusual for a housewife of my age – but of course I stayed home to devote myself to Piers and the children. I think, on the whole, women should do that. Don't you? Why don't you answer my questions? Isn't that what you're supposed to do? Explain me to myself? No?

I must explain myself to myself! Oh.

Behind every great man stands a woman. I believe that. Piers is a Nobel Prize winner. Would he have done it without me? I expect so. He just wouldn't have had me, would he, or the four children? They're all doing very well. Piers was away quite a lot when the children were young – he's a particle physicist, as I'm sure you know. He had to be away. They don't keep cyclotrons in suitably domestic places, and the money had to be earned somehow. But we all always had these holidays together, in France. How we loved France. How well we knew it. Piers would drive; I'd navigate; the four children piled in the back! Of course these days we fly. There's just Piers and me. It's glamorous and exciting, and people know who he is so the service is good. Waiters don't mind so much… Mind what?… I thought you weren't supposed to ask questions. I was talking about holidays, in the past, long ago. Well, not so long ago. We went on till the youngest was fifteen; Brutus that is, and he's only twenty now. Can it be only five years?

I miss those summer dockside scenes: the cars lined up at dusk or dawn waiting for the ferry home: sunburned families, careless and exhausted after weeks in the sun. By careless I don't mean without care – just without caring any more. They'll sleep all night in their cars to be first in the queue for the ferry, and not worry about it; on the journey out they'd have gone berserk. Brown faces and brittle blonde hair and grubby children; and the roof-racks with the tents and the water cans and the boxes of wine and strings of garlic. Volvos and Cortinas and Volkswagen vans.

Of course our cars never looked smart: we even started out once with a new one, but by the time we came back it was dented and bumped and battered. French drivers are so dreadful, aren't they; and their road signs are impossible.

How did the paralysis start? It was completely unexpected. There were no warning signs – no numbness, no dizziness, nothing like that. It was our thirtieth wedding anniversary. To celebrate we were going to do a tour of France in Piers' new MG. It can do 110 mph, you know, but Piers doesn't often go at more than fifty-five – that's the speed limit in the States, you know, and he says they know what they're doing – it's the best speed for maximum safety – but he likes to have cars that can go fast. To get out of trouble in an emergency, Piers says. We were going on the Weymouth/Cherbourg route – I'm usually happier with Dover/Calais – the sea journey's shorter for one thing, and somehow the longer the journey through England the more likely Piers is to forget to drive on the right once we're in France. I've noticed it. But I don't argue about things like that. Piers knows what he's doing – I never backseat drive. I'm his wife, he's my husband. We love each other.

So we were setting out for Weymouth, the bags were packed, the individual route maps from the AA in the glove

compartment – they'd arrived on time, for once. (I'd taken a Valium in good time – my heart tends to beat rather fast, almost to the point of palpitations, when I'm navigating.) I was wearing a practical non-crease dress – you know what long journeys are like – you always end up a little stained. Piers loves melons and likes me to feed him wedges as we drive along – and you know how ripe a ripe French melon can be. Piers will spend hours choosing one from a market stall. He'll test every single one on display – you know, sniffing and pressing the ends for just the right degree of tenderness – until he's found one that's absolutely perfect. Sometimes, before he's satisfied, he'll go through the fruit boxes at the back of the stall as well. The French like you to be particular, Piers says. They'll despise you if you accept just anything. And then, of course, if the melon's not to go over the top, they have to be eaten quite quickly – in the car as often as not...
Anyway, as I was saying, I was about to step into the car when my legs just kind of folded and I sank down on to the pavement, and that was six months ago, and I haven't walked since. No, no palpitations since either. I can't remember if I had palpitations before I was married – I've been married for ever!

And there was no holiday. Just me paralysed. No tour of France. Beautiful France. I adore the Loire and the châteaux, don't you? The children loved the West Coast: those stretches of piny woods and the long, long beaches and the great Atlantic rollers – but after the middle of August the winds change and everything gets dusty and somehow grizzly. When the children were small we camped, but every year the sites got more formal and more crowded and more full of *frites* and Piers didn't like that. He enjoyed what he called 'wilderness camping'. In the camping guides which describe the sites there's always an area section – that is, the area allowed for each tent. Point five of a hectare is crowded: two hectares perfectly possible. Piers liked ten hectares, which meant a hillside somewhere and no television room for the children or *frites* stall – and that meant more work for me, not that I grudged it: a change of venue for cooking – such lovely portable calor gas stoves we had: you could do a three-course meal on just two burners if you were clever, if the wind wasn't too high – is as good as a rest from cooking. It was just that the children preferred the crowded sites, and I did sometimes think they were better for the children's French. An English sparrow and a French sparrow sing pretty much the same song. But there you are, Piers loved the wilderness. He'd always measure the actual hectarage available for our tent, and if it didn't coincide with what was in the book would take it up with the relevant authorities. I remember it once ending up with people having to move their tents at ten in the evening to make proper room for ours – we'd driven three hundred miles that day and Brutus was only two. That wasn't Piers' fault: it was the camp proprietor's. Piers merely knocked him up to point out that our site wasn't the dimension it ought to be, and he over-reacted quite dreadfully. I was glad to get away from that site in the morning, I can tell you. It really wasn't Piers' fault; just one of those things. I'm glad it was only a stop-over. The other campers just watched us go, in complete silence. It was weird. And Fanny cried all the way to Poitiers.

Such a tearful little thing, Fanny. Piers liked to have a picnic lunch at about three o'clock – the French roads clear at mid-day while everyone goes off to gorge themselves on lunch, so you can make really good time wherever you're going. Some-times I did wonder where it was we *were* going to, or *why* we had to make such time, but on the other hand those wonderful white empty B roads, poplar-lined, at a steady 55 mph...

anyway, we'd buy our lunch at mid-day – wine and pâté and long French bread and orangina for the children, and then at three start looking for a nice place to picnic. Nothing's harder! If the place is right, the traffic's wrong. Someone's on your tail hooting – how those French drivers do hoot – they can see the GB plates – they know it means the driver's bound to forget and go round roundabouts the wrong way – and before you know it the ideal site is passed. The ideal site has a view, no snakes, some sun and some shade, and I like to feel the car's right off the road – especially if it's a Route Nationale – though Piers doesn't worry too much. Once actually some idiot did drive right into it – he didn't brake in time – but as Piers had left our car in gear, and not put on the handbrake or anything silly, it just shot forward and not much damage was done. How is it that other cars always look so smooth and somehow new? I suppose their owners must just keep them in garages all the time having the bumps knocked out and re-sprays – well, fools and their money are often parted, as Piers keeps saying.

What was I talking about? Stopping for lunch. Sometimes it would be four thirty before we found somewhere really nice, and by four you could always rely on Fanny to start crying. I'd give her water from the Pschitt bottle – how the children giggled – Pschitt – every year a ritual, lovely giggle – and break off bread from the loaf for her, but still she grizzled: and Daddy would stop and start and stare over hedges and go a little way down lanes and find them impossible and back out on to the main road, and the children would fall silent, except for Fanny. Aren't French drivers rude? Had you noticed? I'd look sideways at a passing car and the driver would be staring at us, screwing his thumb into his head, or pretending to slit his throat with his finger – and always these honks and hoots, and once someone pulled in and forced us to stop and tried to drag poor Piers out of the car, goodness knows why. Just general Gallic over-excitement, I suppose. Piers is a wonderfully safe driver. I do think he sometimes inconveniences other cars the way he stops at intersections – you know how muddling their road signs are, especially on city ring roads, and how they seem to be telling you to go right or left when actually they mean straight on. And Piers is a scientist – he likes to be sure he's doing the right thing. I have the maps; I do my best: I memorise whole areas of the country, so I will know when passing through, say, Limoges, on the way from Périgueux to Issoudun, and have to make lightning decisions – Piers seems to speed up in towns. No! Not the Tulle road, not the Clermont road, not the Montluçon but the Châteauroux road. Only the Châteauroux road isn't marked! Help! What's its number? Dear God, it's the N20! We'll die! The N147 to Bellac then, and cut through on the B roads to Argenton, La Châtre... So look for the Poitiers sign. Bellac's on the road to Poitiers –

So he stops, if he's not convinced I'm right, and takes the map himself and studies it before going on. Which meant, in later years, finding his magnifying glass. He hates spectacles! And you know what those overhead traffic lights are like in small country towns, impossible to see, so no one takes any notice of them! Goodness knows how French drivers survive at all. We had one or two nasty misses through no fault of our own every holiday; I did in the end feel happier if I took Valium. But I never liked Piers to know I was taking it – it seemed a kind of statement of lack of faith – which is simply untrue. Look at the way he carried me in, cradled me in his arms, laid me on this sofa! I trust him implicitly. I am his wife. He is my husband.

What was I saying? Fanny grizzling. She took off to New

Zealand as soon as she'd finished her college course. A long way away. Almost as far as she could get, I find myself saying, I don't know why. I know she loves us and we certainly love her. She writes frequently. David's a racing car driver. Piers and I are very upset about this. Such a dangerous occupation. Those cars get up to 200 mph – and Piers does so hate speed. Angela's doing psychiatric nursing. They say she has a real gift for it.

I remember once I said to Piers – we were on the ring road round Angers – turn left here, meaning the T-junction we were approaching – but he swung straight left across the other carriageway, spying a little side road there – empty because all the traffic was round the corner, held up by the lights, ready to surge forward. He realised what he'd done, and stopped, leaving us broadside across the main road. 'Reverse!' I shrieked, breaking my rule about no backseat driving, and he did, and we were just out of the way when the expected wall of traffic bore down. 'You should have said second left,' he said, 'that was very nearly a multiple pile-up!' You can't be too careful in France. They're mad drivers, as everyone knows. And with the children in the car too –

But it was all such fun. Piers always knew how to get the best out of waiters and chefs. He'd go right through the menu with the waiter, asking him to explain each dish. If the waiter couldn't do it – and it's amazing how many waiters can't – he would send for the chef and ask him. It did get a little embarrassing sometimes, if the restaurant was very busy, but as Piers said, the French understand food and really appreciate it if you do too. I can make up my mind in a flash what I want to eat: Piers takes ages. As I say, he hates to get things wrong. We'd usually be last to leave any restaurant we ate in, but Piers doesn't believe in hurrying. As he says, a) it's bad for the digestion and b) they don't mind: they're glad to see us appreciating what they have to offer. So many people don't. French waiters are such a rude breed, don't you think? They always seem to have kind of glassy eyes. Goodness knows what they're like if you're *not* appreciating what they have to offer!

And then wine. Piers believes in sending wine back as well as food. Standards have to be maintained. He doesn't believe in serving red wines chilled in the modern fashion, no matter how new they are. And that a bottle of wine under eight francs is as worth discussing as one at thirty francs. He's always very polite: just sends for the wine waiter to discuss the matter, but of course he doesn't speak French, so difficulties sometimes arise. Acrimony almost. And this kind of funny silence while we leave.

And always when we paid the bill before leaving our hotel, Piers would check and re-check every item. He's got rather short-sighted over the years: he has to use a magnifying glass. The children and I would sit waiting in the car for up to an hour while they discussed the cost of hot water and what a reasonable profit was, and why it being a fête holiday should make a difference. I do sometimes think, I admit, that Piers has a love/hate relationship with France. He loves the country; he won't go holidaying in Italy or Spain, only France – and yet, you know, those *Dégustation-Libres* that have sprung up all over the place – 'free disgustings', as the children call them – where you taste the wine before choosing? Piers goes in, tastes everything, and if he likes nothing – which is quite often – buys nothing. That, after all, is what they are offering. *Free* wine-tasting. He likes me to go in with him, to taste with him, so that we can compare notes, and I watch the enthusiasm dying in the proprietor's eyes, as he is asked to fetch first this, then that, then the other down from the top shelf, and Piers sips and raises his eyebrows and shakes his head, and then hostility dawns in the shopkeeper's eye, and then boredom, and then I almost think something which borders on derision – and I must tell you, Miss Jacobs, I don't like it, and in the end, whenever we passed a *Dégustation-Libre* and I saw the glint in his eye, and his foot went on the brake – he never looked in his mirror – there was no point, since it was always adjusted to show the car roof – I'd take another Valium – because I think otherwise I would scream, I couldn't help myself. It wasn't that I didn't love and trust and admire Piers, it was the look in the French eye –

Why don't I scream? What are you after? Abreaction? I know the terms – my daughter Angela's a psychiatric nurse, as I told you, and doing very well. You think I was finally traumatised at the last *Dégustation*? And that's why I can't walk? You'd like to believe that, wouldn't you? I expect you're a feminist – I notice you're wearing a trouser suit – and like to think everything in this world is the man's fault. You want me to scream out tension and rage and terror and horror? I won't! I tell you, France is a joyous place and we all loved those holidays and had some wonderful meals and some knock-out wines, thanks to Piers, and as for his driving, we're all alive, aren't we? Piers, me, David, Angela, Fanny, Brutus. All alive! That must prove something. It's just I don't seem able to walk, and if you would be so kind as to call Piers, he will shift me from your sofa to the chair and wheel me home. Talking will get us nowhere. I do love my husband.

1984

Down the Clinical Disco

You never know where you'll meet your own true love. I met mine down the clinical disco. That's him over there, the thin guy with the jeans, the navy jumper and the red woolly cap. He looks pretty much like anyone else, don't you think? That's hard work on his part, not to mention mine, but we got there in the end. Do you want a drink? Gin? Tonic? Fine. I'll just have an orange juice. I don't drink. Got to be careful. You never know who's watching. They're everywhere. Sorry, forget I said that. Even a joke can be paranoia. Do you like my hair? That's a golden gloss rinse. Not my style really: I have this scar down my cheek: see, if I turn to the light? A good short crop is what suits me best, always has been: I suppose I've got what you'd call a strong face. Oops, sorry, dear, didn't mean to spill your gin; it's the heels. I do my best but I can never quite manage stilettos. But it's an ill wind; anyone watching would think I'm ever so slightly tipsy, and that's normal, isn't it. It is not absolutely A-okay not to drink alcohol. On the obsessive side. *Darling, of course there are people watching.*

Let me tell you about the clinical disco while Eddie finishes his game of darts. He hates darts but darts are what men do in pubs, okay? The clinical disco is what they have once a month at Broadmoor. (Yes, that place. Broadmoor. The secure hospital for the criminally insane.) You didn't know they had women there? They do. One woman to every nine men. They often don't look all that like women when they go in but they sure as hell look like them when (and if, if, if, if, if, if) they go out.

How did I get to be in there? You really want to know? I'd been having this crummy time at home and this crummy time at work. I was pregnant and married to this guy I loved, God knows why, in retrospect, but I did, only he fancied my mother, and he got her pregnant too – while I was out at work – did you know women can get pregnant at fifty? He didn't, she didn't, I didn't – but she was! My mum said he only married me to be near her anyway and I was the one who ought to have an abortion. So I did. It went wrong and messed me up inside, so I couldn't have babies, and my mum said what did it matter, I was a lesbian anyway, just look at me. I got the scar in a road accident, in case you're wondering. And I thought what the hell, who wants a man, who wants a mother, and walked out on them. And I was working at the Royal Opera House for this man who was a real pain, and you know how these places get: the dramas and the rows and the overwork and the underpay and the show must go on though you're dropping dead. Dropping dead babies. No, I'm not crying. What do you think I am, a depressive? I'm as normal as the next person.

What I did was set fire to the office. Just an impulse. I was having these terrible pains and he made me work late. He said it was my fault Der Rosenkavalier's wig didn't fit: he said I'd made his opera house a laughing stock: the wig slipped and the *New York Times* noticed and jeered. But it wasn't my fault about the wig: wardrobe had put the message through to props, not administration. And I sat in front of the VDU – the union is against them: they cause infertility in women but what employer's going to worry about a thing like that – they'd prefer everyone childless any day – and thought about my husband and my mum, five months pregnant, and lit a cigarette. I'd given up smoking for a whole year but this business at home had made me start again. Have you ever had an abortion at five months? No? Not many have.

How's your drink? How's Eddie getting on with the darts? Started another game? That's A-okay, that's fine by me, that's normal.

So what were we saying, Linda? Oh yes, arson. That's what they called it. I just moved my cigarette lighter under the curtains and they went up, whoosh, and they caught some kind of soundproof ceiling infill they use these days instead of plaster. Up it all went. Whoosh again. Four hundred pounds' worth of damage. Or so they said. If you ask me, they were glad of the excuse to redecorate.

Like a fool, instead of lying and just saying it was an accident, I said I'd done it on purpose, I was glad I had, opera was a waste of public funds, and working late a waste of my life. That was before I got to court. The solicitor laddie warned me off. He said arson was no laughing matter, they came down very hard on arson. I thought a fine, perhaps: he said no, prison. Years not months.

You know my mum didn't even come to the hearing? She had a baby girl. I thought there might be something wrong with it, my mum being so old, but there wasn't. Perhaps the father being so young made up for it.

There was a barrister chappie. He said look you've been upset, you are upset, all this business at home. The thing for you to do is plead insane; we'll get you sent to Broadmoor, it's the best place in the country for psychiatric care, they'll have you right in the head in no time. Otherwise it's Holloway, and that's all strip cells and major tranquillizers, and not so much of a short sharp shock as a long sharp shock. Years, it could be, arson.

So that's what I did, I pleaded insane, and got an indefinite sentence, which meant into Broadmoor until such time as I was cured and safe to be let out into the world again. I never was unsafe. You know what one of those famous opera singers said when she heard what I'd done? 'Good for Philly,' she said. 'Best thing that could possibly happen: the whole place razed to the ground.' Only of course it wasn't razed to the ground, there was just one room already in need of redecoration slightly blackened. When did I realize I'd made a mistake? The minute I saw Broadmoor: a great black pile: the second I got into this reception room. There were three women nurses in there, standing around a bath of hot water; great hefty women, and male nurses too, and they were talking and laughing. Well, not exactly laughing, but an Inside equivalent; a sort of heavy grunting ha-ha-ha they manage, halfway between sex and hate. They didn't even look at me as I came in. I was terrified, you can imagine. One of them said 'strip' over her shoulder and I just stood there not believing it. So she barked 'strip' again, so I took off a cardigan and my shoes, and then one of them just ripped everything off me and pushed my legs apart and yanked out a Tampax – sorry about this, Linda – and threw it in a bin and dunked me in the bath without even seeing me. Do you know what's worse than being naked and seen by strangers, including men strangers? It's being naked and unseen, because you don't even count as a woman. Why men? In case the women patients are uncontrollable. The bath was dirty. So were the nurses. I asked for a sanitary towel but no one replied. I don't know if they were being cruel: I don't think they thought that what came out of my mouth were words. Well I was mad, wasn't I? That's why I was there. I was mad because I was a patient, I was wicked because I was a prisoner: they were sane because they were nurses and good because they could go home after work.

Linda, is that guy over there in the suit watching? No? You're sure?

They didn't go far, mind you, most of them. They lived, breathed, slept The Hospital. Whole families of nurses live in houses at the foot of the great Broadmoor wall. They intermarry. Complain about one and you find you're talking to the cousin, aunt, lover or best friend of the complainee. You learn to shut up: you learn to smile. I was a tea bag for the whole of one day and I never stopped smiling from dawn to dusk. That's right, I was a tea bag. Nurse Kelly put a wooden frame round my shoulders and hung a piece of gauze front and back and said 'You be a tea bag all day' so I was. How we all laughed. Why did he want me to be a tea bag? It was his little joke. They get bored, you see. They look to the patients for entertainment.

Treatment? Linda, I saw one psychiatrist six times and I was there three years. The men do better. They have rehabilitation programmes, ping-pong, carpentry and we all get videos. Only the men get to choose the video and they always choose blue films. They have to choose them to show they're normal, and the women have to choose not to see them to show the same. You have to be normal to get out. Sister in the ward fills in the report cards. She's the one who decides whether or not you're sane enough to go before the Parole Committee. The trouble is, she's not so sane herself. She's more institutionalized than the patients.

Eddie, come and join us! How was your game? You won? Better not do that too often. You don't want to be seen as an over-achiever. This is Linda, I'm telling her how we met. At the clinical disco. Shall we do a little dance, just the pair of us, in the middle of everything and everyone, just to celebrate being out? No, you're right, that would be just plain mad. Eddie and I love each other, Linda, we met at the clinical disco, down Broadmoor way. Who knows, the doctor may have been wrong about me not having babies; stranger things happen. My mum ran out on my ex, leaving him to look after the baby: he came to visit me in Broadmoor once and asked me to go back to him, but I wouldn't. Sister put me back for that: a proper woman wants to go back to her husband, even though he's her little sister's father. And after he'd gone I cried. You must never cry in Broadmoor. It means you're depressed; and that's the worst madness of all. The staff all love it in there, and think you're really crazy if you don't. I guess they get kind of offended if you cry. So it's on with the lipstick and smile, smile, smile, though everyone around you is ballooning with largactyl and barking like the dogs they think they are.

I tell you something, Linda, these places are mad-houses. Never, never plead the balance of your mind is disturbed in court: get a prison sentence and relax, and wait for time to pass and one day you'll be free. Once you're in a secure hospital, you may never get out at all, and they fill the women up with so many tranquillizers, you may never be fit to. The drugs give you brain damage. But I reckon I'm all right; my hands tremble a bit, and my mouth twitches sometimes, but it's not too bad. And I'm still *me*, aren't I. Eddie's fine – they don't give men so much, sometimes none at all. Only you never know what's in the tea. But you can't be seen not drinking it, because that's paranoia.

Eddie says I should sue the barrister, with his fine talk of therapy and treatment in Broadmoor, but I reckon I won't. Once you've been in you're never safe. They can pop you back inside if you cause any trouble at all, and they're the ones who decide what trouble is. So we keep our mouths shut and our noses clean, we ex-inmates of Broadmoor.

Are you sure that man's not watching? Is there something wrong with us? Eddie? You're not wearing your earring, are you? Turn your head. No, that's all right. We look just like everyone else. Don't we? Is my lipstick smudged? Christ, I hate wearing it. It makes my eyes look small.

At the clinical disco! They hold them at Broadmoor every month. Lots of the men in there are sex offenders, rapists, mass murderers, torturers, child abusers, flashers. The staff like to see how they're getting on, how they react to the opposite sex, and on the morning of the disco Sister turns up and says 'you go' and 'you' and 'you' and of course you can't say no, no matter how scared you are. Because you're supposed to want to dance. And the male staff gee up the men – hey, look at those titties! Wouldn't you like to look up *that* skirt – and stand by looking forward to the trouble, a bit of living porno, better than a blue film any day. And they gee up the women too: wow, there's a handsome hunk of male: and you have to act interested, because that's normal: if they think you're a lezzie you never get out. And the men have to act interested, but not too interested. Eddie and I met at the clinical disco, acting just gently interested. Eddie felt up my titties, and I rubbed myself against him and the staff watched and all of a sudden he said 'Hey, I mean really,' and I said 'Hi,' and he said 'Sorry about this, keep smiling,' and I said, 'Ditto, what are you in for?' and he said 'I got a job as a woman teacher. Six little girls framed me. But I love teaching, not little girls. There was just no job for a man,' and I believed him: nobody else ever had. And I told him about my mum and my ex, and he seemed to understand. Didn't you, Eddie! That's love, you see. Love at first sight. You're just on the other person's side, and if you can find someone else like that about you, everything falls into place. We were both out in three months. It didn't matter for once if I wore lipstick, it didn't matter to him if he had to watch blue films: you stop thinking that acting sane is driving you mad: you don't have not to cry because you stop wanting to cry: the barking and howling and screeching stop worrying you; I guess when you're in love you're just happy so they have to turn you out; because your being happy shows them up. If you're happy, what does sane or insane mean, what are their lives all about? They can't bear to see it.

Linda, it's been great meeting you. Eddie and I are off home now. I've talked too much. Sorry. When we're our side of our front door I scrub off the make-up and get into jeans and he gets into drag, and we're ourselves, and we just hope no one comes knocking on the door to say, hey that's not normal, back to Broadmoor, but I reckon love's a talisman. If we hold on to that we'll be okay.

1985

A Gentle Tonic Effect

'What did you say your name was?' asked Morna Casey. 'Miss Jacobs? Just a miss? Not a doctor or anything? Well, *chacun à son goût*. But tell me, do you need planning permission, or can anyone just set up in their front room and start in the shrinking business?'

Morna Casey frowned at what she thought might be a hangnail, and looked at her little gold watch with the link chain, and waited for Miss Jacobs' reply, which did not come.

'I have very little time for people who go to therapists,' added Morna Casey. 'I'm sorry, but there it is. It's so sort of self-absorbed, don't you think? I can't stand people who make a fuss about nothing. If it wasn't that my dreams were interfering with my work I wouldn't be here.'

Still no response came from Miss Jacobs: she did not even lift her pencil from the little round mahogany table at her side.

'You charge quite a lot', observed Morna Casey, 'for someone who says so little and takes no notes. But if you can get away with it, good for you. I suppose on the whole people are just mentally lazy: they employ analysts to think about them rather than do it themselves.'

Morna Casey waited. Presently Miss Jacobs spoke. She said, 'This first consultation is free. Then we will see whether it is worth both our whiles embarking on a course of treatment.'

'I don't know why,' said Morna Casey, 'but you remind me of the owl in *Squirrel Nutkin*.'

A slight smile glimmered over Miss Jacobs' lips. Morna Casey noticed, of course she did. She had declined to lie down on the leather couch, with her head at Miss Jacobs' end, as patients were expected to do.

'I suppose', acknowledged Morna Casey, 'it's because I feel like Squirrel Nutkin, dancing up and down in front of wise old owl, making jokes and being rude. But you won't get to gobble me up: I'm too quick and fast for the likes of you.'

Morna Casey was a willowy blonde in her late thirties: elegantly turned out, executive style. Her eyes were wide and sexy, and her teeth white, even and capped. She wore a lot of gold jewellery of the kind you can buy in Duty Free shops at major airports. Her skirt was short and her legs were long and her heels were high.

'I went to see a doctor,' said Morna Casey, 'which is a thing I hardly ever do – I can't stand all that poking and fussing about. But the nightmares kept waking me up; and if you're going to do a good job of work it's imperative to have a good night's sleep. I've always insisted on my beauty sleep – when Rider was a baby I used ear plugs: he soon learned to sleep through.'

Rider was Morna Casey's son. He was seventeen and active in the school potholing club.

Morna Casey leaned forward so that her shapely bosom glowed pink beneath her thin white tailored shirt. She wore the kind of bra which lets the nipples show through. 'The fool of a doctor gave me sleeping pills, and though I quadrupled the dose it still didn't stop me waking up screaming once or twice a night. And Hector wasn't much help. But then he never is.'

Hector was Morna Casey's husband. He was head of market research at the advertising agency where Morna worked. She was a PR executive for Maltman Ltd, a firm which originally sold whisky but had lately diversified into pharmaceuticals.

'Helping simply isn't Hector's forte,' said Morna Casey. 'You ask what is? A word too crude for your ears, Miss Jacobs, probably beyond your understanding; that's what Hector's forte is. I first set eyes on Hector in a pub one night, eighteen years ago: I said to my then husband, "Who's that man with the big nose?" and Hector followed us home that night and we haven't been apart since.'

Miss Jacobs looked quite startled, or perhaps Morna Casey thought she did.

'People say "Didn't your husband mind?" and I reply, "Well, he didn't like it much but what could he do?"' said Morna Casey. 'He moved out, which suited me and Hector very well. It was a nice house: we bought him out. Hector's one of the most boring people I know: he has no conversation apart from statistics and a very limited mind, but he suits me okay. And I suit him: he doesn't understand a word I say. When I tell him about the dreams, all he says is, "Well, what's so terrible about dreaming that?" It was the doctor who suggested I came to see you: doctors do that, don't they? If they're stumped they say it's stress. Well, of course I'm stressed: I've always been stressed: I have a difficult and demanding job. But I haven't always had the dreams. I told the doctor I was perfectly capable of analysing myself thank you very much and he said he didn't doubt it but a therapist might save me some time, and time was money, which is true enough, and that's the reason I'm here. At least all you do is poke about in my head and not between my legs.'

Miss Jacobs took up her notepad and wrote something in it.

'What's that?' asked Morna Casey, nastily. 'Your shopping list for tonight's dinner? Liver? Brussels sprouts?'

'If you'd lie down on the couch,' said Miss Jacobs, 'you wouldn't see me writing and it wouldn't bother you.'

'It doesn't bother me,' said Morna Casey. 'Sorry. Nothing you do bothers me one little bit, one way or another. And nothing will make me lie down on your couch. Reminds me of my father. My father was a doctor. He smoked eighty cigarettes a day and died of lung cancer when he was forty-three and I was seventeen. He'd cough and spit and gasp and light another cigarette. Then he'd inhale and cough some more. I remember saying to my Uncle Desmond – he was a doctor too – "Do you think it's sensible for Daddy to smoke so much?" and Uncle Desmond replied, "Nothing wrong with tobacco: it acts as a mild disinfectant, and has a gentle tonic effect." I tend to believe that, in spite of all that research – paid for by the confectionery companies, I wouldn't be surprised – about the tobacco–lung-cancer link. It's never been properly proved. The public is easily panicked, as those of us in PR know. My father enjoyed smoking. He went out in his prime. He wouldn't have wanted to be old.

'But I'm not here to waste time talking about my father. When you're dead you're dead and there's no point discussing you. I'm here to talk about my dream. It comes in two halves: in the first half Rider is miniaturized – about twenty inches long – and he's clinging on by his fingertips to the inside of the toilet, and crying, so I lean on the handle and flush him away. I can't bear to see men crying – and at seventeen you're a man, aren't you. That part of the dream just makes me uneasy; but then out of the toilet rise up all these kind of deformed people – with no arms or two heads or their nerves outside their skin not inside so they have a kind of flayed look – and they sort of loom over me and that's the bit I don't like: that's when I wake up screaming.'

Morna Casey was silent for a little. She stretched her leg and admired her ankle.

'I think I understand the first part of the dream,' said Morna Casey presently. 'I gave birth to Rider in the toilet bowl at home. I wouldn't go to hospital. I wasn't going to have all those strangers staring up between my legs, so when I went into labour I didn't tell a soul, just gritted my teeth and got on with it, and it ended up with Hector having to fish the baby out of the water. Now Rider climbs about in potholes – he actually likes being spreadeagled flat against slimy rock faces, holding on with his fingertips. His best friend was killed last year in a fall but I don't worry. I've never worried about Rider. What's the point? When your number's up your number's up. Sometimes I do get to worry about the way I don't worry. I don't seem to be quite like other people in this respect. Not that

I'd want to be. I guess I'm just not the maternal type. But Rider grew up perfectly okay: he was never much of a bother. He's going to university. If he wants to go potholing that's his affair. Do we stop for coffee and biscuits? No? Not that I'd take the biscuits but I like to be offered. Food is an essential part of PR. The laws of hospitality are very strong. No one likes to bite the hand that feeds them. That's one of the first things you learn in my job. You should really seriously think about it, Miss Jacobs.'

Morna Casey pondered for a while. A fly buzzed round her head but thought better of it and flew off.

'I don't understand the second part of the dream at all,' said Morna Casey presently. 'Who are all these deformed idiots who come shrieking out of the toilet bowl at me? I really hate the handicapped. So do most people only they haven't the guts to say so. If there'd been one single thing wrong with Rider, an ear out of place, oesophagus missing, the smallest thing, I'd have pushed him under, not let Hector fish him out. Don't you like Rider as a name? The rider of storms, the rider of seas? No one knows how poetic I am: they look as I go by and whistle and say, there goes a good-looking blonde of the smart kind not the silly kind, and they have no idea at all what I'm really about. I like that. One day I'm going to give it all up and be a poet. When Hector's old and past it I'm going to push him under a bus. I can't abide dribbly old men. When I'm old Rider will look after me. He loves me. He only clambers about underground to make me notice him. What he wants me to say is what I've never said: "I worry about you, Rider." But I don't. How can I say it; it isn't true.'

Miss Jacobs raised an eyebrow. Morna Casey looked at her watch.

'I have a meeting at three thirty,' said Morna Casey. 'I mustn't let this overrun. I'm on a rather important special project at the moment, you may be interested to know. I'm handling the press over the Artefax scare.'

Artefax was a new vitamin-derivative drug hailed as a wonder cure for addictions of all kinds, manufactured by Maltman and considered by some to be responsible for a recent spate of monstrous births – though Maltman's lawyers had argued successfully in the courts that, as the outbreaks were clustered, the Chernobyl fallout must be to blame – particles of caesium entering the water table in certain areas and not in others.

'So you'll understand it's all go at the moment,' said Morna Casey. 'We have to restore public confidence. Artefax is wonderful, and absolutely harmless – you can even take it safely through pregnancy; you're not addicted to anything, and all it does is have a mild tonic effect. Our main PR drive is through the doctors.'

Morna Casey was silent for a little. Miss Jacobs stared out of the window.

'Well yes,' said Morna Casey presently. 'I see. If I changed my job the dreams would stop. But if I changed my job I wouldn't worry about the dreams because it wouldn't matter about the job, would it. All the same I might consider a shift in career direction. I don't really like working for the same outfit as Hector. It does rather cramp my style – not that he can do much about it. I do as I like. He knows how boring he is; what can he expect?'

'There's a good opening coming up,' said Morna Casey, 'or so

I've heard on the grapevine, as head of PR at Britnuc; that's the new nuclear energy firm. I think I'd feel quite at home with radioactivity: it's like nicotine and Artefax – in reasonable quantities it has this gentle tonic effect. Of course in large quantities I daresay it's different. But so's anything. Like aspirin. One does you good, two cure your headache, twenty kill you. In the Soviet Union the spas offer radioactive mud baths. Radon-rich, they say. They're very popular.'

'Thank you for the consultation, Dr – sorry, Miss – Jacobs. I won't be needing to see you again. I'm much obliged to you for your time and patience: though of course one can always do this kind of thing for oneself. If I ever give up PR I might consider setting up as a therapist. No planning permission required! A truly jolly *pièce de* rich *gâteau,* if you ask me.'

And Morna Casey adjusted her short taupe skirt over her narrow hips and walked out, legs long on high heels, and Miss Jacobs, whose hand had been hovering over her appointment book, put down her pencil.

1986

Chew You Up and Spit You Out

A cautionary tale

'Well, yes,' said the house to the journalist, in the manner of interviewees everywhere, 'it is rather a triumph, after all I've been through!' The journalist, a young woman, couldn't quite make out the words for the stirring of the ivy on the chimney and the shirring of doves in the dovecote. She was not of the kind to be responsive to the talk of houses – and who would want to be who wished to sleep easy at night? – but she heard enough to feel there was some kind of story here. She'd come with a photographer from *House & Garden*: they were doing a feature on the past retold, on rescued houses, though to tell the truth she thought all such houses were boring as hell. Let the past look after the past was her motto. She was twenty-three and beautiful and lived in a Bauhaus flat with a composer boyfriend who paid the rent and preferred something new to something old any day.

'Let's just get it over with,' she said, 'earn our living and leg it back to town.'

But she stood over the photographer carefully enough, to make sure he didn't miss a mullioned window, thatched outhouse, Jacobean beam or Elizabethan chimney: the things that readers loved to stare at: she was conscientious enough. She meant to get on in the world. She tapped her designer boot on original flagstone and waited while he changed his film, and wondered why she felt uneasy, and what the strange muffled breathing in her ears could mean. That's how houses speak, halfway between a draught and a creak, when they've been brought back to life by the well-intentioned, rescued from decay and demolition. You hear it sometimes when you wake in the middle of the night in an old house, and think the place is haunted. But it's not, it's just the house itself speaking.

The journalist found Harriet Simley making coffee in the kitchen. The original built-in dresser had been stripped and polished, finished to the last detail, though only half the floor was tiled, and where it was not the ground was murky and wet. Harriet's hair fell mousy and flat around a sweet and earnest face.

'No coffee for me,' said the journalist. 'Caffeine's so bad for one! What a wonderful old oak beam!' The owners of old houses love to hear their beams praised.

'Twenty-three feet long,' said Harriet proudly. 'Probably the backbone of some beached man o' war. Fascinating, the interweaving of military history and our forest story! Of course, these days you can't get a properly seasoned oak beam over twelve feet anywhere in the country. You have to go to Normandy to find them, and it costs you an arm and a leg. And all our capital's gone. Still, it's worth it, isn't it! Bringing old houses back to life!' The girl nodded politely and wrote it all down, though she'd heard it a hundred times before, up and down the country; of cottages, farmhouses, manors, mansions, long houses: 'Costs you an arm and a leg. Still, it's worth it. Bringing old houses back to life!' Spoken by the half-dead, so far as she could see, but then she was of the Bauhaus, by her very nature.

'What's the matter with your hands?' the journalist asked, and wished she hadn't.

'Rheumatoid arthritis, I'm afraid,' Harriet said. She couldn't have been more than forty. 'It was five years before we got the central heating in. Every time we took up a floorboard there'd be some disaster underneath. Well, we got the damp out of the house in the end, but it seems to have got into my hands.' And she laughed as if it were funny, but the journalist knew it was not. She shuddered and looked at her own city-smooth red-tipped fingers. Harriet's knuckles stood out on her hands, as if she made a fist against the world, and a deformed fist at that.

'So dark and gloomy in here,' the journalist thought and made her excuses and went out again into the sun to look up at the house, but it didn't warm her: no, the shudder turned into almost a shiver, she didn't know why. The house spoke to her, but the breeze in the creepers which fronded the upstairs windows distorted the words. Or perhaps the Bauhaus had made her deaf.

'You should have seen me only thirty years ago!' said the house. 'What a ruin. I must have fallen asleep. I woke to find myself a shambles. Chimney through the roof, dry rot in the laundry extension, rabbits living in the walls along with the mice, deathwatch beetle in the minstrels' gallery, the land drains blocked and water pushing up the kitchen tiles, and so overgrown with ivy I couldn't even be seen from the road. What woke me? Why, a young couple pushing open the front door – how it creaked; enough to wake the dead. They looked strong, young and healthy. They had a Volvo. They came from the city: they had dogs, cats and babies. They'll do, I thought; it's better if they come with their smalls: they'll see to the essentials first. My previous dwellers? They'd been old, so old, one family through generations: they left in their coffins: there was no strength in them; mine drained away. That's why I fell asleep, not even bothered to shrug off the ivy. I woke only in the nick of time. Well, I thought, can't let that happen again. So now I put out my charm and lure the young ones in, the new breed from the city, strong and resourceful. They fall in love with me; they give me all their money: but they have no stamina; I kept the first lot twelve years, then they had to go. Pity. But I tripped a small down the back stairs, to punish it for rattling the stained glass in its bedroom door, and it lay still for months, and the parents neglected me and cursed me so I got rid of them. But I found new dwellers soon enough, tougher, stronger, richer, who did for a time. Oh yes, I'm a success story! Now see, even the press takes an interest in my triumph! Journalists, photographers!' And the house preened itself in the late summer sun, in the glowing evening light.

'I say,' said the photographer to Julian Simley, as he wheelbarrowed a load of red roof-tiles from the yard to the cider house, 'you should get the ivy off the chimney; it'll break down the cement.' The photographer knew a thing or two – he'd just put in an offer for a house in the country himself. An old rectory: a lot to do to it, of course, but he was a dab hand at DIY, and with his new girlfriend working he could afford to spend a bit. A snip, a snip – and worth twice as much, three times, when he was through. Even the surveyor said so.

The house read his mind and sang, 'When *we're* through with *you*, when *we're* through with *you*: you can call yourself an owner, who are but a slave, you who come and go within our walls, for all old houses are the same and think alike,' and the photographer smiled admiringly up at the doves in the creeper, as they stirred and whirred, and only the journalist shivered and said, 'There's something wrong with my ears. I hear music in them, a creaky kind of music, I don't like it at all.'
'Wax', said the photographer absently, 'can sound like that.'

Julian Simley said, 'Christ, is that ivy back again? That's the last straw,' which is not what you're supposed to say when you're telling the press a success story of restoration, or renovation, in return for a hundred-pound fee, which you desperately need, for reclaimed old brick and groceries. 'I haven't the head for heights I had.'

'You fool, you fool,' snarled the house, overhearing. 'You pathetic weak-backed mortal. Let the ivy grow, will you? Turn me into weeds and landscape? Leave me a heap of rubble, would you! Wretched, poverty-stricken creature: grubbing around for money! You and your poor crippled wife, who'd rather fit a dresser handle than tile the kitchen floor! I've no more patience with you: I've finished with you!' and as Julian Simley stood on a windowsill to open a mullioned pane so the photographer could get the effect of glancing light he wanted, the sill crumbled and Julian fell and his back clicked and there was his disc slipped again, and he lay on the ground, and Harriet rang for the ambulance, and *House & Garden* waited with them. It was the least they could do.

'He should have replaced the sill,' thought the photographer, 'I would have done,' and the house hugged itself to itself in triumph.

'We can't manage any longer,' said Julian to Harriet, as he lay on the ground. 'It's no use, we'll have to sell, even at a loss.'

'It's not the money I mind about,' grieved Harriet. 'It's just I love this house so much.'

'Don't you think I do,' said Julian, and gritted his teeth against the stabs of pain which ran up his legs to his back. He thought this time he'd done some extra-complicating damage. 'But I get the feeling it's unrequited love.' The house sniggered.

'But how will we know the next people will carry on as we

have? They'll cover up the kitchen floor and not let it dry out properly, I know they will.' Harriet wept. Julian groaned. The ambulance came. The journalist and the photographer drove off.

'You want to know the secret?' the house shrieked after them. 'The secret of my success? It's chew them up and spit them out! One after the other! And I'll have you next,' it screamed at the photographer, who looked back at the house as they circled the drive, and thought, 'So beautiful! I'll withdraw the offer on the rectory, and make a bid on this one. I reckon I'll get it cheap, in the circumstances. That looked like a broken back, not a slipped disc, to me,' and the house settled back cosily into its excellent, well-drained, sheltered site – the original builders knew what they were doing – and smiled to itself, and whispered to the doves who stirred and whirred their wings in its creepers. 'Flesh and blood, that's all. Flesh and blood withers and dies. But a house like me can go on for ever, if it has its wits about it.'

1988

Ind Aff
or
Out of Love in Sarajevo

This is a sad story. It has to be. It rained in Sarajevo, and we had expected fine weather.

The rain filled up Sarajevo's pride, two footprints set into a pavement, marking the spot where the young assassin Princip stood to shoot the Archduke Ferdinand and his wife. (Don't forget his wife: everyone forgets his wife, the Archduchess.) That happened in the summer of 1914. Sarajevo is a pretty town, Balkan style, mountain-rimmed. A broad, swift, shallow river runs through its centre, carrying the mountain snows away. The river is arched by many bridges and the one nearest the two footprints has been named The Princip Bridge. The young man is a hero in these parts. Not only does he bring in the tourists – look, look, the spot, the very spot! – but by his action, as everyone knows, he lit the spark which fired the timber which caused World War I which crumbled the Austro-Hungarian Empire, the crumbling of which made modern Yugoslavia possible. Forty million dead (or was it thirty?), but who cares? So long as he loved his country.

The river, they say, can run so shallow in the summer it's known derisively as 'the wet road'. Today, from what I could see through the sheets of falling rain, it seemed full enough. Yugoslavian streets are always busy – no one stays home if they can help it (thus can an indecent shortage of housing space create a sociable nation) and it seemed that as if by common consent a shield of bobbing umbrellas had been erected two metres high to keep the rain off the streets. But the shield hadn't worked around Princip's corner, that was plain.

'Come all this way,' said Peter, who was a Professor of Classical History, 'and you can't even see the footprints properly, just two undistinguished puddles.' Ah, but I loved him. I shivered for his disappointment. He was supervising my thesis on varying concepts of morality and duty in the early Greek states as evidenced in their poetry and drama. I was dependent upon him for my academic future. Peter said I had a good mind but not a first-class mind, and somehow I didn't take it as an insult. I had a feeling first-class minds weren't all that good in bed.

Sarajevo is in Bosnia, in the centre of Yugoslavia, that grouping of unlikely states, that distillation of languages into the phonetic reasonableness of Serbo-Croat. We'd sheltered from the rain in an ancient mosque in Serbian Belgrade: done the same in a monastery in Croatia: now we spent a wet couple of days in Sarajevo beneath other people's umbrellas. We planned to go on to Montenegro, on the coast, where the fish and the artists come from, to swim and lie in the sun, and recover from the exhaustion caused by the sexual and moral torments of the last year. It couldn't possibly go on raining for ever. Could it? Satellite pictures showed black cloud swishing gently all over Europe, over the Balkans, into Asia – practically all the way from Moscow to London, in fact. It wasn't that Peter and I were being singled out. No. It was raining on his wife, too, back in Cambridge.

Peter was trying to make the decision, as he had been for the past year, between his wife and myself as his permanent life partner. To this end we had gone away, off the beaten track, for a holiday: if not with his wife's blessing, at least with her knowledge. Were we really, truly suited? We had to be sure, you see, that this was more than just any old professor-student romance: that it was the Real Thing, because the longer the indecision went on the longer Mrs Piper, Peter said, would be left dangling in uncertainty and distress. He and she had been married for twenty-four years; they'd stopped loving each other a long time ago, naturally – but there would be a fearful personal and practical upheaval entailed if he decided to leave permanently and shack up, as he put it, with me. Which I wanted him to do, because I loved him. And so far I was winning hands down. It didn't seem much of a contest at all, in fact. I'd been cool and thin and informed on the seat next to him in a Zagreb theatre (Mrs Piper was sweaty and only liked TV), was now eager and anxious for social and political instruction in Sarajevo (Mrs Piper spat in the face of knowledge, Peter had once told me), and planned to be lissom and topless – I hadn't quite decided: it might be counterproductive to underline the age differential – while I splashed and shrieked like a bathing belle in the shallows of the craggy Croatian coast (Mrs Piper was a swimming coach: I imagined she smelt permanently of chlorine).

So far as I could see it was no contest at all between his wife and myself. How could he possibly choose her while I was on offer? But Peter liked to luxuriate in guilt and indecision. And I loved him with an inordinate affection, and indulged him in this luxury.

Princip's footprints are a metre apart, placed like the feet of a modern cop on a training shoot-out – the left in front at a slight outward angle, the right behind, facing forward. There seemed great energy focused here. Both hands on the gun, run, stop, plant the feet, aim, fire! I could see the footprints well enough, in spite of Peter's complaint. They were clear enough to me, albeit puddled.

We went to a restaurant for lunch, since it was too wet to do what we loved to do: that is, buy bread, cheese, sausage, wine and go off somewhere in our hired car, into the woods or the hills, and picnic and make love. It was a private restaurant – Yugoslavia went over to a mixed capitalist–communist economy years back, so you get either the best or the worst of both systems, depending on your mood – that is to say, we knew we would pay more but be given a choice. We chose the wild boar.

'Probably ordinary pork soaked in red cabbage water to darken it,' said Peter. He was not in a good mood. Cucumber salad was served first.

'Everything in this country comes with cucumber salad,' complained Peter. I noticed I had become used to his complaining. I supposed that when you had been married a while you simply wouldn't hear it. He was forty-six and I was twenty-five.

'They grow a lot of cucumber,' I said.

'If they can grow cucumbers,' Peter then asked, 'why can't they grow mange-tout?' It seemed a why-can't-they-eat-cake sort of argument to me, but not knowing enough about horticulture not to be outflanked if I debated the point, I moved the subject on to safer ground.

'I suppose Princip's action couldn't really have started World

War One,' I remarked. 'Otherwise, what a thing to have on your conscience! One little shot and the deaths of thirty million on your shoulders.'

'Forty,' he corrected me. Though how they reckon these things and get them right I can't imagine. 'Of course Princip didn't start the war. That's just a simple tale to keep the children quiet. It takes more than an assassination to start a war. What happened was that the build-up of political and economic tensions in the Balkans was such that it had to find some release.'

'So it was merely the shot that lit the spark that fired the timber that started the war, et cetera?'

'Quite,' he said. 'World War One would have had to have started sooner or later.'

'A bit later or a bit sooner', I said, 'might have made the difference of a million or so: if it was you on the battlefield in the mud and the rain you'd notice: exactly when they fired the starting-pistol: exactly when they blew the final whistle. Is that what they do when a war ends: blow a whistle? So that everyone just comes in from the trenches?'

But he wasn't listening. He was parting the flesh of the soft collapsed orangey-red pepper which sat in the middle of his cucumber salad; he was carefully extracting the pips. He didn't like eating pepper pips. His Nan had once told him they could never be digested, would stick to the wall of his stomach and do terrible damage. I loved him for his vulnerability, the bit of him that was forever little boy: I loved him for his dexterity and patience with his knife and fork. I'd finished my salad yonks ago, pips and all. I was hungry. I wanted my wild boar.

Peter might have been forty-six but he was six foot two and well-muscled and grizzled with it, in a dark-eyed, intelligent, broad-jawed kind of way. I adored him. I loved to be seen with him. 'Muscular-academic, not weedy-academic,' as my younger sister Clare once said. 'Muscular-academic is just a generally superior human being: everything works well from the brain to the toes. Weedy-academic is when there isn't enough vital energy in the person, and the brain drains all the strength from the other parts.' Well, Clare should know. Clare is only twenty-three, but of the superior human kind herself, vividly pretty, bright and competent – somewhere behind a heavy curtain of vibrant, as they say, red hair, which she only parts for effect. She had her first degree at twenty. Now she's married to a Harvard Professor of Economics seconded to the United Nations. She can even cook. I gave up competing when she was fourteen and I was sixteen. Though she too is capable of self-deception. I would say her husband was definitely of the weedy-academic rather than the muscular-academic type. And they have to live in Brussels.

The Archduke's chauffeur had lost his way, and was parked on the corner trying to recover his nerve when Princip came running out of a café, planted his feet, aimed and fired. Princip was seventeen – too young to hang. But they sent him to prison for life and, since he had TB to begin with, he only lasted three years. He died in 1917, in a Swiss prison. Or perhaps it was more than TB: perhaps they gave him a hard time, not learning till later, when the Austro-Hungarian Empire collapsed, that he was a hero. Poor Princip, too young to die – like so many other millions. Dying for love of a country.

'I love you,' I said to Peter, my living man, progenitor already of three children by his chlorinated, swimming-coach wife.
'How much do you love me?'
'Inordinately! I love you with inordinate affection.'

It was a joke between us. Ind Aff!
'Inordinate affection is a sin,' he'd told me. 'According to the Wesleyans. John Wesley himself worried about it to such a degree that he ended up abbreviating it in his diaries. Ind Aff. He maintained that what he felt for young Sophy, the eighteen-year-old in his congregation, was not Ind Aff, which bears the spirit away from God towards the flesh: no, what he felt was a pure and spiritual, if passionate, concern for Sophy's soul.'
Peter said now, as we waited for our wild boar, and he picked over his pepper, 'Your Ind Aff is my wife's sorrow, that's the trouble.' He wanted, I knew, one of the long half wrangles, half soul-sharings that we could keep going for hours, and led to piercing pains in the heart which could only be made better in bed. But our bedroom at the Hotel Europa was small and dark and looked out into the well of the building – a punishment room if ever there was one. (Reception staff did sometimes take against us.) When Peter had tried to change it in his quasi-Serbo-Croat, they'd shrugged their Bosnian shoulders and pretended not to understand, so we'd decided to put up with it. I did not fancy pushing hard single beds together – it seemed easier not to have the pain in the heart in the first place.
'Look,' I said, 'this holiday is supposed to be just the two of us, not Mrs Piper as well. Shall we talk about something else?'

Do not think that the Archduke's chauffeur was merely careless, an inefficient chauffeur, when he took the wrong turning. He was, I imagine, in a state of shock, fright and confusion. There had been two previous attempts on the Archduke's life since the cavalcade had entered town. The first was a bomb which got the car in front and killed its driver. The second was a shot, fired by none other than young Princip, which had missed. Princip had vanished into the crowd and gone to sit down in a corner café, where he ordered coffee to calm his nerves. I expect his hand trembled at the best of times – he did have TB. (Not the best choice of assassin, but no doubt those who arrange these things have to make do with what they can get.) The Archduke's chauffeur panicked, took the wrong road, realized what he'd done, and stopped to await rescue and instructions just, as it happened, outside the café where Princip sat drinking his coffee.

'What shall we talk about?' asked Peter, in even less of a good mood.
'The collapse of the Austro-Hungarian Empire?' I suggested. 'How does an Empire collapse? Is there no money to pay the military or the police, so everyone goes home? Or what?' He liked to be asked questions.
'The Hungro-Austrian Empire,' said Peter to me, 'didn't so much collapse as fail to exist any more. War destroys social organizations. The same thing happened after World War Two. There being no organizing bodies left between Moscow and London – and for London read Washington, then as now – it was left to these two to put in their own puppet governments. Yalta, 1944. It's taken the best part of forty-five years for nations of Western and Eastern Europe to remember who they are.'
'Austro-Hungarian,' I said, 'not Hungro-Austrian.'
'I didn't say Hungro-Austrian,' he said.
'You did,' I said.
'Didn't,' he said. 'What the hell are they doing about our wild boar? Are they out in the hills shooting it?'

My sister Clare had been surprisingly understanding about Peter. When I worried about him being older, she pooh-poohed it; when I worried about him being married, she said, 'Just go for it, sister. If you can unhinge a marriage, it's ripe for unhinging; it would happen sooner or later; it might as well be you. See a catch, go ahead and catch! Go for it!'

Princip saw the Archduke's car parked outside, and went for it. Second chances are rare in life: they must be responded to. Except perhaps his second chance was missing in the first place? He could have taken his cue from fate, and just sat and finished his coffee, and gone home to his mother. But what's a man to do when he loves his country? Fate delivered the Archduke into his hands: how could he resist it? A parked car, a uniformed and medalled chest, the persecutor of his country – how could Princip, believing God to be on his side, not see this as His intervention, push his coffee aside and leap to his feet?

Two waiters stood idly by and watched us waiting for our wild boar. One was young and handsome in a mountainous Bosnian way – flashing eyes, hooked nose, luxuriant black hair, sensuous mouth. He was about my age. He smiled. His teeth were even and white. I smiled back and, instead of the pain in the heart I'd become accustomed to as an erotic sensation, now felt, quite violently, an associated yet different pang which got my lower stomach. The true, the real pain of Ind Aff!

'Fancy him?' asked Peter.

'No,' I said. 'I just thought if I smiled the wild boar might come quicker.'

The other waiter was older and gentler: his eyes were soft and kind. I thought he looked at me reproachfully. I could see why. In a world which for once, after centuries of savagery, was finally full of young men, unslaughtered, what was I doing with this man with thinning hair?

'What are you thinking of?' Professor Piper asked me. He liked to be in my head.
'How much I love you,' I said automatically, and was finally aware how much I lied. 'And about the Archduke's assassination,' I went on, to cover the kind of tremble in my head as I came to my senses, 'and let's not forget his wife, she died too – how can you say World War One would have happened anyway? If Princip hadn't shot the Archduke something else, some undisclosed, unsuspected variable, might have come along and defused the whole political/military situation, and neither World War One nor Two would ever have happened. We'll just never know, will we?'

I had my passport and my traveller's cheques with me. (Peter felt it was less confusing if we each paid our own way.) I stood up, and took my raincoat from the peg.
'Where are you going?' he asked, startled.
'Home,' I said. I kissed the top of his head, where it was balding. It smelt gently of chlorine, which may have come from thinking about his wife so much, but might merely have been because he'd taken a shower that morning. ('The water all over Yugoslavia, though safe to drink, is unusually highly chlorinated': guide book.) As I left to catch a taxi to the airport the younger of the two waiters emerged from the kitchen with two piled plates of roasted wild boar, potatoes duchesse, and stewed peppers. ('Yugoslavian diet is unusually rich in proteins and fats': guide book.) I could tell from the glisten of oil that the food was no longer hot, and I was not tempted to stay, hungry though I was. Thus fate – or was it Bosnian wilfulness? – confirmed the wisdom of my intent.

And that was how I fell out of love with my professor, in

Sarajevo, a city to which I am grateful to this day, though I never got to see much of it, because of the rain.

It was a silly sad thing to do, in the first place, to confuse mere passing academic ambition with love: to try and outdo my sister Clare. (Professor Piper was spiteful, as it happened, and did his best to have my thesis refused, but I went to appeal, which he never thought I'd dare to do, and won. I had a first-class mind after all.) A silly sad episode, which I regret. As silly and sad as Princip, poor young man, with his feverish mind, his bright tubercular cheeks, and his inordinate affection for his country, pushing aside his cup of coffee, leaping to his feet, taking his gun in both hands, planting his feet, aiming and firing – one, two, three shots and starting World War I. The first one missed, the second got the wife (never forget the wife), and the third got the Archduke and a whole generation, and their children, and their children's children, and on and on for ever. If he'd just hung on a bit, there in Sarajevo that August day, he might have come to his senses. People do, sometimes quite quickly.

1988

Baked Alaska

You know what it's like, Miss Jacobs, when you're having an affair? Forgetting appointments, neglecting children, running off to the hairdresser, having your eyelashes dyed; stopping and staring in mirrors instead of passing by with averted eyes – as if all of a sudden the fact that you're alive and have a body *matters* – and you're back with the sense of Mystical Connection. I'm an addict to extra-marital love: an addictive personality: one whiff of a cigarette and I'm off again: a drop of sherry in the Bombe Surprise and I'm out of my skull by dawn. I can feel your eyebrows shooting up, Miss Jacobs, even though I can't see them. I have to lie here on this couch, which is a little too hard and rather short. What do your men clients do? Dangle their legs? Or perhaps you only get to see dwarves? I haven't been to see you for eight weeks. I'd quite forgotten how dreadful it is – talking into space like this.

What you always forget is that just because you're connected, the object of your love is not necessarily, let alone permanently, so. As if you'd made a telephone call and the other person has spoken for a little and then wandered off, and not hung up, so that not only can't you speak to them, but you can't use the phone either, for anyone else –

I know I told you I was going to Alaska, on business. That my employers had sent me on a trip to learn about Alaskan business methods. It was a lie. You mean it sounded *true*? So unlikely as to be true? Wonderful! Affairs are all lies: one gets really good at them.

I daresay even you have lovers, Miss Jacobs. There's someone for everyone: somewhere out there are men who will admire the stony bleakness of your regard, the ferocious tugging back of your hair, the toughness of your blemished skin, your unsmiling mouth. I envy you. You couldn't even begin to pretend: you are all truth and permanence as I am all frivolity and change. I know only the silly side of the coin: what it is to be loved for blonde curls and sulky looks, and that peculiar gift for idiotic discrimination I foster, which certain men find so entrancing. 'Oh no, I can't possibly go there, or eat this, or see that!' With a flick of red fingernail, despising this, adoring that – men love the carry-on, for a while at least: then they get bored.

During the last eight weeks I have gone at least twice a week to the hairdresser. Nothing to prevent me blow-drying my own hair: it's just at such times you feel the need to be ministered unto. As if it takes a bevy of supporting beauties just to get one woman to meet her lover! As if she carries with her the concentrated energy of women everywhere – their desires, their fulfilment, not just her own. Takes a dozen girls to adorn one bride.

* * *

My stylist Joanna had just come back from New York with tales of high life and a mind generally at the end of its tether. The kind of stories that make you think you'd better defect: that they do things better in Moscow. I can only say that kind of thing to you, Miss Jacobs; husband Roland, well, ex-(possibly) husband Roland, being so politically serious. He married me the better to despise my frivolity. He told me only this morning that in fact he now despises me so thoroughly he is obliged to divorce me: I'll telephone home – home? – when I've finished this session with you and if there's an answer he hasn't left and he's still my husband, and if there isn't, he's gone and he's not. Never a dull moment. I've been putting off calling home or ex-home all day. It's all right if you keep moving and keep talking – it's only with stillness and silence that the panic sets in.

Now what Joanna said – her hair is so long she can sit on it, though I can't think why she'd want to – was that in New York cannibalism is all the rage. Not whole people – *parts* of people; amputated limbs and so forth. At least I hope that's what she said. I do have this incapacity sometimes to hear what is actually being spoken. In retrospect, I can hardly have been hearing with any accuracy what Anton – that's my love, my lover: that is to say, my love, my ex-lover as from precisely seven days ago – was saying, or the end of the affair would not have been quite so unexpected; from bed to nothing in ten swift minutes. Anyway, according to Joanna, human flesh, either discarded bits of body, or – I suppose we have to face it – whole bodies, and tender young bodies at that, especially acquired for the occasion in some appalling and unthinkable fashion, are selling in New York for $2,000 a pound, and served stewed at all the best parties. And the other currently fashionable epicurean delicacy, Joanna says, is the brains of living monkeys, eaten with special long-handled silver teaspoons. Just tether your monkey and slice off the top of its skull and there you are.

I tried not to think about it. I thought about Anton instead, about wrapping my legs round his thin body and pleasuring him as he pleasured me. About a curl here and a streak there and whether a fringe is really what I need: if the hair is back from the face the character may indeed show, but was it character Anton wanted? I doubted it. And, when it came to it, what he wanted was a space in his head filled; some little wounded part made good, some little chilliness warmed. He had fun with the small words that indicated love, concern, possession, even permanence: he liked me to listen to them. He knew, I fear, that I was waiting and hoping for them –

And I? I wanted everything. I can't help it. Men run away from me in droves, as others come running towards me. I am the far end of the swimming pool: the side you have to touch before turning and swimming back. As fast as you can towards: as fast as you can away.

Doesn't it frighten you, Miss Jacobs, to think how soon we're going to die? No, nothing frightens you, because your heart is pure, your soul is good.

Monkeys' brains and long silver teaspoons. Shall I describe Anton to you? His beautiful haggard face, his lean body, his brilliant eyes, his quicksilver mind, his charm? Dear God, his worldly importance! Anton never walked if he could run. Yet I'm sure his wife saw him with more accuracy than I ever did: she would see him as I see Roland; as sheer living, walking, snoring, predictable, day-to-day folly. She would see in Anton a man re-running, decade after decade, without any alteration but with much surface embellishment, five glorious years of youth. A man for ever between twenty-eight and thirty-three, as life and event rolled by. Yes, of course, Miss Jacobs, he had a *wife.* Has a wife. Why are you surprised? Men like Anton have wives. In this brave new cannibalistic world of ours, all proper men are married, all proper women too. It's our prudence, our reality, our safe familiarity while we nibble and guzzle the private parts of comparative strangers. Oh strange new wondrous delicacies!

I try to forget amputated limbs at $2,000 a pound; I try to forget the monkeys' brains, as I try to forget, as my husband can't, the missiles gathering, forget the whole frightening insanity of the world. I try to relish only this: the conjunction of man with woman, in the face of common sense and decency.

I tell you I loved him, Miss Jacobs: it is how I sanctified disgrace: how I justified the dangerous absurdity of our behaviour: this running through the machine of a different and forbidden tape. I set up this terrible, painful affair, the little short-lived merry haphazard affair, as an actual alternative, an actual radical alternative, Miss Jacobs, and not as the optional extra that Anton saw it to be. I took it seriously. It was my escape route from death.

* * *

And yet how many times have I not myself seen my accomplice in sex as an optional extra, the affair as a trivial in-and-out relationship, when the man has believed it to be world-shaking, shattering and permanent. Ah, the biter bit!

Why Alaska, you ask suddenly? Are you keeping up with me? Why did I tell you I was going to Alaska? Because Alaska is *cold,* cold, Miss Jacobs, and one senses the ice already encroaching upon the fire, before it is even lit.

Because my mother used to make Baked Alaska, a fundamentally boring dish. Whale-fat ice cream (in her case) encased in meringue made from a packet; contents: dried egg white, stalibiser, emulsifier, permitted (who says?) artificial flavouring and colouring, put in the oven the better to shock the palate with cold and hot – nothing else is going to.

Anton was great on restaurants; accused me of being unsophisticated because I would not spend £80 on an indifferent meal for two; would rather give it to charity or feed the ducks. He would spend $2,000, I bet you, on a spoonful of the brains of living monkeys, should opportunity present.

Baked Alaska. My mother. My mother served Baked Alaska and I should be grateful. She was trying to tell us something, I think. Life is not what you think. This warm cosy meringue will turn into cold ice cream and set your metal teeth-fillings zinging!

Alaska again. Yes. Well, Anton was warm outside and cold inside. He was not swayed by feeling. By a passing curiosity, I think, because I'd got my name in the papers and he loves celebrity. Didn't I tell you that? I won the Secretary of the Year Award. Yes, little me. I can book-keep like an angel, write shorthand like a dervish, take board room minutes like a High Priestess. I could also stand on my head and run a multi-national corporation if I wanted to, only I can't be bothered. (That's what you feel like when you've won an Award – it goes to your head.) It was when I'd told Anton I could do his job better than he could – Anton is a director of an oil company, did I explain that? – he became a little cool, and then I complained of his coolness and he became colder, and then I wept and said I loved him, which of course was fatal and the end of the affair. He is the kind of man who must woo and never win. And what am I when it comes to it? Miss PA of the year.

Life, love, Miss Jacobs. Love is all we have left, and its excitements, while (as Roland keeps reminding me – you know how involved he is in the peace movement; he is so busy loving peace he has no time to love me: no wonder I run around with other men) while, as I say, the nuclear missiles gather, from Alaska to the Western Australian desert. Love. Sex. Missiles. Penises. Yes, of course there is phallic imagery here, Miss Jacobs; did you doubt it? A penetrative fear. I am the victim who invites attack. If I did not invite attack, the missiles would not gather; the men would pass by prudently; the world would be at peace. Mea culpa. Only, Miss Jacobs, this is the energy that makes the world go round, gets the children born: I can't control it. Takes more than me.

* * *

I have lied and cheated and lost over a trivial affair of the heart – because my heart was involved and Anton's was not, and that is the nub of the humiliation I now feel – and what can any of this matter? 'I cannot feel,' Anton said to me, 'about you the way you clearly feel about me. I'm sorry but there it is. I did not mean to hurt you.'

But he did. It's better to feast on the living than the dead. The taste is better. That's why I got fed upon. But this may be the last time. What I feel like now, Miss Jacobs, is the monkey. I tethered myself with my own desire. I invited Anton under my skin with his scalpel blade: slice! he went; oh sharp, sharp – and then with a long teaspoon he supped off my living brains, trying them out for flavour and then, finding them really not good enough after all for his epicurean fancy, he spat them out with disdain. And the monkey chatters a little, automatically, and dies. I shall go home to my husband now and calm him down. I bet you anything he's still there.

1988

GUP
or
Falling in Love in Helsinki

You'll never guess what happened to me in Helsinki. How my life changed, when I was there last October. Let me tell you! The trees in that much-islanded, much- forested Northern country – you've never seen so many islands, so much forest, so low and misty and large an autumn sun – were just on the turn; the rather boring universal green giving up and suddenly glowing into reds and yellows and browns. 'Ruska' is what the Finns call this annual triumph of variety over uniformity; something so dramatic they even have this special name for it. It is, I suppose, the last flaring surge of summer: like a woman of fifty who throws out the black shoes she's worn all her life and shoes herself in greens and pinks, feeling she'd better make the best of things while she can. Not that I'm fifty, in case you're wondering, I'm twenty-nine; but twenty-nine can feel pretty old. Older, I imagine, than fifty, because around thirty the tick-tock of the biological clock can sound pretty loud in a woman's ear.

My mother wants me to stay home, get married, have children.
'Settle down, Jude,' she'd plead. 'It's what I want for you.'
'I can't think why,' I'd say. 'You never did.'

'That's different,' she'd say, and pour another whisky and light up her cigar. My mother is a professional golf coach, and has been ever since my father walked out twenty-five years ago. She had to do something to earn a living. She's a healthy and athletic woman, though she must be over sixty, and men are still for ever knocking at her door, though she doesn't often let them in. The whisky and cigar syndrome is no problem (or only to my sister Chris). I see it as just my mother's rather old-fashioned way of saying to a man, 'I'm as good as you. What do I want you for?'

'Christ,' I say to my sister, 'Mother's whisky is always well watered. The cigar goes out after ten seconds. What are you worrying about?' But Chris is a nurse. She was seven when my father left. I was four.

My mother's determination that I should settle down seems to me a fine example of GUP. What do I mean by GUP? It's the Great Universal Paradox which rules our lives. See it at work in any obstetric ward, at the very beginning of things. There you'll find a woman who only ever wanted a baby but hers was stillborn, and another who's just had a living baby she doesn't want, and someone in for a sterilisation and another for a termination, and another with a threatened miscarriage, and another resting up before sextuplets, having taken too much fertility drug – and all will be weeping. All want different things so passionately; and nature takes no notice at all of what they want. Nature just rumbles on insanely, refining the race.

What you want you can't have: what you do have, you don't want. That's GUP.

* * *

When I arrived in Helsinki I was in love with Andreas Anders, who didn't love me. And I was loved by Tony Schuster, whom

I didn't love. My loving of Andreas Anders loomed large in my life, and had done so for six years. Tony Schuster loving me, which he had for all of seven days, meant to me next to nothing; that's the way GUP goes. Andreas Anders not loving me made me feel fat and stupid: so if Tony Schuster was capable of loving someone as fat and stupid as me, what did that make Tony Schuster? Some sort of wimp? In other words, as famously spoken by Marx (not Karl, but the third brother) tearing up the long-sought invitation to join – 'Who wants to belong to a club of which I'm a member?' GUP.

Finland is just across a strip of sea from the Soviet Union, though the government is of a rather different kind and in Finland women seem to run everything, whereas in Russia it's the men. Finland is noble but Russia is exciting. Little Finnish children always look so healthy, bright-eyed, well-mittened and properly fed to keep out the cold. Yes, yes, I know. I'm broody. Bright, bright clothes they wear, in Helsinki. Terrifically fashionable. Lots of suede, so soft it looks and acts like linen.

We were in Helsinki to make a six-part thriller called *Lenin in Love* for BBC TV. Helsinki's Great Square is the same period, same proportions, same size as Moscow's Red Square, so it gets used by film companies a great deal. Filming in Red Square itself is always a hassle: there's a lot of worried security men about and they like to read the script and object if it says anything detrimental about the Soviet Union – and the script usually does: that being the whole *point* of cold-war thrillers. Their wrongness, our rightness. The queue for Lenin's tomb is always getting into shot, and you can hardly ask the punters to move on, when they've railed all the way in from Tashkent or Samarkand to be there. So off everyone goes to Helsinki to film the Moscow bits. *Doctor Zhivago* was made in Finland.

Andreas Anders is the Director of *Lenin in Love*. Tony Schuster is the cameraman. I'm the PA. I have a degree in Politics and Economics and moved over from Research to Production five years ago; seeing I had a better chance of being close to Andreas Anders. You'd think a bright girl like me would think about something other than love, but at twenty-nine it gets you, it gets you! Twenty-nine years old and no children or live-in-lover, let alone a husband. Not that I actually wanted any of those things. In the film and TV world there's not all that much permanent in-living. You just have to pack up and go, when the call comes, even when you're in the middle of scrambling his breakfast eggs. Or he, yours. Men tend to do the cooking, these days, in the circles in which I live. Let's not say 'live'. Let's say 'move'.

I'd been the researcher on Andreas Anders' first film. I was twenty-three then and straight out of college. It was a teledrama called *Mary's Son*, about a woman's fertility problems. It was during the first week of filming – Andreas took me along with him: he said he needed a researcher on set though actually he wanted me in his bed – that I both developed my theory on GUP and fell in love with him. At the end of the second week Andreas fell in love with his star, Caroline Christopherson, the girl who was playing Mary. And I was courteously and instantly dismissed from his bed. Nightmare time. I'd got all through college repelling all boarders: now this.

But Andreas Anders! His face is pale and haunted: he has wide, kind, set-apart grey eyes, and he's tall, and broad-shouldered. He has long, fine hands, and what could I do? I loved him. That he should look at me, little me, in the first place! Pick me out from all the others? Even for a minute, let alone a week, let alone a fortnight, what a marvel! At least when he fell for Caroline Christopherson it was serious. They got married. And now she's world-famous and plays the lead in big budget movies, and is a box-office draw, which irritates Andreas, since he's so obviously the one with the talent, the creativity, and the brains: Caroline just has star quality. When it gets bad for Andreas, why there I am in bed with him again and he's telling me all about it. They have a child, Phoebe, who gets left behind with nannies. Andreas doesn't like that either. I don't say, 'But you're the one doing the leaving too,' because I seldom say to him what I really think. That's what this one-sided love does to you. Turns you into an idiot. I hate myself but I'm tongue-tied.

How can I compete with C.C., as he calls her? That kind of film-starry quality is real enough: a kind of glowing magnetism: a way of moving – just a gesture of a hand, the flick of an eye – which draws other eyes to itself. I don't look too bad, I tell myself. Though I suppose where C.C. looks slim I just look sturdy. Both our hair frizzes out all over the place, but hers shines at the same time as frizzing. I do not know how that effect is achieved. If I did, friend, I would let you know. I look more intelligent than she does, but that's not the point. On the contrary. Andreas Anders once complained I always looked judgemental. That was when we were doing a studio play up at the BBC's Pebble Mill studios, *Light from the Bedroom*. My first PA job. C.C. was giving birth to little Phoebe in Paris while we were taping in Birmingham. Andreas couldn't leave the show: well, how could he? He and I stayed at the Holiday Inn. He is the most amazing lover.

I don't let on how much I care. I pretend it means nothing to me. If he thought it hurt, he'd stay clear of me. He doesn't mean to be unkind. I just act kind of light and worldly. I don't want to put him off. Would you? GUP again! If you love them, don't let them know it. 'I love you' is the great turn-off to the uncommitted man.

And now here's Tony Schuster saying 'I love you' to me, publicly, leaning down from his dolly as he glides about in the misty air of Helsinki's Great Square. The mist's driving the lighting man crazy. The scenes are intended to be dreamlike, but all prefer the man-made kind of mist to the one God has on offer. Man's is easier to control.

'Let's leave this life,' Tony says. 'Let's run off together to a Desert Island.'

'You mean like *Castaway*?' I ask. I know film people. Everything relates back to celluloid.

'How did you guess?' He looks surprised. He's not all that bright. Or perhaps I'm just too bright for everyone's comfort. For all his gliding to and fro on his great new black macho electronic camera with its built-in Citroën-type suspension – 'This camera cost £250,000,' he snaps, if anyone so much as touches the great shiny thing – I can't take Tony seriously. He has quite an ordinary, pleasant, everyday face. He's thirty-nine, and has a lot of wiry black hair. Andreas's hair is fair and fine. 'I love you!' Tony Schuster yells, for all the world to hear. 'Run off with me, do!'

I think his loving me so publicly annoys Andreas, but he doesn't show it. Tony's one of the top cameramen around: they can be temperamental. It's as well for a Director to hold his fire, unless it's something that really matters – a smooth fifty-second track in for example – not like love, or desire, which everyone knows is just some kind of by-product of all the creative energy floating around a set.

'I love you' is a great turn-off for the female committed elsewhere. GUP.

Sometimes I do agree to have a drink with Tony, when it's a wrap for the day, and we all stagger back to the bar of the Hesperia. Except for Andreas, who's staying at the Helsinki Inter-Continental. When I heard C.C. was coming to join her husband and hold his hand through the whole month of Helsinki shooting, I put them in a different hotel (I do location accommodation, *inter alia*) from the rest of us. I thought I couldn't bear their happiness too near me. We'd be going off to Rome presently, anyway, and C.C. wouldn't be following us there. She'd be going, not back to little Phoebe, but to Hollywood for some rubbishy block-busting new series, which Andreas despised. He had the Art, she made the money.

'It's so clichéd I can't bear it,' Tony would moan.
'The PA in love with the Director! You're worth more than that.'
More than being in love with Andreas? How could such a thing be possible?

Tony's wife had just left him, taking the children. He'd been away from home just once too often. When she wanted him where was he? Up the Himalayas filming *Snowy Waste* or under the Atlantic with *Sonar Soundings* or in the Philippines with *Lolly a Go-Go*. When he didn't turn down *Lenin in Love* because he couldn't miss an opportunity of working with Andreas Anders, the Great Director, Sara waited for him to say 'yes' to the call from his agent, and he did, of course, having said he'd say no, and at that point she packed. The wives do.

'You love films more than me,' she said. And so Tony did. Now he thought he was in love with me. I knew what was going on. His wife had left, he was sad and worried; love on the set's a great diversion. On the whole, you last as long as the project does; not a moment longer. Sometimes it sticks – look at Andreas and C.C.; me and Andreas – but mostly it's all, as I say, just surplus energy taking sexual/romantic form. I know so much, and so little too. GUP!

'You have no pattern for a happy married life,' laments my mother. 'All my fault.'

'I don't want to be married,' I say. If I was married how could I follow Andreas round the world? But I don't tell her that. His favourite PA! I'm good at my job: by God, I'm good at it. He won't find fault with me.

'Without you!' he once said (that was *Love in a Hot Climate*: we were in a really ritzy room at the Meriden in Lisbon: C.C. was off in Sydney and Andreas thought she was having an affair with the male lead), 'Without you, Jude, I wouldn't be half the director I am!' A real working partnership we have, Andreas and me, oh, yes! His fingers running through my hair when there's nothing else to do, and hotel rooms in strange cities can be lonely; you need your friends around.

Before I left for Helsinki my mother said something strange. 'Your father ran off with a girl from Finland,' she said. 'Our au pair. Just make sure you come back.' Now my mother never said anything at all about my father if she could help it. And my sister Chris and I seldom asked. Questions about our dad upset her. And it doesn't do to upset a woman who is a golf coach by profession. She gets put off her stroke, and if she loses her job, how will any of you live? Our house went with the job. On the edge of the golf course. Thwack, thwee, muted shouts – to me the sound of childhood.

I expect if your husband ran off with the Finnish au pair you wouldn't want to dwell on it much. This was the first I'd heard of it. Chris and I had tried to trace our father, when she was twenty-one and I was eighteen, but we never got very far. I can't say we tried hard. Who wants to be in touch with a father who doesn't want to be in touch with you? Apart from the fun of the thing, I suppose. Sister Chris had been oddly worried about my going to Helsinki.

'You and your lifestyle!' she said, when I rang the Nurses' Home to say I was off to work on *Lenin in Love*. She'd just been made Night Sister of Men's Orthopaedic. Quite a cheerful ward, she said. At least they mostly got better. 'Can't you ever stay in one place, Jude. You'll get AIDS if you don't watch out. You film-people!' Chris had my lifestyle all wrong. I was astonishingly sedate. There'd only ever been Andreas Anders, apart from a few forgettables. It was pathetic, really. But somehow men seem to know if your emotions are occupied elsewhere. You send out 'I belong to someone bigger than you' signals, just as much if you're wretchedly involved as if you're happily married.

My mother and sister were right to worry, as it happened. Because a strange thing did happen to me in Helsinki. I was walking with Tony in the Rural Life Museum one Sunday and explaining why I wouldn't go to bed with him, and what was wrong with his psyche. He was looking quite wretched and pale, as men will in such circumstances. The Museum is in fact an open-air park devoted to the artefacts of Finland's past. We were admiring an elegant wooden church boat which could hold a hundred people – entire villages would row themselves to church in these boats if they so chose – when my attention was caught by one of those familiar groups of people, complete with cameras and sound equipment. This lot were clustered round and filming one of the enormous orange toadstools with yellow spots they have in these parts. Proper traditional pixie toadstools. Hallucinogenic, they say.

And the sound man put down his gear – he was taking white sound, I presumed: a toadstool hardly makes much noise, even in its growing, which can be pretty rapid – and walked over to me. He wasn't young. Sixty or so, I suppose. Quite heavy round his middle: pleasant looking: intelligent: glasses.
'Hello,' he said, in English.
'Hello,' I said, and I thought where have I seen that face before? And then I realised, why! whenever I look in the mirror, or when I look at Chris: that's where I've seen it. More the latter, because both Chris and he were overweight. It looked worse on her. He was really quite attractive.
'You're with the English film crew, aren't you?' he said.
'I saw you in the Square yesterday. It had to be you. Jude Iscarry.'
'Or Judas Iscariot or Jude the Obscure,' I said, playing for time, because my heart was pounding. 'Take your pick!'
'Your mother said you'd gone into films,' he said. 'Chip off the old block.'
'You're my father,' I said.
''Fraid so,' he said.
'I didn't know she was in touch with you,' I said. It was all I could say. Tony just stood and looked on. Moments in a person's life!
'I passed by five years back,' my father said, 'but she advised me strongly to keep away, so I did. Though I'd have liked to have stayed. Quite a powerful stroke, your mother.'
'She's had to develop it,' I said.
'Um,' he said. 'But she always was independent, wanted to be father and mother too.'

'That's no excuse,' I said.

Tony left us and he, my father, whose name was Saul Iscarry, took me out to lunch. We had pancakes, caviar and sour cream, washed down by tots of vodka. The best food in the world. The Finns have the highest heart disease rate in the world. So Chris had assured me, before I set off for Helsinki.

My father had eventually married his Vieno, my mother's au pair, and actually gone to the Moscow Film School, and now he was one of the best sound men in the world (he said) and had Finnish nationality, but lived in Leningrad. Vieno was a doctor, they had three children, and what with visa problems and general business and so forth there hadn't been much point in keeping in touch, let alone the time. (Roubles are just one of those currencies that make it difficult for a father to support his abandoned children.) But he'd thought of Chris and me a lot.
Big deal, I thought, but said nothing. What was the point?

Now we were in touch, he said, we must keep in touch. He was glad I was in films. The best life in the world, he said, if you had the temperament. But why was I only a PA? Why wasn't I a producer, at the very least? Ah. Well. He said he'd like to see Chris. How was she? Just fine, I said. She'd have to come over and see him some time, since visas for him were so complicated. If you ask me visas are as complicated as you care to make them, but I didn't say that either.
I said Chris would be over to see him next Easter. That gave her six months to lose three stone. She should be able to do that. A girl likes to be at her best when she meets up with her old dad.

'You've grown up a fine handsome girl, Jude,' he said. 'I'm proud of you,' and you know, that meant a great deal to me. More than it should have. If anyone was to take the credit for the way I was it should have been my mother. Oh, Great Universal Paradox which runs our lives – that what should please us doesn't, and what does please us, shouldn't!

He had to go back to work, my father said. The pixie toadstool called. The crew could not be kept waiting. When could it ever, in any country, in any language in the world? We exchanged addresses. He went.

And I took myself off to the little Greek Orthodox church that's tucked away behind the Great Square, and there I sat down. I had to be quiet: absorb what had just happened. I didn't kneel. I'm not very religious. I just sat, and thought, and rested. The unexpected is tiring.

It's a small, ancient building: a chapel rather than a church. But it blazes with intricate icons and gold leaf and crimson velvet; everything shimmers: there's no way it can't: there must be a thousand candles at least stuck all around, lit by the faithful at their own expense. It's a sensuous, somehow Mediterranean place, stuck here as if by accident in this cold northern land. The air was heavy with incense: that and candle smoke smarted the eyes: or was I crying? And in the ears was the gentle murmur of the faithful, the click click of the telling of beads. Yes, I was crying. But I don't think from wretchedness. Relief, happiness almost, at something completed. My father: no longer fantasy, just a man.

* * *

And there in front of me, a couple of rows nearer the great glittery altar, was sitting Andreas Anders. He looked round and saw me. I wish he hadn't. I wanted to just go on sitting there, alone, thinking. But he got up and came to sit next to me. How good-looking he was. His bright eyes glittered in the candlelight.

'Well,' he said, 'she's not coming to Helsinki after all. Had you heard?'

By 'she' he always meant Caroline Christopherson. 'I think,' he said, 'I'd better give her up altogether, don't you? Divorce, or something drastic. I can't stand the strain.'

'Let's go outside,' I said. 'This isn't the place for such conversations.' Nor was it. As I say, I'm not one for religion, but some sort of God was here in this place, albeit in heavy disguise, and didn't want to hear all this soggy, emotional mish-mash.

So we went out, Andreas and me. And he tucked his arm into mine and said, 'Shall we go back to the Inter-Continental, just you and me?' and I pulled my arm away and said, 'No, I won't. What a monster you are!' and heard myself saying it, and knew I meant it, and there I was, out of love with him. Just like that. 'A monster?' he asked, hurt and confused. But I didn't even want to discuss it. It wasn't worth it. I'd see the *Lenin in Love* through, of course, because I was a professional, but that was all. The man was an egocentric maniac.

I left him staring after me, his worm turned, and I went back to the Hesperia and found Tony in my bedroom and told him to stop messing about and for heaven's sake somehow get his wife and children back. If he wanted to get out of the business, let him do it with the proper person.

'Is this what finding a long lost father can do?' he asked, as he left. 'And I had such high hopes…'

And all I could do was suppose it was: that, and simply Finland itself.

In the past Finland has always been conquered or annexed or governed by someone else – this vast flat stretch, on top of the world, of islands and forests – but now it has its own identity, its own pride: it looks not to its previous masters, Sweden and Russia, but to itself. How odd, to identify so with a nation! Perhaps it's hereditary, in the genes: like ending up in the film business. My dad ran off with a Finn: one mustn't forget that. Perhaps he somehow felt the same connection, and can be forgiven.

And that's the strange thing that happened to me in Helsinki, last October, and how my life has changed. And I called this story 'Falling in Love in Helsinki', not 'Out of Love', because although it's true I fell out of love with Andreas, out of love with love (which is a real blight), somehow I fell into love with life. Or with God, call it what you will, there in that chapel. Whatever, I found myself sufficiently enamoured of just the sheer dignity of creation to realise I shouldn't offend it the way I had been doing. I think everything's going to be all right now. I'll make out. I might even leave the film business altogether. Not go into a convent, or anything so extreme. But I might try politics. It's what I'm trained for.

* * *

As for GUP, the Great Universal Paradox, that's real enough. What I marvel at now is how happy so many of us manage to be, so much of the time, in spite of it.

1989

Love Amongst the Artists

'Happy Christmas, my own true love,' said Lucy to Pierre, on the morning of December 25, 1899. She woke amongst a flurry of white sheets and feather pillows and this was the nearest she would get to seasonal and romantic snow, for the day was mild and they were in the South of France, not Connecticut, which was Lucy's home, or Paris which was Pierre's.

Pierre stirred but did not wake. Lucy whispered in his ear again. 'Happy Christmas, my own true love,' and this time he murmured a reply.
'If you and I are to be free souls, Lucy,' said Pierre with a clarity apparently quite undiminished by slumber, 'we must put all such religious cant behind us,' and closed his eyes again and slept on. His arms lay brown and young amongst the sheets and his dark hair was wild and curly on the pillow and she loved him. But she loved Christmas too, and always had.

Morning sun shone in through the little square window and bounced back from the whitewashed walls. She smoothed down her white cambric nightgown and wound her hair back around her head and pinned it up, and climbed down from the high bed, and crossed the bare wooden floor and looked out of the undraped window. She could see across a river valley to vineyards which marched across hills like soldiers going to their death. She put the image from her mind. And if there was a smell of rottenness in the air, as if all the grapes which should have been gathered in the autumn to make wine had been allowed to fall and fester on the ground instead, that was nothing worse than French plumbing. Some things had to be bad, Pierre said, so bad there was nothing left for them to do but get better.

'Religion is the opiate of the people,' said Pierre from his pillow. 'God is a drug fed by the masters to the poor and hungry, so they are content with poverty and hunger. Jesus was never born: heaven does not exist. Blind belief is a thorn in the side of mankind and we will pluck it out.'

In one more week it would be 1900, the dawn of the twentieth century, and into that dawn would strike through the light of new hope and new liberty, and all the energy of free thought and free love, untrammelled by convention, and Lucy's soul soared at the thought that Pierre and she were part of it: that he and she were one step ahead of that new dawn. They would be in Paris by New Year's Eve to be amongst the anarchists; they would gather there together to drink to the future: the passionate brotherhood of the enlightened, and their sisters in that passion.

What a different stroke of midnight it would be from the one she would have envisaged just a few months back: a single glass of wine raised solemnly at the first stroke, in the parlour, in the company of Edwin her husband and Joseph her brother, and then to bed. And each stroke sounding its annual dirge to lost hope and failing passion: its welcome to the triumph of boredom and the death of the soul.

Pierre left the bed and stood beside her. He was naked. Lucy could not become accustomed to it. She had been married to Edwin for fourteen years and had never caught more than a flash of white limb in the bathroom, a movement of bare flesh above her in the bed. Now Pierre unpinned her hair so it flowed around her shoulders.

'So never name that day again,' said Pierre, 'or it will drag you back to the Lord of the Dark Domain,' and they both laughed. Lord of the Dark Domain was their name for Edwin. Lucy's husband wrote novels for a living; once every five years or so, to the acclaim of serious critics, he would have published an extremely melancholy book, the text so closely printed that Lucy had no patience with it, but then she was not expected to. Edwin loved Lucy for her folly; she was his child bride, his pretty wife: now he would see how he had misjudged her! Now he would find out: now that another man understood her talent, her intelligence, her quality, her passion.

'All the same,' said Lucy, 'it comes as a shock! No mince pies, no gifts and ribbons and best dresses? Never more?'

'Never more,' said Pierre, 'or you will be dragged back into the Hell of Domesticity, which is the Death of Art.'

Pierre was a composer of fine if difficult song cycles which so few people in the world could understand that when Pierre came to New York from Paris to perform, the concert hall was all but empty, the tour was cancelled and Pierre left penniless and stranded in a strange land. Edwin, as an act of kindness, had offered him work for the summer, teaching Bessie and Bertie the piano. Bessie was twelve and Bertie was ten. They would wake this Christmas morning to a house which lacked a mother. Lucy put that image from her too. Bessie had Edwin's beetling brows; Bertie aped Edwin's clipped, dry manner of speech. They were Edwin's children more than Lucy's. Pierre

saw it. Edwin claimed it. The law acknowledge
have its way.

'An artist needs freedom, not a family,' said Pier
easily read her mind. She felt his warm breath
'The artist's duty is to all mankind; he must br
chains of convention. And women can be arti
are, Lucy, remember that!'

The first time Pierre had heard Lucy sing, in he
untrained voice, helping Bessie's fumbling notes
claimed her as an artist; the one he had been waiting for, the one who could truly bring his music to life. Poor Bessie was forgotten: she could hardly get to the piano: Lucy and Pierre were always there: as she worked to catch the notes between notes he found so significant he could make them include the whole universe. Edwin was on the last chapter of a novel: a time he found particularly tense. There was to be piano-playing only between two and four o'clock of an afternoon. He said so with some force. The house trembled. People wept.
'He has you in prison,' said Pierre of Edwin then. 'For what is a home but a man's prison for a woman, and what is a wife but an unpaid whore? She lies on her back for her keep, bears children and cooks dinner likewise.' And when Lucy had recovered from her shock, the more she thought of it the more she perceived that what Pierre said was true. Lucy understood now that the sapphire necklace she wore round her neck was the symbol of her imprisonment: that her ruby ear-rings marked her as an instrument of lust, that the gold charms on her bracelet were for Edwin's benefit, not her own; for is not a willing slave more useful than one who is unwilling?
'You would not be my slave,' said Pierre, 'you would be my love.'

Lucy's eyes went to the suitcase, and she wondered whether she should check that they were still there, in the suitcase, tucked in tissue in a dancing shoe: the sapphire, the rubies and the gold. But of course they were. Why should they not be? And they were hers by right, every one, payment for years of servitude. In the new world women would have equal dignity with men. When the workers of the world rose up, they would lift up women with them.

'All the same,' said Lucy, 'on this day of all days, allow me to feel like a mother, not an artist, and cry just a little.'

'You should be ashamed to even consider such a betrayal,' said Pierre. 'Weeping is something which women of the *haute bourgeoisie* do the better to control men,' and Lucy was glad to understand that he was joking, for Edwin had scolded her and chided her and made her feel foolish from the day he had met her, and never ever joked about anything.

Pierre called down to the landlady to bring breakfast up to the room. He stood naked at the top of the stairs and dodged behind the door when the woman arrived with the tray: she seemed to Lucy too small and old to carry such a weight. The servants at home were stout and strong.

'Don't upset her too much,' said Lucy when she had stopped laughing. 'We owe her too much rent for that. I don't know why you put off paying her.'

But Pierre said they would wait for dark and then slip away unnoticed and pick up the Paris train before anyone realised, and he didn't want any silly nonsense from Lucy: the landlady was an old witch who took advantage of travellers and overcharged, and deserved what she got.

Lucy said nothing, but after she'd eaten the breakfast the landlady brought – hot coffee and fresh frothy milk, long crisp

bread, and farm butter and apricot preserve – she said, 'I'd really rather pay her, Pierre.'
'What with?' asked Pierre. 'We have no francs left. The journey across France is costing more than I thought. An artist shouldn't be bothered by such sordid things as money: I don't want to talk about it any more. We'll send her some from Paris if you insist when we've sold your jewellery, but she doesn't deserve it. She is a lackey of the masters, that's all she is.'

Lucy felt her eyes mist with tears: she couldn't tell the difference between the frothy milk and the thick white china jug. They merged together. At home the milk jugs were of fine porcelain, and had little flowers upon them. One of them came from Limoges. She wondered where Limoges was, and if she'd ever go there. She could see such an event was more likely now that she was Pierre's lover, no longer Edwin's wife; on the other hand, any such journey would be accomplished in less comfort. She did not understand money: it seemed necessary for all kinds of things she had thought just happened – such as being warm, or welcomed, or treated with politeness by porters, and gendarmes, shop keepers and landladies. But money did not buy love, or freedom, or truth, or hope, or any of the important things in life.
'Don't cry,' said Pierre. 'You're homesick, that's all it is,' and he leaned towards her and removed a crumb from her lip, and her heart melted; the act was so tender and true. Edwin would have mentioned the crumb, not removed it. Pierre put on his shirt and she was glad, though she knew she shouldn't be.
'I'm not homesick,' Lucy said, 'not one bit. You've no idea how dank and drear the woods around the house are at this time of year. How they drip and drizzle!'
'Worse than Bessie on a bad day,' murmured Pierre, nuzzling into her hair, and she thought why is he allowed to mention

Bessie's name, and I am not, but Lucy laughed too, to keep Pierre company, to be of one accord in mind, as they were in body. Bessie was a plain girl and had not been blessed with a musical ear so Pierre could not take her seriously, and that made it hard for Lucy, now Bessie was at a distance, to do so either. Lucy could see that love unconfined, love outside convention, might well make a woman an unfit mother; you were one kind of woman or another: you were good or you were bad, as the world saw it, and no stations in between. They allowed you to choose; you could be the maternal or the erotic, but not a bit of both. The latter made you forget the former. Men married the maternal and then longed for the erotic. Or they married the erotic by mistake, and set about making it into the maternal, and then were just as disappointed. Edwin had married a child and tried to stop her choosing, but now thanks to Pierre she had grown up and made her own choice.

She hoped Edwin would keep Christmas without her. She hoped he would remember, when he brought in the Christmas Tree, the little fir which had grown in its pot on the step since the first year of the marriage, that it had to be watered well. She hoped he knew the boxes in the attic where the decorations were. Lucy added a new one every year – would he remember that? Would he realise you had to balance the golden horses with their silver riders? And part of her hoped he'd get it all wrong. Part of her hoped that now she was not there, he would have no heart for any of it, he would be so sorry she had gone. She would find a letter from him in Paris, forgiving her, asking her to go home. Of course she would not go.

'A penny for your thoughts,' said Pierre, but he wouldn't have liked them if he heard them so Lucy said, 'I'm really glad I'm not at home, Pierre. This time of year. When the days are really short, and winter hasn't quite caught up with them and the skies just seem to sulk. Why, they sulk even worse than Bertie on a bad day,' and she laughed again, betraying her other child, for the sake of love. 'And the rooms of the house are so crowded and sad,' said Lucy, 'and here everything is simple and graceful and plain. I promise you I don't miss a thing. You make up for it all, Pierre.'

Lucy's brother Joseph would have arrived on Christmas Eve, as was his custom, bearing gifts. They would be the wrong gifts: an impossible doll, an unworkable cannon; a scarf she hated, the kind of pen Edwin never used. Joseph's talent for the wrong gifts was a marvel: it was a joke she and Edwin shared: a look between them every year, no more: that much they had at least: this equality of shared experience, which grew every year as the Christmas Tree grew, so slowly you could never see it, soil never quite right, too wet or too dry, so you feared for it; but every Christmas an inch or so higher. This year it would have to go on its side to get through the front door, and could only stand in the window arch – would Edwin and Joseph talk about Lucy, or would her name not be mentioned? An impossible subject, an inexplicable situation: a woman lost to duty, lost to honour, lost to motherhood: a woman altogether vanished away, erased from the mind, nameless. A subdued source of sorrow, of better-never-born-dom.

'No children to tug at my skirts,' said Lucy, 'no brother at my sympathy, no husband at my conscience. A day like any other, dawning bright and fair on our new life together. Just you and I, and art, and beauty, and love, and music. All the things that passed poor stuffy old Edwin by!'
'I pity Edwin,' said Pierre. 'He had no ear. A man who rations

music to two hours a day has no ear and a man who locks a piano has no soul!'

* * *

The better to enforce his ruling, Edwin had kept the piano closed; unlocking it at two o'clock after lunch: emerging from his study at four o'clock to close it once again. In the mornings, thus freed from practice, Lucy and Pierre had walked in the woods, and talked about music, and presently love, and then more than talked, and Pierre had explained to Lucy how unhappy she was, and how her way of life stifled her, and how he could not be a great artist without her, and Bessie had seen them in the woods and Lucy had forged one of Edwin's cheques and paid both their passages over; and left Edwin a note and was gone, taking her jewellery because Pierre said she must, and the way not to think about any of it was to be in bed with Pierre. They had scarcely left the cabin on the way over: they had been the talk of the ship and she hadn't cared. To fly in the face of all things respectable intensified the pleasure she had with Pierre: what was forbidden was sweet: she hoped they would never reach Paris, where everyone felt as she and Pierre did, but of course that was silly of her: what was forbidden could not be kept up for long and in any case had to be sandwiched between the permitted in order to count – why had there been no one to stop her? If you were a child wasn't that what happened? That someone stopped you? She'd relied on Edwin for that all her grown life, but since she couldn't tell him about Pierre how could he have helped her? But she blamed him because he hadn't, because he'd been so busy with his book he hadn't even noticed the time she was spending with Pierre: it was Edwin's fault she had left.

She wondered what she and Pierre would do all day. When they were out of bed there seemed not very much to do, except wait for other days to arrive, or messages to come which didn't come from friends she had only heard of, never seen. If she was at home on this day she would be so busy – it would be all best clothes and mince pies and the gifts beneath the Christmas Tree, and a formal kiss from Edwin before the unwrapping ceremony began –

Pierre said, 'We'll smuggle the suitcase out after lunch, when Madame takes her nap. She sleeps well: she doesn't care how the rest of the world toils for her profit! Then in the evening you dress as me and I'll dress as you, and that will be the best disguise in the world, and we'll escape. We'll be so clever!'
Lucy thought it was probably better as an idea than it would be as an actuality – she could get into his coat but her jacket would never stretch over his shoulders – but didn't say so. It was the kind of prank Bertie would think of. Pierre had explained to her how Edwin was a father/husband – but what did she have now instead – a son/lover? Was such a thing possible?

'I could offer her a gold charm from my bracelet,' said Lucy. 'In fact I think I'll do that.'
And to her astonishment Pierre hit her, or she thought that was what had happened, since there was a sudden kind of stinging blackness around her head, but how could she know, no one had ever hit her before. For a second or so she couldn't see, and was perhaps suffering from amnesia, for she couldn't quite remember where she was; but yes, it wasn't home, it was indeed an inn somewhere in the South of France, and she was leaning against a whitewashed wall, while a strange man rather younger than herself apologised for something rather

trivial, and she could hear a kind of knock, knock, knock, which she thought was Edwin chopping down the Christmas Tree, the one that had started little and grown deep and strong. Edwin divided it root from branch, because it spoke of a celebration Lucy could no longer name, and anyway it spoke a lie. But of course the sound was only the knock, knock, knock of the landlady at the door, demanding money she and Pierre didn't have, speaking in a language Lucy didn't understand, but who knew them better than they knew themselves. She could see that to look after yourself you would have to know yourself, but who was there in that land, in that time, to hear such a thing if it were said?

1991

Lily Bart's Hat Shop

It is said that Gustave Flaubert wove his novel *Madame Bovary* around a press cutting he read in a local newspaper- the sorry tale of a provincial doctor's wife who, unable to face the consequences of debt and adultery, took poison and committed suicide. It is my belief that gloom, and a passion to punish the frivolous Madame Bovary for the vulgarity of her sins, clouded the great writer's judgment. He was reading about attempted suicide, not suicide. The story has come down to me through members of my own family, that though in shame and desperation Emma did indeed cram arsenic into her pretty mouth, Justin the apprentice had wisely taken the precaution of liberally mixing the stuff with sugar and she survived. Black bile poured out of her mouth, true: her limbs for a time were mottled brown, the desecration of her marriage vows took visible and outward form – but there God and Flaubert's punishment ended – Emma lived. And if man's punishment came hot upon the Almighty's – poor pretty Emma went to prison for two years for her sin – to attempt suicide was at the time both a mortal and a criminal offence - there came an end to that too, and fortunately before she had altogether lost her looks.

My grandfather taught Emma's great grandchild the violin at the New York conservatoire, which is how I happen to know the truth of the matter. Perhaps the story has become garbled through the generations, for certainly the timescale is a little strange: but the fictional universe has its own rules as it brushes up against our own. I am happy enough to accept the family version.

Flaubert, having dismissed Emma to the grave, in an elaborate coffin which her husband Charles could ill afford, chose to visit unmitigated disaster on the whole Bovary family. The debts Emma had incurred in life had to be met by Charles in what remained of his, and he was left in penury. His eventual discovery of Emma's love letters to Leon and Rodolphe upset him dreadfully – the maid Felicite having already badly damaged his faith in human nature by stealing all Emma's clothes and running off with them - and the poor man died of grief. Emma's little girl Berthe, orphaned, went to live with her grandmother, and on the old woman's death ended up working in a cotton mill, and that was the end of the Bovarys.

The version handed down by my family is far more benign. After poor Emma went to prison in Rouen, Charles visited her weekly for a time – but dressed in drab as she was, her hair pulled back and greasy, her skin still blotchy from the effects of arsenic – his adoration for her quickly waned, and his visits became infrequent and then ceased. The servant Felicite, far from stealing Emma's clothes, simply wore them around the house to keep Charles happy, and was very soon replacing Emma in her master's bed. There is some reason to believe that Felicite's affair with Charles had been going on secretly for some years, and under Emma's nose. Charles had more or less pushed Leon and Rodolphe into Emma's arms and this is a sure sign of a guilty man. But perhaps it was no bad thing. Felicite made a gift of her considerable savings to Charles and financial disaster was replaced by prosperity. Under the girl's solicitous care little Berthe bloomed and was happy. Nor was the village unduly censorious.

Although Charles found Emma plain and unappealing, the Prison Governor at Rouen did not. Much moved by Emma's plight, he allowed her many special privileges. She ate and slept in his quarters and having a gift for sewing and a love of fabric was kept more than busy embroidering his fine uniforms. Word of Charles's involvement with Felicite having come to Emma, she did not hesitate to accept the Governor's offer when her prison term was up, of a boat fare to New York. He was after all a married man.

In New York Emma quickly found work in Lily Bart's Hat Shop. Lily Bart, you may remember from the Edith Wharton novel *The House of Mirth* – most eloquently filmed in Hollywood, starring the delectable Scully from *The X-Files* – was the unfortunate young woman whose single act of sexual indiscretion in High Society led to her downfall. Cast out from decent company and reduced to penury, Lily, according to Wharton, was obliged to take work in a millinery shop but soon died from sheer despond.

My family assure me that Wharton's desire for a pointed tragedy must have got the better of her – the truth, and Wharton knew it well enough, was that Lily, though she could not sew for peanuts, was good at figures and soon took over the business: far from fading away she flourished, as did the hat shop. All the rich dowagers of New York flocked to its doors to buy, as did all the tragic heroines of literature, to work.

Customers would find themselves welcomed by none other than the lovely Anna Karenina from Moscow, who had escaped her author in the nick of time, saved herself from the iron wheels of the suicide train and bought a passage to the new world. Norah Krogstad from Norway, allowed by the forward thinking playwright Ibsen to flee from home rather than destroy herself, found the miracle came true in New York. Earning as much as man she could be at one with man. Effie Brieff from Prussia, spared the fate of social obloquy, made an excellent seamstress and quickly regained her health and youthful high spirits.

Pretty little Emma Bovary was more than happy in this company, and many were the tales of love and loss and new determination that were exchanged amongst the women, and many an account of the villainy of men. All were especially fond of Emma, who, being a most imaginative milliner found great favour with the customers, some of whom, being the wives of meat barons, scarcely knew how to arrange a scarf let alone fix a hat.

There was some small trouble amongst the workforce when on one occasion Mr. Rochester came round to buy a grey bonnet, untrimmed, for his wife Jane Eyre, and Emma was found alone in the back room with him, choosing scarlet ribbons. But Emma, reminded that Rochester had in all probability murdered his first wife by pushing her off a roof, agreed not to pursue the matter. Instead, the better to keep her mind off the delights of illicit love, she remembered her role as mother and sent for little Berthe. Charles and Felicite, now having twin sons of their own, were happy enough to see the girl go: she was too like her mother for comfort. Berthe showed considerable musical talent, was enrolled in the New York conservatoire, and within the year had married Lord Henry Ashton of Lammermoor, a baritone. It is thanks to Berthe and

Henry's eldest daughter, a chatty little thing, to whom my grandfather taught the violin, that I come to know so much about Lily Bart's Hat Shop.

1992

Knock-Knock

'Knock-knock,' said the child into the silence. He was eight. The three adults looked up from their breakfast yoghurt, startled. Harry seldom spoke unless spoken to first. He'd seemed happy enough during the meal. The waiter had fetched him a toy from the hotel kitchens, a miniature Power Ranger out of a cereal packet, and he'd been playing with that, taking no apparent notice of a desultory conversation between Jessica his mother, and Rosemary and Bill, his grandparents.

'Who's there?' asked his mother, obligingly.

'Me,' said Harry, with such finality that the game stopped there. He was a quiet, usually self-effacing child; blonde, bronzed and handsome.

Perhaps he'd been more aware of the content of their talk than they'd realised. It had of course been coded for his benefit, couched in abstract terms. The importance of fidelity, the necessity of trust, different cultural expectations either side of the Atlantic, and so on: its real subject being the matter in doubt – should Jessica go home to her faithless husband in Hollywood, or stay with her loving parents in the Cotswolds. To forgive or not to forgive, that was the question.

They'd tried to keep the story from the child, hidden newspapers and magazines. It wasn't a big scandal, just a little one; not on the Hugh Grant scale: nothing like that, not enough to make TV, just enough to make them all uncomfortable, leave home and take temporary refuge in this staid and stately country hotel, with its willowed drive, its swan-stocked lake, its Laura Ashley interior, where reporters couldn't find them to ask questions. If you answered the questions it was bad, if you didn't answer them it was worse. The solution was simply not to be there at all.

The story, the embryo scandal, goes thus. Young big-shot Hollywood producer Aaron Scheffer sets off on holiday with English wife of ten years, Jessica, and eight-year-old son Harry, to spend the summer with her parents. At the airport he gets a phone call. His film's been brought forward, its budget tripled; rising star Maggie Ives has agreed to play the lead. Aaron shouldn't leave town. He stays, wife and child go. Well, these things happen. Two weeks in and there's a story plus pics in an international show-biz magazine: Aaron Scheffer intimately entwined behind a palm tree on a restaurant balcony. Who with? Maggie Ives. They're an item. Other newspapers pick up the story.

No air conditioning in the grandparental home in England: how could it ever work? Why try? The place is impossible to seal. Too many chimneys: too many people in the habit of flinging up windows and opening doors, even when it's hotter out than in. You'd never stop them. And it's hot, so hot. A heat wave.

Aaron calls Jessica, much distressed. It's a set-up, don't believe a word of it. I have enemies. Jessica replies of course I don't believe it, stay cool, hang loose, I trust you, I love you.

A chat show runs a piece on spouse infidelity: featuring the phoney airport call; how to get the wife out of town without her suspecting a thing. Ha ha ha.

The heat may be good. It has an anaesthetising effect. Or perhaps Jessica's just stunned. She cannot endure her parents' pity: the implicit 'I told you so.'

Harry's happy in the grandparental English garden. He is studying the life cycle of frogs. He helps tadpoles out of their pond, his little fingers beneath their limp back legs, helping them on their way. Once tadpoles breathe air, he says, everything about them stiffens. Jessica feels there's no air around to breathe, it's too hot.

Best friend and neighbour Kate, back in LA, calls to say Jessica, you have to believe it, you need to know, everyone else knows, Aaron's been seeing Maggie for months. That's why she's got the part.

Jessica can't even cry. Her eyes are as parched as the garden. Forget tragedy, forget betrayal, how could she ever live in a land without air conditioning?

Phone calls fly. Her father Bill frets about the cost. Aaron says not to believe a word Kate says. Kate's a woman scorned. By whom? Why, Aaron, the minute Jessica's back is turned. Come home now, Jessica, pleads Aaron, I love you.

* * *

'I'll think about it,' says Jessica. She asks her mother whether it's safer to trust a husband or a best friend? 'Neither,' says her mother. 'And Aaron probably only wants you home for a photo-opportunity, to keep the studio quiet.'

The first reporter turns up on the doorstep. Is she hurt? How does it feel? He has other photographs here: they'd like to publish with her comments. Will she stand by her man? Doors slam. No comment. More phone calls.

Aaron confesses: words twinkle across continents and seas. 'Maggie and I lunched. We drank. We shouldn't have. She asked me back to her place. I went. I shouldn't have. We succumbed. We shouldn't have. We were both upset. I was missing you. I felt you'd put your parents before me. Afterwards we both regretted it. I took her to a restaurant so there'd be no embarrassment, so we could get back to being friends, colleagues, nothing more than that.'
'And there just happened to be photographers around,' Jessica drawls. Heat slows words.
'Her boyfriend spies on her.'
'I'm not surprised,' says Jessica. She's melting. But perhaps that too is just the heat. 'What was Maggie so upset about?'
'I've no idea,' says Aaron. 'I can't remember.'
'That's a good sign,' says Jessica. 'But if you two have to work together, and I can see you can, supposing she gets upset about something else? What then?'
'Why should she?' asks Aaron, 'now she has the part she wants. Please will you come home tomorrow?'
'No,' says Jessica. She feels mean and angry. She'd rather he'd gone on lying. She wants him punished. 'Then I'll come and collect you,' he says. 'Meet me at Heathrow.' She puts the phone down.
More reporters on the step. The family wait for nightfall, then slip away to the hotel. Jessica calls Aaron. He's already left for England, says his secretary. Everyone has three days off.

Maggie Ives is sick. Aaron's due at Heathrow at eleven-thirty, Friday.

Now it's eight-thirty and Friday. And Harry is saying, 'Knock-knock, who's there, me!' And her parents are saying, if she hears them correctly, because they'll never say it outright, don't go to him, stay here with us. Crisis time.

And here was home, where no one said anything outright, so at least everything was open to change. Perhaps she hated Hollywood. Perhaps she hated all America. Perhaps the only people you could trust were family; blood relatives; and husbands weren't even blood relatives. Other people had serial marriages, why shouldn't she?

If only this hotel, which claimed to have air conditioning but had only a hideous roaring box in a corner of the dining-room, was more American: if only her child didn't knock at her conscience, saying 'Remember me?' then she could think.

Aaron was in the air now, somewhere up above the frozen seas or the hard unyielding land; on wings of love or self-interest, how could she know which? Knock-knock, who's there? God or the Devil?

Harry put down his spoon and asked politely if he could leave the table. Rosemary said yes before Jessica could speak. He must go to his room to put on sun block first. Harry said OK.

Bill remarked that he was an unusually good child. Jessica said yes, but she'd had him checked out with a therapist, who'd said no problem, except he might be overly mature for his age: Rosemary observed that Hollywood must be a dreadful place to rear a child: either vulgar wealth in Bel Air or shoot-outs in McDonald's, and therapists everywhere. Bill said any child was best reared in green fields in a gentle climate, Jessica should get a cottage in the village near them. Presumably Aaron would look after her financing. They'd be near, as families should be, but would of course respect each other's privacy. And so on.

Harry was now out in the garden: the other side of the long French windows. He threw a ball against the wall, hard: it bounced back off uneven bricks, he'd leap to catch it. Hurl again. The garden was remarkably pretty. English pretty. The high wall was made of slim, ancient, muted red bricks, beneath which were hollyhocks and delphiniums, pleasantly tiered. Drought restrictions were in place, but Bill said he'd looked out of his window in the early hours and seen the gardener using the hose.

'Harry's got a good throw,' said Bill. 'He'll be good at cricket.'

'Or baseball,' said Jessica. Rosemary groaned. Jessica understood, suddenly, what was obvious but she hadn't seen: that she was their only child, Harry their only grandchild. Of course her parents wanted her back in the country. She could hardly look to them for impartial advice. Thud, thud, thud, against the wall. Knock-knock. What about me? Father, lying but loving, v. doting grandparents? Broken home v. green fields and no air conditioning?

'We both like Aaron,' observed Rosemary, 'you know that, but there's no denying he's ambitious!'

What did her mother mean? That no truly ambitious man

would put up with Jessica? That she wasn't bright, beautiful or starry enough for Aaron? That it was a miracle he'd taken her on in the first place? So long as Aaron was the one persuading her to stay while she tried to leave, she could cope. But supposing it went the other way, Aaron decided he preferred Maggie Ives to Jessica? How would she survive then? She was playing games she might regret.

'I could take the car and drive to meet him,' said Jessica to her parents. 'He and I could at least talk. I owe him that. I'd just about make it to the airport in time.'

'I'd have to drive you,' said Bill. 'My car has gears. You can only drive an automatic.'

'Bill can't possibly drive you,' said Rosemary. 'It's much too hot. His heart won't stand it. We don't have air-conditioned cars over here, which is just as well for the ozone layer. And I daresay you think you could afford a driver but where would you find one at such short notice?'

Such silly practicalities! But still they stood in her way. It was Fate. Better, Jessica thought, to stick by her original decision. So public and powerful an insult from husband to wife could not be excused, and that was that. All her friends would agree. The waiter poured more coffee. 'Good to see the little fellow enjoying himself,' he remarked. Everyone nodded politely.

Harry came in from the garden.

'If I died,' he said, 'you'd forget me at once.'

'We wouldn't, we wouldn't,' exclaimed Jessica. 'We all love you so much!'

And even Bill and Rosemary, though talk of such emotion came with difficulty to their lips, assured their grandchild of undying and unflinching love.

'No,' said Harry, refusing their comfort. 'I'm right about this.

I'm just not important to you. In a couple of hours you'd forget all about me. In fact if I were out of your sight for just ten minutes you wouldn't remember who I was.'

And he bowed his head beneath the shower of protests and went back into the garden, to his ball. Thud, thud, thud.

Jessica stood up and said, 'Dad, give me the keys. I'm going to meet Aaron. I'm going to bring him back here, you're going to be nice to him; then we fly back to Hollywood. I'm not leaving Aaron, I'm not divorcing him, I love him. And I have to think of Harry. Every good boy deserves a father; we've made him so dreadfully insecure. I hadn't realised.'

Bill handed over the keys.

'We all have to think of the children,' he said.

'We abide by your decision,' said his wife. 'For Harry's sake.'

'Tell Harry I'll be back with his father,' said Jessica. 'Tell him to stop worrying.'

Bill and Rosemary watched as the car lurched and shuddered on the gravel drive while Jessica got the hang of the gears. Then it shot off into the heat haze, grating and grinding, out of the shade of the willows into the sun. The waiter hovered. Harry stopped throwing and came to stand beside them, watching.

'Where's Mom gone?'

'Mummy,' corrected Rosemary. 'She's gone to meet your father.'

'Um,' said Harry, approving but not especially so. Then he said, 'Knock-knock.'

'Who's there?' asked Rosemary.

'Told you so!' said Harry. 'Forgotten me already! Ten minutes and see, you'd forgotten all about me. Gotcha!'

And Harry laughed uproariously, cracking up, bending over a gold and damask chair to contain his stomach and his mirth, making far more noise than they'd ever heard him make before. And the waiter was bent over laughing too, holding his middle.
'I told him that one,' said the waiter. 'Poor little feller. He needed a laugh! We all do, this time of year.'

When Harry had finished laughing he went serenely back into the garden, for more throwing, thudding, catching. The heat seemed to affect him not one whit.

1993

Wasted Lives

They're turning the City into Disneyland. They're restoring the ancient facades and painting them apple green, firming up the medieval gables and picking out the gargoyles in yellow. They're gold-leafing the church spires. They've boarded up the more stinking alleys until they get round to them and as State property becomes private the shops which were always there are suddenly gone, as if simply painted out. In the eaves above Benetton and The Body Shop cherubs wreathe pale cleaned-stone limbs, and even the great red McDonald's 'M' has been especially muted to rosy pink for this its Central European edition. Don't think crass commerce rules the day as the former communist world opens its arms wide to the seduction of market forces: the good taste of the new capitalist world leaps yowling into the embrace as well, a fresh-faced baby monster, with its yearning to prettify and make the serious quaint, to turn the rat into Mickey Mouse and the wolf into Goofy.

Milena and I walked through knots of tourists towards the famous Processional Bridge, circa 1395. I had always admired its sooty stamina, its dismal persistence, through the turbulence of rising and falling empire. It was my habit to stay with Milena when I came to the City. I'd let Head Office book me into an hotel, to save official embarrassment, then spend my nights with her and some part of my days if courtesy so required. I was fond of her but did not love her, or only in the throes of the sexual excitement she was so good at summoning out of me. She made excellent coffee. If I sound disagreeable and calculating it is because I am attempting to speak the truth about the events on the Processional Bridge that day, and the truth of motive seldom warms the listener's heart. I am generally accepted as a pleasant and kindly enough person. My family loves me, even my wife Joanna, though she and I live apart and are no longer sexually connected. She doesn't have to love me.

Milena is an archivist at the City Film Institute. I work for a US film company, from their London office. I suppose, if you add it up, I have spent some three months in the City, on and off, over the last five years, before and after the fall of the Berlin Wall and the Great Retreat of Communism, a tide sweeping back over shallow sand into an obscure distance. Some three months in all spent with Milena.

Her English was not as good as she thought. Conversation could be difficult. Today she was not dressed warmly enough. It was June but the wind was cold. Perhaps she thought her coat was too shabby to stand the inspection of the bright early summer sun. I was accustomed to seeing her either naked or dressed in black, as was her usual custom, a colour, or lack of it, which suited the gaunt drama of her face, but today, like her City, she wore pastel colours. I wished it were not so.
Beat your head not into the Berlin Wall, but into cotton wool, machine-pleated in interesting baby shades, plastic-wrapped. Suffocation takes many forms.

'You should have brought your coat,' I said.
'It's so old,' she said. 'I am ashamed of it.'

'I like it,' I said.

'It's old,' she repeated, dismissively. 'I would rather freeze.' For Milena the past was all dreary, the future all dread and expectation. A brave face must be put on everything. She smiled up at me. I am six foot three inches and bulky: she was all of five and a half foot, and skinny with it. The jumper was too tight: I could see her ribs through the stretched fabric, and the nipples too. In the old days she would never have allowed that to happen. She would have let her availability be known in other, more subtle ways. Her teeth were bad: one in the front broken, a couple grey. When she wore black their eccentricity seemed a matter of course; a delight even. Now she wore green they were yellowy, and seemed a perverse tribute to years of neglect, poverty and bad diet. Eastern teeth, not Western. I wished she would not smile, and trust me so.

The Castle still looks down over the City, and the extension to that turreted tourist delight, the long low stone building with its rows of identical windows, tier upon tier of them, blank and anonymous, to demonstrate the way brute force gives way to the subtler but yet more stifling energies of bureaucracy. You can't do this, you can't live like that, not because I have a sword to run you through, but because Our Masters frown on it. And your papers have not risen to the top of the pile.

* * *

Up there in the Castle that day a newly-elected government were trying to piece together from the flesh of this nation, the bones of that, a new living, changing organism, a new constitution. New, new, new. I wished them every luck with it, but they could not make Milena's bad teeth good, or stop her smiling at me as if she wanted something. I wondered what it was. She'd used not to smile like this: it was a new trick: it sat badly on her doleful face.

We reached the Processional Bridge, which crosses the river between the Palace and the Cathedral. 'The oldest bridge in Europe,' said Milena. We had walked across it many times before. She had made this remark many times before. Look left down the river and you could see where it carved its way through the mountains which form the natural boundaries to this small nation: look right and you looked into mist. On either bank the ancient City crowded in, in its crumbly, pre-Disney form, all eaves, spires and casements, spared from the blasts of war for one reason or another, or perhaps just plain miracle. But Emperors and Popes must have somewhere decent to be crowned, and Dictators too need a background for pomp and circumstance, crave some acknowledgement from history: a name engraved in gold in a Cathedral, a majestic tomb in a gracious square still standing. It can't be all rubble or what's the point?

I offered Milena my coat. It seemed to me that she and I were at some crucial point in not just our story, but everyone's; that the decisions we made here today had some general relevance to the way the world was going. I could at least share some warmth with her. My monthly Western salary would keep her in comfort for a year, but what could I do about that? Not my doing. If she wanted a new coat from me it would have nothing to do with her desire to be warm, but as a token of my love. She didn't mind shivering. Her discomfort was both a demonstration of martyrdom and a symbol of pride.
'I am not cold,' she said.

The City is a favourite location for film companies. The place is cheap; its money valueless in the real world and its appetite for hard currency voracious, which means good deals can be had. The quaint, colourful locations are inexpensively historicised – though the satellite dishes are these days becoming too numerous to dodge easily. And there are few parking problems, highly-trained post-production technicians, efficient labs, excellent cameramen, sensitive sound-men, and so on – and cheap, so cheap. Those who lived in the City had escaped the fate of so much of the hitherto Russian-dominated lands – the sullen refusal of the oppressed and exploited to do anything right, to be anything other than inefficient, sloppy and lazy, in the hope that the colonising power would simply give up and go away, shaking the dust of the conquered land from its feet. And the power it had amassed lay not of course in the strength of the ideology it professed, as the West in its muddled way assumed, but in the strength of arms and organisation of that single, colonising, ambitious nation, Russia. Ask anyone between Budapest and Samarkand, Tbilisi and the Siberian flatlands, and they would tell you who they feared and hated. Russia, the motherland, announcing itself to a gullible world as the Soviet Union. Harsh mother, pretending kindness, using Marxist-Leninism as the religious tool of government and exploitation, as once in the South Americas Spain had used Christianity.

In the City they kept their wits about them; too sophisticated for the numbing rituals of mind-control ever to quite work: the concrete of the workers' blocks to quite take over from the tubercular gables and back alleys, to stifle the whispers of dissent, to quieten the gossip and mirth of café society. McDonald's has achieved that now with its bright, forbidding jollity, and who in the brave new world of freedom can afford a cup of coffee anyway, has anything interesting or persuasive to say now that everyone has what they wanted. Better, better by far to travel hopefully than to arrive, to have to face the fact that the journey is not out of blackness into light, but from one murky confusion into another. Happiness and fulfilment lie in our affections for one another, not in the forms that our societies take. If only I was in love with Milena, this walk across the bridge would be a delight. I would feel the air bright with the happiness of the hopeful young.

Be that as it may, the City was always better than anywhere else for filming, Castle and all. Go to Rumania and you'd find the castles still full of manacled prisoners clanking their chains; try Poland and you'd have to fly in special food for your stars; in Hungary the cameraman would have artistic tantrums; but here in the City there would be gaiety, fun, sometimes even sparkle, the clatter of high heels on cobblestones, sultry looks from sultry eyes, and of course nights with Milena in the fringy, shabby apartment, with the high, white-mantled brass bed, and good strong coffee in porcelain cups for breakfast. Milena, forever languidly busy, about my body or about her work, off to the Institute or back from it. Women worked hard in this country, as women were accustomed to all over the Soviet Union. Equality for women meant an equal obligation to work, the official direction of your labour, sleeping with your boss if he so required, the placement of your child in a crèche, as well as the cultural expectation that you get married, run a home and empty the brimming ashtrays while your husband put his feet up. Joanna would have none of that kind of thing; for the male visitor from the West the Eastern European woman is paradise, if you can hack it, if your conscience can stand it: if you can bear being able to buy affection and constancy.

I hadn't been with Milena for three months or so. Now, like her City, I found her changed. I wondered about her constancy. It occurred to me that it was foolish of me to expect it. As did the rest of the nation, she now paid at least lip service to market forces: perhaps these worked sexually as well. Rumour had it that there were now twenty-five thousand prostitutes in the City and an equal number of pimps, as men and women decided to make the best financial use of available resources. I discovered I was not so much jealous as rather hoping for evidence of Milena's infidelity, which would let me off whatever vague hook it was I found myself upon. Not so difficult a hook. She and I had always been discreet: I had not mentioned our relationship to a soul back home. Milena was in another country; she did not really count: her high bouncing bosom, her narrow ribcage and fleshless hips vanished from my erotic imagination as the plane reached the far side of the mountain tops – the turbulence serving as some rite of passage – to re-imprint itself only as it passed over them once again, on my return.

The cleaning processes had not yet reached the bridge, I was glad to see. The stone saints who lined it were still black with the accumulated grime of the past.

'Who are these saints?' I asked, but Milena didn't know. Some hold books, others candles; noses are weather-flattened. Milena apologised for her ignorance. She had not, she said, had the opportunity of a religious education: she hoped her son Milo would. Her son lived with Milena's mother, who was a good Catholic, in the Southern province – a place about to secede, to become independent, to ethnic-cleanse in its own time, in its own way.

'I didn't know you had a son,' I said. I was surprised, and ashamed at myself for being so uncurious about her. 'Why didn't you tell me?'

'It's my problem,' Milena said. 'I don't want to burden you. He's ten now. When he was born I was not well, and times were hard. It seemed better that he go to my mother. But she's getting old now and there's trouble in the Southern province. They are not nice people down there.'

Once the City's dislike and suspicion had been reserved for the Russians. Now it had been unleashed and spread everywhere. The day the Berlin Wall fell Milena and I had been sitting next to each other in the small Institute cinema, watching the show reels of politically-sound directors on the Institute's books, in the strange, flickering half-dark of such places. Her small white hand had strayed unexpectedly on to my thigh, unashamedly direct in its approach. But then exhilaration and expectation, mixed with fear, was in the air. Sex seemed the natural expression of such emotions, such events. And perhaps that was why I never quite trusted her, never quite loved her, found it so easy to forget her when she wasn't under my nose – I despised her because it was she who had approached me, not I her. If Joanna and I are apart it's because, or so she says, I'm so conditioned in the old, pre-feminist ways of thinking I'm impossible for a civilised woman to live with. I am honest, that is to say, and scrupulous in the investigation of my feelings and opinions.

'Why didn't you put the child into a crèche?' I asked. It shocked me that Milena, that any woman, could give a child away so easily.

'I was in a crèche,' she said bleakly. 'It's the same for nearly everyone in this City under forty. The crèche was our real home, our parents were strangers. I didn't want it to happen to Milo. He was better with my mother, though there are too many Muslims down there. More and more of them. It's like a disease.'

I caught the stony eye of baby Jesus on St Joseph's shoulder – that one at least I knew – and one or the other sent me a vision, not that I believed in such things, as I looked down at the greeny, sickly waters of the river. I saw, ranked and rippling, row upon row of infants, small, pale children, institutionalised, deprived, pasty-faced from the atrocious City food – meat, starch, fat, no fruit, no vegetables – and understood that I was looking at the destruction of a people. They turned their little faces to me in despair, and I looked quickly up and away and back at Milena to shake off the vision; but there behind her, where the river met the sky, saw that nation grown up, marching towards me into the mists of its future, a sad mockery of those sunny early Social Realist posters which decked my local once-Marxist, now Leftish bookshop back home: the proletariat marching square-jawed and determined into the new dawn, scythes and spanners at the ready, only here there were no square jaws, only wretchedness; the quivering lip of the English ex-public schoolboy, wrenched from his home at a tender age, now made general; the same profound puzzled sorrow spread through an entire young population, male and female. See it in the easy, surface emotion, the facile sexuality, the rush of tears to the eyes, uncontrolled and uncontrollable, pleading for a recognition that never comes, a comfort that is unavailable. Pity me, the unspoken words upon a nation's lips, because I am indeed pitiable. I have been deprived of freedom, yes, of course, all that. And of proper food and of fancy things, consumer durables and material wealth of every kind, all that; but mostly I have been robbed of my birthright, my mother, my father, my home. And how can I ever recover from that? Murmur as a last despairing cry the latest prayer, market forces, market forces, say it over and over as once the Hail Mary was said, to ward off all ills and rescue the soul, but we know in our hearts it won't work. There is no magic here contained. Wasted lives, lost souls, unfixable. Pity me, pity me, pity me.

'I think the fog's coming down,' said Milena, and so it was. The new dawn faded into it. A young man on the bridge was selling black rubber spiders: you hurled them against a board and they crept down, leg over leg; stillness alternating with sudden movement. No one was buying.

'Well,' I said, 'I expect you made the right decision about Milo. What happened to his father?' I turned to button her cardigan. I wanted her warmed. This much at least I could do. Perhaps if she was warm, she would not feel so much hate for the Southern province and its people.

'We are divorced,' she said. 'I am free to marry again. Look there's Jesus crucified. Hanging from nails in his hands. At least the communists took down the crosses. Why should we have to think about torture all the time? It was the Russians taught our secret police their tricks: we would never have come to it on our own.'

I commented on the contradiction between her wanting her son to have a Catholic upbringing, and her dislike of the Christian symbol, the tortured man upon the cross, but she shrugged it off: she did not want the point pursued. She was not interested in it. She saw no virtue in consistency. First you had this feeling; then that: that was all there was to it. No parent had ever intervened between the tantrum and its cause; no doubt Milena along with her generation had been slapped into silence, when protesting frustration and outrage. She was wounded: she was damaged: not her fault, but there it was. What I'd seen as childlike, as charming, in the early stages of a relationship, was in the end merely irritating. I could not stir myself to become interested in her son or in a marriage which had ended in divorce. I could not take her initial commitment seriously.

* * *

'I'm pregnant,' Milena now says. 'Last time you were here we made a baby. Isn't that wonderful? Now you will marry me, and take me to London, and we will live happily ever after.'

Fiends come surging up the river through the mist, past me, gaunt, thin, soundlessly shrieking. These are the ghosts of the insulted, the injured, the wronged and tortured, whose efforts have been in vain. Those whose language has been taken away, whose bodies have been starved; they are the wrongfully dead. All the great rivers of the world carry these images with them, over time they have infected me by their existence. They breathe all around me. I take in their exhalations. I am their persecutor, their ruler, the origin of their woes: the one who despises. They shake their ghoulish locks at me; they mock me with their sightless eyes, snapping to attention as they pass. Eyes right! Blind eyes, forever staring. They honour me, the living.

'Is something the matter?' asks Milena. 'Aren't you happy? You told me you loved me.' Did I? Probably. I remind her that I've also told her that I'm married.

'But you will divorce her,' she says. 'Why not? Your children are grown. She doesn't need you any more. I do.' Her eyes are large in their hollows: she fears disaster. Of course she does. It so often happens. I can hardly tell whether she is alive or dead. To bear a child by a ghost!

Milena is perfectly right. Joanna doesn't need me. Milena does. The first night I went with Milena she was wearing a purple velvet bra. It fired me sexually, it was so extraordinary, but put too great an element of pity into what otherwise could have been love. There seemed something more valuable in my wife Joanna's white Marks & Spencer bra with its valiant label, 40A. Broad-backed, that is, and flat-chested. I supposed Milena's to be a 36C. English women lean towards the pear-shaped; the City women towards the top heavy. It's unfashionable, dangerous even, to make comparisons between the characteristics of the peoples of the world, this tribe, that tribe, this religion or that. The ghouls that people the river, who send their dying breath back, day after day, in the form of the fog that blights the place, mists up the new Disney facades with mystery droplets, met their end because people like me, whispered, nudged and made odious comparisons, and the odium grew and grew and ended up in torture, murder, slaughter, genocide. Nevertheless, I must insist: it is true. Pear-shaped that lot, top heavy this. And if I suspected Milena's purple velvet bra of being some kind of secret police state issue, or part of the Film Institute's plan to attract hard currency and Western business, an end to which their young female staff were encouraged, even paid, it is not surprising. Had I been of her nationality, I knew well enough, her hand would not have strayed across my thigh in the film-flickering dark. I was offended that the Gods of Freedom, good health, good teeth, good nourishment, prosperity and market forces, whom I myself did not worship, endowed me with this wondrous capacity to attract. I could snap my fingers and all the girls in Eastern Europe would come trotting, and fall on their knees.

'Milena,' I said, and I was only temporising, 'I have no way of knowing this baby is mine, if baby there be.'

Milena threw her hands into the air, and cried aloud, a thin, horrid squeal, chin to the heavens, lips drawn back in a harsh grimace. There were few people left on the bridge. The fog had driven them away. The seller of rubber spiders had given up and gone home. Milena ran towards the parapet, and wriggled and crawled until she lay along its top on the cold stone, and then she simply rolled off and fell into the water below; this in the most casual way possible. From my straightforward question to this dramatic answer only fifteen seconds can have intervened. I was too stunned to feel alarm. I found myself leaning over the parapet to look downwards; the fog was patchy. I saw a police launch veer off course and make for the spot where Milena fell. No doubt she had seen it coming or she would not have done what she did, launched herself into thick air, thin, swirling water. I had confidence in her ability to survive. Authorities of one kind or another, as merciful in succour as they were cruel in the detection of sedition, would pull her out of the wet murk, dry her, wrap her in blankets, warm her, return her to her apartment. She would be all right.

I walked to the end of the bridge, unsure as to whether I would then turn left to the police pier and Milena or to the right and the taxi rank. Why had the woman done it? Hysteria, despair, or some convenient social way of terminating unwanted pregnancies? I could take a flight back home, if I chose, forty-eight hours earlier than I had intended. The flights were full, but I would get a priority booking, as benefitted my status, however whimsical, as a provider of hard currency. The powerful are indeed whimsical: they leave their elegant droppings where they choose – be they Milena's baby, Benetton, the Marlborough ads which now dominate the City: no end even now to the wheezing, the coughing, the death rattling along the river.

I turned to the right, where the taxis stood waiting for stray foreigners, anxious to get out of the fog, back to their hotels.

'The airport,' I said. He understood. 'To the airport' are golden words to taxi drivers all over the world. This way at least I created a smile. To have turned left would have meant endless trouble. I was thoroughly out of love with Milena. I wanted to help, of course I did, but the child in the Southern provinces would have had to be fetched by the Catholic mother, taken in. There would be no end to it. My children would not accept a new family: Joanna would have been made thoroughly miserable. To do good to one is to do bad to another. But you don't need to hear my excuses. They are the same that everyone makes to themselves when faced with the misery of others, and though they would like to do the right thing, simply fail to do so, but look after themselves instead.

1993

A Knife for Cutting Mangoes

When I moved in his wife's belongings were still there, all around me, even to the sheets on the bed. She didn't so much as bother to change them, and very pretty, impractical sheets they were; fine white linen with scalloped edges and self-embroidery, the kind which have to be ironed after the wash. What an absurdity! Who has anything these days but drip-dry? She moved out saying she didn't want anything of the past: she wanted to start again: she was desperate to have a new life, she couldn't be her true self while married to him. I wish her every luck, but perhaps she didn't have much of a true self to begin with. It's easy to blame others for one's own shortcomings.

Using her saucepans, drinking from her coffee cups, going through the house and switching on her brass lamps as evening fell didn't bother me. Why should it? The saucepans were heavy and expensive, not the tinny things I was accustomed to: food didn't catch and burn if you stopped stirring. It made me feel quite dainty to drink black coffee from little cups with saucers, instead of from Safeways' mugs. The lamps turned out to be real antiques – student's lamps, Victorian. I found a cutting in a kitchen drawer all about them, so they were good not just for light to read by, but as a talking point when guests came.

One night she lay between the sheets, the next night I did. She couldn't have liked them all that much, or she'd have come back for them. Wouldn't she? Scalloped edges and self-embroidery and all. The things she spent money on that I never would! She was so hopelessly extravagant. She even had a knife for cutting and peeling mangoes. Mangoes are things I can do without, believe me. So messy and time-consuming. But I did quite like moving among her bits and pieces, I suppose, pushing aside her party dresses to make room for my jeans and T-shirts. All that silk and crushed velvet giving way to denim and lycra. It gave me a sense of victory. I expect soldiers feel like that when they sack and loot a town after a long war.

I've never worried about finding my true self, personally. I don't think I have an inner me and if I have I don't particularly want to meet her. And he certainly doesn't want me to waste time searching, when I could be in bed with him. Look at the trouble he had with Chloe, for ever trying. That was his wife's name. Chloe. Quite pretty, really. Mine is Jane, and very plain, but plain girls often win. And his is Jub, rub-a-dub-dub: Jub-Jub for short or for long. He says the sex between them was never very good, but men do say that, don't they.

No, of course I don't want us to get married. Marriage is for the birds. Look what happened to her, look what happened to my parents, look what happens to stay-at-home wives who have time to buy antiques and iron sheets. Divorce happens, because they get to be so dull, and end up buying mango knives. I took my father's side in the divorce, not my mother's. I wanted them divorced so I could go and live with my father and look after him and he wouldn't yawn all the time, showing his back teeth. Of course it didn't work out like that. I ended up living with my mother and my father married a real bitch of a girl I didn't even know about. But all that's in the past. This is now.

Trying to find her inner self, the real her. What a fool Chloe was. She deserved what happened. Why did she think she was more than she was? I'm sure I don't. I am the sum of my parts, of what I do and what I say, I don't add up to more. Feelings change all the time, it's part of being alive. It's dangerous to try and nail them. Define who you are and all you do is throw chunks of your life away. And what's a self anyway? Nobody knows, do they: the psychologists and the philosophers argue about it all the time. What is the brain, what is the mind, what constitutes our identity? Since we don't know, why bother. There's everyday life to get on with.

And I am so happy, and there is nothing to go wrong. The sun shines upon our love, all things are beautiful. Chloe doesn't bother me. It's not as if she were dead. I wouldn't like that, if she'd killed herself or something. Then I might get really spooked. As it is she's just off searching for her true self, after the great gesture of leaving it all behind, even to the knickers in her drawers. I guess it took all her strength, just to go.

So here I am, happy as Larry. I once had an affair with a Larry, and I can't say he was all that happy, rather depressed, in fact. I don't suffer from depression; every morning I wake up full of the joys of spring, and summer too, and autumn and winter in addition, whatever season it happens to be. You know some religions say the object of life is to be happy. That being the case I am a very good person indeed.

I tell a lie. Not totally happy. Chloe left her cat behind when she went. *Jub-Jub and Chloe together's cat.* I wasn't at all happy about it, but I took the creature on. Jub insisted. 'We are going to keep the cat,' he said, 'and that's that. No, we are not going to take it down to the vet.' I've always been perfectly kind to the animal, I never kick it or anything or keep it out all night as some people do, but it has never liked me, and I have to say the feeling is mutual. Sometimes when Jub-Jub strokes the cat so gently and carefully I get the feeling perhaps he loves me but he doesn't quite like me.

* * *

Little by little the things she abandoned stopped being hers-left-behind and began to feel like mine, and the sense of her presence altogether faded. I bought some more sheets in a summer sale last week and I took hers down to the charity shop, because I'm working and have no time to iron and I'm tired of wasting money sending them out to be laundered. The lady in the shop shook her head and said, 'Oh, they're the kind that need ironing. We'll have trouble shifting them.'
'Look at the hems,' I cried, 'look at the stitching,' and she did, and was impressed, and took them in the end. I felt quite proud for Chloe at that moment. I think my dreams have been easier since, but I don't see why they should be, I have done nothing wrong. I had only done what others do: we were both being true to our feelings, Jub-Jub and I. Why should there be punishment?

Jub and Jane, happy together. Life flows tranquilly by. If you don't count the dreams. But I take sleeping pills now, which blurs them okay. Can we grow new skins? Become different people? Or are we doomed to stay the same bawling, devious little creatures we were when we were born? Nothing singular about us, all the same? Perhaps that's why I could never feel properly maternal. When I looked at my child, I looked at me. Anyway my child's doing just fine, I'd have heard if she weren't.

Because I brought nothing out of my past either. I too wanted to leave everything behind. My husband was better than I was with our child, and the therapist said make a clean break, so I did. How strange the word husband sounds, all duty and obligation and female cowardice. 'Please don't leave me on my own.' It hurt at the time, breaking free the way I did, but I gritted my teeth and was able to follow through my feelings for Jub, rub-a-dub-dub, and this is the real life not the one I left behind. That's gone. I don't think of it if I can.

The one thing I brought with me was an alarm clock. Isn't it strange how difficult it is to find a reliable alarm clock that works and goes on working? You'd think it would be easy in this technological age. But they clatter and chatter and you don't hear them; they shriek their noises in your head and you sleep on, or else they don't go off at all. And you miss your flight and your one great chance in life.

What's so strange? Many women nowadays leave their children. As I say, I wasn't the maternal type: my husband was always more involved. I think that's what made me go off him. I just can't love a man who likes to wash dishes and gets involved with the school nativity play. I'd cringe with embarrassment at the soppy bits, while genuine tears would run down his cheeks. It wouldn't do.

A victory? Yes, I suppose it is a victory, that's how I described it earlier. To take a man from someone else. From his wife. To win his affections. Not that I set out to do it. I just was, and he just was, and there we were, and she wanted to be herself anyway, didn't she. That's what she said. Find her true self. It's been two years. I heard a noise from the back of the linen cupboard the other day: I looked, the noise drew me to it, such a little delicate clang, clang clanging, like a fairy fire bell. It was her alarm clock, I hadn't known it was there, tucked away. Such a pretty little clock, with a tiny gold bell for an alarm, and the dial had flowers painted on it. That spooked me a bit. It was hers, left over. She was still lurking in the house. Perhaps she'd forgiven me. Perhaps she was trying to warn me. More likely something had just fallen on the alarm switch, and set it off. Perhaps the cat had disturbed it, looking for somewhere safe to have kittens. She's pregnant again, that's the second litter since I moved in and I have to find homes for all the kittens. As if I don't have enough to do.

I probably didn't tell you she found us in bed together but that wasn't why she left, of course it wasn't. Something like that wouldn't be important if the relationship was good. She'd left the house before I'd even got out of bed and she never came back. She wrote a letter or two. We threw them away unopened. Why should she damage our happiness? And now I'm here. We're here. Jub, rub-a-dub-dub, I think perhaps he's rub-a dub-dubbing with someone else. The doctor's given me different sleeping pills. They're stronger. The dreams are back. I wander in a grey, still, flat landscape, without beginning or end. Sometimes the dreams creep into my waking life, so I can't tell what's real and what isn't.

I think I should have taken the sheets down to the charity shop way back, but they were just so pretty and I'm so plain. I think one day I'll come back from work and there he'll be in the bed with someone else, because perhaps our relationship isn't so good as I believe, and perhaps he does hanker after Chloe, and perhaps he does blame me – you know what men are – so perhaps he'll find someone totally new. And I'll walk out of the house too, saying *I want nothing, I want to start a new life, I have to go in search of myself* and I'll leave everything behind, as she did. I don't think the new woman will like my sheets, though, nearly as much as I liked Chloe's. Mine are thin nylon, easy to wash, drip-dry, non-iron, practical, cheap.

2000

Smoking Chimneys

I am by nature a solitary person. If I were to advertise in a newspaper for a partner – and who hasn't at one time or another been tempted? – the entry would go something like this: *Reclusive blonde young woman (thirty-two), workaholic, sharp-tongued, hates company, children, loud music, country walks, wining and dining, likes crosswords, seeks similarly inclined male. No smokers, no Viagra users.* Nevertheless, when Marigold asked me to Badger House for the Christmas weekend I was glad of the invitation. Aloneness, that normally enviable and superior state, can around Christmas feel suspiciously like loneliness.

'You don't have to talk to anyone,' said Marigold. 'You can sit in a dark corner among the pine needles and wrapping paper, and pretend to be the au pair. My family won't even notice you, I promise.'

Well, I thought, don't be too sure of that. I can make people notice me if I put myself out. I share an office with Marigold: fortunately she, like me, is a silent person. We are both the offspring of noisy, ducal families, who, having taken to drugs in the sixties, dropped babies like flies and failed to make proper arrangements for their upbringing beyond sending them off to boarding schools. Now, for both of us, just to be in a quiet room alone is bliss: I for one seek it perpetually. In the same way, my mother says, those children who were kept short of butter in World War II grew up to slather it on their bread for ever. Thus she excuses her own obesity.

* * *

My mother decamped with a movie maker to California some four years ago, and one by one my younger siblings drifted after her – I was the oldest of five. I could have gone out to join this new ersatz family of mine for the festive season but I declined. I mention this so you don't feel sorry for me or see me as the kind of person who is short of places to go to at Christmas. It's just that I sometimes fail to want to go wherever it is on time, and then end up miserable. I do like to feel I have removed myself from company, not that company has removed itself from me.

I also need, I think, to point out to you that the benefits of my temperament are such that my confinement in this prison cell is not in itself onerous. Don't feel pity for me on this account. I have faith in justice and assume that I will be found innocent of a murder I did not commit, and in the meantime I rejoice that I won't be expected to go to some party to see in the New Year. I understand that here in Holloway we just all sit silently and separately in our cells on the dreaded night, and contemplate the past and the future. Suits me.

No indeed, sir, I did not murder Lady Hester Walpole Delingro. Let me tell my story in my own way, as is normally done, from the beginning. Or are you in some great hurry? Perhaps you Legal Aid solicitors are on piecework? No? When I hear from my mother she'll have the best lawyers in town take over my case: it's just that she's staying oddly silent, so you will have to put up with me for the time being.

Badger House! My heart sank on seeing the place, at the wrong end of a two-hour standing journey on a crowded train, which smelt of alcohol and mince pies. Marigold had showed me photographs of her family home. It looked lovely enough in the summer, with rampant nature creeping up to its door, but in midwinter, standing isolated and denuded of foliage, you could see it all too clearly for what it was. One of those badly sited, dull, ostentatious houses built at the end of the eighteenth century by people with more money than sense. For one thing the house was situated too near the brow of the hill – downdraught would be bound to make the fires smoke – and faced north. Wall the sloping kitchen garden as you might to keep off the bitter wind, there would be endless troubles with drainage and slugs.

Badger House – badgers prefer valleys, actually, but I daresay occasionally wander – was the property of Marigold's grandmother, Lady Hester Walpole Delingro. (Delingro had the money, she had the title; the marriage – her third – lasted six weeks.) But she kept the name, if only because it stood out in the gossip columns, and she loved a smart party, as did all the family. It was here at Badger House, every Christmas, that the whole vast, noisy, extroverted, once-Catholic Walpole family assembled to celebrate if not exactly the birth of Jesus (they had all long ago forgotten Him, except perhaps for Marigold's ninety-three-year-old great-aunt Cecilia, a nun, whose convent, these days, let her out for Christmas) then their survival as a unit for another year.

The taxi let me out by the great front door: it was half past five on Christmas Eve, heavy crimson damask curtains had been closed, but there was an urgent sense of movement and life behind them. I rang three times and no-one answered. I pushed the door open, and went inside. What noise, what brightness, what Babel! I would have turned and left at once and taken my chances on a train back to the city but the taxi had already gone.

In the great hall someone played a grand piano, honky-tonk style, and a group of adults gathered round to sing Christmas carols out of tune: rivalled only by a cluster of teenage children singing the pop world's seasonal offering, *Have Yourself a Hip-Hop Xmas and Other Tunes*, and jigging about in Ecstasy frenzy. Decorations were plentiful but without discrimination, organisation or style.

Dull paper streamers, of the kind made by earnest children, hung droopily over great distances from wall to wall. Vulgar tinsel draped old family portraits, and cheap Woolworth's magic lanterns in gold, silver, scarlet and green hung from chandeliers and doorways wherever the eye fell, without order, without symmetry. Little children ran around to no apparent purpose, the girls dragging Barbie dolls around by their hair, accessories scattering far and wide on the oak floors and never picked up: little boys panicked and shrieked, pursued by clanking and fashionably cursing computer toys they seemed unable or unwilling to control. Fires had been lit in all the rooms and as I had predicted, smoked. I was obliged to pull my scarf up to cover my nose and mouth and breathe through that to save myself from the worst of the fumes.

As I stood dazed and horrified I was approached by Lady

Hester. I recognised her from the pages of *Tatler* and *Hello!* (Yes, she stooped to *Hello!* I assumed that there were financial problems.) Lady Hester was a woman well into her eighties, still tall and gaunt, bright-eyed and vigorous for her age. She wore black leggings and a waisted silver jacket, which would have looked better on a cheerleader. Old legs are old legs and look skinny, not slender, and that's that.

'You must be Marigold's friend Ishtar,' she said. (My parents had been deeply into Indian mysticism around the time of my birth.) 'Welcome! I'm sorry about so much smoke. Very cunning of you to think of the scarf. As soon as the fireplaces warm up, it gets better. It's a problem we have every year. Part of the ritual!' And just as Marigold came running up, I was saying, 'Personally, I'd abandon the ritual and put in central heating,' which Lady Hester obviously did not react well to, if only because it was sensible advice. But Marigold hugged me and said, 'Ishtar, please don't tell the truth, remember it's Christmas. Let us have our illusions, if only for the weekend.'

* * *

I had never seen Marigold like this, as if she were six again, tippy-toed. Her usually pale horse-face was flushed and she looked almost pretty, tinsel in her hair, wearing a low-cut black top which left a bra strap showing, knocking back the punch as if it were Diet Coke, hotly pursued by the Seb she sometimes talked about, a young man with tendrilly-golden curls clinging to a finely sculpted head.

'This is Ishtar,' she was saying to Seb. 'I share an office with her. She had nowhere to go for Christmas, so we've all agreed she can be this year's Outsider.'

Well, thank you very much, Marigold. Who wants to be labelled as an Outsider, an object of pity, the one invited to the Christmas festivities because otherwise they'd be on their own? It seemed to me a gross abuse of the laws of hospitality and if thereafter I did not behave like a perfect guest who can be surprised? Nor had I liked the way Seb's eye had drifted over me and away, even before he heard me described as the Outsider. Prada, to the uninformed eye, can sometimes look too plain, too dowdy.

But what did I do, you ask me, to justify some twenty people and a host of sticky little children bearing false witness against me? Firstly, remember that the Walpoles as a family are notoriously mentally unstable: they have become so through generations of mismarriage, drug-taking, miscegenation and eccentric social mobility. Rest assured that a girl who goes to the best school in the country is more likely to end up with a Rastafarian or a truck driver than a stockbroker or a prince. Secondly, although Marigold maintained that what kept the family together was their adoration of Lady Hester and their reverence for the Christmas ritual, it seemed just as likely to me that all were simply hoping to be first in line for a legacy. Or is this too cynical of me? I hate to be thought cynical, when all I am is realistic.

What did I do to annoy so much? Very little, by my standards, but what I did I made sure was noticeable. Shown to an attic room with three makeshift truckle beds in it, with twigs and soot tumbling down into the empty fireplace every time the door slammed – the chimneys were not even netted against the rooks – I explained that I would have insomnia if I did not have a bedroom to myself, and that I needed sheets and blankets, not a duvet, and after much apology and discussion ended up sleeping in Marigold's room, and her on the sofa under the Christmas tree, so that Seb was unable to join her that night – I am sure that had been their plan – and the children did not get their normal sneak 2.00 a.m. preview of the presents. People should not invite guests if they cannot house them adequately.

Earlier I'd found a gold dress in Marigold's wardrobe and put it on. Well, she offered.
'Isn't that one too tight?' she asked. 'The navy would be more you.'
'Oh no,' I said. It was tight, of course, and incredibly vulgar too, but what does an Outsider know or care? I draped myself round Seb once or twice and pole-danced round a pillar for his entertainment. Then I let him kiss me long and hard under the mistletoe, while everyone watched. Marigold fled from the room weeping and flinging her engagement ring on the floor. People who put up pagan mistletoe at a Christian ceremony must expect orgiastic behaviour.

Before going to bed I used the machines in the utility room to launder the damp towels I had found on the floor of Marigold's bathroom. I had searched the linen cupboard for fresh ones but found none; what else could I do? The washing machine was faulty – there was no warning note to say so: is one meant to read the mind of machines? – and overflowed and caused some kind of electrical havoc to the kitchen electrics, so the deep freeze and the fridges cut out. This was not discovered until well into the next day. People who stuff turkeys with packets of frozen pork and herbs deserve what they get, and must risk E-coli if the power goes off.

* * *

On Christmas morning, leaving Seb in the bed, I rose early when only small hysterical children were about, and restrained the ones who assaulted me too violently, or made me sticky, and escorted them by ear to where their parents slept in their drunken stupors, and asked them to take charge of their offspring. People should not have children if they do not have the moral wherewithal to control them.

I spent the morning assuring enquirers that Seb was nothing worth Marigold having, and in all probability, was not her cousin but her half-brother, and preserving the Christmas presents from the ravages of the children, standing up to their wails and howls. Then came the adult giving ceremony. The custom was for every adult Walpole to bring what they called a tree present, a gift acceptable to all ages and genders, to the value of £15, to place it under the Christmas tree, and when the time came to take another out for themselves. Thus everyone came with a gift and left with a gift. It was a system fraught with dangers: simply by taking one out and not putting one in, I caused mayhem. The nun Cecilia, being slowest on her feet, was left without a gift and made a terrible fuss.

Lunch did not happen until three. Some thirty people sat in a triangle formed by three trestle tables. The table setting, I must admit, was pretty enough, and decorated with Christmas crackers and the heavy family silver had been taken out of storage. But thirty! How this family bred and bred! I had been seated at the jutting end of one of the tables, as befitted the Outsider. This did not improve my mood. I declared myself to be a vegetarian just as the three turkeys – one at each side of the triangle – were being carved. People who have thirty to a meal must surely expect a certain proportion of them to be vegetarians. I mentioned the deep freeze débâcle and a number of the guests converted to vegetarianism there and then – all of these, I noticed, had married into the Walpole Delingros; those born as family were hardier.

* * *

Next to me was Cecilia, rendered incontinent by the morning's upsets. When all were finally served I enquired of everyone what the strange smell could be. A faulty drain, perhaps? Or one of them? A few rose to their feet and the children, seeing the adults rise, found the excuse to leave their chairs and run hither and thither, sniffing around under the table, overexciting the dogs, and pulling crackers out of turn. People should look after the elderly properly and make sure they do not drink too much or lose control of their bladders.

It was at this point that Lady Hester Delingro rose to her feet and, pointing across the festive triangle at me, arm fully extended, asked me to leave her table since it was clearly so unsatisfactory to me. I too rose to my feet.
'Thank you for making me your Outsider,' I said, 'at the annual feast of the Walpole Delingros. I would hate to be an Insider.' Which was no more than the truth. Lady Hester's noble horseface contorted, reddened and went into spasms. She grabbed her heart; her hand fell away, she fell dead into her plate. It was over in five seconds. She can hardly have suffered. Rage and pain get confused. Nevertheless, it was a shock. Silence fell. Even the little children returned to their seats and sat silently.

And then something to me even more shocking occurred. A group of male Walpole Delingros carried off the body to the next room, without so much as checking for a pulse, and stretched it out on the sofa under the Christmas tree. They closed the door, returned to the table, and behaved as if the death had not occurred. Lady Hester's plate was removed, her daughter, Lady Rowan, Marigold's mother, filled her chair. Everyone moved up one, even Cecilia, leaving me isolated, but with one damp, smelly chair next to me.

'Shouldn't someone call a doctor, an ambulance?' I asked. No-one replied. 'You can't just eat Christmas pudding as if nothing had happened.'

* * *

But they could: curtains were drawn, lights put out, heated brandy poured over hot Christmas puddings to be set ablaze and carried in with due ceremony. I was offered none. It was as if I had ceased to exist. Only after coffee had been made and served and crackers pulled – those the children had left – and the dreadful jokes been read out and scorned, and the ritual been declared complete, were the doctor, the ambulance and the police called.

And that, I swear, is what happened. Even if thirty, not twenty, Walpole Delingros allege that the death happened after dinner, and that I took Lady Hester's head and deliberately banged it into the edge of the marble fireplace during the course of an argument about the cause of smoking fireplaces, so she fell dead, suffering a cardiac infarction on the way down, I cannot help it. This was not what happened. If there is, as you say, a nasty dent on the side of Lady Hester's head why then one of the family did it while she lay dead on the sofa, with a blunt instrument, the better to incriminate me. The Walpole Delingros are famous for sticking together, and I would be the first to admit I got up one or two people's noses, even to the extent of their feeling that prison hereafter would be the best place for me. And others might feel that by being so rude to Lady Hester I had caused her death, and natural justice should prevail. It is not the first time people have borne false witness against me. Or again, perhaps one of their number, finding the old lady was still just about alive, and simply wanting to inherit, finished her off and the others closed ranks and decided to get me, in passing? Or is that too cynical a view of human nature?

It won't work, of course, one of the children must surely blab, or perhaps Marigold will remember she is my friend. I believe she is back with Seb. In the meantime, while I wait for my mother's call, I am happy enough in this cell. But perhaps you could arrange to have *The Times* sent in, so I can do the crossword? And if you could ask the Governor, or whoever he is, to stop people playing their radios and TVs so loud? Or at any rate to tune them to the same station? I am feeling a little insecure. I am accustomed to having enemies – the honest and righteous always are – but it was my bad judgement to make so many, in one place, and in that particular season. It is never safe to disturb the ritual, however much fun it may be.

2001

Happy Yuletide Schiphol

And we'd been so clever. We would catch the 15.40 from Schipol on the 24th, and be back in Bristol by 17.55. We'd pick up a hire car and be down the M5 to Okehampton in good time for Christmas Eve dinner with goose, mashed potatoes, red cabbage and a fine Rhone wine. Christmas dinner the next day would be turkey, roast potatoes, sprouts, cranberry sauce and good claret. My daughter and her husband live in Devon and are traditionalists. Chris and I tend to go for salad and a slice of quiche, but that's the way it goes, these days. You go forward into a quicker, lighter future, and the children hop off backwards into the past, staring at you and muttering *weird*. But we love to see our daughter, and we have a new grandchild, and our son and his new fiancée would be joining us.

We'd finished work in Amsterdam and had a host of presents already wrapped, which we'd pack into the suitcase. Yes, very clever. Well organised. My husband does all that. It's his thing, dates and timetables and being at the right place at the right time, and I trot along behind. He does consultancy work for a Dutch property company: I'm a writer: I fit in.

Too clever by half, of course. We'd reckoned without Christmas, or at any rate Yuletide. We'd reckoned without the waywardness of humanity. We had not taken into account the seasonal urgency which sometimes catches us up like a tide, so we move as others do, in a group, and do what we must, not what reason says. Princess Diana's funeral, trolley rage at the supermarket just before the bank holiday. Just the same when Thor cracked his thunder over Northern skies, and everyone jumped the same way at his command. Rituals must be observed. They have their own imperative.

Amsterdam is far enough North to still be partly the land of the Nordic Gods, and Christmas is still Yuletide, their mid-winter festival. I have always suspected Schiphol Airport to be Thor's own place, all that cracking of the skies, the low thunder of aircraft breaking through the clouds, the tremble of the ground as the big jets land. Thor likes it; he hangs around. This year Christmas Day falls on a Thursday, (donderdag in Dutch) Thor's day: all the more likely for him to put in an appearance. When the God roars out over the flat damp land that it's time to shut the doors and bring out the drink, people do as he commands, and who cares what the timetables say. They go home, as instructed.

We got early to the airport and checked in the baggage. We'd allowed ourselves twenty minutes to look round the Rijksmuseum annexe situated between Piers E and F before going to the gate. We like to do that. There is something refreshing, like cool clear water on a hot day, about looking at paintings in an airport. It restores you to sanity. There's currently an exhibition of Rembrandt prints, which Chris particularly wanted to catch before it closed on January 3rd. But my attention was caught by a farmyard painting by Melchior d'Hondecoeter, 1636-1695. Two vain and disdainful peacocks look down their nose at a little pretty silly hen with four fluffy chicks, while a great gobbling turkey, stupid and amazed, looks on. I wondered which of them was most like me.

I asked Chris, hoping, I suppose, for some kind of compliment or reassurance, but instead of answering he said 'We can't be too long here. We don't want to miss our flight. Shall we go?' Now I can't bear to be hurried, Chris can't bear to be late. And I was feeling tetchy and tired: we'd been shopping and wrapping all morning. 'Don't panic.' I said, meanly. 'You are so neurotic about time. They have our luggage, they can't go without us.' And for once I didn't relieve him of his anxiety and turn to go, but lingered, and let him fret. It is the kind of cruelty even the fondest couple sometimes practice on one another. Putting the other in the wrong, creating a double bind, pressing their buttons: it may fall short of an outright row, but it verges on it.

The elegant girl from the Rijksmuseum shop, the only member of staff left on the premises apparently still resistant to the Gods, was beginning to hover and look at her watch. That irritated me too. I am a customer: I have my rights. It was only ten past three: there was a full five minutes before the place was due to close for the six days of the Christmas holiday. I was looking at Art. I shouldn't be hurried.

It was almost twenty past three by the time we left and the poor thing could hiss the doors shut behind us. She stalked past us as we left, long legged: she carried crimson and gold parcels, prettily tied with Rijkmuseum ribbon. She was one of the peacocks, disdainful.

In the space of fifteen minutes Schiphol had stopped being a busy, noisy, excited place and become a lonely expanse of empty walkways. Shops had closed, passengers gone their ways. Lights were muted. Even the all-pervasive smell of coffee was fading. *Yuletide!* said the notices, *Happy Christmas! Bon*

Noel, but here and there New Year Sale signs had gone up. The passport booth was closed and empty: barriers were up. We had to find another one, and the Information desk was closed. Chris began to run. The moving walkway slowed and stopped while we were on it. The girlish warning voice dropped a tone and was silent. I ran too. We loped down a flight of steps – the escalator had stopped – to gate C4, where our flight was closing. Even as we ran we heard a gate change. Now it was Gate C6. We ran some more. And then we sat, because when we got there, there was no urgency, the flight was delayed. One minute we were racing: the next we were staring into space. Airports are like that. And we sat, and sat and sat.

'We could have taken our time,' said Chris. He is very good. He could have said earlier, as we ran 'told you so.' But he didn't. There were six of us. One little old lady who had been drinking, one shabby business man who looked as if he had been up all night, and a young engaged couple. She was plump and blonde and fidgety and reminded me of the busy little hen in the painting. He was the turkey, cross and awkward, with a nose too big and a chin too small. But he loved her. He kept trying to hold her hand but she'd push it away. She was upset. There were tears in her eyes. I don't know what they had quarrelled about but it seemed quite bad. Two hours passed.

Pretty soon I had tears in my eyes too. The flight had been cancelled. There had been a technical fault. Thor was punishing me. I had been mean to Chris: I had been mean to the girl in the shop. I had not heeded the clarion call to the midwinter ritual. The last flights to Heathrow had gone. There was no way we could leave Schiphol that night. They were running a skeleton service. They would put us up in the airport hotel. They apologised for the inconvenience caused. We would be compensated. No, baggage could not be returned. There had been an industrial dispute, and the baggage handlers had gone home. There was a strange underwater feeling to everything. I could hear Schiphol breathing, or was it the air conditioning in the great echoey empty halls. In and out, very slowly. Thor's breathe. Airline staff were polite, but looked at their watches. Everyone wanted to be off. Christmas. Yuletide. Donderdag coming.

We were all silent. 'A Fokker 70,' said the business man, looking out the window, as it taxied away, cute and ansty, as if the brand made a difference. There was a crack of thunder from outside and lightning – only one second between the two – but no rain. 'Nice little aircraft,' he observed. I think he was stunned. So was I. 'Cityhopper. Doesn't usually go wrong.'

But that was no comfort to us. The blonde girl, whose name was Penny, threw the engagement ring across the floor. It skittered and bounced. The boy, whose name was Darrell, set his jaw and didn't go after it. 'That's it,' Penny said. 'That's it,' 'Yes it is,' he said. 'Goodbye you and goodbye Christmas.'

It seemed a great pity to me, the way the whole world had to suffer from the weight of my sin. The ring glittered under a plastic chair. I thought it was diamond. The old lady said it was all right by her, she didn't like Christmas anyway. I longed to be at home in bed.

They bussed us to the airport hotel. The rain broke as we stood outside waiting for it to arrive. We were soaked. Thor was letting me know who ran things round here. I had no face cream: Chris had no sleeping pills. The young couple still weren't talking. I was distressed for them. It seemed such a waste of life. They'd never find anyone better than the other. I told Chris so. He said it was projection, personally he was distressed for us. The hotel was crowded. Industrial dispute, fog and storm had wreaked havoc with flights. They gave us tickets so we could be called in order to the reception desk. A girl from the airline came over and said they would try to get us out first thing the next morning. Christmas Day. She was the other peacock from the painting, disdainful. They go round in pairs.

'Now I must be off,' she said. 'In Holland we take Christmas Eve seriously.'

We made phone calls. We said don't expect us tonight, we'd been delayed, we'd be in touch when we knew more. There were plates of free food in the bar, but I wasn't hungry, not even for little marzipan cakes with windmills imprinted on the chocolate. Chris gnawed a chicken leg. Our numbers came up. There was one room left, a double: they gave it to Chris and me. Everyone else would have to sleep in armchairs and sofas in the lobby. I said to Chris, 'Please can we give the room to them,' meaning the young couple, and he looked at them and he looked at me and said 'Okay.' He is not a man of many words. They went upstairs, not touching. We slept and partly slept and outside the storm died down.

In the morning everyone said 'Happy Christmas,' to each other, and there was big notice up with an arrow saying 'Yuletide breakfast this way,' and there was, too. Fresh bread and good coffee and fine eggs. The young couple came down from their bedroom. They had made it up. They leant into each other and smiled soppily at everyone. Chris looked in his pocket and handed them the ring. He had actually stopped to pick it up. 'I kept it safely,' he said. 'I'd have given it to Oxfam.'

The young couple leant into each other in the Cityhopper, the Fokker 70, all the way home. An oil seal had been mended. We had missed Christmas Eve goose and the hire car depot was closed, but my son-in-law would pick us up and we'd be in time for Christmas lunch. We even had the presents with us.

'Look at you!' said Chris, as we disembarked into brilliant morning sun. Thor doesn't have much pull down here in the old West Country. 'You're even smarter than a peacock, nicer than a mother hen, and not one bit like the turkey,' and the world seemed pretty ideal to me.

2003

Why Did She Do That?

Sooner or later all roads lead to Schiphol Airport, if only for an hour or so, on the way from here to there, in transit. It is a vast place. Today we perched on our high stools at the oyster bar where Zones C and D meet. My husband had a new-season herring and a glass of beer, and I had a brown shrimp sandwich and a modest glass of white wine. After that we planned to do our usual thing and go to the art exhibition in the new Schiphol extension of the Rijksmuseum, situated where Zone E meets Zone F. The exhibits change every month or so, and there is always some new skating scene, some famous soldier on a horse, some soothing Dutch interior to be seen, some long dead artist's glimpse of the love and trust that exists within families, or between mankind and nature. Thus fortified, we would fly on to Oslo, or Copenhagen, or on occasion further afield, along those curving, separating lines on the KLM map – Bombay, Los Angeles, Rio de Janeiro, Perth, wherever. And if you are lucky, on the return journey the Rijksmuseum exhibits will have been changed, and there will be yet more to see. That is, of course, if delays and security checks allow you the time you expect to have to spare in that strange no-man's land called Transit.

Lucky, I say, but thinking about it I am not sure. The paintings in the Rijksmuseum pull you out of the trance which sensible people enter while travelling, checking out from real life the moment they step into the airport, coming back to full consciousness only when once more entering their front door. The technical name for the state is de-realisation, or dissociative disorder: too much of it, they say, and you can actually shrink your hippocampus – that part of the brain from which the emotions fan like airline flight paths on the map – never to recover. It might be wiser just to stare at the departure board like anyone else. But I am with my husband, a rare bird who has never in his life experienced a dissociative state, and is enjoying his herring, and I am emerging from mine in preparation for the Rijksmuseum, and am even vaguely wondering whether I am drinking Chardonnay or Chablis, when there is a sudden commotion amongst the throng of passengers.

The herring stall is by a jeweller's booth, where today there are diamonds on special offer. '*The new multi-faceted computer cut*' – whatever that might be: presumably habitual buyers of diamonds know. But can there be so many of them as the existence of this shop suggests? So many enthusiastic or remorseful husbands or lovers around, who want to buy peace at any price, and stop off to purchase these tokens of respect and adoration? Though I daresay these days travelling women buy diamonds for themselves.

Next to the diamond boutique is a shop selling luggage, and a booth offering amaryllis bulbs at ten euros for two. As a point-of- sale feature I see they're using a reproduction of that wonderful early Mondrian painting you can see in the Museum of Modern Art in New York. '*Red Amaryllis with blue background*.' I bet that cost them a bit. It's midday by now and comparatively quiet in Schiphol: few customers and lots of staff, like a church when they congregation has left after a big service and the clerics are busy snuffing out candles and changing altar cloths. How do these places ever make a living? It defeats me.

A woman and her husband walk past us in the direction of departure gates C5-C57. They are in their forties, I suppose. I notice her because she walks just a little behind him and I tend to do the same, whenever I am with a man. It is a habit which annoys husbands, suggesting as it does too much dependency, too little togetherness, but in a crowded place it seems to me practical. You don't have to cut a swathe through potentially hostile crowds, and passage can be effected in single file. Couples who face the world side by side, I am prepared to argue, assert coupledom at the expense of efficiency. And it must be remembered that Jacob sent his womenfolk to walk before him when angry neighbours obliged him to return to the family farm – so that the wrath of his brother Esau would fall first upon the wives, and not upon him. As it happened Esau wasn't in the least angry about the business of the potage and was simply glad to see his long lost brother again. But lagging behind is always safest, in a world scattered with landmines, real and metaphorical. This woman seemed well aware of their existence.

I was hard put to it to decide their nationality; probably British, certainly Northern European. They had a troubled air, as if worried by too much debt and too little time ever to do quite what they wanted to do, always grasping for something out of reach, disappointed by the world, not as young as they'd like to be, or as rich as they deserved to be. I blame the Calvinists and the work ethic: people from the warmer South have easier ways, less conscience and more generous hearts. Something at any rate was wrong. The flight had been delayed, or it was the wrong flight, or they didn't really want to go where they were going, or they didn't want to go together, or she was thinking of her lover or he of his mistress. But I didn't expect what was to happen next.

She was I suppose in her mid-forties: a respectable, rather pudding-faced, high-complexioned, slightly overweight, stolid blonde with good legs and expensive hair piled up untidily in a bun. She was trying too hard. Her skirt was too tight and her heels too high and slim for comfortable travel. She wore a pastel pink suit with large gold buttons. The jacket stretched a little over a middle-aged bosom: that is to day it was no longer perky but bulged rather at the edges. She carried a large shiny black plastic bag. The husband who walked before looked like a not very successful business man: he wore jeans, a tie and a leather jacket, not High Street, but not Armani either, and you felt he would be happier in a suit. His face was set in an expression of dissatisfaction, his hair was thinning: he had the air of one beset by responsibilities and the follies of others. There was no doubt in my mind but that they were married. How does one always know this? We will leave that as a rhetorical question: it being parried only with another, 'why else would they be together?' and the import of that exchange is too sad to contemplate.

But I thought of that tender 1641 Van Dyck painting of the newly married pair, William Prince of Orange, aged fifteen, and Mary, Princess Royal of England, aged ten, and took comfort. The weight of the world is upon the young pair, and all the troubles of state and domesticity, and they are brave and beautiful in the face of it. And I sipped my Chardonnay, or Chablis, and watched the couple walk by, and wondered about their lives. They were on their way, perhaps, to visit a first grandchild and had never approved of the marriage in the first place: or to visit her parents, whom he had never liked. Something like that.

And then one moment she is walking beside him – well, a little behind him, as I say – and he says something and she suddenly falls on her knees before him: it is quite a movement: she seems to shoot out from behind him to arrive at floor level, twisting to face him. It is the same movement you see in the Pinter play, *Homecoming*, I think it is, the one in which the man proposes to the woman, shooting right across the stage on his knees to entreat her to be his.

A few years back, when Harold Pinter was playing the part himself at the Almeida theatre, he lamented that his knees were no longer up to it. He was sixty. It was at one of those pre-performance meet-the-author sessions. I proposed a solution, namely, that he could alter the part to suit his knees. Just write out the proposal. It was after all his play. Pinter was horrified. The lines were sacrosanct, they had entered into the canon, were no longer Pinter's to change. They dwelt with other scared texts in some dissociated state of their own: stage directions which had to be served and suffered for, by the writer too. I really admired that.

Picture the scene that day at Schipol. Now the woman wails aloud like an animal, a human bereft, a cow that has lost its calf, hands clasped towards her husband in entreaty; her hair toppled around her face, her red lip-sticked mouth smeary and gaping wide, her back teeth dark with old fashioned fillings. Her heels stick out oddly at the end of lean shins, as if someone had broken her bones, but people's legs do look like that sometimes when they kneel at the Communion rail. Her skirt is rucked up, too tight and short for this sudden, passionate, noisy activity. She is not like a virgin, beautiful in prayer; she is a fat middle aged woman with thin legs having a mad fit. She is praying to him, beseeching him, *have mercy, Lord, have mercy.*

At the Oyster Bar glasses pause mid air; people all around pause in their transit and look to see what's going on. The husband takes a pace or two back, embarrassed and bewildered, and stares at the wife. He is trying to look as if she is nothing to do with him. At least he does not disappear into the crowds. Perhaps she has his passport.

Something stranger still happens. Women staff come out of the shops, first hesitantly, then with more deliberation, towards the source of the noise. There are two young girls with bare midriffs, but most are brisk and elegant older women, in crisp white shirts and black skirts and sensible shoes. They cluster round the wife, they help her to her feet, they brush her down and soothe her, soothing, clucking, sympathising. She stops the wailing: she looks round their kindly, consoling faces. She feels better. She manages a tremulous smile.

An armed policeman approaches: he is dismissed by this Greek chorus of female nurturers with a look, a dismissive flick of a hand, a derisive finger, and he melts away. It occurs to me that the Nurturers, ever more difficult to sight than the Norns, who weave the entrails of Nordic heroes to decide their destiny, or those Mediterranean Furies, who drive us mad with guilt – have actually put in an appearance at Schiphol. Like the Lover at the Gate, unseen until the hour of need, who fills up the bed when the husband departs, these benign creatures turn up in an emergency, so long as it is dire enough.

I have always suspected they existed, though unsung in fable, but I had never sighted them until now. And in an airport! I am privileged.

Then, as if this was her destined fate, and this was their purpose, the Nurturers propel her towards her waiting husband. She does not resist. She is tentative and apologetic in demeanour. The expression on his face does not change – '*I am a man much set about by troubles, bravely enduring.*' The nurturers turn back into shop assistants and disappear behind their counters. The couple walk on as if nothing had happened, towards Zone C, she still just a little behind him. She pushes her hair back into its proper shape, and wobbles on her heels. She may have hurt her knees.

Back at the oyster bar things return to normal. Eating and drinking continue. The crowds close behind them. Schiphol flows on. Lunchtime is approaching: Noise levels are increasing.

'Why did she do that?' my husband asks, bewildered. 'Is she mad?'
'He may well have driven her mad,' I say, 'but she will not have got there on her own.' And as we make our way to the Rijksmuseum I tell him how I imagine the day has gone for the blonde woman, and how she has been driven to distraction, to the point of falling upon her knees in a public place and wailing, imploring him to stop, just stop, her state of desperation so extreme that she managed to summon the Nurturers. What I tell him is, of course, only one of a dozen possible scenarios.

'Marcelle,' he said to her this morning –we will call her

Marcelle, she looked like a Marcelle, and we will call him Joseph, perhaps in the spirit of mild irony: Joseph, after all, stood steadily stood by Mary in the hour of her need: he did not take a step back and try to disown her when she embarrassed him so. 'Marcelle, did you remember to call Sylvia about Alec last night?' Marcelle is busy packing, in a suitcase not quite big enough for all her needs. They are up early. They have a flight to catch.

Marcelle and Joseph will live in a detached house with its own thick carpets and good reproduction furniture and a designer kitchen. He will have one married daughter by an earlier marriage and they will have two teenage children between them, and a neat garden, in which anything unruly will have been cut down to size. She will use bark chippings, that ugly stuff, to keep the weeds down. *Joseph: Ugly, what do you mean, ugly? Well, you should know. But I am not made of money: we cannot afford a gardener more than once a week, for God's sake. Just get him to use bark.*' Once long ago, Marcelle dreamed of romance and roses round a cottage door: and once indeed Joseph picked a single cherry in an orchard and brought it to her. That was when she was first pregnant with Alec and Joseph was emotional about it. She kept the pip for ages, and even tried to make it sprout by putting it in water. Then she would have a whole little tree covered with cherries, but nothing happened except that the pip just lay there and the water grew cloudy and sour and she had to throw it out. All that was left was a ring round the glass which no amount of scouring would remove. Still, even that was a consolation. A memento of something good.

She would really like another suitcase especially for her cosmetics, but Joseph doesn't like heaving cases about. Who

does? Jars are heavy and bulky: creams for the eyes and the neck and the lips and the bust, each one magically different, are probably interchangeable, but she is nervous of being without a single one of them. She can't make up her mind. She packs and re-packs: she slips jars into her shoes to save space, but the weight is unavoidable. *Joseph*: *'Couldn't you do without the gunk for just a couple of days and nights? It's not as if they seem to make any difference. You're over forty, nearly fifty. Surely the days when face creams would help have passed? Take them to the Charity Shop and be rid of them.'* As if charity shops took half empty jars of cream, however expensive. What do men know?
'I called but there was no answer,' says Marcelle. She lies.

'Did you leave a message on Sylvia's answer phone?' asks Joseph. He has already packed. It takes him five minutes. He is decisive. *Joseph: 'One of us has to be.'* Now he is brushing his teeth. She cooked him his breakfast but had none herself. He likes a good breakfast; she is never hungry first thing in the morning. Joseph has good teeth: Marcelle spends a lot of time at the dentist. *Joseph: 'My mother made sure I had milk everyday. You really shouldn't let Alec and Carla drink those disgusting sweet drinks all the time. It's not as if you were passing on any particularly good dental genes – at least from your side.'* But how do you stop teenagers from eating and drinking exactly what they want? It wasn't as if Joseph was around all that much at meal times to train them to do anything at all, let alone sit down when they ate and drank.

'I couldn't,' says Marcelle. 'It wasn't switched on.'
'That's strange,' says Joseph. 'Sylvia is usually so efficient.' Sylvia gets called 'Sylvia' a lot, even when 'she' would be more normal. Marcelle notices these little things. According to

Joseph, Sylvia is elegant, Sylvia is intelligent, Sylvia has perfect teeth, what a good dress sense Sylvia has. And so slim! Such a pretty figure. Sylvia is like a sister to Joseph, and tells everyone so, though of course they are no blood relation. Sylvia has twin girls of fifteen: very smart and well behaved and no trouble at all. *Joseph: 'Sylvia knows how to bring up children.'* The only thing wrong with Sylvia is her husband Earle. Joseph thinks Earle is something of a slob, not worthy of Sylvia. Earle and Sylvia are Joseph and Marcelle's best friends, and their children like to spend time together. But over the last five years Earle has crept up the promotion ladder and Joseph has stuck on a certain rung while others clamber up over him.

The fact is, Marcelle does not want to call Sylvia. It was late; she was tired, now thank God it is too early. Seven years ago Joseph spent a night with Sylvia in an hotel, at a sales conference. He had come home in the morning – smelling of Sylvia's scent (*Joseph: 'Why do you never wear scent any more, Marcelle?' Marcelle: 'Because I am too busy. Because I never remember to put any on. It made the babies sneeze and I got out of the habit'*) and had confessed and apologised and she and Sylvia had talked it out, and they had agreed to forget the incident, which had been, well, yes, both unfortunate and unexpected. *Joseph: 'I am so sorry, Marcelle. It should not have happened. But she is such a honey, such a sweet dear, you know how much you like her, and she is having such a hard time with Earle. I can only conclude somebody put something in the drink or it would never have happened. It meant nothing: just a silly physical thing. And she is your friend. I feel much better now I've told you.'* Yes, but in an hotel? A night? Full sex? Behind the filing cabinets would have been more understandable. *Sylvia: 'I am so, so sorry, Marcelle, I would never do anything to hurt you. I will always be open with you. It was a silly drunken thing – someone must have put something in the office drink. Completely out of character and it will never happen again. We both have our marriages and our children to think about, so shall we both just say "closure" and forgive and forget?'* So Marcelle had. Or tried to.

Sylvia was a psychotherapist who worked in the Human Resources Department of the haulage business where Joseph worked as an accountant. Earle was now director of acquisitions at the same firm and earned far more than Joseph, and had an office to himself and a good carpet. He was away from home quite a lot, visiting subsidiary companies abroad. Sylvia was brave about his absences but sometimes she would turn up at Marcelle's door at the weekend with red eyes and talk about nothing in particular and Marcelle felt for her. And Marcelle could see that bedding Sylvia had been a triumph for Joseph: a feather in his cap, so great an event it was now what sustained him in life. '*I was the one who bedded Sylvia, Earle's wife, at the office party seven years ago.*'

But Marcelle still did not want to call Sylvia 'about Alec.' Alec had been found taking drugs in school and was in danger of expulsion. Joseph reckoned that Sylvia could help with advice and wisdom, she, after all, being so good with young people. The twins would never take drugs, or be anorexic, like Carla. They were calm and orderly and dull.

'I'll call her when we get back from Copenhagen,' Marcelle says to Joseph, looking up from the parade of the jars: different makes, different shapes: some gold topped, some white, some silvery, all enticing. They are going to visit the new baby, and will only be staying two days. She is glad it is not longer. Her stepdaughter has always been a bundle of resentments, at the best of times. Now she will be sleepless, and ordering Marcelle about as if she were the maid. *Joseph: 'What can you expect? You stole me from her. Now you have to put up with it.'* It will not be an easy trip. Joseph does not like the new husband.

'That's all very well,' says Joseph, 'but you promised me you'd call her and now you haven't. I really don't understand you.'

'I expect it will have blown over by the time we get back,' says Marcelle with unusual firmness. 'Schools always over-react. And I really I don't see why Sylvia needs to know every detail of our business.'

'She's a good friend to you,' says Joseph. 'Better than you'll ever know.' What does he mean by that? Has something else happened between Joseph and Sylvia? Has he tried to restart the flirtation and she refused, for Marcelle's sake? Or is that just what Joseph wants Marcelle to think, because he's annoyed? She gives up on the throat cream and then thinks of Sylvia's smooth and perfect neck, and re-packs it. Perhaps she can do without the eye cream? Sylvia is seven years younger than Marcelle. Sylvia has beautiful clear bright eyes, widely spaced and good cheek bones. Flesh seems somehow to have shrouded Marcelle's. She feels suddenly hungry and goes to the kitchen to have a cup of coffee and a piece of toast. Joseph follows her into the kitchen.

'Sylvia says the way to keep slim is never to eat carbohydrates before breakfast,' he observes. 'And I don't think this matter of Alec is simply going to melt away, however much you hope it will. You have such a problem with reality! I don't like to say this of Alec but he does have a family history of criminality. And remember the time when he was eight and you found money missing from your purse? I don't think you dealt with that properly: Sylvia said the whole thing should have been talked through, not just swept under the carpet. Now this drugs business. Where has the boy been getting the money?'

Marcelle's father, a respectable builder, had served a four months sentence in prison for petty theft, shortly after Joseph and Marcelle were married. He had taken a lathe home – he said by accident, but the client had reported it to the police and the magistrate – no doubt in the middle of his own building work – had seen it as a gross breach of trust. Marcelle always had an uneasy suspicion that if her father had turned into a jailbird before the marriage, not after, the wedding would never have taken place. Somehow the feeling was always there that Marcelle was lucky to have caught him – a surgeon's son, well educated, good-looking, an accountant with a degree in mathematics, and she Marcelle, really, was just anyone, out of nowhere. Joseph's family photographs were in real silver frames; Marcelle's were in plastic.

She saw herself with a terrible clarity. Good legs and bosom, but with a tendency to put on weight, no conversation, no dress sense, no brains and no qualifications, a too shrill speaking voice and a vulgar laugh. And both children took after her, not him. They were a disappointment to Joseph. If he'd married someone like Sylvia – one of whose sisters was now the wife of a peer of the realm, albeit non-hereditary – he would have had children as perfect as the twins. Though Earle had once said something really nice, when they were round to dinner. *Earle: 'Say what you like about those children of yours, Marcelle, they're never dull. They're like you. A pleasure to be with.'* She was serving a chocolate mousse at the time. Sylvia never served sweets, only cheese. She didn't believe in sugar. Sylvia had made quite a face when Earle said that to Marcelle and looked disdainfully at the mousse and tried to smirk at Joseph, but Joseph for once took no notice. He even seemed pleased at what Earle had said, as if he too were being complimented. Men were strange: they were pack animals, no doubt about it, and very aware of who was top dog. Sometimes she was surprised that Joseph never actually offered her to Earle, in recompense for the office party incident, just to even things out. She wouldn't have minded too much if he had: she liked Earle. But Sylvia would have seen it as compulsive-obsessional behaviour and liked it not one bit.

She knows Joseph loves her, and she certainly loves him: she feels for him acutely as the world looks by him and over him: she wants to protect him. She knows why he is trying to upset and disturb her: there was a letter in the post recently talking about his pension and the assumption is that he had reached the ceiling his career, and will never earn more than he does now. They will never have a swimming pool like Earle and Sylvia. They will have each other, of course, but that in itself is a disappointment for Joseph. How can it not be? There are so many beautiful and brilliant women in the world that will never be his. She worries for Alec and Carla because Joseph cuts them down to size all the time, as he does her, and she knows that children grow into their parents' plan for them, and wishes that he would just sometimes *pretend* to love and admire them more. It would help them.

'I hope you're going to change before we leave?' he asks. She is wearing black trousers, and a dark blue cashmere sweater, soft and comfortable but rather over washed.

'I wasn't going to,' she says.

'Why don't you wear that nice pink thing? Sylvia always says how much it suits you.'

She changes into the pink suit, which is too tight for her and makes her look vast. She has not worn it for a few months. She can't admit it's unwearable, she will only get a lecture on Sylvia and carbohydrates. She will just have to hope he doesn't notice. She goes back into the kitchen. He looks her up and down and says nothing. He is not looking forward to the trip, either. His son-in-law is a man Joseph does not like or respect. He is a small time Danish architect who came to Marcelle and Joseph's house to discuss plans for a conservatory, in the days when they could have afforded one. The plans came to nothing but he went away with the daughter. *Joseph: 'Marcelle, I can't forgive you for this! When you knew they were seeing each other why didn't you stop them? It's a disaster.'* Now he has to go and see the baby, fruit of this union, and try and look pleased. He never saw himself as a grandfather.

Well I don't want to be a grandmother either, thinks Marcelle, with a sudden burst of inner petulance, two can play at this game, and it's your fault not mine that I am, since I married a man with a child, more fool me. She knows better than to say so: she takes a spoonful of conserve straight from the pot and puts it into her mouth without even bothering about the toast and Joseph gives a sharp intake of shocked breath and leaves the room.

Marcelle solves the beauty problem by slipping such small jars as she can into the case of Joseph's laptop. With any luck he won't notice the extra weight. She wears her highest heels: she knows they are impractical for travel but her morale needs boosting. Since the only good thing about her Joseph is prepared to admit at the moment is her legs, she will make the most of them. Sylvia may have the eyes and the cheekbones and the salary, but Marcelle has the legs.

They get to the airport in good time. Joseph cannot abide being in a rush and Marcelle has learned not to hold him up. She has to pay extra because her bag is so heavy. *Joseph (the week after the wedding). 'Now, about our finances. We will pay each proportionate to our earnings, and keep careful and accurate accounts. I will be paying the lion's share out of the joint account but that is right and proper: I am your husband. I am not complaining. Personal extras must come out of our separate accounts – by extras I mean jaunts to the cafe, your friends to lunch, parking fines, excess luggage, and petrol for unnecessary outings – that sort of thing.'* And Marcelle had agreed, without asking for clarification as to who decided on the interpretation of unnecessary. Her mother had told her at the time to get everything straight within the first week of marriage because if it wasn't done then it never would be. But that had been the week her father had gone to prison and her mother had been told she had cancer. She hadn't been concentrating.

On the Cityhopper flight to Schiphol Joseph said, 'I am disappointed you didn't get through to Sylvia. It's very unusual for her to leave the answer phone switched off. When we get to Amsterdam I'll call her on her mobile and you can talk to her then.'

'Did you bring the number with you?'

'It's on my mobile,' he pointed out.

'Well, it would be, wouldn't it,' she said. That was rash.

'I don't know what's the matter with you,' he said, looking at her with disdain. 'Next thing you'll be wanting to go through my numbers called, to check up on me and Sylvia. It really is sick, Marcelle. You're insanely jealous of your best friend, so you'd risk the future of your own son. And your mascara has gone odd. There are little lumps of it under your left eye. Why do women want to plaster their faces with that stuff? It makes them look worse, not better.'

She could have pointed out that Alec was his son too, and if he was so sure Sylvia would know how to deal with the situation he could always have called her himself. Or popped in to her office for a consultation as to how to conduct his family affairs. No doubt he did that all the time, anyway. But she said nothing. There was a strange kind of bubbling feeling inside her. Was this what blood boiling felt like? Her ears popped as the aircraft began to descend for the landing and she felt more normal again.

Joseph called Sylvia from Schiphol to check up on the status of her phone, and Sylvia reported that it was fine, as far as she knew. Perhaps Marcelle had dialled a wrong number. It was easy to do – they made the keys so small these days: they only suited the young. She'd be delighted to talk to Marcelle about Alec, when they got to Copenhagen, perhaps, and had a little more time. It might be, perhaps, that Marcelle was the troubled one, not Alec?

'Did you hear that, Marcelle?' asked Joseph. 'You might be the troubled one, not Alec. We have to think about that. Sylvia always has a fresh slant on things. I knew we ought to talk to her.'

Joseph and Marcelle make their way towards Gate B for the Copenhagen flight. After the brief good cheer of his conversation with Sylvia his mood was worsening.

'I wish you'd keep up, Marcelle. And why are you wearing those stupid shoes? And pastel pink? For travelling? The skirt's too short for someone your age and weight. You look absurd. The only gold buttons in this whole airport belong to you. Sometimes I think you do it on purpose.'

And that was the point at which Marcelle threw herself on the ground in front of him, on her knees, hands clasped like a supplicant, wailing; '*Stop it, stop it, stop it, come back to me, love of my life*,' so piercingly loud in her heart that the Nurturers heard and came to her rescue and returned her to him, and him to her. These things can happen beneath our very noses. I like to think that so shocked was he, so brought to his senses, he didn't say a single mean thing to Marcelle, or even mention Sylvia, for the rest of the visit. That he even picked up the baby – it was a girl – and smiled at it, and said 'You're a pretty girl, just like your grandmother. And you have her lovely smile.'

'So that's why she did it,' I said to my husband. 'He drove her mad. Thank you for asking.'
'It's obvious you can't resist a happy ending,' he said. 'I felt rather sorry for the poor husband. Dreadful when the wife makes a scene.'

By that time we were at the Rijksmuseum, but found it was closed, because they were changing the paintings.

2003

Christmas on Møn

He supposed that with time you could get used to the strangeness of things. His father didn't live in the same house as he did and after six years he was quite used to that. Having a father who lived in another country now seemed almost normal. His father suddenly having a new wife called Lone – what sort of name was that? – was still a little strange because he'd assumed men only had one wife. But apparently no: you could have any number so long as they were in sequence. He had wanted to go to Denmark and visit his father and the new Lone but his mother said no. He'd tried to argue but his mother cried so he stopped arguing. Now he had to get used to his mother being dead. People said things like 'passed on' or 'with the angels' but the fact was she was dead. Dead as a doornail. Not here. Nowhere else. There was time before and a time after and a clear dividing line, and you had to get used to being on the wrong side of the line. Well, he would, people did. After all he was quite old. He was eleven. He'd had since the summer holidays to get used to her being dead and gone and in a couple of days it would be Christmas.

'You'll have to get used to Christmases in another country,' his grandmother warned him. He had to go and live with his father and Lone in Copenhagen. He would have liked to have stayed with his grandmother and so would she, but a judge somewhere had said no, Neil was to live with his father, because Lone was going to have a baby and it would be a proper home. He'd only met his father a few times since he was small and could never think of anything to say to him when he did. But he expected it would be all right.

'It can't be all that different,' Neil said, and his grandmother said 'Oh yes, it can be.' There'd be no presents waiting when you woke up on Christmas day, Gran said, and no big, noisy, crowded dinner hours late because the turkey wasn't cooked, with mince pies so you didn't stay hungry, and friends and family pulling crackers and putting on silly paper hats.

When the clock struck one on a Christmas day in Denmark, his Gran said, all you would have to eat was cold herring on rye bread. She put some Mars bars in his suitcase so he'd be prepared. She loved him but Neil had the feeling she didn't like his father very much. Not that Danish clocks actually struck, his gran added, everything was too sleek and electronic. Well, Neil would do his best. He would get used to it. He was certainly better off than, say, Oliver Twist. He'd never gone hungry and his shoes didn't let in water.

While she was packing the Mars bars Gran found his Neolithic arrowhead tucked into one his shoes and said why on earth are you taking this old piece of stone?
'I just like it,' he said, not explaining that he had picked it up on a walk with his father and mother when he was five, and they'd taken it to a museum and the curator had said it was a lucky find and he was a clever boy, and it was actually very late, almost bronze age, and people had been living on that hill for thousands and thousands of years. He liked that thought. It made him feel part of something though there wasn't much left to be part of that he could see. But it was a kind of lucky charm.

Now the flint was in the suitcase in the back of the car, and he and Lone were on their way straight from the airport to an island where they had their country house. The island was called Møn, with a line through the middle of the o, unlike Lone. It was not easy to pronounce and Lone laughed when he tried. She was very fair all over and quite broad with large pale blue eyes, and a bump in her middle which was the new baby. He thought perhaps his mother had been right to hate her. Neil had worked out the number of miles from where he lived to Copenhagen – 693 – and begrudged every one of them, and now here they were driving and driving on and on in a stupid little eco-car with no power, further and further away from anything he'd ever known. Presently they came to the end of the land and a flat, flat sea and a long bridge which took them over to the island.

It occurred to Neil that the one thing he could never get used to was the landscape. It was wide and flat somehow smoothed out, and empty.

'You'll love the house,' this Lone said. 'It's right on the edge of the sea. My father built it. He's a famous architect. Your father is a famous architect too, but not as famous as my father.'

Neil smiled at her with his bright brave smile and said nothing.

And Lone looked sideways at Neil, and thought this is not what I meant at all. He was a good looking child with his father's square chin and bright eyes, but dark and gypsy-ish like his mother. And he had a shocked look, almost stunned, as if he had been hit, and a kind of fixed smile which made her uneasy. She wanted to do her best by the child of the man she loved, of course she did, but why Ben had gone to court to get custody she could not understand. Neil was a child, not some kind of unfinished building Ben was obliged to complete. It was very sad that his poor mother had died of cervical cancer, and so suddenly, but his grandmother had been willing to look after him; why couldn't Ben have left it at that? There was the new baby to consider. And within ten minutes of meeting the boy at the airport Ben's Blackberry had summoned him back to some emergency, and she, Lone, was left to undertake the long drive on her own. No, this was not what she had envisaged at all. Life with a stepson who rather clearly hated you. Life with a son – she'd had scans and knew – would be bad enough: she had so wanted a girl.

The next day was going to be busy. The house had to be decorated, food prepared for Christmas Eve, the presents for Neil and his six cousins wrapped – well, step-cousins, three boys from her elder sister, three girls from her younger. Neil was getting a bicycle. Lone thought it would be wise if they all had presents of equal value, but Ben had said no. This year Neil would get a special treat. Lone was tempted to say better to spend time and attention than money, but she didn't. Ben would have looked so shocked and hurt if she had.

When they got to the house, she asked Neil to help her unpack the car, but he said quite rudely no, he was going straight down to the sea before it got dark. She let him go, but it irked her and when he came back excited about a bit of old stone which he claimed was a Neolithic axe head she told him not to be silly and if he was determined to keep it to wash it before it made everything dirty.

When she showed him to his really beautiful room – the best spare bedroom all to himself, with the special Baby Elephant

Feet wallpaper – he asked where his television was and she told him there was no TV in the house but he could have the radio, he said 'What's the use of that. I don't understand Danish, and I never want to,' and closed the door behind him, with just the same hurt and shocked look Ben used to get his own way. She could hear him sobbing on his bed. She tried to lure him out with pate and rye bread, and prawns and mayonnaise but he said he'd rather starve. 'Starve then,' Lone said, and it was her turn to slam the door. Her turn to lie on her bed too, out of frustration and guilt mixed, and weep. She couldn't be sure whether she was more angry with Ben or with his son, or with herself for being pregnant.

The next day went rather better. Ben turned up all apologies – it really had been an emergency: a crane had toppled – and he and Neil went for a walk and came back with some more old stones, and Lone bit back remarks about dirt and mess. Later in the morning, while she prepared the meal and cooked the pork, they went to church and Neil came back saying he liked the paintings like cartoons on the walls but he didn't know the tunes of the hymns. The family arrived and Neil nagged until he was allowed to open his present early, which meant everyone else did too, so that quite spoiled the ritual timing of Christmas Eve. When finally he did get his bicycle he said it was stupid and he didn't know how to ride one anyway. The cousins were astonished and laughed at him but took him out into the crimson and yellow sunset and showed him how it was done. He learned quickly and within a couple of hours was doing wheelies in the lamplight with the best of them. His body language was like his father's, and Lone, watching while she stacked the dishwasher, decided that having a son wasn't necessarily the worst disaster that could happen to a woman.

But the next day, Christmas Day, friends and neighbours arrived and matters got worse. Neil refused to eat smorgasbord saying he wanted something hot, and though Lone piled little potatoes on his plate, with butter, he wouldn't eat a thing and said Danish Christmases were boring, there weren't even any crackers or paper hats. It was embarrassing for everyone.

Ben said 'if you want to go hungry that's fine, all the more for us,' and Neil went to his perfect room wearing his dirty outside boots and stomped about. Then someone saw the old stones on the mantelpiece: Lone had been wrong. They were indeed worked axe and arrow heads from thousands of years ago. So Lone went upstairs and apologised to Neil for being so mean, and Neil came down with his own arrowhead and showed it round and everyone congratulated him, and Ben said perhaps his son would grow up to be an archaeologist; Neil had what Ben called 'a natural talent: an observer's eye.' And once again Neil smiled, with his real smile, not the one that had been forced on him.

Lone felt a surge of affection for the boy and said she would bake mince pies for Boxing Day to make him feel at home. And with a jar of mincemeat – dried fruit and nuts with a dash of brandy: nothing to do with meat: just other countries, other customs – borrowed from an Anglophile neighbour, set about making them. Neil showed Lone how his mother decorated the pastry edges with the back of a fork, and that somehow eased things between them, now the mother had been mentioned.

Neil watched Lone work in silence for a little while, and then said, 'Once upon a time, two hundred thousand years back, there wasn't an English channel at all, just land all the way. I could have walked from here to home, if I'd wanted to. Seven hundred and fifty-three miles. Except there would have been wolves and tigers so it wouldn't have been wise. You can call me Nils if you like.'

At that moment the baby kicked and Lone wanted to sit down and Nils bought her a chair without being asked. 'Thank you Nils,' she said. She thought it was all going to be okay, after all.

2009

THE
TED
DREAMS
A NOVELLA
FAY WELDON
LOVE IS...
NEVER HAVING TO
STAY DEAD

One

It was the night before Christmas, and all through the house, not a creature was stirring, not even a mouse… except a clot of blood, creeping up from Ted's leg to his brain, there to burst and kill him as he slept. He'd been complaining earlier of a swelling and some mild pain in his calf, that was all.

I'd spent the day in a mood of sulky despair wishing that I were somebody else, or at least that I lived with somebody else, and even while I shopped for presents and prepared for the next day's festivities I was planning my escape from what seemed a grievous marriage. Of course as soon as Ted died I forgot all that and the only thing that was grievous was his death. I had loved him. I still loved him. The loss of him was intolerable. I married again as soon as I could.

I can't even remember the exact source of that day's particular grievance. But anything would have done to fuel my resentments and keep poor Ted's faults, rather than his virtues, mulling away in my head almost to the exclusion of all else. I was in a negative state of being, a captious, resentful mood. I do remember that I shopped ineptly that morning and in the afternoon curdled the mayonnaise, and that Ted commented: 'Women are like the weather. Their moods blow in and out like the wind. Time of the month, perhaps?' Which I denied, though of course it was true.

Actually I think our moods blow in with our dreams, and it's dreams which control the matrimonial weather. Ted and I were married when I was eighteen, a week after my adoptive parents died in a car crash: they had been out shopping for her mother-of-the-bride outfit. She appeared to me the following night in a dream in which she wore the dress – pale green with flouncy bits: something of a mistake, I thought, even at the time – though in life she was never to wear it. The outfit – dress, jacket, leafy hat, satin shoes – had been found still in its Debenhams bag in the boot of the semi-submerged car. She had leaned over me where I lay in bed with Ted, and said funeral or not, take no notice of her, the wedding must go ahead. So it had.

I was with Ted for twenty years before death took him from me. There had been a lot of sex and sex usually gave me vivid dreams. When the dreams were good, and he and I lived in a pleasant dreamscape, our days would be happy and productive. When the dreams were bad our days would be clouded. When they were nightmares, when I was pre-menstrual, they would feature Ted as the bad guy even as I lay beside him in the double bed, breath and limbs as one, he sleeping peacefully and innocently enough. In those dreams I would find him in bed with Cynara his partner from the art gallery, or trying to murder Martha and Maude our twin daughters, or lunging at me with a knife while my legs would be rooted to the spot or all my teeth falling out, that sort of thing. Then I would wake up angry with Ted, and spend the whole day furious, and the emotional weather would be set cold, bleak, and judgemental.

Poor Ted, he must have had a hard time from me. I too had a hard time from my heaving hormonal states. Some of us are just more female than others. Life flowed through me in the messiest of ways. Yet to an extent one must be responsible for one's own dreams: they happen in one's own head. Though actually that's the kind of thing I would have said before Robbie appeared on the scene. Now I am not so sure.

Robbie is my current husband. I married him ten months to the day after Ted died, and I've been married to him for ten months. My grief therapist had warned me not to 'embark on a relationship' so soon after my loss, but I'd ignored her. A good man is hard to find, I told her – they don't just hang about on trees like ripe fruit waiting to be plucked – and to me ten months of celibacy seemed a very long time indeed. Robbie has been supportive, kind, generous with money and very good to me, concerned for my welfare to the extent of evening out what he calls my 'hormonal issues'. He's an American and a neuro-pharma-scientist, and works in a science lab with psycho-pharmacist colleagues. The distinction is that Robbie works on drug-induced changes in the cell functioning of the nervous system: the colleagues study the effects drugs have on mood, sensation, thinking and behaviour in the totality of a human being. In other words they know the right pills for someone like me to take so Robbie can have a quiet and tranquil married life and focus on his top-priority, top-secret, top-paying job at Portal Inc. in the Nine Elms area of London.

Even in the early Ted days I had taken Valium, and then for a time Prozac and they had helped. Now the drugs are more sophisticated.

Today I sit on my new leather sofa and wait for Robbie to return home from Portal Inc. It has been a rather extraordinary and exhausting day. I try to clear my head and sort out what emotion is real and what the result of psycho-pharmacology.

That is to say what pills I've been taking, and how many and when, and why. But I'm very tired. Thoughts go round and round, and lapse into dreams.

Before I came to woman's estate and knew better, I imagined dreams came from outside us, 'sent' by either God or the Devil, the good force or the bad, creeping under a cloak of darkness to get into our heads. I developed quite an elaborate cosmology when I was small. I went to a convent school where the nuns would tell me God was always watching: that I could never be alone in a room even though I thought I was: God's eye was on me. I grew out of believing that when I became a teenager and felt the urge to pleasure myself. One believes what it is convenient to believe. I read a lot of Tolkien, and for ages saw the cosmos as largely consisting of Mordor-versus-the-Middle-Kingdom. I came to assume that if there was a good there must be an opposing bad. It was all God versus Devil, poor versus rich, worker versus boss, tenant versus landlord, art versus science. I knew which side I was on.

But since Ted died I've revised my rather simple vision: it seems to me now that evil is not just an absence of good, but a power in itself. A gleeful Devil does the watching the better to catch us out; and every tiny little nasty thing we say or do, every snap of temper, every flicker of meanness, every miserable act of bad faith from each of the myriad of tiny souls who scuttle about on this hurtling ball of rock of ours, is used as grist to his mill. It's tempting to provide bad deeds for the Devil's nourishment: he pays well, as Faust found out. The wicked flourish.

Ted flourished, which is why he now has to spend time struggling in the dark wood. These days I seem to see this place almost nightly in my dreams – a horrid place, dank and drear, but one gets used to it. I witnessed him hacking his way through the forest two or three times in the months after he died – but after I married Robbie I had the dreams more frequently. Ted is certainly in need of forgiveness. That is if Cynara, Robbie's ex-girlfriend, was telling the truth. I had lunch with her today. She hinted she was having an affair with Ted when he died. Well, she is like that. A mine of upsetting disinformation. I have refrained from taking my normal six o'clock pill. I had better face what has to be faced.

I imagine the dark wood is my version of what the nuns of my childhood used to call Purgatory, a place where sinners are set to wandering after death, dogged by the reproaches of others; a forest where creepers cling to you and strangle you, roots trip you up, and devils flit about like mosquitoes, until you finally push through to a clearer, greener parkland where trees stand straight, tall and separate and a sun brighter than you've ever imagined shines through to touch your soul. Finally, I daresay, you pass out of dappled light into full sunshine. But the whole thing is metaphor anyway. I am no believer in the final full stop, mind you. I have had too much evidence to the contrary in my lifetime, though I try to make as little of it as I can.

The longer it is since Ted died the more real he becomes. In my dream last night I watched him stoop to brush away the mud of the dark wood from his shoes. They were the heavy lace-up shoes he wore when he was clearing the brambles that afflicted our nice suburban garden; shabby brown leather, not the smart loafers he wore to the gallery. They were wet from the forest. In the dream he looked straight at me and for once he spoke loud and clear: 'For God's sake leave me alone!'

Then he kind of faded away like the Cheshire cat in *Alice in Wonderland*, only leaving behind more of a snarl than a smile. I was able to tell myself that the dream came from my head not his, which was some comfort, but it was still the kind of thing an ex, or about to be ex, husband might say if one asked him how he was feeling or what he was doing, rather than one who was deceased. And I hadn't said a word. I woke feeling rather shaken.

Robbie and I sleep in the marital bedroom I once shared with Ted. Robbie moved in with me when we married. We did try to sell the house, though no buyers turned up, there being a current threat of compulsory purchase in this neck of North London. We didn't try very hard, I must admit. It was a large, convenient, suburban home and had many happy memories for me, and Robbie said Ted would be rather pleased that I had someone to look after me. I'd accepted that it must be difficult for the twins, in their late adolescence, to have a stepfather sleeping in the bedroom where so recently I'd lain with their father – and only now did it occur to me that Ted might find it difficult too. Perhaps that was why he had spoken to me so harshly in the night? We'd had the room redecorated, bought a new king-size double bed and had the original forest green carpet replaced by pale. The twins had even admired the new décor.

Maude.... A new fresh start, Mum. Can't be bad.
Martha.... Out with the old, in with the new!

Maude and Martha are identical, blonde and beautiful, and thank God now away at college. They were here at home for the Christmas holidays when Ted so suddenly died, when the clot crept up like a thief in the night to steal away his life – at least I think that's what happened. The death certificate had certainly said so. Cynara hinted otherwise at lunch today, but then she was out to upset me, and succeeded. I shouldn't have had lunch with her, but I'd had a sudden fit of paranoia which I thought Cynara might be in a position to relieve. The 'leave me alone' dream must have really disturbed me.

I replayed this morning's scene in my mind. We'd had vigorous sex earlier. The dream had woken me. After a time I'd gone back to sleep, conscious of Robbie's steady breathing beside me, his reassuring warmth, my own body – if not my mind – well satiated and duly grateful. Robbie stirred, woke, swung his legs over the side of the bed to get up. And then he stopped. There was a lump of wet mud – about the size of the heel of a man's shoe – on our pale green bedroom carpet.

'What's this?' Robbie asked. He bent down and sniffed at the mud which seemed unnecessary, but then he is a scientist, the kind of man to whom detail and order is important, a left-brainer, rational and dutiful. (I'm a right-brainer, a fuzzy thinker, muddled but creative.) I'd have just chucked it out and thought no more about it, but anything out of place or unusual and Robbie was on to it like a terrier.

'Ted must have brought it in with him last night,' I said, without thinking. 'It was raining in the dark wood.'

'Ted is dead,' Robbie said flatly, not in any spirit of protest, or reproach, but with what seemed a kind of quiet satisfaction. On the few occasions Robbie neglects me and I sleep longer and undisturbed I have fewer nightmares. Well, nothing is for nothing. Bad dreams, good sex, one or the other. I know which I choose.

'I know that,' I said. 'I'm being silly. But Ted was so real in last night's dream it gets hard to remember.'

'Did he say anything?'

'No,' I said. 'He never does.' I don't know why I lied. Except – loyalty to my one-time husband and our life together still lingering, I didn't want Robbie to see Ted in bad light.
'Would you say the dreams are getting stronger?' he'd asked.
'I don't know about strong,' I said, 'but they used to be quite nice. Now they're not.' And it was true. In the days of my celibacy, before I hooked up with Robbie I'd rather liked the dreams. I would go to sleep hoping to catch a glimpse of Ted battling with thickets and thorns in the dark wood, struggling towards the light, knowing that one day he'd finally be through to the other side and would turn and smile at me. Waking, I'd feel comforted and reassured. Make of that what you will. But now the Ted dreams came thick and fast and registered more as nightmare. Ted seemed annoyed by my presence, prowling round a clearing like a trapped animal rather than journeying on. '*Leave me alone!*' – the only words he'd said to me since he died. Well I wasn't going to tell Robbie that, was I?

Then Robbie did something that startled me. He took his Samsung Singularity S20 – ever the brightest, best and newest, as provided by Portal Inc – from the bedside table and snapped away at the small slab of mud on the carpet. He had the phone in 3D mode.

Then he ran downstairs, still naked, his half-erect penis waving ahead like a flag, came back with a freezer bag from the kitchen drawer, got my tweezers from the bathroom, and used them to place the slab of mud inside the bag, which he then put into his laptop case. It occurred to me he was treating the mud as he would some valuable piece of evidence from, say, a murder scene.

I don't know why this so disturbed me but it did. I continued pulling on my leggings as if his behaviour was nothing untoward, but my flesh and my mind had gone oddly and suddenly cold and cautious. Perhaps Robbie was a little mad? I knew so little about him. My body not my brain was doing the warning. My conscious mind could do little else these days but shrug and accept and feel good. Yet my body was telling me something somewhere was terribly, terribly wrong. Well, first rule when danger's detected: keep calm, act normal, carry on as usual. Second rule: give yourself time to think. Third rule: escape while the going's good. So that's what I did.

'Tell you what, Philly,' he said to me when he came back into the bedroom. 'These dreams of yours are beginning to be a real problem. Don't you think you should see someone?'

'Like who?' I asked. I am not a talking cure kind of person, which he should surely know by now. The grief therapist was an aberration. There is no such thing as 'closure'.

'Like whom,' he corrected. As I said, he is a left-brainer. 'Like my psychologist colleague Dr Ben Marcus. I suggest you drop by Portal Inc and see him one day soon. I do a lot of work with him. His speciality is the connection between post-traumatic stress syndrome and the dreaming self.'

'Oh I see,' I said. 'The trauma being your predecessor Ted's death.'

'Exactly,' he said. 'Ben's brilliant, out of this world. A sixer. Known him since Harvard.'

A sixer; in Robbie's terminology someone with an IQ of between 140 and 145. His being 141. (I, untested, had to make do with an estimated 134, but Robbie said that was pretty high for a woman.) You have to be really very clever to get into the Harvard neurology programme. Robbie's current area of research is into intellectual impairment in women affected by

PMDD – pre-menstrual dysphoric disorder; in other words, me. Mind you, I never thought my fits of sulks and bad temper suggested mental impairment, on the contrary, just rather more mental acuteness than was comfortable. The real me might very well be the disagreeable, argumentative, one-week-a-lunar-month me, not the nice three-weeks-a-lunar month version. On the other hand, I could see the first version of me was quite difficult to live with, so I'd asked Robbie if he could think of anything I could take to even out the mood swings, and Robbie had obliged with a medication from his lab which so far has seemed to work. One little pink pill night and morning, and I now felt generally benign and tranquil. I saw no need at all to 'see someone'.
I said as much, rather snappily and Robbie looked at me oddly and said 'Did you forget to take last night's pill?' and I lied and said no.

But it had occurred to me only the previous evening that the change of feeling tone in the Ted dreams might be something to do with Robbie's two-a-day tablets. As the conscious distress calmed, so the unconscious was playing up. There'd be no harm in halving the dose and seeing what happened. I'd dropped the tablet down the loo and forgotten about it. And what had happened? I'd had the best sex ever, the worst dream ever, had a fit of paranoiac shivers over Robbie's reaction to slab of mud. How did one start to sort these things out? That was how my day started and I hadn't even got to lunch with Cynara, Robbie's one-time squeeze. No wonder I was exhausted.

I'd done my best to keep things normal as I made coffee as usual, while Robbie prepared his oatmeal and grated apple as usual. He kissed me goodbye as usual and I waved to him from the door. But as I watched him leave the house I was uneasy. He seemed more like a stranger than a husband, this gangly, attractive, bespectacled, Armani-suited, highly-sexed American who now occupied my bed and leapt from it each morning to go to his job at Portal Inc. What did I really know about him – what he thought, what he felt, what was the wellspring of his being? It was as though I'd acquired a kind of male manikin to take Ted's place in my bed, bathroom and kitchen. I knew the manikin's sexual habits and had grown very fond of them. Robbie was great deal less – how shall I put it? – languid than Ted had ever been.

I knew how Robbie brushed his teeth, but I didn't know the state of every individual tooth as I had with Ted. I knew Robbie was as happy with frozen food as with fresh; Ted would be appalled at the thought of a frozen lasagne. I was suddenly not sure I even liked Robbie, let alone loved him.

But what was the matter with me? There was so much to love and like. Robbie declared love and longing frequently, listening to my boring dreams and even taking notes, watching what I ate and drank, concerned about my health and welfare. But perhaps he was pretending? I should feel grateful, and suddenly I wasn't one bit. Yet the doubt and suspicion in itself was familiar – a return to the monthly fits of paranoiac ill temper that had that so blighted my life with Ted and the twins. Were Robbie's little pink pills really so fast acting and so powerful?

I've always had vivid dreams. When I was small, about six or seven, a lady in a white dress would come and sit on my bed while I went to sleep. She had strange blonde hair which kept fading into nothingness and that Cheshire cat smile left behind when she faded away, but I didn't mind her sitting there, pulsing in and out of existence, any more than at first I'd minded seeing Ted wandering about in the dark wood. It was only later others told me the blonde lady 'must have been a ghost'. But children do see things that aren't really there: the young brain has a whole set of new experiences to make sense of and sometimes gets them wrong.

I was an adopted child, and I knew the reason for the adoption. When I was four my father shot and killed my mother then turned the gun on me, but fortunately changed his mind and shot himself instead. Childhood amnesia only partially sets in at that age, and I remember the broad strokes of this traumatic event, if not the detail. I daresay such a trauma rivals waking up and finding your husband dead in bed beside you, but not by all that much. The ghost at the foot of my bed was in all probability my mother, but my adoptive parents – who were kindness itself, but not very bright – did what they could to steer me away from what they called 'spookiness'. Odd, considering my adoptive mother made quite a name for herself as a fortune-teller in the village fête world. To me, believing you can foretell the future using cards and tea leaves is weirder than anything. But I tried to oblige my new Mum and Dad, who were very good to me, and I got into the habit of keeping silence about any weird spookiness of my own.

Then when I was about ten, playing on the foot of the war memorial in the grounds of our local church, I saw a young soldier wearing puttees sitting on the steps and someone old said, 'Oh, that'll be poor Joe Morland. He died in 1915. He was only twenty-two.' I reckoned it was a kind of time slip: I was seeing Joe Morland at twenty-two as he was then, not him now coming back from the dead or anything like that. Such time slips continued to happen from time to time but if I saw people who didn't look as if they were quite there, or were dressed in odd clothes, I learned to shut up about it.

As I grew older I'd do rather less of this 'seeing people'. I once watched someone's cat die in the road after being run over, and the difference between the living animal and the dead was so great it certainly gave me the feeling that the spirit left the body and went somewhere else. But one sees what one expects to see (ask any conjurer), and events in the real world can be even more disturbing than any number of visions, dreams and phantasms.

I looked in the trash can as soon as Robbie had left for work to make sure he hadn't dumped the plastic bag before he left, but he hadn't. He'd taken the mud to work for some kind of forensic report. But was I being paranoid in assuming so, or was Robbie being that in doing so? It was perfectly possible that I'd brought the lump of mud into the house on my trainers before I'd gone to bed, that I'd noticed it subconsciously and done nothing about it which was why the mud had featured in my dream. I might well be turning into a really feckless housewife. Nothing to do with Ted stepping over into our reality: how could he? True, the natural laws of the nano-world differ from ours in ways we do not understand, though thanks to the Hadron Collider and such, no doubt we soon will. But even acknowledging the reality of alternative universes, and living in the quantum-conscious age we do, no-one is yet suggesting material objects can pass from one dimension to another. Robbie has *Scientific American* and *Nature* delivered every week, and I find them as fascinating as in the Ted days I had found *Vogue* and *Elle*.

My uneasiness got worse not better, and by mid-morning I

found myself punching in Cynara's number. I hadn't spoken to her for months: she was the last person I wanted to talk to – the weeks after Ted had died were still too painful for too much remembering. But Cynara had been Robbie's lover before he so suddenly deserted her and married me, and she would surely have something to say about what actually went on at Portal Inc's developmental facility, and I thought I deserved to know.

I shared a domestic life with Robbie – I shared an intensive and concentrated exchange of bodily fluids night after night, but I knew surprisingly little about his work. Cynara might be prepared, if only out of spite, to tell me something I didn't know. Robbie was an American, not an Englishman, and people from outside one's own culture are often hard to read – but maybe he was just too good to be true?

And then I put down the phone. This was madness. I had so many reasons to be grateful to poor Robbie. Had he not come to my rescue when I was floundering about as a widow, wooed me, entranced me with his lovemaking, told me he adored me, married me, restarted the engine of my life so that after a few chokes and groans it ran smoothly? Hadn't he paid off my mortgage, got the roof mended, settled the twins' college fees? I was ungrateful, unreasonable, suspicious, hormonally disturbed and dysfunctional. Had I not lived with Robbie in peace, harmony and order for many months? He did not deserve this sudden distrust on my part. All he had done was pick up a piece of wet mud in tweezers and take it off to a lab to be examined. Surely he had his own reasons, which could be perfectly well explained if only I were in the mood for explanations. Again I picked up the phone, and then again put it down.

'For Christ's sake, Philly, look before you leap!' I heard Ted in my head, clear as a bell. It wasn't really Ted talking, of course, but me talking to me using Ted's voice, urging common sense. Though come to think of it I never say 'for Christ's sake', it's what Ted says. Only sometimes when driven to distraction I'll let out a mild 'for 'God's sake'; 'Christ' seems somehow extreme, male.

I do hear voices in my head from time to time, but not the kind the mad have: mine are perfectly benign, they don't tell me to kill anyone, anything like that; they just give me advice, usually quite sensible if not what I want to hear. I will feel my birth-mother, long dead, hold my hand as I pour myself another drink, and hear her say, *'You've had quite enough, Philly!'*, and sometimes I'll take notice and sometimes not. But I at least know it's me talking to myself. I can't deny that after Ted died, when I was really distressed and traumatised, there were a couple of weeks when I heard all too clearly what other people were thinking. Fortunately this fit of intense telepathy, if one might call it that, lasted only a couple of weeks and then everything snapped back to normal. I was glad: it is horrible being so aware of what others think of you.

Not that one necessarily needs voices in the head to let one know. After Robbie started staying the night I have no doubt it was all: *'I wonder if she'd been having an affair with him all along,'* and: *'Those poor twins, and their father only just dead,'* and at the Judd Street wedding: *'Talk about warmed-up funeral baked meats.'* Things like that. Gossip is what makes the world go round. But it's not nice. Anyway, I, or at any rate the sensible part of me, told myself I was being stupidly impetuous and on instruction from whomsoever – my guardian angel? – put the phone down before Cynara could answer.

I had been freaked when Robbie had invited Cynara to our wedding. She wouldn't wish us well: she'd be jealous and angry. I certainly would be in her place. Robbie had gone with Cynara to the party; she'd been wearing his ring, but he'd left hand-in-hand with me, the merry widow. I'd been going through a for-God's-sake-I-need-a-fuck phase, and didn't care what others thought. I'd been conscious at the time of a fair amount of whisperings and nudgings, but the sense of cosmic inevitability, the across-a-crowded-room syndrome, had been overwhelming. Eyes met eyes, hand met hand, and that was it.
'Don't worry about it, Philly,' Robbie had said, once the first flush of primal urge had been assuaged. 'Cynara's just a bed buddy. You're different.'
'But what about her engagement ring?'
'Oh, that. It was given to her by her late husband.'
'No way an engagement to you?'
'Good God no. I'm totally free. I wouldn't want to marry Cynara. She's good fun but she's mostly high as a kite.'
Fun or not, I still didn't want him inviting an ex-girlfriend to my wedding.
'But everyone thinks she was having an affair with Ted,' I tried to explain. 'It isn't true, but they'll think I'm having my own back by marrying you.'
'You mean *you* think that, honey; nobody else does. It's your hormonal dysphoria speaking. What do you want other people to think? That you're the one who's jealous and angry?'

Of course he was right and Cynara came to our wedding and behaved perfectly well, just as she had at Ted's funeral. Then she had been suitably and calmly sad – as one would be when a friend and business partner has died, not when a lover has been snatched away by a cruel fate. I hadn't, by the way, sent her an invitation. She just turned up.

Cynara had come into Ted's and my life some eighteen months before he died. The young widow of a very rich old man, she had been an occasional customer at the art gallery we ran in Cork Street. We sold fake artworks by reputable forgers. You might not think there was much of a market in these, and it was indeed beginning to dwindle when the economy picked up. We had been worryingly undercapitalised until Cynara came to the rescue. She had invested £200,000 and saved our bacon. She was younger than me, not even thirty – a lissom, leonine thing (she'd started out as a dancer) long-legged, slim-hipped, with a great mane of reddish gold hair. She was all the things I wasn't – impeccably dressed, manicured and shod, charming, at ease with herself and the world. I could hardly be expected to like her, though her interest in fake artworks was genuine enough. Some of her husband's artworks – Vermeers, Picassos, Monets, Van Dycks – had turned out to be forgeries, or looted masterpieces which had to be returned to their rightful owners. Ted had been able to help and advise. They could pool their knowledge, enthusiasms, and above all their business contacts.

Ted was fascinated by Cynara, of course he was, while ruefully recognising that she was out of his league: 'She's top totty; she goes for Alpha males; I'm arty bog Irish, Beta plus, don't worry about it, Philly.' But of course I did, a bit. Cynara spent more and more time in the shop, sold her own stock out of her house in Holland Park, and was soon buying and selling along with Ted. And then when Ted died she bought out my ten per cent stake at a knock-down price and started buying work by young artists which sold well and with a much higher mark-up.

On my part it was hardly a close or very genial acquaintance.

Ted died on Christmas Eve. I'd met Cynara in the gallery on several occasions before that event. She turned up at his funeral in January. I saw her in March when I signed away the gallery, and then not again until September when I went to a private view in Cork Street – my friend Ali the Nigerian sculptress – and Cynara was there, cynosure of all eyes, her escort a handsome young neuroscientist from Harvard. Ali's sculpture was all grey and stone and tasteful; Cynara was in primary colours: a sleeveless Prada silk dress in bright red and strong green, a pale blue bag, thick white-wool knee-highs, pink flats, and a superb diamond on her finger – on the arm of this tall blond American. He took one look at me and I at him and we bonded there and then. He came back to my house; the children were out; he stayed the night. We were married a month later. It was madness.

Robbie did ask Cynara to the wedding. But being in a generous mood I'd attempted a kind of apology for having so crudely snatched her boyfriend.

'Cynara, I do feel rather bad. One doesn't usually behave, so, well, impetuously, at a private view.'

'Oh darling, one simply does, sometimes,' she said. 'I totally adore you, you know that. And you're so much Robbie's type. I never was. And I was so very fond of dear Ted.'

I puzzled about that rather, but one does not waste time pursuing subtleties at one's own wedding reception. She gave Robbie a rather full and prolonged kiss on the mouth with her slightly pouty collagen lips, and then a little slap on the cheek which I suppose indicated forgiveness and the righting of wrongs. Otherwise she behaved unremarkably. She had even, if rather obviously, dressed down so as not to outshine me; that is to say she didn't wear crimson-soled Louboutin platform pumps but a plain navy silk dress which might have cost £25 or £2,000, how could one tell, and perfectly ordinary flats like my own. Her legs could stand them, mine couldn't really. The ceremony had been a very quiet affair at the Camden Register Office near King's Cross. Robbie's boss, and a clutch of his work colleagues came along, my two former research employees Carole and Luella, Ali the sculptress, and my grief therapist Bambi Bennett. That was all. Afterwards we all went and had an Indian meal.

Bambi had been most disapproving. She thought that after one relationship ended you should learn to live on your own before you tried again. I thought this was nuts: a recipe for loneliness and boredom. Some people like to pretend sex isn't crucial, but a kind of optional extra to one's existence. Maybe it's a therapist thing; they tend not to be sensuous people, but great advocates of sensible thinking. Bambi denied the reality of loneliness, saying one had rather to see it as 'aloneness', as if that were something to be desired. But at least she came to the wedding, if under protest.

Our twins, Maude and Martha, did not come, nor did I pressure them to do so. It was too soon after their father's death. My urgencies – sex and comfort: love, even – were not theirs. All they could see, along I fear with many others, was that the baked meats were barely cold, their widowed mother was remarrying and it was an insult to their father. I told myself that they had finished their college courses, got their degrees and left home: what happened in their old home scarcely mattered. They shared a flat in Camberwell. Both had, so they said, found jobs with the Arts Council. Their new lives had started.

When they came to visit they might have a stepfather sitting at the end of a table where once their beloved father had sat, but he would be a stepfather who would help fund their first steps onto the housing ladder – which was rather more than their real father would have done. I would hereafter be no kind of emotional burden to them. Could they not be glad for themselves, if not for me? But no.

Martha.... Marriage is for the procreation of children, Mum.
Maude.... And best done in your twenties.
Martha.... Our friends will refer to you as the cougar.
Maude.... A cradle snatcher.

Robbie was thirty-nine, four years younger than me. I had the twins when I was twenty-two. Children can be very difficult. When they're born you think you will have them for twenty years or so and that'll be it – but it's not the case. They have you for ever. Maternal guilt and anxiety doesn't abate with time, not does the child's resentment against the parent: you didn't make their life perfect and you can never be wholly forgiven. Just as one can't forgive one's own parents. My birth parents put themselves out of court, mind you, by my father shooting my mother; my adoptive parents did their best but brought me up to believe that truth and reality were dangerous things. At least the ghost of my birth mother had the grace to sit on my bed and croon to me; my adoptive mother went into the good night after the merest smile, the touch of a blessing: if my birth father said goodbye I did not catch it – he had blown the top of his head off; and my adoptive father went without saying anything – but then he had been drinking. And Ted – Ted just walked off into the dark wood without so much as a look behind, as if I had been no part of his life at all.

The twins were polite to Robbie, but were no longer wholly trusting of me. They had always seemed to make common cause with Cynara, when she first turned up in the gallery.

Maude.... She is so good with clothes, Mum, and she knows everyone who's anyone.
Martha.... She's going to help us find jobs when we leave college.
Maude.... She says never, ever, use soap and water on the face: it dries out the skin.
Martha.... All the kinds of useful things she knows about and you don't.
And even after Ted died they'd go round to see her from time to time. They'd turn up at the gallery and she'd leave early if she could and take them round the corner to the Ritz for hamburgers. The twins would call me up to let me know and invite me to come along, but I always said I was busy. Perhaps that was stupid and narrow-minded of me. Was I the one at fault? Their new lives had started.

I picked up the phone one more time and got through to her at the gallery straight away.
'Hi, Cynara,' I said, 'This is Phyllis Whitman, remember Phyllis, Ted's wife?'

'Ah. Oh yes. Of course. Philly. How could one forget? White witch Philly.' I felt an acute pang of jealousy, which ran like a shiver from my crotch to my scalp. Stupid, unsophisticated me. Second husbands have ex-girlfriends; first husbands have no doubt confided and joked with women other than their wives. I told myself Ted was well dead; what had happened when he was alive between Cynara and he was hardly of any consequence. Everything fades into the mists of time, anyway. But white witch Phyllis? Ted had sometimes described me to the children as 'your mother the white witch', but as a kind of intimate family joke.

It's what he'd call me when sometimes I seemed to know what was going on behind my back with the children – the way surely any mother does. But Ted liked to see it as magic. And it was true that once or twice a mug I disliked – too garish or too vulgar – had leaped off the shelf and plunged to its destruction, just when I was saying so. I'd have put it too near the edge, that was all. Or the garden tap once or twice ran red like blood, but it must have been rust; or a letter ready for the post disappeared and then appeared in another place, the silly things that happen in households from time to time. But now 'white witch Phyllis', and from the mouth of Cynara? How could Ted have blabbed so? Yes, they'd had an affair.

'That's the one,' I said, trying to keep the tremor out of my voice. 'Phyllis the white witch. The one who married Robbie.' One point to me. 'I know this is out of the blue and I may be the last person you want to see. But could you have lunch with me?'

'Okay,' she said, not ingratiating, not dismissive. 'When?'

'Today?' I was pushing my luck.

'We'll say my local at one, then.' she said, without a moment's hesitation. 'What's happened? Fallen out of love already? Darling, I do so hope not!'

There was something instantly appealing about Cynara. She was up for anything. The elderly art collector who had married her and left her all his money and his collection had made a good choice. She exuded energy and good cheer: she was charming, clever and without apparent malice; she kept her word, and had an eye for art – and had to all accounts nursed her old husband devotedly through his terminal illness. Just as Ted had made a good choice in accepting her into the business. She was not the gold digger I had assumed her to be. Ted had been praising me, not mocking me, when he called me a white witch. But why was I thinking like this? A second ago I had been thinking just the opposite. What was happening to me? Somehow I must get my moods under control – these sudden swings between hate and love, fear and over-confidence, between unreasonable trust and unwarranted suspicion.

But what Cynara had said was true. I'd indeed fallen out of love with Robbie, just like that, like some silly girl, and within the hour. I clung to this understanding as a drowning woman might cling to a log swirling down some swollen river in Ted's dark forest. I must not dismiss Robbie as some silly boy: he might well be an actual danger to me. Why else the shiver up my spine, why else was I calling up Cynara, the least likely of all allies, looking to her for help?

Two

The Caprice in St James turned out to be Cynara's local. (Ted used to go to The Tavern in Shepherd Market for beer and pork belly.) She arrived ten minutes late, wearing a reddish gold *faux*-leather dress which matched the colour of her hair. I couldn't decide on the make. Jason Wu? True, I once spent a month as an intern at *Vogue Italia* but new couturiers spring up like wildfire in a drought and one has better things to do than try and keep up. I had decided not to compete, in any case: what was the point? Cynara outclassed and outranked me so totally that the best I could do was look anonymous. I wore a five-year-old M&S sensible spotted blue-and-white dress, and no doubt looked like one of those PR people, or even a dresser, who's got into the shot by accident, whose job is to be a foil to the glamorous while looking mildly pleasant and supportive.

Cynara ordered fish and chips for both of us, which she said were the best in London. I was grateful. My instinct when worried is to eat everything in sight, and I was indeed nervous.

Over our vodka martinis I said I had a few things I needed to get clear in my head: I was sorry I had dragged her out on such short notice.

'Robbie texted me,' Cynara said, 'to say if you were in touch I should take you to the Caprice for lunch, but on no account to say too much. I texted back nobody tells me what to do and I'd say whatever I fucking felt like. These boys think they can get away with murder. We girls must stick together, don't you think?'

I couldn't reply: I was spluttering and choking. I had no idea Robbie was in touch with Cynara – I had thought she was safely in the past: but apparently not. Waiters hovered around and looked concerned, if only because I was with Cynara and she was obviously someone of consequence. She looked at me with kindly concern. Waiters brought me water while others slapped my back. I recovered. She leaned forward and dabbed tears from my cheeks.

'Poor darling,' she said. 'You are such an innocent. Robbie keeps in touch with me. He has to; I know where the bodies are buried. Don't worry so: we were only ever bed buddies. And nothing sexual at all any more, darling, it's just work, though he is quite a dish and I'm sometimes tempted. But I was fond of Ted and I owe you something, we all do, so I'm here. But I have to get back to the gallery by two-fifteen. Someone's bringing in a fake Picasso, so I'll make this fast. You know Robbie's with the NSA?'

'The NSA' I asked. 'What does that stand for?' It was dawning on me that she was on drugs – why else was she so bright, glittery and fast?

'You're kidding me. The National Security Agency,' she said and looked at me with pity. 'Portal Inc are best buddies with the NSA though rumour has it ADA's involved.'

'ADA?'

'Search engine. Oh, forget it! An actual physical cable running through from the Bay Area to the new US embassy.'

I was mystified.

'But I thought everything these days was wireless.'

'Cable's unhackable,' Cynara said, 'or so they hope.'

'It's all beyond me,' I said, all innocence. The dumb one Robbie went and married. 'Anyway Robbie works for Portal Inc as a scientist not some kind of spy.'

'A neuroscientist,' she corrected. 'Neuro-schmeuro and now well into psycho-pharms. It's where the funding is. Doxies, all that.'

'Doxies?' But Cynara did not elaborate. She was talking fast. It struck me she was as nervous as I was. She kept looking past my shoulder, but perhaps only to see which celebrity had just walked in.

'Robbie serves strange new masters, Phyllis. Portal Inc poached him from Pfizer in the first place. Easy-peasy, no-one earns much anymore in pure neuro. Scientists follow the money. Who doesn't? Say Portal Inc and you might as well be saying NSA.'

'But that doesn't make Robbie some kind of spy.'

'I work for the NSA, and that doesn't make me a spy either. But I'm an art dealer, and we can all do with a little government subsidy. Were you followed on your way here?'

'I hardly think so,' I said.

'Did you check?'

'Of course not.'

'I did, because Robbie texted me to meet you here if you asked. But I didn't see anyone,' Cynara said. 'They're very clever.'

Paranoiac, too. Her teeth would be receiving messages next. She'd had them done in the US. They were very large and very white, like Robbie's. I was conscious of the thin, translucent flimsiness of my own.

'I don't think anyone would find it worth their while following either of us,' I observed.

'Oh darling, you've no idea, have you,' she said, 'just how important you are to the future: that is to say, how much money they're prepared to spend on you. Same thing. But I think we're probably safe, as it happens. Not enough time to plant mikes. He only texted this morning.'

It is very pleasant to be told you are important, but rather alarming to have someone suggest you are being spied upon. Our fish and chips came. I asked for extra mayonnaise; the tartare sauce does for the fish but what about the chips?
'I do so adore you! Chips! Simply no-one eats chips.'

I did not remind her that she was the one who ordered them. She ignored her chips and removed the batter carefully from the pure, white, flaky, non-fattening fish, though she was to get through all the tartare sauce in its little silver gravy boat, and manage at least a teaspoon of the accompanying pea purée. I had a feeling she was perpetually hungry, as so many really slim women are. I was glad Robbie preferred women with a little more flesh on them. I had traipsed all this way and all Cynara was prepared to tell me was drug-driven paranoiac nonsense. I might have known it. The batter went on to Cynara's side plate and she gestured to the waiter to take it away. He did, and took her dish of chips away too without even asking. Evidently she was a regular customer, and he was used to her ways. She preferred to have the chips taken away on request, rather than just not come in the first place. It made her feel virtuous.

'Do you want to know how I met Robbie?' she asked. I said I was more interested in why I was important to the future but there was no stopping her. Robbie, she said, had come into the gallery about a Van Meegeren Vermeer they had in the window at £5,500 and tried to beat her down to £3,000. They had ended up in bed together. Robbie had been taking Doxies so she hadn't stood a chance and the next morning she'd let him have the painting for £3,250. Ted had been furious.

'Really?' I was trying to be polite. It didn't sound at all like the Robbie I knew.

'What happens when you take Doxies?'

'Sod all happens if the woman takes them, but when the man does he passes on extra SSRI in his cum, and she ends up so passive, pleased and loving she'll do anything he asks. The lab keeps them under lock and key but Robbie nicked some. I told Ted he should be grateful I even earned us £250, but he wasn't having any. He'd no idea about Doxies.' Cynara at least lowered her rather piercing voice so the whole restaurant didn't hear. 'But then he didn't need them. Dear sweet Ted, I so miss him. Well, I suppose you do too, white witch. Do you mind being called that?'

'It's minimally better than black witch,' I said coolly. I wondered exactly what it was she missed about dear sweet Ted. 'These Doxies seem to be really something.'

'Viagra is so yesterday!' She was attracting looks from all over the room. She was the poshest totty in the room, evidently. 'Viagra makes them good in bed, Doxies make women fall in love with them.'

D-OXY-S. I worked it out: Dopamine, Oxytocin, Serotonin. Happiness hormones all, known in the tranquiliser world as SSRIs, serotonin re-uptake inhibitors, the world's favourite pleasure enhancers, depression avoiders. It all figured. Take the pill and pass it on through the male ejaculate. Bond with him, lady – *I love you* – then melt: *whatever you say, dear. Take the painting cheap. Take anything. Take everything. You want to hit me? Oh please, please do!* This was the future, which the NSA, according to Cynara, was spending money bringing about. It was progress; it was bound to happen. I ate another couple of chips. Was it happening to me? The more sex, the more tranquillised I was? Addicted to Robbie? A Robbie on Doxies? At least he didn't hit me.

'Are lots of men on them?' I asked. I hardly knew what else to say.

'Good God no,' she said. 'They only go out to male agents on surveillance work. Really bad form on Robbie's part, nicking them just to save himself a measly two thou. Portal Inc found out – I realised what had happened and told them: there was such a terrible row but what could I do? I was working for the NSA myself; I owed them something. You know they can trace practically every stolen artwork in the word? Good to have them on one's side.'

'I expect it is,' I said, reeling. 'Cynara, you did say something about me being important to the future. Little me. Why would that be?'

'You're such a little solipsist, darling,' she complained. 'It's all me, me, me.'

But she did consent to explain it was because telepaths were two a penny, so were mediums, but telekineticists were in short supply. I must have looked at her with blank astonishment.

'Poor dear Ted always said you were in denial,' she said. 'The rest of us knew if you didn't like a mug it just committed harakiri on the spot. Ted used to tell me and I told Robbie. It fascinated him.'

'That's just absurd,' I said. 'I once put a mug too near the edge of some shelf, and it juddered itself off, that's all. We're near the railway; the container trains are very heavy. The normal laws of physics apply.'

But she wasn't listening.

'Whatever. It wasn't just household crockery: you'd hear voices, see ghosts, there was always a parking space. Real witchy stuff. You and the paranormal are just like that.' She entwined her fingers to make her point. 'You were very close to Ted when he died. If anyone could get a genuine word from the other side it'd be you. And that's what they're after. They want the dead to start yielding up their secrets. I'm not saying they bumped Ted off just to try it out, but it wouldn't surprise me. They Doxied Robbie up to the eyebrows and put him in to keep an eye on you. And they were right. It's paying off. Last night you materialised a piece of mud from the other side. They're very excited. Mud today, a revenant tomorrow.'

She had moved her lovely head close to me. She was whispering in my ear. Her eyes were large and luminous, her breath smelt faintly of fish. I moved away. She was mad and it might be catching. I humoured her, even as I hated her.

'But Cynara, why would "they" want to raise people from the dead? Do you mean your employers?'

'Darling it isn't just the NSA. It's all of them. ADA, Nile, Gateway, LoveBill, Whispring, all the big boys, all in it together. They mean to live forever. Make Hell's foundations quiver, the gates to fall, death to have no dominion. They're very rich. What, have it all end in nothingness? Unacceptable! So now it's all immortality, daily changes of blood, brain transplants, contacting the other side. String theory, white holes, oneirology, alternative universes – pursue the dead and the dreaming to the other side of the cosmos. They're trying the lot. Millions, billions going into Portal Inc. They want a revenant to pick his brains, so how about fetching your Ted back from the dead. You're the key. They need you.'

I finished my chips.

'Oh eat, eat,' Cynara said, 'You need your strength, you sweet old-fashioned girl you. You've gained at least a couple of stone since you married Robbie. It quite suits you; you look better placid.'

Cynara was trying to upset me, and succeeding. So much was clear: anything would do: my previous husband had been murdered, my current husband had been 'put in' to marry me by forces unknown and unknowable: her affair with Robbie was still ongoing; she had been having one with Ted when he died (poor dear Ted!) if all else failed I had put on weight. This was her revenge for my having stolen Robbie from her at Ali's private view. She didn't do things by half. I realised how little I cared if Robbie was still seeing her, but how much I still cared whether or not she had once 'seen' Ted. Which was absurd because Robbie was very much alive and my body, so frequent was our intercourse, seemed almost merged with his. Yet still the handful of ashes that was Ted raised more passion.

'Six pounds at the most,' I said. I lied, as one does, accepting a guilt too obvious to deny while palliating its degree.

A kind of seismic shift was taking place in me; I had no doubt it would be followed in due course by a tsunami of tears. But my inner landscape was changing: valleys became mountains, mountains became valleys. I was back to where I was when Ted died. It was a relief. The time between Ted's death and now had been a kind of madness, an illusion of happiness, a complicated deceit, a void filled up with Robbie who, even as I sat here talking to Cynara, was dwindling, evaporating. It was the kind of relief someone feels when they've been living for a week in the utmost luxury, a five-star hotel paid for by an insurance company after a flood, or a fire, some kind of disaster, and can at last return to the ordinary desultoriness of home.

And then, because I couldn't help it I asked, 'Did you and Ted have an actual affair? I'm sorry, but I need to know.'
'My poppet,' she said. 'Teddy was absolutely and utterly devoted to you. Of course we didn't.'
Teddy? He hated being called Teddy. Cynara opened her luminous eyes – I wondered if she'd had surgery to make them that big – and stared at me with a so honest a look I knew at once she was lying, and more, that she wanted me to think she was. Cynara would never oblige me with the truth. There was no way I would ever know what happened, unless, heaven forfend, I brought Ted back from the dead. And then he too would probably be telling lies. The Other World offers our own only misinformation. Perhaps the living and the dead are in some kind of rivalry; perhaps the other side does what it can to discourage our meddling. You get on with your side; we'll get on with ours. Never act as your horoscope advises, it will do you no good. Never seek help from a soothsayer. Foretold fortune turns to dust in your hands. The love potion merely brings on a fever, or is fatally toxic. Snatch the Ouija board from your teenagers' hands: they will summon up more than they bargained for. They are right to feel frightened. I am. I do what I can to steer clear of all things paranormal, and still unease nips at my heels like some little terrier which won't be shaken off. Reality is an illusion and a dangerous one at that.

'Not that we weren't tempted,' Cynara added, 'but I wouldn't.' By which she wanted me to know Ted had made advances and she had repelled them. Oh, thanks a lot! 'I'd met you, and that always makes a difference. You had children with Ted, and I hate upsetting children.'
I had no children with Robbie, she was reminding me. Well she was welcome, the cow.

'That man over there,' she said. 'He's one of them. NSA. Smile and look cheerful.'

I did my best. 'That man over there' looked like so many of the Caprice's customers. Well-dressed and well-fed with one of those slightly anarchic lopsided faces; someone doing well in the entertainment business, or with artistic pretensions. The kind who would sleep with a female art dealer to get a fake Vermeer cheap. Yes, he might well be NSA.

'I'm off,' Cynara said, and rose up in front of me, brown and tawny, a vision of soft beauty and high fashion. 'Any dessert for you? Coffee? No? Sorry this has had to be so quick, but we'll do it again, shall we? And soon. I'll be in touch. Remember someone's always listening. If not Robbie, one of his minions. They have so much invested in all this. And be careful, darling. Dream well, with me!'

That startled me. What did that mean? Did she too dream of Ted? I rose to my feet and touched her arm. A tiny charge, a tremor of electricity passed from her to me. Static, it must be. Her dress was a man-made fibre. The carpet was nylon. She felt it too and laughed.

And then she was gone, without paying the bill. A hundred and fifteen quid for two fish and chips; no wine, no coffee. It seemed excessive. But we'd had two martinis, they'd bought us mixed breads which we hadn't asked for or touched, and I'd had water, I suppose, when I choked. It was still an outrage. Or perhaps it was me, suddenly so thoroughly outraged by fate and fortune I would take offence at anything at all.

I went home. There was nowhere else to go. There was the same front door, as it had been since Ted and I moved in with the twins – then aged fourteen – but now painted dark blue, not black. The same stairs Ted and I had climbed, but a different stair carpet; the same master bedroom – the same bedhead but at least not the same mattress Ted and I had once shared. I still have some sensitivity. Robbie had gone along with my home décor whims happily enough, while being rather surprised at my various insistences. He was a tad autistic, he told me, a single-tasker; he needed help in knowing what other people felt, especially creatives like me: fuzzy thinkers.

I lay on the bed. I looked up at the same ceiling I had looked up at with Ted. I could hear his breathing beside me. It steadied mine. What had I been doing? I was some kind of fixture and other people's dramas and happenings swept over me and carried me along in their wake, and nothing was anything to do with me. But what Cynara had said about Ted's death stayed with me, spoken almost in passing, thrown away amid a jumble of facts and suppositions; words I still struggled to interpret. *'I'm not saying they bumped Ted off just to try it out, but it wouldn't surprise me.'*

Who did she mean by 'they'? The universal 'they' so favoured by paranoiacs everywhere, of course, but now not just 'the State' or 'the Jews', or 'the CIA', but the kings of the digital world, so animating to a new breed of conspiracy theorists. The mysterious lab at Portal Inc where you can score Doxies, linked by an NSA cable to ADA's even more mysterious data bunker in San Francisco, where the great search engineers, the social network emperors, the giant software dispensers, the Hadron colliders unite and conspire – the big boys in it together, all those garners of information who having milked this world just about dry are now (if Cynara is to be believed; and I must remember she is a mine of misinformation) putting their feelers out into alternative universes. Portal Inc being their shared point of contact, unscrupulously doling out its passion pills, its dream potions, prepared to analyse at a moment's notice soil samples from the Moon, or Mars, or another cosmos, whatever, and using brilliant left-brainers, unimaginative men like Robbie, fired up by Big Pharma culture, as their tool.

And what about me? So addicted to sex I had noticed nothing? Could Robbie perhaps be an android? No, that was going too far – robots didn't have toothache, of which Robbie occasionally complained. A robot who seeded his wife with bonding hormones nightly, and gave her a hallucinogenic pill twice a day to even out her oestrogen levels – thus making her susceptible to visionary dreams? No, too far by far. Cynara told lies: she was afflicted by some kind of infectious paranoia and I had lunched with her. That was all.

Raking up the past is never a good idea. I had stirred up old memories. I should not have been in touch with Cynara. The passage of time is nature's great gift to the distressed and traumatised, or so I always believed. Remembrance does not heal, in spite of what the therapists say; it merely scrapes scar tissue from wounds best left alone to mend; forgetfulness is the quickest path to tranquillity.

This morning I had called up Cynara – madness, madness! And true to form she'd re-awoken in me the sexual jealousy that had spoiled my last days with Ted and might threaten my happiness with Robbie. She had persuaded me not only that Robbie had not fallen in love with me on first sight as I had with him ('sent in', for fuck's sake!), and worse, that I'd fallen out of love with Robbie. Cynara was the witch, if anyone was.

The breathing I could hear beside me on the bed was Robbie's, not Ted's. I did not dare look. I moved my hand and there was no-one there. Nothing. I looked. No-one. The breathing had been my own.

All at once I was happy again. I'd just been unnerved by lunch with Cynara, and had a fit of the wobbles. Robbie would have the soil analysed and find it was perfectly ordinary garden soil from our flower beds. Perhaps Portal Inc did have something to do with the NSA; perhaps it was just normal surveillance protocol to have any unusual substance analysed. Robbie had bought paintings from Cynara in the past and probably would again. She had probably simply invented his text message about lunch. Sex was just sex, not a drug, not a medication, not a fix. Anyway I was no addict: I did not drink, take drugs or gamble. Robbie was just Robbie, and I loved him. When he eventually came home from work I would warn him about Cynara – she was no friend but a malign force trying to come between us. But then, again, I might not. It might all be better left alone, undisturbed, like a heap of rotten leaves.

I half slept. A silly song came into my head: *There was an old man called Michael Finnigan, he had whiskers on his chinigan, the wind came up and blew them inagain, poor old Michael Finnigan. Beginagain!* Ted would mutter 'Oh Finnigan!' when things went wrong, holding back (for the twins' sake rather than mine) the 'Oh fuck!' which sprang more naturally to the lips. I thought perhaps Ted was in my head, trying to tell me something.

My phone burst into life. It was Robbie, in a rush, saying he was delayed; there was a security clamp down; he would sleep in the office and be back for breakfast. Then his phone went dead. The circumstances were such that I trusted him to be telling the truth. I did not think he would be off with Cynara. I got up and made myself some strong coffee. I searched amongst my bureau drawers and found what I was looking for – a few stray wake-up pills in a bottle I'd had for years, which sometimes kept me going when I worked through the night. I took two. I needed to think.

'I'm not saying they bumped Ted off just to try it out, but it wouldn't surprise me.'

I went back to the beginning, and re-thought the circumstances of Ted's death, reviewed my case notes as it were. *Beginagain!*

Three

The Night before Christmas and all through the house, not a creature was stirring, not even a mouse... just the blood clot, creeping silently up from the bottom of Ted's leg to his brain. Did it? I had doubts at the time, I remember now. But everything that happened was so sudden and incredible that when eventually a death certificate arrived, by post, from the Coroner's Office, I opened it, glanced at it, and did my best to forget it. It meant that after weeks of delay I could go ahead with the funeral. The corpse had finally ended back with the local undertaker. There had been an autopsy which involved slicing off the top of Ted's head, taking out his brain, inspecting it, and putting it back in its case again. This is not the kind of thing you want to think about too much. But needs must.

'I'm not saying they bumped Ted off just to try it out, but it wouldn't surprise me'.
Murder, then, not SADS at all: not Sudden Arrhythmic Death Syndrome, which can so suddenly strike down the apparently healthy. Ted did not just fall, he was pushed. No ordinary assassins, Cynara's 'they', but ones who follow you after death. But who was the assassin? How? A ricin pellet? A poisoned umbrella tip? Ted might well feel resentful, snatched from his comfortable life by villains, to be dumped in a dark forest and punished for sins he would hardly realise he had committed. He might well feel inclined to carry mud back from an alternative

universe to his wife's newly furnished bedroom, even months after his death. If that wife of twenty years is now besottedly in love with another man who sleeps in his bed and fucks her out of her brain nightly and her head is all over the place, he might well feel aggrieved. Enough to tell her sleeping self to 'for God's sake leave me alone' – and then change his mind and plant the idea of beginagain in her waking head, so she can at least in due course avenge him.

I have the experience, and I am not alone in it, that when people die they return briefly to say goodbye – you sense it: the feel of a touch on the shoulder, a sudden sharp clear awareness of them at your side, or they come to you in a dream. You have to wait for them – they come first to those they are closest to, and it's not necessarily the order you expected. The merest acquaintance may come to you within a couple of hours, your close relative may take days, to your chagrin, you being low down on their list. Ted took weeks to appear to me. Then when he finally came it was after the funeral, in a dream, but one so clear, sharp-edged, distinct and memorable it was like a vision of something real. It woke me up. It wasn't even to say goodbye, it was more like a formal rejection. '*Know your place. Stay behind!*'

I was in a boat with Ted, and we were scudding along on a sunny lake, with a wind-filled sail, towards a distant shore: we were close, fond, on some kind of adventure together. The sun went behind clouds, darkening the far side of the lake, and I was left in sunlight while Ted was taken off and whisked on over the shadowed lake to a gloomy shore. I watched him trudge up the rocks and sand to where the forest began. I thought he would turn and wave to me or in some way acknowledge me but he didn't, and that was the most painful thing of all. I was an irrelevancy in his life. He walked on, shoulders bowed, into the forest, and was lost in the trees.

Where it seems he still is.

Robbie said to me when I first told him about the Ted dreams: 'You won't forgive him for not turning and looking back at you when he went off into the shadows. Poor bastard. You're so angry you're going to keep him marooned in the dark wood forever.'

Sometimes Robbie seems to understand my thought processes better than I do myself, even though he might, as in this case, get them wrong. He is interested enough to think about them: so few men are. Perhaps this is in itself suspicious; perhaps Robbie is really part of the 'they' conspiracy of Cynara's fevered imagination? But I don't think so. How can he be: he didn't come into the equation until after Ted's death.

Cynara's other bizarre claim about Robbie over lunch: 'they put him in to keep an eye on you' might, I suppose, explain why Robbie sometimes took notes about my dreams, and took this morning's piece of mud off to work, but anything false in Robbie's concern is far more likely to be that he is humouring me because he loves me, than any kind of elaborate conspiracy involving 'they'. Well, there are worse things in the world than being humoured – certified as mad being one of them – which is what happens when people claim to see visions or hear voices. And it was Ted's voice I heard in my head just now 'Finnigan'. In other words, 'beginagain'. It came over as an instruction. I must re-examine the circumstances of Ted's death. Concentrate.

Others think it strange that I live with Robbie in the house where Ted died, but we are both busy people and moving house is traumatic. Dinton Grove's in a nice bourgeois suburb in North London where houses like ours line leafy lanes, but are so hidden behind hedges you don't get much glimpse of their front doors unless you are family, friend, delivery man or robber. Only if you make a real effort do you get to see much of your neighbours. Ted saw all but two of our neighbours as rather foolish and on the whole uncultured, so we tended to stay clear of them. Now I'm with Robbie, people drop by and visit us at weekends. Like Ted, Robbie is courteous. Unlike Ted, Robbie doesn't say or do unexpected things. Ted dressed like the art student he once was, with a taste for interesting fabrics and old clothes. Robbie dresses smartly and conventionally. When I was with Ted I used to worry in case I said something stupid: these days I smile and chatter on like Robbie. How quickly one picks up the attitudes and habits of one's newly espoused!

At the time the alleged SADS struck Ted down the twins were away at college. I had my work cut out running a small research agency from home. It was called Q&A&Co, had a staff of two women on part time, Luella and Carole, whom I paid well, plus holidays and bonuses. We ran and recorded focus groups on changing patterns in high street fashion sales. My skill lay in asking the right questions, and the staff looked up the answers, often on Google, but my clients, relieved to be spared even this labour, seemed happy enough to pay, if never quite enough. It wasn't at all what I'd set out to do – I took a degree in English Literature at the University of East Anglia, where Ted and I met. Ted was doing a PhD in World Art Studies – and I had vague aspirations of becoming a writer, but ending things and coming to a conclusion was always difficult for me, on the page as in life. I gave up literature, trained as a fashion designer and got a job at *Vogue*, while Ted worked for Sotheby's. When the twins came along I gave up the day job and started Q&A&Co.

Ted started his own art dealership at around that time, moving up market over the years to end up with a business in Cork Street in the West End. He goes up to town most days of the week. Slip of the tense – Ted is dead. Ted *went* up to London most days of the week. We were ordinary people, vaguely arty but socially acceptable; not the kind who got themselves murdered. Ted wasn't even dealing in old masters, just an odd branch of the art world where art is reckoned in hundreds, thousands if you're lucky. He was a good-looking easy-going man. He had brown eyes, an olive skin tone – the kind that tans quickly and smoothly; Robbie has blue eyes and a pale New England skin – the kind that reddens and burns. Ted had thinning hair and was stocky and a little fleshy. Robbie has a floppy Hugh Grant thatch, and is tall and skinny. But comparisons are odious – both were, are, good-looking men, attractive to all too many women.

Ted was gregarious when amongst people he thought well of, loved parties and went wherever art buyers congregated, though at home he would too often sink into a gloomy silence, as if blaming me for some fault of mine unspoken by him and unknown to me. (What I like so much about Robbie is that he doesn't hold grudges.) Ted still does, I fear. He seems to have lost weight on the other side, but grown no older, just a bit sadder and recently more resentful. Once again I seem to be failing him. In last night's dream his corporeality seemed stronger than usual: as if when you touched him in affection your hand would not just go through him but rest on resistant flesh – but also that, as in life, he might be in a bad mood and might simply brush the hand away. I suppose it is unreasonable to assume that our loved ones are vastly improved in temper once on the other side. Last night he'd said, *'For God's sake leave me alone'*. He'd said it to me in his lifetime often enough. I have to remind myself that his revenant, his visible ghost, his returning corpse, is coming out of my mind, not his. Tonight I heard, though Ted did not necessarily say, '*beginagain*'.

The night before Christmas Ted went to bed before me. I stayed up until after midnight, stuffing the turkey. The twins were home for Christmas. I was pre-menstrual and feeling hard done-by.

'But you treat this house as a hotel,' I remember myself saying that day, without any sense of cliché because that's exactly what they were doing. 'You bring your dirty washing home and just dump it!'

At other times of the month I'd have been put out if they hadn't done so. But like their father they were used to me, or at least I hope they were, or they must have spent a miserable childhood one week out of every four, when white witch turned into black.

'I know it's your hormones,' was all Ted would say, thus maddening me the more. 'I just sit them out.'

The night he died we'd been round to our next-door neighbours, Richard and Jill Woodward, for pre-supper Christmas Eve drinks. Richard ran some kind of motor agency and talked about cars, and Jill, who lived on the proceeds and had facelifts which went wrong, talked about those and her séance experiences. I'd once rashly told her about various apparitions I'd encountered, which thrilled her to bits. But Richard had once called in at the gallery and spent £675 on a signed, dated and authenticated Andy Warhol lithograph of Mickey Mouse, and since then the Woodwards had passed more as friends than just neighbours. They didn't have a book in the house, unless you include glossy magazines, but Jill's very pretty and silly in the way men like. There wasn't much to say, other than to enthuse about their Christmas decorations from Harvey Nichols, and the shapely black branch with a hanging dull gold ornament which they had for a Christmas tree, and apologise for our taste in cheap tinsel. Ted flirted with Jill and I daresay I flirted with Richard just to keep pace.

I do not imagine that the conduct of either of us was enough to induce murderous intent in our neighbours. It was normal in our circles over Christmas: everyone a little tipsy, a little flushed: Jill going out onto the heated patio with Ted for a smoke, and having at least three; a suggestive reference to a wife swap from Richard in their absence. I taxed Ted with his behaviour as we walked home. He had humiliated me, and so forth, left me open to Richard's awfulness.
'Oh for heaven's sake. Your monthly paranoia's back again,' was all he said, which of course riled me the more because it was true.

But it was such a calm, beautiful night, with stars in the navy sky and a nearly full moon and frost crunching underfoot, that I forgave him and we even held hands as we went home. I am glad that Ted took with him to the grave, or wherever, the memory of this world at its most enchanted. God gives us landscapes and still, bright skies, I sometimes think, to compensate for what He means to do next. When we got to the front door an owl flew down suddenly from our roof with a great whooshing of black feathers and a piercing downscale

shriek, and then a silence, and then the cry of some little night creature as it met death.
'My God,' said Ted. 'What was that?'
'An owl,' I said, 'eating its dinner.'
'But it was black,' he said. 'There aren't any black owls.'
'Yes, there are,' I said, it being that time of the month. 'Though it's true they tend to live in Australia,' I conceded. He could always check; look it up on Wikipedia any time, and he probably would.
'Lucky I'm not easily panicked,' he said, 'or I'd take that as a bad omen. Don't black birds mean a death in the house?'

Death was not a subject I ever wanted to discuss. I'd lost my birth parents in a most unfortunate way, and then when I was eighteen my adoptive parents were killed. Clive had driven off the road into a swollen river; his body and Marion's were found the next day. Clive had been drinking, but he was a very bad driver anyway. I'd had a dream that night that they were waving goodbye. Oddly enough, I never worried that anything would happen to Ted or the twins. More denial, I suppose – things too terrible to contemplate.

'It was an ordinary tawny owl.' I said. 'It just looked black in the lamplight.'
'You're very good at believing what you want to believe,' I remember Ted saying, and my feeling cross about that too, but I couldn't spend too much time resenting his saying it, since it was past midnight and there would be seventeen for Christmas the next day and the turkey not yet stuffed, and presents still to wrap. At least I'd already done the twins' traditional stockings – a pair of my old tights cut down the middle, assorted nail varnishes, make-up, socks, a silver-papered tangerine in the toe, a few nuts and assorted junk food. Even at their great

age they expected to wake up to a Christmas stocking each, and since they were a touch obsessive-compulsive (or so Ted alleged), any change of routine upset them.

I was very short of relatives but Ted had enough for us both. His mother was a good Irish Catholic, and he was one of four. Frank, Hector, Aidan and Ted. Just as small families wither and die out with the years, big families expand; children are born, step-children accumulate, spouses get switched but not abandoned. Aidan was bringing two wives and one of his mothers-in-law. Seventeen were expected. It was not surprising I was up late that night. After I'd finished with the turkey there was all the cutlery and glasses to assemble, and three last-minute presents to wrap – boring-but-needed slippers for Ted, and I've forgotten what I got for the twins. I was pleased by what I achieved – firm, neat edges, paper in various shades of pink, tied with gold string and gift tags written out and firmly tied, I was exhausted by the time I got into bed. Ted had fallen asleep. He'd turned off the heating. I undressed quickly in the dark, and I was grateful for his warmth as I got under the duvet. My horror is that he was dead when I got in beside him, and I only felt the warmth because it was so expected, but I don't think it can have been so. The cold I felt later was so shocking. I had no dreams or any that I can remember. It was a deep dark sleep.

I suppose if I reject the idea of a crime passionnel, *the Woodwards could still have been in the pay of the NSA and slipped Ted some kind of poison and me a Mickey Finn which only cut in four hours later. I certainly slept very heavily that night and Ted did not wake at all. But poison seems unlikely. More likely Cynara is nuts.*

I stirred at seven, looked at the clock and went back to sleep until nine, when I woke, thinking of the Christmas turkey and the seventeen for lunch, and became conscious that the body beside me was a different temperature from mine. Whatever your temperature when you go to bed with someone else, when you wake you share the same warmth. When I went to bed the night before I had been cold and I had experienced his body as warm. Now it was the other way round. With my eyes still closed I searched for an extra blanket to pull over me in order to warm Ted. He had thrown his bedclothes off in the night.

He was lying facing away from me and, still half asleep I tried to turn him towards me which was usually a doddle because he'd cooperate even in his sleep, ever ready for sex, but his body was oddly heavy and inert. I thought *he's dead* without any real evidence for it and got up and went round to the other side of the bed to see his face, and he was lying there looking just as usual with his eyes open, but I was right; there was no life in him. The eyes were unseeing. His soul, as I'd describe it these days, had left the body. Gone somewhere else: this was the immediate impression, as I voiced it at the time, without thinking, without rationality intervening. *He's left me.* Not that he had stopped being, but that he had gone away.

Ted was dead. I felt quite rational and without emotion. I happened to have the mobile number for old Dr Nevis, our family G.P. so I phoned him, and he said he'd come round at once. I sat by the bed and waited in case Ted woke up, but he didn't. Dr Nevis came and said, 'He's gone.' I felt like asking him where to, but I didn't.

The doctor phoned the ambulance and I gave them directions

in a competent and practical way. I knew Ted was dead but modern medicine is such these days that if you get an apparent corpse to a hospital in time even the dead can be brought to life. I was of course in shock. Then I went to wake up the twins but the room they shared was empty: they weren't home from their party. I checked the answer phone.

Maude.... We're sleeping over, Mum.
Martha.... But we'll be home early.
Maude.... To help with the turkey.
Martha.... I'll do the bread sauce.
Maude.... I'll do the brandy butter.
Then they clicked into silence.

Dr Nevis said he was afraid that he had to go, he'd left a small goose in the oven. Then Jill Woodward came in to 'be with me'. I had to calm her down. We put the turkey in my oven. The ambulance came. I couldn't find Ted's mobile with his brothers' numbers on it so there was no way I could stop them and theirs coming for Christmas dinner. I went with the body to the hospital where Ted was registered DOA, and saw him settled in the morgue. I got home at about midday: the twins were back saying 'Where is everybody?' and I had to tell them their father was dead. Jill seemed incapable of saying it. She was busy stripping our bed and putting the sheets into the washing machine at ninety-five degrees.

The twins are identical: long blonde hair, blue eyes, cherub-mouthed, small, neat and perfectly formed, and cool, very cool. They move as one, think as one, and as far as I can tell feel as one; they absorbed the news thoughtfully, joined their little hands together as they would when shocked and surprised, and wept a single tear each. I didn't weep or wail or scream either; perhaps they inherited non-affect from me.

Maude.... Does that mean we won't be going to St Moritz?
'It does,' I said. We'd booked to go skiing as a family in the New Year.
Martha.... That's all right, Mum. We didn't really want to go anyway.
Maude.... We were only doing it for you and Dad.

The twins are very academically clever, and though I have never had them tested I would imagine they'd come out somewhere low on the autistic scale of non-empathic response, just high enough to give some people the heebie-jeebies.

I thanked Jill Woodward and said I had to get on. She wept a little more and left, I think very shocked and dismayed, but then so was I: she just showed it more. The twins and I prepared lunch, silently; we basted the turkey, peeled potatoes for seventeen and prepared the gravy.
Maude.... I'll do the bread sauce.
Martha.... I'll do the cranberry.
They cleared up as they went along, which was in their nature, being particular and methodical. They put in the extra sleeves of the Edwardian dining room table, laid it beautifully – crackers, Christmas napkins, plastic holly centrepiece – and a place setting for Ted at the end of the table, writing 'Dad RIP' on his table mat and going out into the damp garden to find sprigs of holly to make into a wreath to enclose the mat. They are very clever with their fingers.

The phone rang and it was Dr Nevis saying there had to be an autopsy but it was 'difficult' since it was the holiday season and to warn me there might be 'delays'. I told him this wouldn't make much difference to Ted. He asked me how I was and I said I was making Christmas dinner: I explained it was a family gathering; all Ted's relatives were arriving from Ireland. I didn't like to turn them away, and to hold an impromptu wake now would save them all a lot of travelling expense later. Dr Nevis offered me Valium and sleeping pills. I said no.

I went upstairs to put on a clean dress and change my wet shoes. I put the twins on the front door to explain what was going on to the arriving guests: I could hear them from upstairs.

Maude.... We have to tell you our father's dead.

Martha.... Last night in his sleep. Mother's just back from the morgue.

Maude.... The doctor says it's not suspicious.

Martha.... But please do stay for lunch.

Maude.... Mum needs to keep busy.

Martha.... It's the way she copes.

Maude.... We all cooked it together.

Maude-and-Martha.... Do stay! Turkey and all the trimmings. Waste not, want not.

If the twins were being at their most Aspergery it was not surprising; first an all-night party; then their father, there yesterday, gone today. I hurried down. All who arrived stayed. They came in assorted executive cars, provided by their hotel in Knightsbridge. They seemed stunned and upset and took time to settle. They were sombre and embarrassed over the turkey but cheered up over Christmas pudding and drank and toasted and laughed and chattered; even the twins smiled, if only in unison. We all distributed presents as planned. Ted's were put aside on the hall stand, still wrapped, to go straight to charity. Only the present from me to Ted stayed under the Christmas tree. When all the guests were gone I looked at the tag on the slippers I'd wrapped for him the night before, and it was blank, though I remembered very clearly writing out his name. Still, one can be mistaken. But to me it was as if Ted's presence on this earth was being rapidly and steadily obliterated by forces greater than me. Well, odd things happen.

December 25th and 26th were public holidays so I couldn't get down to the Harrow Civic Centre to register the death until Thursday the 27th. When I found I was not entitled to a certificate because the coroner had to sign off the autopsy and I needed various papers I didn't have, I fainted. I was picked up, sat down and given water by a Civic Centre employee wearing a Happy Winter Festive Season broach that flashed on and off very close at eye level. Reality dawned and grief began.

Cynara's words in my head… 'I'm not saying they bumped Ted off just to try it out, but it wouldn't surprise me.'

Why had the body seemed so cold when I woke? Was that natural? Weren't bodies meant to take time to cool down? Could the chill be indicative of some kind of poison? But wouldn't an autopsy pick such a thing up? I came back from the Civic Centre wondering exactly where Ted was. I'd assumed he'd be in the morgue where I'd left him: I rang them and they said they'd signed it out to the undertakers of my choice – oddly named Loam & Leap, chosen from a list the morgue gave me. I called Loam & Leap who referred me back to the medical attendant who had signed the death confirmation, apparently different from a death certificate.

I went round with the twins to the surgery. Old Dr Nevis was 'away on a well-earned holiday' so they gave us an earnest young man who stared goggle-eyed at the twins. Pretty identical twins, especially if they have long blonde hair, are much in demand in the porn industry, and heaven alone knew what erotic fantasies came to his mind. The twins have a lot to put up with – and all my fault, according to the latest findings of the medical profession. Being starved of mitochondria in the maternal womb, their degree of identicality was extreme – ninety-three percent, Robbie reckoned, though I would not let the girls be tested. There are too many scientists wanting to prod and poke identical twins as it is.

Of course the twins are angry with me: I've so often failed them. Once when they were about eight and arguing and giggling in their private language in the back of the car I turned and slapped them both and almost crashed the car. They shut me out after that; they were cold to me, and made do with me as servant, not as a loved and trusted Mummy. They adored Ted. Motherhood can make one mad.

And then of course I'd let Ted die and thus failed in my wifely responsibility of keeping him alive. I'd find them glaring at me in the same way as when they were four, when they'd fallen down in the gravel path and hurt a knee, and I represented a world which had treated them unfairly. Or they'd start one of their peculiar sibling arguments about who was most upset. Sometimes they'd both stop talking in mid-sentence and one or the other would begin to cry great big terrible sobs, usually Martha, because Maude tried harder not to screw up her face, having read an article which her sister seemed not to have, about how weeping developed wrinkles. They worry so about their looks, like so many of their contemporaries and not at all like me. I don't bother much about my appearance. I always seem to have too much to do other than simply comb my hair, drag on clothes and find my shoes in the morning, forget make-up. But that may be just what having twins does to a woman. Pre-motherhood, I'd spent a lot of my youth staring into a mirror, like my girls do today.

Cynara's words in my head: 'I'm not saying they bumped Ted off just to try it out, but it wouldn't surprise me.' But one way and another I did not think the twins were so angry with me they would collude with Cynara's 'they' in the murder of their father, even to obtain the possibility of replacing him with some stepfather who could provide them with all the goodies Ted could not. I could safely remove my girls from suspicion.

But I wasn't happy they were with me when I asked Dr Nevis's young locum about the necessity of an autopsy. It seemed that because Ted had died young, in apparent good health and had not seen the doctor in the last three months of his life, an autopsy was required. An autopsy! The twins were fascinated.
Maude.... Do they think Mum did it?
Martha.... She was the last person to see him.
Maude.... It can't have been us.
Martha.... We have an alibi.
'No-one's suspected of anything,' the young man replied, startled back to his senses, erotic fantasies abandoned. 'They'll assume SADS, Sudden Arrhythmic Death Syndrome. Largely a hereditary condition. Nobody's fault, just most unfortunate.'
Maude.... They actually chop up the body?
Martha.... Not even key-hole surgery?
'They open it up, yes,' said the young man.
Maude.... To get at the brain?
Martha.... They have to use some sort of saw?
The doctor agreed that yes they would. The NHS was

investigating the use of non-invasive forensic techniques where possible but they were not yet operational.

Cynara: 'I'm not saying they bumped Ted off just to try it out, but it wouldn't surprise me.'
Yes, why had Dr Nevis insisted on an autopsy? Ted had been to visit him in August for a malaria jab: Nevis could have stretched a point and ticked the 'been seen by doctor within last three months' easily enough, but he didn't. Had he suspected something? Murder? But then the coroner had eventually signed the death certificate. Could Dr Nevis have been involved in the plot? No, that was absurd, the wake-up pills were doing things to my brain. And God alone knew what Robbie's little pink pills were doing to me.

The twins would be off to college with the new spring term and I'd be glad of it. I didn't want to have to think of the reality of what an autopsy meant, and they would make sure I did. A buzz-saw, splinters of bone and splashes of cold, cold blood. My Ted.
'And then they plonk the top of the skull back on again, I suppose,' one or both of them had said, 'for appearance's sake. And who are these pissy "they" anyway?'
Maude.... Then they pluck out the heart, all dripping—
Martha.... —with blood, like in a horror film.
Then they'd both said 'Sorry, Mum,' for which I was grateful. But whether it was for saying 'pissy' or because they realised I can't stand too much reality I don't know. I took them home as soon as I could, and waited as instructed to hear from the Coroner's office. It was a busy time of year, I was told, and there was a shortage of pathologists prepared to do this specialist work so I should be patient. I resigned myself to waiting, and getting on with all the letters, phone calls, notifications, the

closing of bank accounts and so on that go with a death. Ted's brothers stayed around to help.

Cynara: 'I'm not saying they bumped Ted off just to try it out, but it wouldn't surprise me'.
I waited and waited for Ted to say goodbye, for his spirit to touch me before it departed, but he did not come. There was a kind of heavy silence in the house, a blankness. My deceased birth mother had come to sit on my bed, my adoptive parents had said goodbye as they left; but from Ted, my husband of twenty years, nothing. I'd felt aggrieved at the time but I wonder now if the delay was because Ted was waiting for me to avenge his death but I was doing nothing.

Then Cynara called me out of the blue on New Year's Eve to say how sorry she was to hear of my loss and how fond she had been of Ted. Such a dear, darling man, such a great loss, but she felt better because he'd visited her in a dream the previous night.
'Such a vivid dream, Phyllis. I woke and Ted was standing beside my bed! He smiled at me and said he was okay and wished me well. Then he kind of faded out. I went back to sleep and felt so much better in the morning. As if he'd wiped away my grief.'
'I'm happy for you, Cynara,' I said, though it took considerable effort to say so. I hated her. Why had he come first to her, not me? The answer was horribly clear. Cynara had been more on Ted's mind when he passed on than I had been. A simple affair I could have forgiven; it had happened before and meant nothing in the long run. But this?
'I've been so upset,' Cynara complained. 'And nobody called me to tell me. I was left to find out from strangers.' Her voice was a little slurred. It occurred to me that she was a little

drunk. Many people are at that time of year.
'I've been rather upset too,' I said.
'Of course you have, poor darling. I'm such a selfish bitch. But you must tell me when the funeral is.'
I told her it was not yet settled. Ted's family were over from Ireland. I didn't mention the autopsy; I didn't want to engage with her.
'Oh yes, all those brothers,' she said. 'Me, I'm so alone in the world. And Phyllis, I just have to say this. I didn't have any kind of affair with your Ted. We just worked together. He was my business partner. It was purely business. I want you to know that.'
Which of course made me the surer that she was lying. Why even mention it otherwise? She was feeling guilty.
'Why thank you, Cynara,' I said, cool as cool. 'That's very thoughtful of you. All my best wishes to you both for a happy New Year.' And I put the phone down. I suspected her of not being alone. I resolved not to tell her anything about the funeral: I didn't want her turning up.

Ted's three older brothers all came back to visit in that strange lost time between Christmas and the New Year, when the whole country falls back into a kind of exhausted stupor. All three, left-side dominants (left brain is rational, orderly, analytical – right brain fuzzy, creative, intuitive) had regarded Ted as the arty and confused sibling; the irresponsible one, the right-brainer. Frank and Hector were accountants – or so they described themselves, though I'd have called them hedge-fund managers – and Aidan was a lawyer. They lost no time. They went through Ted's papers. A trendy art gallery in the West End was out of their ken, though they seemed impressed by the mark-up considered normal in the art world. But the gallery was obviously a risky project – a market for fakes people knew were fakes could only be a flash in the pan – and Cynara was a wild card. But I was glad of the brothers' comfort and support.

Their wives and hangers-on were a different matter. They did not take the arrival of New Year as a signal to go away. The wives saw it as their duty to sit with me a lot, though the body itself was away for the autopsy and the funeral couldn't happen until the coroner said so, and of course the New Year sales were on. All had to be fed and watered by me, though all assured me of their willingness to 'help'. There was a lot of running to and from Marks and Spencer on my behalf for chilled food of the expensive kind – they were a well-heeled and classy lot – and no end of sherry, gin and Guinness. They were also quarrelsome, large and noisy and kept turning up the heating, when all I wanted was cold and cool. They'd throw their arms around me and squeeze the breath out of me, weeping for my loss. I needed Ted to come back and say goodbye to me, but how could he, why would he, with all this going on?

They disapproved of so many things –
.... 'Sure and why didn't you keep the body at home, girl? Throwing him out of the house and his body not yet cold. Those morgues are terrible, terrible places.'
.... 'Those girls of yours need to learn not be mean. Those mince-pie fillings were a disgrace. They do everything by halves. We don't have twins on our side of the family.'
.... 'We can't even go down to the morgue to view! You English just love to sweep everything under the carpet, even dead bodies.'
.... 'An autopsy? They want to cut our poor Ted open? This country's a madhouse.'

.... 'But we can't stay around forever waiting for a funeral. Not if we've already had the wake on Christmas Day.'

They took the Christmas baubles down, not waiting for Twelfth Night, saying they were tired of looking at them. I was glad: I couldn't bear the sight of the decorations now, though Ted had always been a great stickler for keeping them up. I didn't have the will power to make the decision to take them down myself and it didn't seem right to ask the twins to do it – they'd put them up in the first place: too much the stuff memories are made of. Martha and Maude sobbed in unison and worried about the effect of tears on the skin beneath the eyes. I didn't do much sobbing, though. I couldn't believe Ted was *dead*, just that he had rather wilfully deserted me.

It was after Cynara's phone call that I began to 'hear' the relatives, still busy embracing and weeping over me, saying things to my face that were simply too rude and callous to be said aloud. I was hearing their thoughts as well as their words. Frank's ex-wife's mother, who seemed to travel everywhere with his new wife, began it at breakfast: 'I didn't sleep a wink. Nylon sheets! Cheap, slippery and hot. And those towels! Thin and scratchy. Ted should never have married her.' I stared at her in disbelief and then realised no-one else seemed to have heard what I had. It got worse:
.... 'People don't just up and die like that for no reason. Must be something *she* did.'
.... 'No instant coffee in the house. A rotten house-keeper she is!'
.... 'Those twins of hers. Spooky! Poor Ted, no wonder he wanted out. I expect she destroyed the suicide note.'
.... 'One person in two bodies, those twins. Like seeing double. In a lot of countries they put them down at birth.'

And then 'she' became 'you', which was worse.

.... 'You're a rotten cook. You do realise that? That omelette would kill anyone.'
.... 'You murdered him! He was having it off with that rich girl in his shop and you didn't like it.'
.... 'Even your daughters call you a witch. You're always seeing things. You probably just looked daggers at him, and he upped and died.'
.... 'Did you put a stone in his mouth to stop him walking, the way his great grandpa did. It runs in the family.'

I suppose it all came out of my own mind, not from theirs, but I still found it hard to forgive them. It was 'rotten cook' that hurt most. I'm actually quite good.

Cynara: 'I'm not saying they bumped Ted off just to try it out, but it wouldn't surprise me'.
It was not out of the question that I was the guilty party and just didn't remember. It's possible to hypnotise people into doing things and then forgetting they've done it. Forget that, re-wind. It's an absurd proposition. Oh Finnigan! as Ted would say. Beginagain!

I made more coffee. I felt perfectly alert. The wake-up pills were working well. I realised that I didn't want to go to sleep anyway in case Ted came walking out of my dreams into my real life. He seemed so much on the verge of doing so. If he did, where would my loyalties lie? Odd that I now loved Robbie as once I'd loved Ted. Cynara had suggested over lunch that love had nothing to do with romance, just with the nature of the sexual relationship. And it is true that many a girl in an arranged marriage will say 'I did not see my husband until my wedding day, but I came to love him almost at once' – she lived happily enough before him, but now can't envisage life without him: she is addicted to him.

Perhaps Cynara is right. Love is the product of a hormonal exchange between two people. An addiction to Robbie has simply replaced an addiction to Ted. Odd too that Robbie had chosen tonight of all nights to be trapped in his office. If indeed he had been. Whatever his motives, whatever 'they' had to do with it – and it was important that I did not let my incipient jealousy of Cynara interfere with my judgement – at least I had a few hours before his return in which to gather my wits.

I went to find the death certificate. I remembered shoving it into the living-room bureau after a brief look at 'cause of death', and thinking I'd deal with it later. Rather to my surprise it was still there. (Robbie had done a great clear-out when we got married because it was to be a new beginning for both of us. The house these days looked the way Robbie liked a home to look, neat, tidy, rather male and without clutter. Robbie favoured disambiguation.) The reality, the finality of the document was rather shocking; it had been filled with a pen hand, not a computer, in a rather thin and tremulous but determined hand, as if by an old person sticking to older ways. It was as I remembered it: 'Cause of Death – apoplexy; query? cerebral thrombosis. Query? arteriovenous malformation.'

The coroner's letter had not arrived until January 21st, and was at odds with what the locum had told us. He had simply assumed SADS. I went down to the surgery with the twins to check it out. Who these days spoke of apoplexy? Ted's family had melted away back to Ireland – most had decided not to come to the funeral; they had surely done their duty by me –

and my sudden acute attach of telepathy evaporated as they did. I could once again hear only what others wanted me to hear, and thanked God for it. Dr Nevis had returned from his 'well-earned holiday'.

'Apoplexy: death by rage?' I complained. 'What kind of medical term is that? No-one talks of apoplexy these days.'

'The Scots still do,' he'd said. 'Up there it's a recognised cause of death. Down here in the South you get more detail.'

'But we are down here in the South,' I said.

But a post mortem had been obligatory, it seemed. The death ranked as 'mysterious' though non-suspicious, and it being the holiday season and very few pathologists around at the best of times – autopsies were a messy job and delay distressing for the loved ones – Dr Nevis had done what he could and found a slot in Scotland. The body had been transferred by ambulance from the Royal Free to the Edinburgh City infirmary and hence by taxi to the city morgue for the autopsy.

'By taxi? Just ordinary taxi?'

'One of the new ones big enough for wheelchairs.' Ted's corpse would have travelled with a nurse attendant. It was a short distance and taxis were quicker, simpler and cheaper than ambulances.

Cynara at lunch: 'Oh darling, you've no idea, have you, just how important you are to the future: that is to say, how much money they're prepared to spend on you.'

So many people had been involved – corners must have been cut, taxi drivers could have been bribed, even pathologists – 'cause of death: apoplexy' in a tremulous hand – filled in by some unpaid intern, or some batty old morgue attendant anxious to get rid of a body and home for his tea. Do coroners keep their blank forms under lock and key? Once you begin to doubt you doubt everything. The cost of anything simply did not apply if you were thinking of the behaviour of social media, or the search engine people, or the great Internet stores – the 'they' to whom Cynara referred. The 'they' who had sent Robbie in to keep an eye on me, because of my alleged closeness to the other side. Blast this bloody wicked paranoiac nonsense, breeding paranoia in me...

I wondered if I should call the twins in the morning and ask them if they thought there was anything strange about their father's death. But then I thought no, they would not, like Hamlet, feel the need to avenge their father's most foul and unnatural murder – if that's what it had been. It was hardly in their interest. They no longer lived with us – they now shared a flat near Lambeth Bridge, overlooking the Thames: Robbie had put down the deposit for them a month or so after we were married. I hadn't asked how much, but it can't have been cheap – three rooms, bathroom, kitchen and a river view in central London? And he'd paid off their student loans, at £9,000 a year each hardly negligible. Was Robbie paid so much that he could afford this kind of thing almost without noticing?

Were 'they' involved in some way, even in this? Had the twins too been bought off – my lovely, light, dancing, two-peas-in-a-pod girls? Mind you, life with the twins wasn't always sweetness and light. On bad days during their childhood, when I was tired and low, I'd resented the fact that I had one child but twice the work. Most identical twins develop differences in looks and temperament as they grow older, but not ours. Martha and Maude just seemed to become more and more alike. I'd said as much to Jill Woodward on the day that Ted died, 'It's all so unfair. All that work with Ted and now he's just gone, and all that work with the twins and still there's only one of them,' and she'd looked at me blankly with her botoxed face. If she felt sorry for me she couldn't show it even if she wanted to. She was unreadable.

In their early teens the twins make a real effort to become more easily recognised as separate individuals, wearing different clothes and following different celebrities but by the time they were nineteen they'd given up – they looked and moved and thought like the same person, ultra, ultra identicals. People accuse me of being telepathic, when all I am is normally empathetic, just over-sensitive to what others must be feeling, but I'm nothing compared to Martha and Maude: their bickerings often end (and they do bicker) just because one of them is using the other's lines and they get confused.

Robbie of course has always wanted to take them off to the Portal Inc lab to 'check out their brain wirings' as he put it, but so far as I know they've never gone along with that. One of Robbie's neurobiologist colleagues is working on twinning, researching the effects of mitochondrial insufficiency on the development of the foetus. (That's me, apparently. Mitochondrially deficient! It figures: when in doubt just blame the mother, ha-ha-ha.) There are degrees of twin-ness in identical twins. Normally mitochondrial traces continue to work on the fertilised foetuses so that as they grow older differences in appearance and personality become more and more pronounced, but not with Martha and Maude. Robbie suggested a link between my (alleged) mitochondrial insufficiency and my oestrogen over-sufficiency, probably contributing to my menstrual mood swings – but I really didn't want to know. Enough is enough. I'm a person, not a bundle of hormones and chemicals, and I'm not going to be defined away by my DNA. It's reductionist. On the other hand, if there could be some link between my mood swings and a dream life which is beginning to oppress me, next time Robbie suggests it maybe I will go and 'see someone' at Portal Inc. It can do no harm.

Oh God, so much is all my fault – my insufficient mitochondria having failed to enable the twins to differentiate as they grew older, and one can only suppose I drove my natural parents to murder and suicide, my father getting fed up and killing my mother. I said earlier that 'he had changed his mind' and shot himself, but actually he did fire at me and I was hospitalised but survived: the police had to shoot him. One way and another I think it's a miracle I'm as sane as I am.

And the twins had always seemed to me to be over-fond of Cynara, almost taking her part against mine. They admired her style, the sheer extravagance of her manners. They'd even met Robbie before I had. They'd happened to drop by to see Ted in the Gallery: he wasn't there, but Cynara, as it happened, was – on the very day when Robbie was there, interested in buying a fake Franz Hals for his office foyer. A strange coincidence. Stranger still, come to think about it, that since we were married Robbie had showed so little interest in paintings. The ones we had on our walls had been bought and hung by Ted: and though I had suggested to Robbie that we simply give them back to the gallery and have done with them (I'd always been a little disconcerted by Ted's interest in fakes) so that Robbie could have his own space on the walls, he'd not taken the suggestion up. Ted's choice of paintings hung stubbornly on our walls. Married life is like that – all compromise.

What else had Cynara said? 'When a man takes Doxies he passes on so much extra SSRI in his cum she ends up so passive, pleased and loving she'll do anything he asks. The lab keeps them under lock and key.' And then I thought, it all makes dreadful sense. I so love Robbie, and he seems to love me. Perhaps Cynara isn't making it all up, isn't deranged. Supposing the love-fix is true, the sex you have to have to keep the addiction going? Supposing it's all true. Ted, murdered just in order to get him back from the dead, myself put in as stalking horse. Cynara: 'If anyone could get a genuine word from the other side it'd be you.' That's what they're after. Me as the stalking horse. No wonder Cynara was doing so well with the gallery: 'Good to have the NSA on one's side.' Again and again:'I'm not saying they bumped Ted off just to try it out, but it wouldn't surprise me.'

Then, after weeks, the letter from the coroner came and we were free to go ahead with the funeral. Ted's brother's Aidan's mother-in-law from his first marriage came over to help me with the arrangements. I tried to apologise for the nylon sheets and scratchy towels she'd been given last time, but she looked surprised and said she hadn't even noticed. Everyone had just been upset I realised. The relatives had not been particularly unkind: just thinking what people will think, but don't say, if I really had been overhearing their thoughts.

Cynara called me white witch Philly. How dare she!

When we finally got the body back it looked okay in its coffin. You could hardly see the join, according to family members who'd gone down to see it at the undertakers before it was cremated. I had no desire to do so, though one of the brothers told me I ought, otherwise I would have trouble believing Ted was dead.

A cat once died in my arms: I was a child. It belonged to our neighbour. In one second it turned from a living, wailing, struggling creature to a scrap of rather dusty limp fur, which might as well go in the dustbin. When my adoptive mother died the police gave me her handbag to sort out, sodden with river water as it was – it had been trapped in the car – and the same thing had happened to that. The life had left it. The bag, so much part of her, was denatured: changed from a watched and guarded possession – '*Where's my bag? Oh, where's my bag?*' – to a piece of limp washed-out leather, and even the cards and coins inside seemed worthless: my mother had taken their significance with her and the bag didn't even have a soul. I tell you the spirit goes. The bits and pieces become as nothing.

When I'd seen Ted dead in his bed the spirit had already gone, and I accepted his death as much as I ever would. Interesting, that as soon as his body was back in the locality where it had died I'd had the dream, or as I now saw it the vision, of Ted walking away. I can see now why it is so important the world over to have corpses back and close at hand. Edinburgh was simply too far away. In my mind now Ted was not dead, but wandering and stumbling in the dark wood waiting for salvation, or at any rate hoping for it. I should have gone down to the icy morgue and prayed over his body and helped him on his way, on the principle held by mediaeval theologians that the prayers of the living hastened the sinner out of purgatory – so the priests had taught my adoptive mother and so she had taught me. But I delayed and delayed, and then I heard that Cynara had been to view Ted's body, so any indecision was at an end. If she visited, then I wouldn't.

By the time Ted's corpse was back and sufficiently restored to receive visitors, I was in what my grief therapist Bambi

Bennett called the second state of grieving: out of denial and into anger. The twins had gone down to the morgue without waiting for me to decide if I was going to go, and come back to report that they had seen Cynara there.
Maude.... Leaning over Dad's body, Mum.
Martha.... Touching his body, Mum.
Maude.... She put her finger to her own lips.
Martha.... And then she put her finger to his.
Maude.... She looked so soppy.
That was enough for me.

For her outing to the morgue Cynara had been wearing thigh-length pale brown leather boots, a very short skirt and a yellow beret. Maude thought her coat was Stella McCartney. Martha agreed. The next day the twins came back from Brent Cross both wearing yellow berets from Miss Selfridge. In the days before Robbie that was all they could afford. These days they'd have probably got round to designer coats as well.

Ted and she had been having an affair, I'd convinced myself of that, though in retrospect I can see the evidence was rather flimsy. Cynara could make a drama out of anything. I'd had suspicions at the time, which Ted had laughed out of court. 'Time of the month fantasies.' But two heads close together in the gallery; a couple of flushed faces when I turned up unexpectedly; his telling me over and over what a most remarkable business head she had, how well she dressed and how good she was with customers, 'and of course she has the figure to carry it off' – had had me reacting one day and then an outburst, me stamping and crying and accusing.
'For God's sake, Phyllis, you're not telling me you're jealous of Cynara? You and your bloody moods. You see sex in everything. She's my – she's our business partner. You have

a chunk of the business too, though you don't give it any attention.'

Which had sent me spinning off into my normal feelings of inadequacy – I knew so little about art and Cynara seemed to know so much. My share of the business had always been a mere token – the few thousand pounds my adoptive parents had left – and frankly I found staring at paintings boring and meaningless. More sensible and virtuous, surely, for me to keep the home show on the road, and building up Q&A&Co, doing the most boring work in the world, earning a steady if not lavish living for us all. While Ted and Cynara swanned about looking at bad fakes and talking of the truth behind the false and listening to farts from the Courtauld giving lectures. 'Why would Cynara be interested in me?' Ted had protested. 'Or I in her? I've got a lovely wife and she's got a perfectly good boyfriend. Some well-heeled brain surgeon from the States in a fancy suit. Much more her style. And a wonder in bed, she tells me.'
Did she indeed? That was the sort of conversation he had with his 'business colleague'? Yeah, sure.

But as my surging monthly hormones subsided so did my level of disbelief. It was too disturbing to my emotional equilibrium to act on mere suspicions. I kept the acknowledgement that it was in Ted's nature to have affairs well below my conscious threshold. If I didn't know about Ted's affairs, then he wouldn't know about mine. Of course I had them, though hardly affairs, one-night stands mostly: a quick fuck and they'd run away. Long-term intrigues with women married with children are too risky for most men – they might get too serious.

Women used to fall in love with Ted: I was aware of that. I just accepted that my life with him was peppered with mysterious phone calls, 'wrong numbers', sobbing women running away from the front door when I opened it. He'd always have an explanation: he'd be angry at my lack of trust; he'd flatter me and soothe me and take me to bed and I'd lose all interest in checking details. I loved Ted. He didn't need the mythical Doxies of Cynara's imagination; he'd had his own ample natural supply of hormones.

That was the first time I'd heard of Robbie's existence. A wonder in bed, as described by Cynara to Ted, reported to me mid-marital-row, then forgotten. Or filed away by me and why I fell for Robbie so instantly at Ali's first night? Who's to say? But yah boo sucks to you Cynara anyway: I got him. 'Don't worry so, we were only ever bed buddies' – so you told me over lunch. And you lied, along with your other fantastical tales of the new all-powerful rulers of the social media universe who had their sights on me, little me. What could I have been thinking, believing you even for a second?

Paranoia had been returning, I realised, reinforced by the keep–awake pills? What else were these recurring *who-murdered-Ted* fantasies I was enduring? Ted had had a normal unsuspicious death, and I even had a certificate to prove it.

Last night I'd rashly flushed my little pink pill down the loo. Now I got up from the chair where I'd been sitting staring into space with my brain so uncomfortably and wildly speculating, went to the bedroom and took another pink pill. Then an extra one to be on the safe side. I needed to calm down. I went down to the kitchen and had some coffee and my fears all flared up again. One never learns.

I hadn't thought Cynara would have the nerve to go to the funeral as well, but she did. Mistresses usually keep out of the way of new widows. When our mourning group was waiting at Golders Green Crematorium – such a sorry black-garbed cluster – to go into the chapel of rest – these things run by clockwork: one group out, one group in; no hanging about – I spotted Cynara who was wearing dazzling black-and-white Missoni stepping out of a taxi escorted by a tall handsome man in an Armani-looking suit, the whitest of white shirts and the blackest of black ties. I was in my old black M&S raincoat. I waited to exchange a few polite words with Cynara for the sake of onlookers, and then I just fainted and thus excused myself from the funeral itself. If she was going I would not.

'The widow was prostrated by grief,' the local paper reported, 'and could not attend the funeral.' Actually I think I was prostrated by a kind of generalised rage, accompanied by a fit of the oestrogen blues. Ted had left me without warning and without consideration and had contacted Cynara before he contacted me. I was dimly aware I was taking it out on Cynara.

After the funeral, after the messages of affection and goodwill had stopped and I was left alone, I swung like a weather vane between acceptance and rage. I'd tell myself there was no evidence other than gossip that Ted had any kind of carnal relationship with Cynara: she was his business partner and knew him well, and it was perfectly reasonable that she should visit him in the morgue and come to the funeral. Then it would strike me as a total outrage.

The twins got their share of my fury for having so callously returned to college, though I'd gone to great lengths to persuade them to do just that. My workforce got it, for not turning up when I'd actually told them not to. My customers got it, for asking me to pay their bills. I wound down the Q&A&Co business. I couldn't concentrate on it. I was having trouble making ends meet; there'd been no life insurance, nothing sensible like that – but that was hardly my clients' fault. Most of all Ted got the full blast of my rage, just for being dead. The occasional Ted dreams – at this time they were only once a week or so – were comparatively easy to dismiss.

Nor could I find it in myself pray for him. I'm sure it makes good therapeutic as well as theological sense to pray for the dead – how often the recommendations of both disciplines coincide; only the metaphors are different. I'm sure it helps reconcile the living to life without the deceased, but I was too angry. But nor had I put a stone in his mouth, as one of the relatives had urged me to do (if only by telepathic means) in the confused days after Ted's death. One way or another, if I were a superstitious person, it would not be surprising to me that Ted should 'walk'. I wanted him to walk – it meant he was not dead. He would be a revenant, a dead person returned from the other side, walking on this earth. Even if he had to bring the other side back with him, manifested by mud from his shoe.

The mind struggles to make sense of the peculiar and uses imagery it knows and understands. In South America space aliens appear as little green men, in North America they have large eyes and wear white polo necks, in Mediterranean countries people see the Virgin Mary: around Glastonbury choirs of angels are seen in the skies, across the sea in Ireland they'll tell you about the Wild Hunt. When there's something weird and wonderful going on we interpret it as best we can.

Most rational people blank off when you talk in these terms; one of the endearing things about Robbie is that he's always been prepared to listen when I tell him about my dreams. I now love Robbie as once I loved Ted. Cynara may well be right. Love is not all you need, love is the result of a hormonal exchange between a man and a woman, to which the woman is more sensitive. Any girl who doesn't want to fall in love would be wise to insist on a condom.

Ted, in that initial dream, had left me in sunlight, but a fine sort of sunlight it then turned out to be: my new life was just lonely and humdrum. Once the captains and the kings departed I was left alone with my girls and I felt embarrassed and didn't know what to say to them. They had more than enough to say to me: their general feeling seemed to be that I had wilfully deprived them of a father by some monstrous act of carelessness: somehow I should have saved him, and thus them, from their loss. They said aloud what the other had just thought. Why hadn't I watched his diet? Why hadn't I stopped him smoking, drinking, eating chocolate? There's a competitive element in family grieving, a *this-hurts-me-more-than-it-hurts-you* syndrome. I ended up shouting at them. I was a widow, I screamed, they should leave me be, they were merely half-orphans, I was a quadruple orphan: their lives were before them, mine was ebbing fast. Then I apologised. The twins were shamefaced and confused and both went to bed early after sessions on social media with their 'friends'. But I felt quite selfish about my right to despair. They had each other, I was just me. Family relations were mended; they went back to their college rooms with a smile and a kiss. But nothing was quite the same between us. And they would sometimes call by the gallery and see Cynara, I knew, which struck me as egregious disloyalty.

Then Robbie came into my life. In one short day a life changes. What was grey and gloomy suddenly seems bright, full of hope and possibility. Robbie's colleagues explain it away as a rush of oxytocin and its friend vasopressin – large, 'excitable', bonding neuro-endocrines which 'generate action potential' – into the blood. All those young lovers clasping each other under street lights, his bio-nerd friends would argue, are merely glued together by bonding hormones. But they would say that, wouldn't they? Me, I was in love. I felt ten years younger, my hair shone and my complexion glowed. I smiled all the time. Men caught my eye on the tube instead of looking through me. In September Robbie came to Ali's sculpture show with Cynara, and left with me. *Quelle victoire!*

'Why me?' I asked him at the time. Of course I did. He could have had anyone, this tall, good-looking, benignly intelligent, expensively dressed, clearly affluent man with his long-fingered hands, well-manicured nails – and heterosexual to boot – who took one look at me, and fell in love.

'I've no idea,' he said, 'Except you're an alpha female and I'm an alpha male and there aren't too many of us. And you understand what I'm talking about, and you're not thin as a rake like all the others. And I adore your hair. And I want you to have my children.'

'They might be twins,' I warned him, sounding apologetic.

'Better and better,' he said 'Just make sure they're identical! Fascinating. I'm your man when it comes to cloning.'

And I was gone, held. Why would I doubt him? His love-making was ardent, long-lasting and confident enough to subsume any initial embarrassments and self-doubt into the larger, dreamy category of love-at-first-sight. It was as if the universe worked through Robbie, easily and naturally, with its steady, insistent beat. *'A wonder in bed.'* I was surprised and gratified – usually the left-brainier the man, the more tentative he tends to be and it's the artistic types, the right-brainers, who excel in bed. I was wise enough to be on the pill. Even though Ted was gone I'd kept on taking it. Widowed I might be, and sad, and depressed, but I saw no reason to live a sexless life. Perhaps it was just Cynara's Doxies drugging Robbie, and so me too, making us feel things we wouldn't normally feel. Given a choice between the drunkenness of love and the sobriety of truth, I'd choose intoxication any day.

The truth is so hard to put a finger on. It's like the little ball of silvery mercury that comes from a broken thermometer – or did when I was a child; nowadays they all seem to be digital. Touch it and it splits into a hundred tinier versions of itself. Sweep the tiny balls with your finger – mercury is a poison, just dreadfully pretty, not to mention expensive – and they dart together again, as if really anxious to be reabsorbed into the whole. There's attraction for you. But once reunited, little scraps of the dust gathered on their adventure will cling to the surface of the mother ball and quite spoil it.

What had Cynara said? 'All the big boys, all in it together. They mean to live forever. Make Hell's foundations quiver, the gates to fall, death to have no dominion.' Perhaps Ted was still alive, the dream the illusion. Some hired assassin crept in while I was downstairs wrapping presents on the night before Christmas, and jabbed Ted with a needle full of a drug which made the body cold, but did not induce death. The living body then conveniently whisked away 'to Edinburgh': a brain transplant for a dying Californian software tycoon with a passion for 'art' – why not? They've already done it with rats and monkeys; heaven knows what they can do to people over at Portal Inc or even here at

Dinton Grove. Something else she'd said: 'But you hear voices, dead people appear to you. Stuff like that. You're at home with the paranormal. You have the gift.'

I suppose I'd better face it, though it's three in the morning: stuff like that.

Four

That other stuff: the last thing I want to think about. The dead visiting their nearest and dearest to say goodbye and soften the blow of their departure is a common enough experience, and one which has much preoccupied me lately. But our degree of importance to the deceased may turn out not to be what we thought. Take the example of Althea Bishop. Ted and I had met her only once, and casually, at my friend Ali's and we'd instantly both liked her, but that was all. I'd scarcely known her, but she chose me to come to first.

I was watching *Shrek 2* with the twins at the O2 multiplex in Finchley Road when Althea came mid-performance and sat in the empty aisle seat beside me, touched me on my arm, and smiled when I turned my head. A slight whiff of alcohol came on her breath. I didn't recognise her at first.

'What are you doing here?' I asked in surprise. 'Is this your kind of film?'

'I just came to say goodbye,' she said, 'I'm not staying. I have to be off now.' And she patted me on my arm, got up and went up the aisle towards the exit.

'See you, Althea,' I called out after her.

'Do shut up, Mum, you're talking to yourself again,' chorused the twins. They were sixteen at the time.

There seemed no difference between the level of reality offered by the film, which everyone could see, and Althea, whom I alone saw. I looked at my watch – the twins loved the film but it didn't really absorb me, and I longed for it to be over – and it was nine-forty. The audience was singing along to *Holding Out For a Hero*, not very well.

The next day I called Ali to say I'd run into Althea at the cinema, but Ali could hardly listen. She was crying. Althea had been killed the night before in a road accident.
'What time did she die?' I asked.
'What the bloody difference can that make?' Ali was quite cross. But she told me that just after nine-thirty Althea had stepped off a kerb without looking and a motorcyclist had got her. There'd be no prosecution, there were witnesses. Althea had boyfriend trouble: she'd been upset, had had four vodkas and Red Bulls at the pub.
'She was smiling when I saw her,' I remember saying.

I reckon I was the first person Althea visited: perhaps she happened to be thinking of me at the time of the accident instead of concentrating on crossing the road. Or perhaps she and I were more closely connected in some way I don't properly understand – in the way the same people turn up in our lives again and again, for no apparent reason. We live with coincidence – we are invited to a stranger's house and it turns out to be the house where we were born: we run into a childhood friend in a small hotel in a foreign land – we remark upon the strange ways of fate and dismiss them. Synchronicity, Jung called it. Interlocking gears. I have no doubt Cynara's 'they', those who want to make Hell's foundations quiver and live forever, are number-crunching even as I speak to find out what goes on.

'I have to be off now,' Althea had said, and it certainly seemed to me she had somewhere to go. But where? She seemed too easy and uncomplicated to end up in the dark wood like Ted. She was less of a spell-in-purgatory than a straight-to-heaven person, though what do I know? And as for heaven, I can't see it in terms of playing harps and sitting on clouds – that's just a metaphor to explain the inexplicable – any more than I can see it as just more-of-the-same in some other dimension.

When Ted came back from the gallery that evening I told him about Althea's farewell. I usually kept quiet about the occasional weird things that happened around me: the lost clothes that materialised in the wardrobe, words that vanished from a letter I'd been writing and reappeared, keys which changed places of their own accord and so forth. I hated it when Ted went into his I-married-a-witch mode, which he tended to when he was tired or cross. He looked at me in disbelief: the soft brown eyes which could look so kindly hardening just a little.

'It didn't happen,' he said. 'You're upset. It's called confabulation. The opposite of retrograde amnesia. Philly, you remember things that didn't happen. Perhaps you should see someone.' My life seems full of husbands who suggest I 'see someone', when all that happens is I see something others don't.

'I called out to Althea. The twins heard me. It was exactly when she died,' I said.

'The police got the time wrong. Or she'd left the party and gone to the cinema.'

'She died in Clapham in South London. We were in the Finchley Road, in *North* London. Oh, what does it matter? She's dead! I'm just glad she said goodbye. Forget it.'

Home life gets reported and embellished in the office. My

Althea incident could have been fine grist to the gossip mill as reported to Cynara by Ted. '*My wife the witch: can't even go and see a kids' movie without seeing a ghost!*' And Cynara would have passed it on as small talk to her favourite customer Robbie if only in the interest of a good sale, or in pillow talk in her Mayfair bedroom – she lived well, did Cynara – and Robbie would have taken it all back to his masters, with their growing interest in the Other Side: that I was a 'sensitive'.

At the turn of the last century it was considered that just as a few were born great artists, or dancers, or writers, a very few were born mediums, sensitives, for whom the wall between the living and the dead was thin, who slipped more easily between alternative realities than most. Like I do, I suppose.

'Oh darling, you've no idea, have you, just how important you are,' Cynara had said over our fish and no chips for her at the Caprice. It's all very well for her. But I need food to weigh me down, to keep my physical presence strongly based. Most mediums are overweight. I'm a size twelve.

Yes, it figured. 'They' might be gathering samples like me from here, there and everywhere. Big Data could locate us, the few amongst millions. And how long had Cynara been part of it? Why did Cynara buy me out of the gallery after Ted died? Simple greed on her part, perhaps? Within the month I'd accepted a miserable offer from her solicitors. I should have asked for three times as much and probably I'd have got it. Or if I'd stayed a sleeping partner I'd be rich by now. She's branched out from old master fakes into works of art 'by' celebrities, but ghosted by notable 'named' artists. The gallery is no longer becalmed but steaming ahead. Cynara has friends in high places. *'I'm with the NSA too'*, while I was choking and gasping over our dry martinis.

In retrospect I can see that Cynara timed her offer well: I was in no position to argue. Ted had left me inadequately provided for, which she knew. Her call to me days after Ted's death to say he had appeared to her in a dream thoroughly unsettled me, and had perhaps been intended so to do. Though I can also see that if she was sleeping with Robbie and he was on Doxies, she too was likely to have powerful dreams.

Until Robbie came to live with me the Ted dreams were erratic, and with nothing like the intensity of the first vision – when I was left poised in sunlight while Ted was whisked on in dark shadow to a gloomy shore. After that I'd just see Ted from a distance, stumbling amongst gnarled roots, held back by brambles and thickets like Snow White in the Disney film, but with the feeling that if only he got through the wood there would be something better on the other side. Now I must remind myself that Ted's revenant, his visible ghost, his returning corpse, is coming from my mind, not his, and not through some malicious external force. This is not a curse, this is not black magic.

My dreams: I wake from them, even if they became more difficult to forget. There is a difference between a dream (defined as a series of thoughts, visions, or feelings that happen during sleep, from which one is said to 'wake') and a hallucination (defined as an image, sound, or smell that seems real but does not really exist, from which you don't 'wake', but is simply here one minute, gone the next). More, hallucinations are usually caused by mental illness or the effect of a drug, or so the dictionary tells me. But I suppose you could have a hallucination of a dream, which if there is any truth in Cynara's wild assertions about Robbie taking Doxies, might well be the case. What I am having is both. His declarations of love for me might be as hallucinatory and as drug-fabricated as mine for him. Ted's '*for God's sake leave me alone*' at least had a ring of familiarity.

Two days after Robbie and I had met at Ali's and I spent the night with him he turned up at my house with roses and quantities of smoked salmon. He was doing some serious wooing – that much was obvious. Then he said, 'You won't believe this, but your Ted appeared to me in a dream, and asked me to make a decent woman of you.'
'I don't believe you,' I'd said. I wasn't too pleased. He was linking my present with a past I wanted to put behind me.
'I can't help that though,' said Robbie. 'What happened, happened.' He pulled me to him and we resumed our kissings and clutchings and the one trying to be part of the other, like teenagers. It was wonderful after the months of celibacy.

Robbie did quite a lot of kissing with his perfect, shiny north-American teeth, so well set back behind well-shaped George Clooney lips. He favoured suit fabrics that were good to bury one's head into – nothing cheap or man-made. He also ponged delicately of something called Homme de Chasse No 1, which he said Portal Inc always gave away as their annual Thanksgiving staff gift. 'We guys can choose a twenty-pound turkey instead. I've always gone for the man-scent but come next Thanksgiving, when we're married, I'll take the turkey.'
'Married? It's only been two days,' I said. 'You may change your mind. And the twins are vegetarian.'
'Dammit,' he said. 'Nothing's perfect.' I loved him.

Robbie was so new to me, so un-Ted-like. Ted just smelt as he smelt, dressed as he dressed, was happy enough to buy his clothes from the charity shop, kissed little, fucked much. I'd have hesitated to nuzzle my nose into an old leather jacket that in all likelihood had been handed in by the initial wearer's widow. And Ted would not have dreamed of wearing scent – last week's bonfire was good enough for him. Ted's bonfires smelt of wood; Robbie's of paper and plastic.

And then about a week after we'd met Robbie told me he'd dreamed of Ted too.

'You're making that up,' I said.

'No, I'm not,' he said. 'I couldn't have made it up. It was too detailed. Ted was wearing a black-leather biker jacket with a brown fur collar and striped yellow socks. He was looking at a painting of the *Mona Lisa* and she was smiling. He waved at me and said, "Look after her".'

I admit this gave me a shiver. Ted *had* bought such a jacket at a charity shop, and it was dear to his heart. I'd sent it back to the shop it came from, a couple of weeks after his death, when the clearing up had started. And how could Robbie know about the striped socks? Ted wore them in the garden, never to the gallery. Too gaudy.

'I bet the *Mona Lisa* was a fake,' I said.

'She was sure as shit really smiling,' he said. 'Not just a simper. She was wishing us well.'

And that dream, genuine or not, was the end of any doubts I had about the matter of marriage. Ted had given permission. Neither he nor I wanted the other to get away, that was the truth of it. Robbie never mentioned his own relatives. Ted's family were horrified at the speed of events. You didn't need to read their minds to know what others were thinking. A raise of the eyebrows, a sniff and a snigger said it all. *'Out of one bed and into another!' 'It's indecent! Those poor twins – what they must feel!' 'What on earth can he see in her?'* and so on.

But in the here and now sleep was beginning to overcome me. The wake-up pills were wearing off. I wouldn't wait up for Robbie. I'd go to bed alone in the confidence I wouldn't dream if I didn't have sex with him. Ted wouldn't be able to come walking out of his world into mine. In the morning Robbie would be there, and he would sit on the bed and stroke my cheek, and his declarations of love and concern for me would ring as true to me as mine did for him: *Let me not to the marriage of true minds, Admit impediments…* Forget Cynara and her improbable impediments… I slept.

I awoke from a dreamless sleep around nine a.m. feeling alert and rational. That is to say I couldn't remember having any dreams, and my own view of myself was that I was alert and rational; but that too may have been illusion. There was no sign of Robbie, but I felt no pang of loss, no withdrawal symptoms resulting from the absence of his attentions. My conversation with Cynara had been the bad dream: lunch with an anorexic maniac. The room was full of light: the sun had been up for hours; I pulled the blind up and got the full blast of its brilliance in my eyes. I was dazzled and couldn't see properly at first, then my eyes adjusted.

On the floor between the bathroom and the chest of drawers, seeming to grow out of our new fitted pale green carpet (John Lewis, wool-rich woven celery velvet, £52 the square metre) which now replaced Ted's and my pale pink one (John Lewis, wool and nylon mauve twisted pile, £19 the square metre) was a little sapling. It was about six inches high, with a brown stem hardly thick enough to call a trunk. It had branching arms hung with bright green clusters of something between leaves and fronds, and with black roots descending like tentacles and digging into the velvety pile of the carpet. It was a miniature version of one of the Arthur Rackham trees Ted wrestled with in my dreams of the great forest. It looked as though it had every intention of growing.

I hadn't had a dream and I hadn't seen Ted, I'd just been asleep. No, I thought, this is a hallucination. This is not something that's grown, sprung up overnight like an evil mushroom; this is some horror I have produced myself, out of my addled imagination.

I tiptoed round the little tree carefully and went through to the bathroom; brushed my hair, my teeth, put on lipstick. If I ignored it perhaps it would go away. When I went down to the kitchen there was a strong smell of coffee and frying bacon, and there was Robbie, limber and fully dressed and perfectly lively. He smiled at me. His perfect teeth gleamed; his glasses caught the sun and glinted back at me. Everything glittered. It was a beautiful spring morning. Robbie was like a man on a Calvin Klein poster, all clean-cut and pent-up vigour, not a crumple anywhere. I didn't run to him and clasp and wriggle: I pecked him affectionately on the cheek. I felt affectionate. A woman who hallucinates – but whose twins are housed by her husband, whose dream kitchen is paid for by him, whose Dualit toaster cost £195, and whose sexual needs are more than matched, does well to show affection even if their husband has been out all night, even if his jealous 'ex-bed-buddy' has had nasty things to say.

'Sorry not to get back earlier,' Robbie said. 'I called but

couldn't get through. I hope you weren't worried. There was a major security lockdown at the Embassy.' The new American Embassy, next to Portal Inc at Nine Elms. That great sparkly glamorous prism on the Thames skyline, all facets and angles, that citadel that seemed to hover rather than stand; that miracle of rare device, with its closed-loop water supply, its blast-resistant glass, its controlled climate! Robbie certainly had a thrilling life. To be near to it, close to it, trapped inside it, could justify all eventualities, neutralise all grievances. 'The big guys flew in an hour early, ahead of schedule. The Portal crew, yours truly included, were stranded the wrong side of the doors and that was it for the night.'

'That's awful,' I said. 'Wasn't it alarming?' But I was impressed. I couldn't help it. My Robbie, so close to the centre of power! It is dreadful the way status and wealth impinge on the female psyche.

'A nuisance,' he said. 'But we were safer in there than any place else. I've cooked pancetta; I prefer it to the back bacon.'

'I do too,' I said.

I knew better than to ask who the big guys were, or why their flying in triggered a security shut down.

'I hope you got some sleep,' I said.

'Oh, they looked after us. I'm not used to sleeping alone, though.' He gave me a little pinch on the bottom. I quite liked that. It's nice to be owned, good to be acknowledged; I gave him a little pinch back. 'In fact I'm feeling great – they handed out Juves by way of apology. It was a great honour to be there. I was privileged.' He looked at me and he smiled. It was the smile of the evangelist, of one who knows he will have eternal life, and deserves it.

'Juves?'

'Rejuvenating capsules. CDF hormones, good for heart-function and general wellbeing.'

'Like Doxies?'
He seemed taken aback. He shook his head.
'No. Not at all like Doxies. Doxies are extremely complex psycho-pharms. Juves are junior league.' And then: 'But what do you know about Doxies? They won't be let out on sale for a good five years and then only on prescription.'
'Cynara told me at lunch.'
He said Cynara was a naughty naughty girl, but he didn't deny the existence of Doxies. The Juves, whatever they were, appeared to me to have the same effect as cocaine; that is to say rendered the taker wide awake, lively and friendly, but without any accompanying anxiety.

He asked me how I had got on with Cynara. He wanted his two favourite girls to be friends.
'Don't take that amiss,' he said, since I must have shown from my face that I did.
'The most she ever was to me was a bed buddy.' That phrase again. Were they both talking from the same script? 'You are my wife and I love you. But she was fun.'
The Juves seemed to be acting as a truth drug, so I took the opportunity of asking him whether he thought Cynara had had an affair with Ted when they worked together at the gallery. I dropped it in casually as a kind of afterthought, but some basic wariness in him lingered. He lived in a top secret world. He was not going to tell me.
'Phyllis honey,' he said. 'I thought we were living our new life together, not forever raking over old times. My predecessor in your bed was an attractive fellow, but what's dead and gone is dead and gone.'

I said I didn't think that was necessarily the case and suggested he go upstairs to the bedroom and have a look at what was growing there. He bounded upstairs.

A few seconds of silence. And then a shout.

'Oh my God, Philly, what have you done?'

That's right, I felt like saying: when in doubt, fucking blame the woman. But Robbie was already on the phone. I took the pan off the cooker. I didn't think we'd be getting any breakfast.

Five

By ten o'clock we were on the underground on our way to the new award-winning, art-deco-maroon-and-white-tiled station at Nine Elms, having taken a ticket to Vauxhall. Robbie explained we would not actually get off at Vauxhall, but would stay on the train and pay the extra, the better to forestall watchers. He did not say who 'watchers' were. Juve-induced paranoia, I supposed.

Robbie had to use the kitchen scissors to disentangle the roots of the little tree from the carpet – it was a tender sapling scarcely a hand tall but already an inch taller than when I had first seen it – so tightly and firmly had they dug themselves in. He did it with energy and verve. I would have to put a rug down to cover the damage. But it was a small price to pay for getting the thing out of the house. I didn't like the tree at all, and obviously neither did Robbie. He had placed it, along with its small quantity of muddy soil and some extra tufts of green carpet, inside a sealed zip bag, then put that into his brief case. He carried it with him, rather gingerly now, I thought, as if it was an unexploded bomb. But he remained inordinately cheerful.

After the phone calls, and after he'd showered and found a clean shirt, a fresh suit and a new tie – rather wide and bright yellow, which seemed to echo his cheerful and active mood –

he'd suggested I come along with him to the office.
'It would be good for you to meet everyone,' he'd said. 'And my friend Ben Marcus in the neurological department wants to have a word with you about trauma nightmares.'

It seemed as well to co-operate. If Ted had stepped into my reality last night without so much as the courtesy of a dream, and brought with him not just a scrap of mud but a living entity, and this colleague Ben could stop the dreams, then I must let him, whatever else lurked at Portal Inc. I would step into the mouth of the dragon.
'Because you do love me, don't you,' he said, oddly child-like as I helped him with his tie. It took me only ten minutes to get ready: a clean dress, and sandals. No eye make-up.
'Of course I do,' I'd said, but I wasn't sure. An adult Robbie on Doxies was easy enough to love: Robbie, on Juves as well, was fast developing a child-like, trusting quality, which came over as non-erotic, and I wasn't used to it. But then I'd taken another wake-up pill and they helped me think clearly. I'd only had four hours' sleep and I could see it was going to be a long, breakfast-less day.

Oddly enough, I rather enjoyed the journey, into the mouth of dragon though it might be. We sat next to each other. I felt at home and safe and liked the feel of his haunch against mine; I was wearing a rather pretty white cotton dress with red poppies on it and I knew I looked good. On our way to the station Robbie had taken another pill from his inside breast pocket, chewed it, and swallowed. He seldom kept things in his pockets, for fear or spoiling the hang of his suits.
'A Juve,' he explained, 'I swiped a couple of extras last night. I've had quite a tough time lately; things are hotting up at Portal. Fucking funding priorities.'

'All the more reason to look after your heart muscles, darling,' I said. I had never heard him swear before; he was acting like some college boy. But then it was not in my nature to call men 'darling'. Perhaps it was the wake-up pills. 'They do say it's stress that wears them out.'

We were at Archway before he replied. I sat silent. I thought, well, Robbie is a single-tasker. He does not usually talk and catch trains at the same time.

'It's not just about fucking heart muscles,' he said. 'Juves can make a guy, well, impetuous. But I'm well under control. Not like some I know. I'm not saying a thing. Juves kinda screw up a guy's ability to keep his cards close to his chest. An anti-lie mechanism kicks in. Not a good idea in this business. They sure put a spring in your step, but they can make you stupid too, so you gotta know how to handle them, d'you get it?'

'I get it.' I said. And so I had. I was looking at the psycho-pharma future, where nobody was quite what they seemed. The depressed laughed, the frivolous ceased to smile, pundits believed their own lies. The crazy looked sane and the sane crazy. Doxies made you mistake sex for love and love for sex; Juves made you lose years of wisdom; my little pink pills evened me out into a false serenity. I no longer knew who I was. I'd given up knowing who Robbie was.

At least my wake-up pills helped me think, turned me from passive to active. They were also making me walk fearless into jeopardy. Of course Portal Inc wanted to bring me in. I was their contact with the other side, unwitting and unwilling as I might be, and their robot-slave Robbie had been sent to pull me in. Portal Inc wanted to make the dead walk. Well, fuck them. Maybe I'd rather join the dead than collude. In the meantime I was sitting on a train next to a husband who could not tell lies, and I should make the most of it.

'Perhaps Cynara had taken a Juve yesterday?' I asked. 'She told me all kinds of things at lunch she shouldn't have.' Robbie thought about that a little.
'It's possible,' he said. 'Stock control is appalling at Portal Inc – they just dole stuff out. They're far too sanguine about Juves. They're dangerous in the wrong hands.' 'Are you telling the truth?' I asked.
'Probably,' he said cheerfully. 'It's just so much easier to tell the truth: lies are so exhausting. Checking yourself all the time.'
'I see,' I said, and then I asked, as casually as I could, 'are you taking Doxies?'
'One every night before bed,' he said. 'Those are my instructions.'
'Whose instructions?' It was like one of those quiz games when you only have so many questions before time's up. Any moment now and Robbie might decide lies were less troublesome than truth.
'Portal's of course. I have my bosses, like everyone else on this earth. Bob Dylan got it right,' and he began to sing Dylan's *Gotta Serve Somebody*, with a bit of air guitar. He was well away.

He stopped and looked at me earnestly. Along the half-empty carriage people shuffled and took up their print or e-reading matter. A well-dressed and handsome man with his cleft jaw and rosy lips and springy clean hair, on drugs or drink or both, and behaving strangely. But no-one did anything. All on psycho-pharms too probably.
'But it's nice being in love, Philly, isn't it?'
'Oh yes, very,' I agreed.
'Strange stuff, Doxies. Pass it through the man and the woman falls in love. The Vikings used to pass fly-agaric mushrooms through their womenfolk, drink their urine and end up with

berserker rages. The women did the twitching and got the head pains but mostly lived to see another day.'

'Just great,' I said. 'But with the Doxies the man doesn't get head pains?'

'Oh no,' Robbie said. 'Just a good fuck.'

'Doesn't seem quite fair,' I said.

'Whatever was?' he asked. 'They were right about one thing. The dreams came thick and fast. Doxy sex seemed to bypass the thalamus and get right through to the epiphysis cerebri, where all that hallucinogenic stuff is stored. It was a screwy theory but it got the funding.'

'I'm so glad,' I said. 'So Cynara was right: you're my minder.'

He looked troubled, like a child trying to remember.

'I wouldn't put it quite like that,' he said. 'You always looked so pretty and nice. I do love the dress. Lucky you, being a five. We sixes have our problems. At least you can be happy. I like to make you happy.'

'Are we talking IQ points here, Robbie?'

His hand was creeping round to my bosom. He fingered the nipple and gave it a tweak. I subdued a little scream.

'What else? Sixes are too clever for their own good, I'm a six. 140 plus. I have trouble with empathy. University entrance is only four, 120 plus. You're a five, I reckon: that's between 130 and 140. Lower end, I should think. Most mediums are three's: below 110. You're an exception. Fives are nice. I love you.'

'Okay. What's Cynara?'

'Five veering to six, that's why she's so difficult.' I moved his hand. He didn't seem to notice. Up and down the carriage people relaxed.

'Female sixes are very rare. They're not easily employable. Lost in their own clouds. At seven Asperger's drifts into autism. So no female eights. The female bell curve is steeper. You don't get the extremes either end of the scale.'

'And the ones who flew in yesterday and triggered a lockdown?'

'Little Miss Curious,' he said, frowning and suddenly suspicious.

Sooty tunnel walls of impacted London dirt and ancient brick flashed past the windows. We held hands. His mood lightened. He raised my fingers to his lips and looked at me with slow, dreamy, teenage eyes. I felt absurdly flattered.

'I adore you,' he said.

'What does Portal Inc *do* exactly,' I asked.

'That's easy,' he said. 'We study the links between the new psychoactive substances and such traditional paranormal phenomena as fall within the scope of entheology and neurobiology. Keep your voice down. We're being watched, you realise? That guy standing over there by the door is the NSA.' He was whispering, but smiling at the same time. It was an odd combination.

'What is Portal's connection with the NSA?' Robbie didn't take fright as I thought he might. He was too far gone.

'None, really. We're currently most favoured company, that's all. They fund, we deliver the research. We're the old CIA's Stargate resuscitated. Within certain constraints we're independent.'

'That's really good,' I said, brightly. 'What's entheology when it's at home?'

'Entheogens – oh you little five, I adore you – are any psychoactive substances used in a religious or shamanic context – all that incense and chanting, all those voodoo drums and smoky fires and dancing about. You don't even need the props, you sweetheart.'

I supposed I would get home again. They might prefer me as an in-house specimen, a guinea-pig, monitor me like an egg about to hatch something rare and valuable. On the other hand my credentials were in Robbie's brief case: a plant, one could only infer, from the other side. Keep me in familiar surroundings, and who knew what I might not produce? A sapling today, a revenant tomorrow? I would play innocent, case the joint, go home, divorce Robbie and dream no more.

Robbie took off his glasses and polished them on the sleeve of my dress – it was a nice soft cotton and would do the lenses no harm. His unshielded eyes looked very blue and kind and luminous. He had a full, curved, sensuous mouth. Ted's had been rather thin and could look mean.
'When all this is over,' he asked, 'can we stay together?'

I read once about a man with a memory of thirty seconds. When his wife visited him he'd embrace her tenderly, crying, 'Darling, how wonderful to see you, I love you so much!' before falling back into baffled melancholy. He was on a memory loop and it was an automated response: anterograde and retrograde amnesia, poor man, he was stuck in that loop for ever. Still, it was nice to be asked, and Robbie took my hand again and we were just like authentic lovers.
'Of course,' I replied.

We were at Waterloo: only two stops to Nine Elms, and three to Battersea. I tried again with the seminal question. 'Did Ted sleep with Cynara?'
'I'm sorry about Ted.' Robbie's blue eyes were filling. A final jolt of empathy. 'It wasn't meant to happen. Nothing to do with us.'
'No? Well, that's good.'
'It was our neighbour Jill, not the sharpest knife in the drawer. In fact you might say if intelligence was a disease she'd be

the healthiest girl in town!' He laughed heartily, and I sort of laughed along too.

'She's one of ours. I recruited her. Your Ted had eyes for her, and we had our eye on you from way back.'

It seemed our house was bugged, and had been for years.

'Even the bedroom?'

'Well, of course the bedroom.'

But visitors from the other side had not shown up, though room temperatures could fall dramatically on nights I had Ted dreams. Then Robbie said things that really shook me. When our neighbours the Woodwards had called in at the gallery to buy their Warhol Mickey Mouse Jill had fallen for Ted in a big way. Richard had gone back to his showroom to fetch his debit card and Ted had fucked Jill in the back room in the fifteen minutes the cat was away.

'Quite a guy, your Ted. Boris Becker had nothing on him. A natural font of SSRI's. We had his hair combings analysed. A few men are like that. But it wasn't fair on you, baby.'

It had gone on, on and off, for a couple of years. The night Ted died Jill had taken a Doxy. They'd been out in the moonlight, listening to the nightingales or whatever and having a quickie while they were at it.

'We don't know how she got hold of them. Cynara, probably,' Robbie said. 'Taken by a woman they can trigger an allergic reaction in the man a few hours later and that's what happened. We had to get our own post mortem done. I'm sorry for your loss,' he added as an afterthought. I presumed Portal Inc offered empathy training to all those sixes on its staff.

'That's all right,' I said, but it wasn't. That it was two years since Ted died didn't seem to help much. Jill Woodward was so boring: we'd both despised her. How could he? And Jill, with Ted's death on her hands. Bitch. No wonder she had been so upset when we were stuffing the turkey.

'Ted did get about,' was all I said.

We were at Kennington. The station had been redecorated, all silver tiles engraved with discreet stars and stripes. The train glided off smoothly and swiftly to its destination on new rails.
'I admired your previous husband, Philly,' Robbie said. 'I want you to know that.'
'I'm glad,' I said.
'Doxy love,' he said sadly, 'is nothing like true love. True love follows a man to the Other Side.'
We stopped at Nine Elms. Next stop Battersea.
'Was Ted sleeping with Cynara as well as with Jill?'
'Yeah, of course,' said Robbie. 'Cynara was anyone's. Wouldn't you if you were a guy? We none of us took her seriously. High maintenance too, mind you: all those dress bills on expenses.'
Robbie's voice was slowing, his eyes losing their youthful lustre. The Juves were wearing off. But I had what I wanted, even though I didn't like it. We were at Battersea. We sped on slinky shiny walkways to the return platform, to go back to Nine Elms, a change of plan which would not show up on our Oyster cards.

Ted, murdered by the neighbour he despised but shagged. I couldn't run to the police. I'd seem delusionary, out of my mind: 'Phyllis, the white witch next door who hears voices in her head and complained of poltergeists in her kitchen.' Jill Woodward would look at the enquiring detective with steady, calm, sane, bourgeois eyes opened wide by an expensive plastic surgeon and tell lies and they would believe her.

Screwed by Ted – me, Cynara, Jill Woodward, and no doubt a whole host of others.
Fathered by Ted – Aspergery twins who didn't tell lies.

Screwed by Robbie – Cynara, me, who else, the twins? It was a possibility.
Fucked by me – Ted, Robbie , and yes, others. I was the self-righteous bitch. I wasn't without guilt. I hadn't been totally faithful to Ted during the marriage – a passing Swedish professor when I was a student, a boss when I was an intern, a meeting on a train, a colleague at a conference. Sex with the stranger was always a draw, how you got to know the world outside your little circle of acquaintance. But always for me with the greatest discretion, never as a threat to the marriage. I'd always had a little doubt about the fatherhood of the twins. The Swede was a possible contender, though it was far more likely to have been Ted; we were young at the time, at it all day and every day, and the professor was only the once. Actually it had been one small source of relief when Ted was finally cremated and his DNA destroyed – the twins might well at some stage have wanted to have Ted's paternity scientifically proved. I hadn't reckoned on Robbie getting hold of an ancient hair-combing. But this was the old paranoia, a fear too far. As if I didn't have enough to worry about. We'd arrived at Nine Elms and the new American Embassy was just across the way.

Six

It was good to be above ground again. We walked together to Robbie's workplace. It turned out to be a very ordinary-looking office block, four-square and a mere four stories high, sheltering in the lee of the great glittering prism of the new Embassy. '*Forward into the Future * Shrine of Science*' was engraved in stone above the entrance. I had begun to imagine something far more sinister.

This was just a visit to my husband's office for a consultation with a colleague about the oppressive dreams I had been having lately. I even looked forward to it – it would be a kind of confessional. I had nothing to be ashamed of, much to be proud of. And of course it went without saying that the sooner the dreams stopped the better. The last thing one wanted was for one sapling to lead to another – for the dam between the dimensions to be carelessly breached, and oneself to be in any way responsible. I could imagine a hundred US Marine security guards having to battle and chop away at a forest of encroaching trees – the same kind poor Ted faced nightly on the other side – as they took root and flourished in the Embassy grounds. It didn't bear thinking about.

Security at Portal Inc was agreeably unobtrusive. I did notice that the amiable girl at reception sat behind a typewriter, not a computer. Indeed, during my stay in the building I saw not one single computer, just card indexes and paper files. Here secrets stayed secrets, one supposed, and were not susceptible to hacking: knowledge was exchanged verbally. Everything seemed relaxed and normal, and rather old fashioned. Only when I got to the diagnostic centre, with its futuristic screens and state of the art equipment, was I conscious of any intrusion by the modern world. Our arrival had been anticipated: cameras had noted our approach. The only thing that struck me as quirky was a small automated trolley of moulded plastic which rolled forward to meet us as the glass doors slipped open at our approach. Robbie dropped his briefcase and cell phone into it and the trolley moved swiftly and silently back and disappeared through a hatch into the bowels of the building.

Robbie was let through by iris recognition, but a verbal *my wife – she's with me* wasn't enough to get me past reception. The building swallowed Robbie up and I was left to have inked fingerprints and these were checked by a human being not a scanner taken – heaven knows where they'd got the originals for comparison. This took an irritatingly long time, and it was half an hour before I was shown in to a waiting room: it was of the formal kind that Harley Street doctors still have, unchanged since the fifties in order to soothe old ladies, all velvet curtains and chintz sofas. Almost at once a red haired and bearded man in a rather dishevelled suit bounced in and introduced himself at Robbie's colleague Professor Ben Marcus. It seemed he'd been expecting me.

He led me down corridors to his office. Robbie was all lean and angular and tidy: this man was fleshy and large and enveloping and looked more like a lumberjack than a neuropsychologist. I liked him at once. I have a weakness for large burly men into whose clasp it seems natural to melt, but now was not at all the time or place.

The office looked like any doctor's consulting room – a desk, a couple of chairs, a photo of a dog, a coffee machine – apart from a typewriter and a big old-fashioned reel-to-reel tape recorder. My breathing came a little oddly. I felt short of air. 'You'll get used to it,' Red Beard said. 'We're climate-controlled, vibration-protected and dust-free. Make yourself at home. I'd like to talk a little with you and take a few notes. After that we'll go into the lab and do a test or two.'
'I'm all yours,' I said. But I felt wary. Robbie might have lured me into this place to hand me over for experimentation. Scientists will be ruthless in the pursuit of knowledge.

Red Beard offered me coffee from the machine, but I was cautious. I asked for hot chocolate if there was any. It was less likely to have been tampered with – to contain a powdered Doxy or Juve than the coffee which they expected me to choose because I'm a girl and hot chocolate is fattening. When it came it was suspiciously sweet. I thought what the hell, and drank it. A phone rang and Red Beard was called away. I was grateful; I could just sit there for a little in neutral surroundings and think.

What Robbie had told me on the train was beginning to register. I was fairly certain he had been telling the truth. He had confirmed what Cynara had told me over lunch, that I was indeed part of an experiment. I was watched, spied upon, drugged up to the eyeballs. The hot chocolate probably contained some fucking truth drug. Red Beard's absence was probably calculated to give it time to work. I no longer quite knew who or what I was, or trusted the validity of anything

I remembered as happening to me, or whether I could even tell the difference between dream and reality. Jill Woodward had caused Ted's death. Ted had betrayed me with both her and Cynara. I had been mistaken in him: believed in the self-congratulatory illusion of 'I love Ted, therefore Ted loves me' for twenty years. 'Love', I realised, had been the staple of my existence. I had defined myself as a woman who loved men. Without that anchor I was adrift in a sea of meaningless sensation; a fluttering of SSRIs in the head did not add up to an identity. I was almost sorry for Robbie: it must have been difficult for him during all these months of Doxies and Juves to keep track of who he was. Somewhere beneath the surface lurked a real self I had never met. Red Beard returned.
'I'm so sorry,' he said. 'The last thing I wanted to do was keep our most important client waiting.'

It occurred to me that he was treating me rather as one treats royalty, with a mixture of deference, fawning, and an intense desire to manipulate. It was quite fun to be at the receiving end of such unaccustomed respect. But he asked myriad questions, and I talked and talked: he took down my answers in what I assumed was shorthand. My adoptive mother, a trained secretary, sometimes used these strange squiggles for grocery and laundry lists. Perhaps Red Beard was so clever that he could diagnose my mental and emotional state with a single squiggle. I was being recorded on the creaky old tape machine too, its twin spools quivering in a bath of climate-controlled air.

Red Beard's questions involved the frequency and intensity of the dreams, whether they were recurring – I told him recurring but with variations, and he listed the variations. Why did I describe them as dreams not visions? What traumas had I had in my life? I referred to my birth parents, which seemed to rather startle him; I realised I probably hadn't mentioned the manner of my adoption to Robbie, all so long ago and dire besides that none of it seemed relevant and all of it too daunting for an ardent suitor. That must have gone on for at least an hour. I felt very relaxed and happy and had some more doctored hot chocolate. Might as well be hanged for a sheep as for a lamb.

Then we went on to list and classify the various minor paranormal experiences I usually kept quiet about, and he seemed particularly interested in the jumping rubber episode. I was about ten and had trained an Indian rubber on my school desk to leap into my hand. I'd been pencilling in the names of all the towns in Britain, and spending a lot of time reaching for my eraser because I'd got them wrong or not written them neatly enough; I was bored and frustrated so I taught the rubber to jump into my hand. Beth Audley in the desk beside me saw it happen and had hysterics and refused to sit next to me anymore. So I stopped training things.

'When you say taught, Mrs Whitman, what exactly do you mean?' I was pleased he called me Mrs Whitman, not Phyllis, Phil or Philly. 'Mrs' might carry the tang of age, but also of due respect. I thought over his question.

'A mixture of concentration, will and impatience.'

'Impatience? Can you clarify?'

I explained that I'd been annoyed with the whole situation. It just saved time having the rubber come to me rather than me having to search for the rubber. In the end I'd been licking the rubber so often and hard the map disintegrated over the city of York anyway. I realised there was always a downside to taking shortcuts between ordinary procedures; knowing what a letter said before it was opened meant it brought bad news:

knowing what the cinema was showing before you got round the corner meant the film would be a disappointment. I was late for a dancing lesson and stopped the town hall clock just by wishing, but then it wouldn't start again for months. Once or twice a tin of tuna or something would end up in my hand when I was looking for it. And then there was the wedding ring. That was really odd, but I could have been mistaken. I'd been on a diet and the ring slipped off in the sink when I was peeling potatoes and went down the waste disposal. I turned it off at the wall and put a hand – I have small ones – down it to fish around for the ring but I couldn't find anything. When I gave up and manoeuvred my hand out the ring was back on my finger, only now on the middle finger, where it fitted better. That was considerate of whatever it was: just sometimes it was on my side.

'What was your mood when it happened?'

'Well, as I said, I was peeling potatoes. Impatient, bored, it had to be done but the sooner it was over the better. That sort of mood.'

'But no sense of training the ring?'

'No, I wasn't thinking at all, just trying to find the bloody thing.'

'Ted's ring, or Robbie's?'

'Ted's, of course.' I was indignant – that got a circle round the squiggle. And so it went on. I was tiring. I accepted another Juve-and-hot-chocolate, or so I assumed it to be. It took more effort to tell lies than the truth. I had nothing to lose. Then the talking stopped, and we moved to the lab and the hospital scenario began.

The lab was wall-to-wall futuristic, monitor displays crouching dormant but alert, softly blinking lights, tiny little bleeps, medical instruments designed to analyse the state of any human body offered for their concern. And very, very hygenic. There were no corners, no firm lines: all was curved and cleanable: screens and lighting inset flat with walls; not a screw head visible, nothing to trap dust. I marvelled that I'd lived so long and so healthily at Dinton Grove, it being so full of the nooks and crannies of domestic life where bacteria multiplied unhindered, and I was surprised the professor had not been asked to shave off his beard; it was bushy and raggedy enough, I thought, to harbour an army of germs.

Technicians and nurses aplenty attended, all in hospital scrubs. There was a series of blood lettings – the automaton trolley hovered, came, received and went. Graphs flashed up on screens. There were internal examinations: I am perfectly sanguine about this kind of thing – once one's had twins most ladylike sensibilities are gone for ever. I allowed my body and mind to pass into the care of others.

Only when I was required to lie in an MRI scanner in a lead-lined side-room did I feel nervous. Forty minutes, they told me. I hate the things. They strip one of all metal and one is enclosed, helpless, at the mercy of others while they try and deafen you in the name of science. Clang, clang, clang they go in your ear, driving all sense out of you. But I went like a sacrificial victim naked to the slaughter. My clothes were folded neatly on the chair beside the great hooded pink plastic cylinder. Red Beard made himself scarce. I was left with two technicians, Billy and Mo. They were very talkative:

Mo.... It's a 7.5 Tesla. Most are only 1.5. This can see everything you're made of. Really state of the art, so expensive there's only one in the whole country; a magnetic resonance so strong it can pull the metal fillings out of your teeth. You're our first

patient. Aren't you the lucky one!
He clucked and fussed around my naked body. He waxed enthusiastic with pride. I was happy to assure them that my fillings were all composite.
Billy.... We know that.
Me.... But what are you going to be looking at?
Mo.... Just taking a little peek at your conarium or epiphysis cerebri, in old-fashioned terms your pineal gland.

But that was my precious third eye! I felt protective of it at once. I remembered it well from my time with the Theosophists. What Billy and Mo planned to inspect was the invisible eye in the centre of my forehead in front of the pineal gland, the portal that leads to inner realms and spaces of higher consciousness. My adoptive mother Marion became a member of the Theosophical Society when I was fifteen, and I would be sent off with the Young Theosophists to have apple juice and biscuits while the adults pondered on the Oneness of Everything. All talk was of the 'atrophied third eye' with which the ancients saw a higher range of reality. Mine was less atrophied than most, it seemed, and I was outed as 'a seer' after pretending to see the ghost of the recently deceased treasurer. I refused to go to meetings after that; it all seemed so silly. The biscuits were whole-wheat and homemade, the boys were pimply and the girls wore long scratchy hand-woven woollen skirts. Fortunately my adoptive mother was not averse to giving up the meetings either: there were some things we agreed on. She always preferred a glass of champagne to fizzy apple juice.

But I could see that today my third eye would have to look after itself. It would have been churlish to object; Billy and Mo were so excited about their new 7.5 Tesla toy. The pink plastic cylinder opened up like a mummy's sarcophagus; they sedated me, put muffs over my ears, closed the lid down on my prostrate body and slid me into a dim pink void. Every claustrophobic nerve in my body cried out in alarm.

'Don't move,' I'd been told, and sheer fear kept me immobile. I began to hear what the technicians were saying, through pink plastic walls, through ear muffs, and despite a strange clanging noise which grew progressively louder and sounded to me like hammering on the gates of Hell. There was no way I could actually hear what they were saying, yet I did: in the same way I could hear the thought voices of Ted's relatives after he died. I had gone into telepathic mode. My pineal gland was being stimulated, no bloody doubt about that.

Mo.... Shit! Something hit me!

Billy.... Ferromagnetic projectile. Sodding shrapnel. Better note that for the records – what was it?

Mo.... She had a safety pin keeping her bra together.

Billy.... Idle slut.

Mo.... What's up with her pineal?

Billy.... God knows. Seat of extra-sensory perception. Hears voices? Sees things? They reckon this 7.5 will sort it. They'll get a cell-by-cell picture.

Mo.... Resonance at this strength heats anything up. Everything inside is going to hop about like a box of frogs.

Billy.... If it doesn't implode.

Mo.... This machine frightens me.

Billy.... But it's state of the art.

Mo.... It's already tried to kill me. Supposing she'd left the safety pin open? It could have got my jugular.

Billy.... Perils of modern life.

Mo.... Pretty girl though. Fit! You'd never have thought she'd had twins.

Then they stopped talking or I stopped hearing them, I'm not sure which. The banging got louder; and now I was through into the forest, where Ted was in the clearing, but now beginning to make headway through his normal impenetrable tangle of foliage. I began to help him, chopping away like him at the branches and creepers which stopped him getting through. We were making some progress: there was light at the end of a tunnel though it seemed to me we were going in the wrong direction, away from it not towards. I began to feel frightened. I shouldn't be in here. Ted's head, arms and shoulders were at last free. The twins were there too, busy, untangling vines with nimble fingers. They were for all the world like the young Norns of Norse mythology, weaving the fate of mankind from the entrails of dead warriors, deciding who would live and who would die. Ted's right foot was free now, but his left foot was still trapped by a net of foliage, made up of little saplings like the one which had grown in our carpet last night. Perhaps Ted had visited me in a dream I'd not remembered, bringing with him a seed the same way he'd carried mud in on his shoe the night before – only that time he had brought something that was living and growing. I shouldn't have taken a sleeping pill. They didn't stop dreams happening, they just stopped one from remembering them?

We were through now to a place where trees grew more sparsely and Ted could move freely. Now the twins went into Cheshire-cat mode and faded away. Ted turned to me and said: '*The great juggernaut of progress is not easily held back. You have what you want,*' and I thought: '*but you're dead and I'm alive; what can you possibly know what I want?*' The dream world is nothing to do with ours, I realised, it is an alternative universe, and perhaps those that dwell there share it with the dead and they all don't get on too well. Ted wrenched his foot free: he simply stepped out of the open sarcophagus into the lead-lined booth and walked off through the wall, leaving me trapped and immobile, prostrate in my hospital gown with the dreadful cacophony still attacking my ear drums, stopping all thought and all fear. Just when I thought I really couldn't stand any more the clanging began to slow and quieten, and finally stopped altogether, and Billy and Mo slid me out blinking into the open.

Then there was a spell of general dazed blank dizziness until I was back on my chair in the consulting room and Robbie was shaking me saying, 'Wake up, wake up!': which was odd because I had assumed I was awake. I was dressed and decent, if without my bra. I supposed it had been listed and kept as evidence; just another case of a magneto-ferrous projectile. Robbie seemed agitated. The investigation was at an end, Red Beard was busy clearing away, wiping down, or whatever one did in a climate-controlled, vibration-protected, dust-free environment. Mostly it seemed to be feeding records into the shredder. He too seemed unduly agitated and kept stopping and patting his beard in the mirror to quieten it. The trolley was flitting to and fro, apparently without purpose. That seemed as spooky as anything.

'Philly, you feel all right, darling?' Now Robbie was easing the tension between my shoulderblades. I felt a surprising surge of sexual desire. But again this was hardly the time and place. I felt light-headed and cheerful.
'They've asked you to come in for an interview. We must hurry. They're already in session. We weren't expecting this.'
'Who?' I asked.
'The big guys,' Robbie said. 'The LIFLs and the ADFs who flew in and caused the lockdown. They're conferring upstairs.'

'I call 'em the Live Forever Lads and the After Death Freaks,' said Red Beard.

'Don't worry about it,' Robbie said.

'Why should I?' I asked. 'I have nothing to hide.'

'When was that ever a reason not to worry,' said Robbie, with a flash of shrewdness which reminded me of Ted. Did all husbands, in the end, merge into the one?

I asked what the acronyms really stood for. Robbie and Ben looked at one another as if wondering whether or not to trust me.

'Tell her,' said Ben. 'She knows more than enough already. So much for security.'

They sighed, in unison: I was a mere five. I was reminded of the twins. It was as if the word 'wife' kept one out of important matters – decorative and useful for dull, practical matters, and for the satisfaction of lusts, but one was basically replaceable. If I'd been the one to die, not Ted, who would have replaced me? Cynara? Jill next door? Probably neither. Robbie would have explored new possibilities entirely: and the twins would have shed a tear and gone on to eat food cooked by the new wife and lie in sheets laundered by her and the waters would have closed over me, and Robbie and Ben would get on with their work lamenting the loss of one interesting guinea pig. As for Robbie, I now simply discounted him. All those nights of passion? Nothing, nothing: Doxy dreams, every one.

They explained. LIFLs were Life is for Living adherents, a movement whose ambition was to lengthen telomeres via stem-cell technology and with the aid of spare-part bioengineering, rattle hell's foundations and conquer death's domain so that humans could live forever – or at least those members of it who had money to pay, which would keep numbers down quite severely. The ADFs were a voluble splinter group, the

After Death Friendship society, who felt death was inevitable, and it was important to reach out to 'the other side'.

Frivolously, I asked whose side we were on.

'The ADFs, of course,' said Robbie. 'They're the ones who fund us.'

I tried to take them seriously, but it was difficult, and I giggled.

'And the "big guys"?' I asked at last. But I knew. The ones who rule our lives and know our secrets. What we buy and what we think, every passing whim and feeling categorised and turned into mega data to be algorithm-ised. The young ones sauntering about in California in the sun, who mean to live forever , or, plan B, swap universes and set up their palaces in Lethe. Red Beard was offering me a pill.

'I think not,' I said.

'No worries,' said Red Beard. 'This is just ordinary caffeine to wake you up.'

I realised only then that that he was an Australian. That figured. He had the burly amiability yet stubbornness of a man whose beard would not be denied. I realised I was being swept with a wave of frivolity which would probably do me no good in an interview, whoever it was with: one should never joke with policemen, security guards or an interviewing committee. It is one of the rules of modern society that one does not joke with officials.

I accepted the pill. Really, I had little to lose, no secrets left. Waking up was certainly a good idea. Robbie seemed to have lost his normal languid composure. Both Red Beard and he were all of a flutter, competing for a view of themselves in the mirror, straightening ties and smoothing hair. They might have been biker girls waiting for the leader of the pack. They seemed to have forgotten me.

'The Committee are holding a special convocation ahead of

tonight's AGM,' said Robbie. He was breathless and babbling. 'They opened up the cathedral the minute the analysis of the tree came through. The ADFs are using it as evidence.'
'It's fairly conclusive. Percholate of unknown origin, most likely other dimensional. Where a tree goes a revenant can follow.' said Red Beard.

'When was a committee ever rational? They might jump this way, might jump that. And Phyllis as a star witness—' said Robbie.
'I'll say whatever you like,' I said, feeling obliging again, but they didn't seem to notice.
'Someone patched through the lab results to them,' said Robbie.
'Fuck,' said Red Beard. 'The techs pushed the machine up to 6.5. I told them not to go past 6. The gradients were way too steep. Her epiphysis cerebri readings were all over the place. Something crook happened. "Stare into the abyss and the abyss stares back at you?"'
'Or it could have been the sapling,' said Robbie.
'Pity it ever made it to the lab, then,' said Red Beard. 'Better if we'd deep-sixed it. Shit. Just when we were getting somewhere.'
'A bit too fast for my liking, and possibly theirs.' said Robbie. 'Did you give Phil a Juve?'
'Plenty,' said Red Beard.
'Pity about that,' said Robbie. 'There'll be no discretion on Philly's part, then.'
'And some normal Ritalin.'
'That's why she's so cheerful.'
I expected Ted to walk through the door at any moment but what the hell.

I said I wanted something to eat. Just a sandwich would do. It had been a long day and I'd had no breakfast. Robbie trotted off to the canteen. He was being very attentive, as if I needed to be placated at all costs. 'Normal Ritalin', forsooth, and telling me it was caffeine! But it did make me feel rather good; alert and jokey, a great combination.

I was soon chewing on a limp cheese and tomato wheatgerm roll: all the canteen had left, but it restored me. I assumed it wasn't poisoned. Who would bother to do such a thing?

'I can't face a committee not wearing a bra,' I said, and explained the garment had been taken as evidence of the murderous intent of expensive RMI machines. The hooks had torn off when I put it on that morning in a hurry: therefore the safety pin. I didn't want the bra back, it was old anyway: I just didn't want to look sloppy and droopy in front of some ethics committee.

Robbie said I looked just fine to him without a bra, but when I persisted said he imagined I was much the same size as Cynara and she was in the building somewhere. If she was wearing one today – and it was fifty-fifty; she often went without one – she might be induced to part with hers. I smiled and nodded.

My first thought was where had Ted had gone when he stepped over the rim, rashly freed by me and the twins? Off to find Cynara? My second thought was that I didn't care one bit if he had, and the third thought was astonishment – I was not troubled at all by Robbie's apparent intimacy with the state of Cynara's underwear. I no longer craved any man's approval. I was unburdened – no longer bowed down by useless longing. I was free! I brushed the crumbs from my mouth and stood up to face the world.

It was news to me that Cynara was in the building, but presumably she worked at least part-time for Portal Inc. Nothing was what it seemed. I was amazed at my own naïveté, but excused myself. I had been going round in drug-induced haze for almost a year. Of course Robbie knew about the state of Cynara's underwear. Why would he not? How much did any woman whose partner went off to work every morning with a clean shirt and polished shoes know about what happened when he got there, on the way, or on the way back?

When Robbie returned with the bra I asked him if he had another Juve and he said he had not.

Seven

I could see why they called their meeting a convocation and the place it was in a cathedral; it was as much like a small-scale Chartres as steel and glass, and a glaring mosaic maze on the floor could manage. It took up the entire height of the building. Everything seemed to reach skywards in a pattern of gothic arches and mirrored glass: as a temple to everlasting life on earth it seemed to me faintly ridiculous. They were trying too hard. The place had no age to it – it seemed brittle, an ad-man's delight.

They sat me to wait on my own in the equivalent of a vestry. If I was a witness I was the only one. In the far corner a cluster of uniformed staff stood waiting for the crowd to surge out of the inner sanctum for their tea and coffee and the various health drinks on offer. I went over to them and asked for an orange juice, but this caused considerable consternation – I wasn't on their list and they had no instructions. I said don't bother, and went back to my seat to sit and snooze and wait, but for what? I presumed there was a preliminary meeting of some kind going on next door.

Two security guards in sinister black appeared out of nowhere and hurried towards me; they were carrying what looked like assault rifles, though I know very little about arms. Their weapons looked lethal, and their owners only too happy to use them. I was still in my red poppy cotton dress and what I assumed was Cynara's bra: it fitted, but not as well as my own. Heaven knew where my bag had gone but there'd been nothing important in it anyway. I'd had very little sleep the night before, but though I might not look my best I hoped I looked harmless. The black-clad ones took up their positions in front of me, and I was relieved to see that their brief seemed to be to herd and protect me like attentive sheep dogs, rather than to assault me in any way.

A soft broadcast voice announced 'Recess, Recess', the near set of double doors flew open, the organ struck up Bach's *Sheep May Safely Graze*, and a procession of men emerged: I counted twelve. They wore long scarlet velvet robes and buckled shoes and walked two by two with due solemnity. One could suppose they were cardinals or professors except that they all looked young and healthy, not at all worn out by too much thought or the normal burdens of office: almost like Olympic contestants, strong, confident, and moved by an athletic grace. The Illuminati, I supposed them to be, the 'big guys' – the Ethics Committee who were to interview me.

Only when they got nearer did it strike me that their outer and inner appearances did not match. They were old men in new bodies: their eyes did not open wide with the enthusiasms of youth, but were narrowed and watery as if they had seen too much, knew too much. Yet all seemed in bursting good health, with that smooth, polished skin and confident air of those not plagued by money worries. You might attribute the wisdom of experience to them, while yet fearing the enthusiasm of their youth.

So these were the ones not prepared to accept their own

mortality that Cynara had spoken of, whom Ben and Robbie had called the Live Forever Lads, and exactly half of them – Portal's sponsors – who favoured contacting the Beyond were the After Death Freaks. And all consulting little me, I thought: this is a great opportunity, and a great responsibility.

And then they passed by me, just a few feet away, on into a side room, where I guessed that, in the interests of life extension and even immortality they would rest, and perhaps indulge in a well-deserved blood change to lengthen the telomeres, munch blueberries and carp liver, sip green juices, or whatever the latest longevity craze was. Maybe they just all lay down together for a rest in agreeable togetherness.

The organ died away, the other set of double doors were flung wide and a whole crowd of young men and women, dozens of them, flocked through for tea, coffee and health drinks. They had the kind of happy, earnest and animated faces I'd seen years ago at the Young Theosophists – devotees all. All seemed to be on their phones, or moving nimble fingers over tablets. All were dressed in white or pastel shades. Among the first out were Cynara, Jill Woodward and the twins. I cried out in surprise. I was upset, and the shock was enough to break through my drug-induced non-affect and mental acuity that had protected me so well throughout the day. I found myself on my feet, but the two security men who flanked me suggested by look, gesture and weapon that I sat still, kept quiet, and behaved. I sat down again quietly, composed myself, and thought.

Cynara, Jill Woodward, Martha and Maude. What did the four of them have in common? Why, Ted, Robbie, the NSA (presumably the twins also were now on its books –

why else the riverside flat?) and myself. They didn't seem to have noticed me; all were too busy with each other and their cellphones and their strange green drinks. I hoped that their being dressed in white did not mean that they were potential brides. Martha and Maude, their blonde heads close together, were no doubt on the phone to one another. They did that a lot: I think it made them feel more like separate entities if they communicated electronically. My reason was returning: I recognised all this was actuality, not a dream.

Seeing the four of them together had been startling, but I could at least understand what had happened. The death had acted like a divorce; friends and family had split and taken sides – sometimes the most painful thing about a divorce is not just the damage done to the children, but the way good friends will take sides. Ted had died and I had become the guilty party, betraying my husband by bedding Robbie. All of them loved Ted and all had taken up arms against me. Jill Woodward might have killed Ted, but only by accident: there was no point in blaming her. Ted was the one I should be angry with. The night before Christmas he had betrayed me with her by thought and word, and deed. In all probability he'd been over at her place for a quickie while I was out on my forlorn Christmas Eve shopping trip. And Jill had taken a Doxy in anticipation of his visit, the poor silly bitch. I won't blame the woman; in such circumstances I blame the man.

As for Cynara, she loved Ted, and for all I knew Ted loved her sincerely and passionately. Why not? Why would he love me, the wife of decades, the older woman back home, the bad-tempered, un-generous, un-fun me. I must accept it. As for the twins, they loved their father. I had bedded Robbie too soon, and though they took the gifts their stepfather brought them, they never could forgive either him, or me, their mother.

And perhaps I was not the only one to have Ted dreams. Perhaps all five of us did; perhaps we all knew he was not dead, only halfway dead? And for all I knew Ted was walking amongst us here, now. Had he not stepped out of his sarcophagus shell, set free by me, as the 7.5 MRI machine had agitated my pineal gland out of its stupor. It had done what it was meant to do all too well. Too steep the gradient!

I did feel very odd. There was an empty chair beside me. I had a sudden feeling Ted was sitting in it. I could almost see him, but not quite. The air quivered there as it had around the tape reels. Ted was there. I stretched out my hand to touch, but it went right through him. It was almost him, though not quite a solid him, as if he were a hologram. Then he got up and walked away. The security guards did not notice: no-one did.

Ted seemed to join the group of four – Cynara, Jill and the twins – and laughed and joked with them. Why wouldn't he? All were part of him and he of them. The twins were his children. The women were joined to him by sexual contact. Whomever women have unprotected sex with affect them just a little – I'm convinced of that. Animal breeders say the bitch who 'gets out' never breeds true again; no wonder men used to be so fussy about marrying virgin brides. And the harder I gazed at Ted the less he seemed to be there, winking in and out as if there were something wrong with my eyes.

The organ struck up again: with a loud, fulsome, triumphant sound the hymn from Beethoven's ninth, *Joyful, joyful, we adore thee*. The twelve scarlet-robed members of the Ethics Committee were filing back in after their twenty-minute break. They looked even healthier and younger than they had when they'd gone out, but it might have been my imagination. Ted peeled away from the others, and joined the end of the procession. He did not look at all out of place. He too was wearing a scarlet gown and buckled shoes. The chattering brides quietened for a moment of awe and adoration before filing back themselves in a brisk and orderly fashion to take their seats in the hall. A trusting and dedicated lot, I thought: one could tell they were worshipers all at the shrine of longevity, conscious of the possibility of immortality, of death without its sting at last, grave without its victory, the world to come. And Ted was to be one of those deciding the direction mankind was to be led. I could only hope his time in another reality had given him some added wisdom. He had not necessarily spent all his time in a forest jungle.

The two guys in black uniforms left my side, as Robbie and Red Beard came to join me in the now emptying vestry; the coffee staff wheeled their trolleys away to wherever they belonged. We were alone. They looked calm and composed: more like competent modern executives than mad scientists. But what struck me was how tentative, flawed and pallid both looked in comparison to the manly vigour of twelve red-robed Committee members. We all sat quietly for a minute or two. Robbie took my hand.

'Okay?' he asked.

'I'm fine,' I said.

'She's fine,' said Red Beard.

I'd rather wanted Red Beard not Robbie to take my hand, but I subdued the thought: *so* not the time or place.

'Mrs Phyllis Whitman, please come to the stand,' said the loudspeaker. We all jumped.

'Good luck,' said Red Beard
'Tell the truth,' said Robbie.
'I haven't much choice,' I said. (I wondered if it was possible to manufacture Juves without the dangerous truth component – and Ritalin without the habit-forming propensity – how enormously popular with public speakers the world over such pills would be: an end to sleepless nights and stage fright.) I found I was not at all nervous, just glad to have Robbie and Red Beard for support – they both loved me! SRRI's of one kind or another had not completely worked their way out of my system.

The committee was sitting in a semi-circle on a daïs, facing an audience of a hundred or so of young, good-looking, clear-complexioned and attentive young persons, like a picture of the hopeful utopian world they strove to bring about. I took my place facing the panel and counted them again. Thirteen, not twelve: or had I miscounted? The panel member to my far left, presumably the last one in, looked very like Ted. I was almost sure yet not quite sure that it was. Revenants seem to have a way of always looking rather like someone else, if only temporarily.

I took my time to settle. All assembled waited patiently, then the Chairman addressed me. He sat in the centre of the semi-circle, a charming man with a big nose and deep set if slightly rheumy eyes. He exuded power and grace.
'Our thanks to you for coming in to speak to the Ethics Committee, Mrs Whitman,' he said to me, in his rich, kindly voice. 'We are honoured and flattered.' On cue the organ next door struck up a chord or two. This was an absurdly over stage-managed event. 'You have worked long and hard for us in our outreach programme and contributed your outstanding

talents towards a greater understanding of the nature of the barriers that exist between the living and the dead. Future generations will be grateful to you.' I couldn't point out that my hard work had consisted mainly of sex and sleeping: it's only courteous to accept compliments when they come one's way. 'And now we have some questions for you, Mrs Whitman.'

Audience and panel applauded politely, as if I was a jazz player who'd just finished a satisfactory though not very noteworthy solo. I wished I could take these people more seriously. Frivolity still kept welling up in me. The chairman fell silent. I could see I was expected to respond, to play my part and speak in similar spirit.

'Honoured? Flattered?' I asked. 'Very nice of you and all that. But why? What for?'

My voice was picked up by a microphone somewhere and I could hear it ripple around the hall. The lighting of the daïs dimmed: if Ted was still there I could not be sure of it. The lighting in the auditorium brightened so that when I looked behind me I was dazzled, and couldn't see faces; I myself sat in a pool of light. I was a Juve addict amongst Juve addicts, a Doxy addict amongst Doxy addicts, dweller in the new Pharmocracy and it was great.

'Mrs Whitman, we have recognised your talent for quite some time, and marvelled at it. As Mozart is a musician amongst musicians, Rembrandt an artist among artists, you are a medium among mediums, a genius. You are the one in billions picked out through metadata procedures, and before you the traditional barriers of space and time dissolve.'

'Oh, I see,' I said. 'All that.'

What, a few ghostly sightings, a spasm of telepathy, a spurt of telekinesis, a blossoming of poltergeists, all no doubt exaggerated in the telling, in transit from me to Ted, to Cynara, to Robbie, a few leapings and fallings of my lit-up pineal gland, and I was placed in honour before these, the powers that be. Me, with my mitochondrial insufficiency, bearer of twins, with my over-active epiphysis cerebri: a medium amongst mediums? Hardly. Look in the small ads of *Psychic News* and you'd find a dozen better qualified.

'Yes, Phyllis – all that,' said the panel member sitting on the right of the Chairman, evidently the second in command. 'We've been watching you for some time. We know each other, though you may not remember. But I do, and very clearly. We were both fifteen and young Theosophists. My father had just died; you summoned him back from the other side. In front of witnesses he spoke to me with words of wisdom I've not forgotten, that have led me on the road to where I am today. Fame and fortune, as you predicted, came to me.'

I remembered the incident vaguely. But I'd been making it all up: he'd been the pimply lad whose father had just died. The Theosophists were such gullible, amiable idiots, always looking for a miracle. It had seemed a simple kindness to him to provide one: his father with a message from the other side.

'Since those early days,' he said, 'you have gone from strength to strength; the lovely young seer becomes the shaman. The shaman becomes the Goddess.'

'Thank you for your witness, brother,' said the Chairman, briskly, as if the delegate was about to be overcome by emotion. 'Mrs Whitman, the committee has asked me to offer their condolences upon the loss of your previous husband. It was most regrettable, and of course not by our design. A case of human error and greatly to be deplored, but lessons have been learned. This tragedy is one of the reasons we are here today.

But we want to assure you, and others like you who have sacrificed so much in the fight for the ultimate perfection of humanity, that the loss of one is felt as deeply by us as is the loss of many. On your return home, Phyllis – I may call you Phyllis? – you will find compensation has been made, a redress. It is the least we can do. Acceptance of this sum will be in full and final settlement of the whole sorry business. In the battle for human understanding, in the war against ignorance, the fight against old age and even death itself, there will always be casualties on the way, but the greater good is nearly here – the day when the doors of perception will fall open.'

There was enthusiastic applause from the audience, and muted clapping from the dais. The lights there had gone up again, and yes – it was Ted there on the platform. I had never heard a more self-serving speech, and nor I imagined had he. I knew it was Ted because he was wearing his favourite shoes, the ones he wore when he was meeting important clients, his rather fancy John Lobbs. Yet earlier I had noticed his mediaeval-style buckled shoes. He was not yet fully adjusted to his new circumstances: still settling. But he was taller, straighter than I remembered him: his hood was pushed back and he had a wodge of thick hair. It was Ted in his youth; in is mid-twenties, not in his early forties: more like my son than my lover, more like the twin's brother than their father. Not like the young-old on the platform, with their blood changes, their 3D printed spare parts and their stem-cell jabs and their blood transfusion and spinach- nourished telomeres. This was not the Ted of the forest clearing, Ted was truly young again.

The Chairman was still speaking. 'Phyllis – this committee, with its due oversight of the affairs of mankind as it goes forward into the new digital future, stands at a crossroads. We need your testimony to point the way. You are the voice of the humble multitude; through you Everyman, Everywoman, speaks.'

There was a short burst of organ music. The light on me intensified so I was utterly blinded. I was the woman from *Revelations*, 6, clothed with the sun, with the moon under her feet and a crown of twelve stars on her head. Only now there were thirteen. Ted was with them, the new apostle, the casting vote, and it was no-one's fault but their own. They should not have interfered, not have taken my minor slippages into other dimensions and encouraged, recorded and enhanced them, and in their monstrous questing appetite for algorithms made the preposterous come true.

'So do we open the doors of perception, Phyllis, or shall we keep them firmly closed?' The voice from the throne was loud and clear in my poor befuddled ears.

I hesitated. I was duly impressed. I thought of Robbie and his good job and my comfortable life; I thought of Doxies and sexual pleasure and Juves and freedom of expression, of Ritalin and its fitful acuity, of Red Beard's bearish hug, of Cynara and her thriving gallery, of the twins' river-view apartment, and I understood that what I said would change everything for everyone. 'They' had pushed open the doors of perception a crack, and Ted had slipped through and that now Ted had found the way others would follow; the dead would be upon us. Did I want this? Did I really want my lost, dead loved ones about me – my sweet mother, perhaps, but my murderous father, Ted's parents, my drony adopted father...? Never. '*If the doors of perception were cleansed,*' William Blake had said, '*every thing would appear to man as it is, infinite. For man has closed himself up, till he sees all things thro' narrow chinks of his cavern.'* And just as well, I thought, we were safer in our cavern.

I spoke up.

'Look,' I said, 'The thing you need to understand about the paranormal is that everything it touches becomes second-rate, useless. I train an eraser to jump into my hand and all it does is rub out the map I'm working on: the spoons that Uri Geller bends can no longer be used to eat your soup or pudding; the keys he twists no longer fit the lock; his stopped watches no longer tell the time. So much for bending the laws of physics. Even if you can, where's the point? When a clairvoyant channels Mozart or Beethoven from the Other Side the music they compose is poor pastiche. Mediums end up with shapeless bodies and bad breath. Occult energy degrades all it passes through. If the dead tell you something they're bound to be lying: information becomes disinformation. Open the doors of perception and God knows what will come through. Go where the laws of nature no longer apply, and water flows upwards, trees grow upside down, and yesterday becomes tomorrow. The abyss stares back at you. My advice to you is slam the bloody doors of perception shut, if it's not too late, and keep them fucking closed.'

It was quite a speech but it didn't go down at all well. I shouldn't have sworn, but it wasn't just that. The spotlight left me. Faces all around had fallen. I was the wet blanket of wet blankets. Phyllis Whitman, medium, now public enemy number one, telling a truth no-one present wanted to hear.

The Chairman's voice was tremulous. One can get one's vocal chords tightened like guitar strings so one speaks with a younger voice. Maybe he hadn't got round to it yet.

'Thank you, Phyllis, you may stand down. Your remarks have been noted.'
I stood down. I was escorted out.

I was shivery. Red Beard lent me his leather jacket. We left the building in quite a hurry. I suggested to Robbie before we left that we take as many Doxies and Juves home as possible while we could, and perhaps some Ritalin, but Robbie said Security were already in the pharmacy cleaning up the place. Two of the Portal Inc pharmacists had been taken away in handcuffs. It was alleged that they'd been trading illicitly.
'But you two weren't trading?'
'Of course not,' said Robbie, indignantly. He and Red Beard had been acting under instruction; their attempts to break through to the other side had been properly sanctioned, but political power was shifting at the top. Hence the arrest of the pharmacists that morning. The Ethics Committee would be disappointed by my testimony but would report it back at the AGM that evening when the vote was taken.

They asked a little anxiously whether anything had 'happened' during my stint with the MRI machine, and I said no, and I think they were relieved. I didn't mention Ted's stepping out of the apparatus over the sill. Some residual loyalty to him remained, like a mother's to a son, but thank God without the tormented agitation of sexual jealousy and possessiveness which had overlaid our earlier relationship. If his was to be the casting vote I thought he would vote to keep the doors of perception closed: to bar more investigation of the other side, other alternative universes. He would be like so many immigrants; he had got through but would not want others to follow and queer his pitch.

I stayed quiet and Robbie said I was not to reproach myself. There'd been no time to prepare or brief me, and I was only a five. Nevertheless the dissolution of Portal Inc was possible if the vote went against the ADF tonight and funding was withdrawn. Robbie and Red Beard might well find themselves made redundant. They did not seem unduly distressed. There were other jobs waiting, though in places where access to the new generation pharms could be difficult.

I hope I showed proper sympathy. It seemed Red Beard was already planning a sideways step into Godix Inc, sister institution to Portal Inc, where work was being done on the ergodic nature of the multiverse: the mathematical approach. Robbie hoped to join him there. Psycho-pharms had been fun, but fun must have a stop. We were all grownups again now.

And Ted is walking amongst us, I thought, but did not say.

Eight

Robbie and I went to bed that night with my best Chinese rug from the living room covering up the carpet where the perchlorate sapling had rooted. We slept holding each other with great affection but without feeling the need for sex. So much for life without Doxies. It wasn't heaven but it would do.

That night I dreamt of the forest again. Sunlight streamed into the clearing. There was birdsong. Trails of white clematis hung from high trees. Even the net of saplings underfoot looked benign.

And Ted was not to be seen. Of course not. I had set him free. I hadn't prayed for his release from Purgatory but I'd done the next best thing. I had forgiven him and not forgotten him. Ted was satisfied. I suspected that it was the last Ted dream I'd ever have. I was right. My third eye, after its final excitation, had been irretrievably dimmed, and just as well. I was no longer the heroine of the metadata, no goddess, no medium, just an ordinary working wife and mother of twins.

I had made my bed with Robbie and now must lie upon it, with as much content as it provided. It was hardly Robbie's fault that he had acted as he had. He was a six, and like many a six was Aspergery: but what he lacked in empathy he made up for in a generalised goodwill. Ted would be around to divert

Cynara's attention from him. The twins had grown up, left home and had each other and the NSA. Working in the world of Security would suit them very well. They were judgemental by nature, and if they joined some LFL harem it was none of my business. One could only hope 3D computer-printed spare body parts were properly rewarding.

For myself I resolved to rebuild the Q&A&Co business and keep myself busy. I would keep off pills of all kinds. We might be living in a pharmocracy, but it was up to individuals to resist. I might even start a movement.

In the morning the phone rang. It was the Ethics Committee chairman. He thanked me for my contribution to yesterday's proceedings and said that as a result of last night's vote Portal Inc was being wound down: the project 'had not shown sufficient intelligence benefit or financial dividend to justify its continuance'. It had been a close vote, carried by one. He personally regretted the decision but could see it was prudent. Then, he asked, and I knew he was angling for confirmation of some kind:
'I hope you had a quiet night, Phyllis? You must have had quite an exhausting day yesterday.'
'Perfectly quiet, thank you. Poor Ted was still there in his forest,' I lied, 'stumbling round as ever. He's in some kind of mental loop, I suppose. But as a dream it no longer bothers me.'
'Well, we could keep in touch, Phyllis,' he said, as he rang off. 'We must have lunch one day. Such a pleasure to meet you.'

I thought he sounded rather relieved. As indeed was I – to find that the Juves had finally worn off and I could tell lies so easily. When Robbie asked me the same question as the chairman I replied in the same way: no change in the Ted dreams, and with any luck, I said, if Robbie refrained from taking Doxies, no doubt the dreams would taper off.

I had no wish to set more hares running. The future would have to look after itself. Ted was not likely to bother me again, though he might well have found a path others could still follow, shaking little sapling seeds or even more malignant things from their clothing as they went. I could see that Ted might well have unfinished business with Jill Woodward – she had murdered him, if only inadvertently. But if he haunted anyone, it would be Cynara, whom he had screwed and – I could finally admit it – loved. Well, she'd have to deal with it. Perhaps even now he was sitting in her gallery telling her what to do and how to do it.

A couple of days later an envelope turned up in the post. It contained a lottery ticket – although I never play the lottery – and when Robbie checked on the Internet he told me I was one of three winners: I had all six numbers, plus the bonus. He reckoned we had won something in the region of four million dollars, for it was just over two and a half million pounds. Robbie clasped me to him. The illuminati of the Ethics Committee had been true to their word and seen me right. Even with house prices as they were, we could afford to move out of Dinton Close and leave Ted behind us for ever. It was just as well; I had tried to vacuum really thoroughly that morning, only to find tiny green saplings growing all over the place and the dust bag clogged with little leaves.

Original Publication Details

The dates the published stories first appeared in print:
Angel, All Innocence was first published in *The Thirteenth Ghost Book* [Barrie and Jenkins, 1977]; *Alopecia* in *Winter's Tale*, [Macmillan, 1976]; *The Man with No Eyes* in *New Stories 2*, Arts Council, 1977; *Breakages* in *The Midnight Ghost Book* [Barrie and Jenkins, 1978]; *Weekend* in *Cosmopolitan*, 1978 and BBC radio, 1979; *Delights of France* or *Horrors of the Road* in *Cosmopolitan*, 1984; *A Gentle Tonic Effect* in *Marie Claire*, 1988; *Chew You Up and Spit You Out* in *Woman*, 1989; *Baked Alaska* in *Wicked Women* [HarperCollins, 1995]; *Down the Clinical Disco* in *The New Statesman*, 1985; *GUP* or *Falling in love in Helsinki* in *Leader of the Band* [HarperCollins, 1989]; *Knock-Knock* on BBC Radio, 1993; *Ind Aff* or *Out of Love in Sarajevo* in *The Observer*, 1988; *Wasted Lives* in *The New Yorker*, 1993; *Love Amongst the Artists* in *The Times*, 1991; *A Knife for Cutting Mangoes* on BBC Radio, 2000; *Smoking Chimneys* in *Harpers and Queen*, 2001; *Happy Yuletide Schiphol* in *The Times*, 2003; *Christmas on Møn* in *Politiken*, 2009.

The dates the published stories were first collected:
Angel All Innocence, *Alopecia*, *The Man With No Eyes*, *Breakages*, and *Weekend* were first anthologised in *Watching Me, Watching You* [Hodder and Stoughton, 1981]; *Delights of France* or *Horrors of the Road* in *Polaris* [Hodder and Stoughton, 1985]; *Down the Clinical Disco*, *A Gentle Tonic Effect*, *Chew

You Up and Spit You Out and *Ind Aff* or *Out of Love in Sarajevo* in *Moon over Minneapolis* [HarperCollins, 1991]; *Baked Alaska, Love Amongst the Artists* and *Wasted Lives* in *Wicked Women* [HarperCollins, 1995]; *GUP* or *Falling in love in Helsinki*, and *Knock-Knock* in *A Hard Time to be a Father* [HarperCollins, 1998]; *A Knife for Cutting Mangoes* and *Smoking Chimneys* in *Nothing to Wear and Nowhere to Hide* [HarperCollins, 2002].